GODPLAYERS

GODPLAYERS

DAMIEN BRODERICK

THUNDER'S MOUTH PRESS • NEW YORK

GODPLAYERS

Published by
Thunder's Mouth Press
An Imprint of Avalon Publishing Group Inc.
245 West 17th St., 11th Floor
New York, NY 10011

AVALON
publishing group incorporated

This project has been assisted by the Australian government through the Australia Council, its arts funding and advisory body.

Library of Congress Cataloging-in-Publication Data is available.

ISBN 1-56025-670-2

9 8 7 6 5 4 3 2 1

Book design by Maria E. Torres

Printed in the United States
Distributed by Publishers Group West

To the memory of Peter Mac
and to Mariann McNamara
with thanks for encouragement
and kindnesses over the years

According to the Eddas, there was once no heaven above nor earth beneath, but only a bottomless deep, and a world of mist in which flowed a fountain. Twelve rivers issued from this fountain, and when they had flowed far from their source, they froze into ice, and one layer accumulating over another, the great deep was filled up.

—Thomas Bulfinch, *The Age of Fable*

Human beings are temporal dynamics of Shannon information in physical states. There is no "stuff." Stuff is an illusion generated by a brain adapted to deal with complex regularities of the macroscopic world as if they were substances. You are dynamics of information in a probability distribution, dynamics distributed over an unimaginable number of changes and interactions, stretched over an incredibly long time period. If you are the same person you were 10^{43} Planck increments ago, even though all of the matter waves in your body have shifted places, why would you not be the same person after a slightly different interaction within the same huge wavefunction?

—Eliezer S. Yudkowsky

August

PROLOGUE

THERE'S A WORLD I know where the women are a head taller than the men, and file their ferocious teeth to points. The men are just as fierce.

A different world, yet the same, another earth, has luminous rings spread brilliantly across the whole sky, bright as a full moon. Those rings are all that remained of the moon when it fell chaotically too close to the world and got torn apart by tidal forces. There are no people there, only about twenty million different kinds of dinosaurs in a range of sizes and colors. Lots of them are meat eaters, with shockingly bad breath.

On a third world, the people are lean and lightly furred. The pale pupils of their eyes are slitted vertically. I believe their remote ancestors, maybe fifteen million years ago, were the great Ice Age cats now extinct in our world. All the apes and humans are extinct in theirs. Has any of them managed the trick of slipping here through the mirrored cracks between the worlds? If so, perhaps they gave rise to legends of vampires or werewolves. I don't think any of them came here, though. They love the taste of simian blood, which is why the apes and humans are extinct in their earth. We'd have noticed them, trust me.

On a fourth, the humans are gone, but machines are everywhere. Evolution by other means. Same old, same old, but different. Always different.

And in all of them, by and by, we Players stroll, connive, or run for our lives. So do the K-machines, driven by malign motives we can scarcely guess at. I like to kill the bastards, I really do.

The endless hazard, of course, is that they'll kill me first, and those I love. That's no abstract threat. I've been alive and I've been dead. Alive is better.

Sorry, that sounds like cynical gallows humor. But I'm not being facetious. It's the literal and exact truth. I find it hard to recall the filthy noise and confusion of my death. It is simply too painful, and besides your synaptic web doesn't work terrifically well once your brain has been torn to shreds. Luckily, I've always been a cheerful if guarded fellow, equable under stress, buoyant and, you know, simply *happy* if I'm given half a chance. Even so, death is no picnic. Well, death is a picnic, but the dead tend to be the luckless meat in the sandwich.

But I see I've jumped too far ahead too soon. Let me start again.

I don't suppose I have the appearance of a Player in the Contest of Worlds. You wouldn't think it, to look at me. Well, that's not true, of course, since that's *exactly* how I look—but if you knew about us, you'd probably expect a Player to resemble premium Bruce Willis, all bruised muscles and weary but romantic hard-bitten sarcasm. Or maybe you'd think we look like those macho but insanely handsome Hollywood guys with ponytails who spend most of the day working up their lats and pecs and biceps, and fine-tuning their flashy karate kicks.

Nah—I'm just this tall Aussie walking down the street, booting a loose plastic bottle top into the gutter, hands in my pockets, floppy hair in my brown eyes, looking a bit wary. True, I have a soft leather glove on my right hand, but people assume it's a personal quirk like a nosering, or a data wearable, or maybe that it hides a nasty burn, which I guess comes closest. Other than that, just another graduate philosophy student dressed in black: fashion uniform, in this place.

Let me tell you how this thing came to pass. Start with Lune.

Lune

ONE

AS SHE LISTENED from a small side table to the house crooner sing "Moon River" in a smoky room of perfume and fumes of brandy and Scotch, something new snared Lune's attention. Not the low irritating stench of the deformer at the table near the front with his noisy cronies. Neither was it the expected tingle of a Contest Player's glamor—not quite, and it put her on edge. Guardedly she scanned the room, saw a young man approach the bar and order a drink. Shadowed, this tall, rangy man with the broad shoulders was presumably her Player: that dark hair, eyes brown as old gold.

With a nod and smile he took his glass from the cornrowed barkeep, leaned his back against the polished timber countertop, surveying the crowd of revelers from behind those long dark sleepy lashes. He drank a little, held the glass easily. She pressed through the tables in the shadows, carrying an empty cocktail glass that had held only Perrier water. At the bar she stood beside him, accepted his relaxed, approving regard. The faintest penumbra of glamour. He narrowed his eyes, smiled faintly, gave her a slow secret smile. After a moment's beat he said, "Ember Seebeck."

Now that she looked at him more closely, the apparent freshness of his youth was lost in the abrasions of time, in perhaps a thousand years of memories and bruising encounters with the worlds, with joys, pains, mortifications unimaginable to the young. It gave him depth, naturally, but experience enshrouded the clarity of the self as a shroud masked glamour.

"You are very beautiful." He shifted his drink to his left hand, extended his right.

"Thank you. Lune," she told him. "Lune Katha Sarit Sagara. You're hunting," she said. "So am I. I've been watching the creature over there." She frowned.

He released her hand, watching her. "I wonder that we've never met."

"So many worlds," she said, and found her tone had grown abruptly brittle, "so little time."

Another cat smile. "What are you drinking?"

"Shanghai Astor Hotel special this time, please."

The barkeep frowned. "Boss don't like the hired help drinkin', even if customers treat 'em."

"Thomas, I wouldn't want to get you in trouble. But I'm not working for Mr. Rogerson, not yet."

"I'll chance it, if'n you will." He flashed her a grin. "I never heard of that cocktail, though, ma'am. Somethin' from New Orleans?"

"Lot farther away than that. Jigger of cognac, teaspoon of maraschino," she said. "You have absinthe, of course? Half a jigger."

He nodded, shrugged.

"And an egg?"

"Uh-huh."

"Two teaspoons of albumen, then. Shake them with half a teaspoon of lemon and some cracked ice. Top off with chilled soda, not too much."

A man at the front table frowned over his shoulder, nudged the despoiler, a big-shouldered man in an expensive suit who looked like a prosperous bank manager. The fog-voiced torch singer seemed not to be bothered by their quiet exchanges, putting his heart and soul into "September Song." Lune took the glass, sipped, ignored them.

Her eyes flicked to the front table, as did Ember's, and he nodded. She said mockingly, "Is it . . . *mere coincidence* . . . that we meet here?"

"No such thing, as you know, my dear."

"So we were meant to meet in this place, however belatedly?"

"I would that it were so. Often I feel more like a chess piece than a Player of the Accord. You know, the 'destiny that shapes our ends—'"

"'—Rough-hew them how we will.' Ember, that view," said Lune, ever the scholar, "was declared heretical in the Accord, *avant la lettre.*" Not that this fact bothered her, for the Accord had been hammered out by Thomas Aquinas in 1271 in the Paris Chapterhouse of the Ensemble, long before the emerging physical and mathematical sciences of the Metric Renaissance had deepened sufficiently to show how ill-fitted his theological apparatus had been to the task. Still, tradition had its uses; one retained what worked, and worked around its encrusted shell.

Ember shrugged.

She had been expecting a companion in arms for this night's task, had depended on it. A small shudder passed through her.

In a soft, velvet voice, Thomas told her, "Boss wants you up on stage now, Miss Lune. Good luck."

"Thanks." She put the glass on the counter, walked through tables to the front. The room was small enough that she needed no mike. In the afternoon, she'd had a brief opportunity to run the house band through her audition repertoire; they nodded to her now, offhand but friendly. They were good and knew it, even if the horn man was a little too eager for his solos. Half-cut after work, business types looked up blearily. The deformer thing stared at her with barely contained detestation. She nodded to the band leader, went into Dylan, Tom Waits, and finished with a wailing, pure-throated reading of Roy Orbison's "I Drove All Night" that woke up the salarymen and had them singing along in manic chorus.

"You're good, babe," the sleazy manager said, trying to cop a feel. Faintly sweaty and pleased with herself, her throat dry, Lune chose not to injure him. She'd already done what she had to in order to draw just the right amount of attention to herself. Deftly she avoided his groping hand, smiled, shrugged. "Well, so anyway, yeah," he said, resigned, "you've got a gig here."

"Thanks, Mr. Rogerson."

"And no drinking with the customers."

"Oh, were you going to pay me for tonight?"

He frowned, twitched his eyes to one side. "Hey, tonight you can do what you like, honey. But if you're gonna screw the john, do it outside in the alley, not in here. This is a decent Mithran joint."

She gave him a dazzling smile. "Thank you for the job, Mr. Rogerson. I'll be here tomorrow night at nine sharp." Knowing she would never see his puffy face again, nor his unpleasant cognate world, was satisfaction enough. By the time she had made her way back to the bar, swaying slightly as she passed the despoiler's table, Ember Seebeck had found them a table and set her cocktail on it.

"You're brilliant," he told her.

"I know. Thanks." The Astor wasn't up to Singapore standards, but Thomas had done his best. People were giving them unpleasant looks, even though the band had settled down to a drink of their own. "So are we going to kill that thing up front?"

"I thought you'd know."

"Nope. I guess this is an improv. Situational. The atmosphere's kind of dirty."

"I don't think it's likely to happen in here."

"The owner recommends that I take my johns out into the alley. Might have been a hint. Care to join me there?"

"Nothing would please me more. Let's finish our drinks first."

"Of course. Sometimes I'm paired with Maybelline Seebeck. Your sister, I take it."

He shrugged. "One of them."

She felt a burst of envy. "A large family."

"As an old family riddle has it, 'Brothers and sisters have I ten, six doughty wenches, four strapping men.' Yeah, larger than the usual, these days, one of us for every month of the year. Then again, Mom and Pop had plenty of time."

Something suddenly came clear. Maybe it was the jingle. Lune found herself chanting another, a childhood mnemonic for recalling months and holidays:

"'Thirty-three days each from September, To June and July, fire to ember,'" and she nodded in his direction with a smile, which he acknowledged, "'Plus one extra day each for summer and winter, And every fourth year a leap-day to remember.'"

Ember grinned broadly. "Exactly. Have to suppose they planned our birthdays with exquisite self-control. And you?"

Me what? Oh, family. "A singleton, alas," Lune said. "I lost track of my parents when the Ensemble admitted me."

"A good crowd, the Ensemble. A trifle jaded, perhaps. You'll bring them a breath of fresh air."

"I'm not *that* young, Ember. But thank you. Shall we go?"

"My pleasure." He crooked his arm, she placed her hand lightly there, and they made their way down the narrow curving stairway, more filthy looks and mutters attending their passage. Maybe nobody liked singers, but in that case why would they pay good pelf to sit here and drink? They went out the back way, into the alley, and waited for a minute or less holding hands decorously, watching the sky, the cobblestones, the polluted brick wall of a factory. The large man in the bank manager suit came out of the same door and instantly flung himself at them.

"Filthy nigra slut," he shouted, and tried to strike her. Despite his slurred speech, he was not even slightly intoxicated, so that when Lune moved to evade his drunken blow it was not where she'd expected and caught her numbingly on the jaw. "You some kinda coon-fucker, you shithead," he was screaming at Ember. Dazed, she saw through a streaky haze Ember's arm extend. A small weapon made almost no sound, and the deformer fell to the cobbles, half his head blown away.

"Crap!" he said, "Sorry, I was slow. Shouldn't have had that drink."

"Never mind," Lune said. "Get hold of the bastard's feet, I'll find a nexus point." She spoke to the Schwelle operating system, and a threshold opened. With a noise like a fire hydrant hit by a truck, water smashed out at them, a torrent of blackness in the dark alley. It struck them both bent over, toppled them along the cobblestones, foamed and rushed, dragging the corpse out of their grip and flinging it high against the factory bricks. Lune, choking and drenched, screamed command words. The Schwelle closed, and the noise was cut by a tenth. Water surged back and forth along the alley, slapping walls, draining out into the nearest street and down gutters. Voices were yelping. A light went on above the club.

"Mithra's bull!" Bedraggled and shocked, Ember was scrabbling through the ebbing tide to recapture their prize. Lune kicked off her shoes, gasping at the chill of the water. She helped him hoist the corpse into a fireman's lift.

"Bastards must have found that nexus," Lune told him, "flooded the whole damned valley. Overkill, but effective."

"Egypt? Indonesia?"

"China. They like those gigantic hydraulic projects. Damn it, I was there only a decade ago."

"Do you want me to find one?"

"No, no, I have a dozen drop-offs. Just a moment." She was breathing heavily. So was Ember; the corpse was heavy and ungainly. She spoke another command. With a tearing noise, a fresh Schwelle opened in the darkness, with equal darkness beyond. At their back, Rogerson burst out from the club, a shotgun raised, ready for mayhem, followed by the K-machine's flunkies.

"Shit, move it, Lune."

"I'm gone," she said, and went across. He lumbered after her, weighed down, and she instantly closed the threshold. Another urban myth in the making. Lune hoped there had been fish or frogs carried in on the brief deluge. With a thud, Ember Seebeck dumped the dead thing off his shoulders. They stood beneath unfamiliar stars in a field of sweet clover. Somewhere nearby a large animal whuffled, maybe a mammal, maybe something stranger. An owl-like avian swooped overhead, eyes catching the moon's whiteness. It settled in a dark tree. Lune took a barefoot step, felt warmth creep into her toes, and a less appealing odor filled her nostrils.

"As you put it so eloquently, shit," she said. "I really hate the countryside." She took a careful step backward and wiped her foot on soft clover.

"The city doesn't seem such a great improvement," he said, laughing lightly. He had a penlight in his hand, examining the headless corpse. Blood and meat and other stuff more like the insides of a machine. Undoubtedly dead, if you imagine the things ever being alive to begin with. "I wonder why they tend to come stocked with such vile bigotry."

Lune nodded her agreement. "They might as well wear T-shirts with branded signs like EVIL MOTHERFUCKER. One thing Maybelline and I offed was screaming about dirty dykes." She rolled her eyes.

There was a moment's silence. The light went off. "Well, in May's case—"

"You know perfectly well what I mean."

"Yeah. Okay, let's take this across to your nexus, and hand it over to a disposer."

They did that thing, and then she went home alone, despite some elegant pleading on Ember's part, had a long, relaxing soak, ate a scratch meal out of the fridge, watched some trash TV, slept for six hours.

Two

FOR ME, THOUGH, it started with Tansy.

I was studying medicine, not philosophy, about a million years ago after I got back to Australia from Chicago. I fell in love, fell out again, played some music, studied like a dog, and at the end of my third-year academics Great-aunt Tansy, with whom I'd shared a big old empty house since my parents disappeared over Thailand, waved me off as I headed for the outback to do a little jackarooing. That's tending huge herds of beef cattle or sheep that roam across dry grassland spreads the size of small European nations. It's not done on horseback these days, not much. Helicopters and 4WDs are the preferred method. I learned to round up a few thousand head of cattle at a time from the back of a bounding Suzuki bike, 800 ccs and lean as a greyhound. On a blazing 41-degree-Celsius Summer Day (which in Chicago was Winter Day, or would be in a few hours' time when December 33 was done), I ate ritual damper and rum cake with the other jackaroos and two hotly pursued jillaroos, drinking Bundy rum and Coke and singing western laments. American West, that is. Nothing is more unnerving that hearing three black aboriginal stockmen whose ancestors had dwelled in that part of the country for upward of 50,000 years singing "The Streets of Laredo" in totally unself-conscious American hillbilly accents. That's how they heard it on the radio, that's the way they sang it.

I drove home all one day and most of the night late in January in the old 4WD Pajero I'd won on a lucky hand of poker, with a swag of tax-free cash in each of my high-top R. M. Williams boots. At a drive-through booze shop I'd bought a bottle of Bundaberg Rum for myself, for old times' sake, and a bottle of premium sherry for Aunt Tansy. Dugald O'Brien, her old golden Labrador, met me joyously at the gate, tail wagging. How did he do it? Mysteriously, he always seemed to know when I'd be arriving, and welcomed me with his simple, blessed affection. I wondered if Tansy tipped him off, using her occult powers.

"Do Good, my man," I told him, "likewise," and scratched his ears, then crouched to give him a proper hug, dropping my swag but holding the bottles carefully. The poor chap was growing old, and he limped a little as he followed me into the hallway.

The comforting smells of Tansy's home welcomed me in like a warm memory. It made me embarrassed: I was grimy, and I'm sure I stank like a skunk. I found her in the enormous kitchen, gave her a kiss, deferring the hug for later, and told her I was headed upstairs for a shower. She lifted the remote with a floury hand and flipped off her TV set.

"I'm sorry, dear, you can't."

"Huh?" I paused halfway up. I'd driven 1500 kilometers with not much more than fuel breaks; I was numb with fatigue, starting to see double.

Great-aunt Tansy began cutting pastry mixture with a metal template shaped like a heart. She looked up at me, eyes wide and watery blue and honest. "This is Saturday night."

"What there is left of it. I know, I should phone around, catch up with people, Tansy, but I'm bone tired. After I've have a good soak, I think I'll just slip into—"

"No, darling, that's what I'm saying. You can't have a shower upstairs. Every Saturday night, recently, there's been a corpse in that bathroom."

Rather carefully, I came all the way down the stairs again, not clattering, and poured a cup of coffee and waited. Tansy did her magic with strawberry jam, popped the tray into the hot oven, began blending a fresh mix for date scones. She made the best jam tarts since the Queen of Hearts, which I guess made me the Knave, since I'd pilfered plenty of them over the years. She sat perched on a three-legged stool beside the heavy oak kitchen table, rolling an amorphous lump of putty in flour with an old-fashioned rolling pin. As ever, no conscious effort went into the expert motions of her hands: It was a tantra, as graceful and automatic as my martial-arts kata when I was in the zone. Absentminded as an old hen, Great-aunt Tansy, and twice as industrious.

After a time, I said, "I can't have a bath tonight because you have a dead man in the bath." Anyone else, I'd have laughed, or said something scathing. But it was Aunt Tansy's testimony, and she was in her eighties, as fragile as expensive glassware.

"You can use mine, August, downstairs. In fact, I think you should, and the sooner the better." Her white bun of ancient silky hair bobbed. "The fact of the matter is, my dear, you stink like a polecat." I watched her press down on the white, datey dough, and the clean round shapes of the scones came out of that putty and sat snugly on the tray she had waiting for them. I felt the sleepy contentment of that large old eccentric nineteenth-century house closing around me again, and my mind phased away from her mad statement. It was easy to forget at Aunt Tansy's, which is why I so greatly enjoyed my—I yanked myself out of distraction, forced myself to think about a corpse in a bathroom.

"Always the same corpse, is it?" I drained the last of my cool coffee.

"Heavens no, child, don't be absurd. There's a fresh one every week." She took the scones over to the oven, slid them in above the tarts. The tray rattled. "All shapes and sizes. Last week it was a nice-looking young fellow in a tweed suit." She came back to the table and held out her shaky cup; I poured more coffee. The poor thing was trembling, and it wasn't the caffeine; she was scared stiff. My bemusement turned to dismay. They keep promising a cure for Alzheimer's, but as far as I knew firm kindness seemed the only available prescription. Tansy had done a lot for me.

"What happens to these bodies?" Pretty difficult, humoring an old lady's delusions without making it obvious. And Tansy was sharp.

"They're always gone in the morning. Sometimes a bit of blood, you know, but I wash out the tub with citric cleanser and you'd never know there's been a body there."

Her cup clattered faintly on its saucer. I was getting scared myself.

"How long's this been going on?"

"It started just after you left for the bush. Let's see—six of them so far. And another one tonight, I expect."

I had seen some strange things in my life, not the least of them my lunatic school friend Davers running about an Adelaide football field in cleated boots and his sister's frilly dress, pursued by jocks, but never anything so weird or bloodcurdling as quiet little Great-aunt Tansy talking about corpses in her upstairs bathroom.

"You've told the police, I suppose?"

She gave me a scornful look.

"August, they'd have me committed to an insane asylum."

Her trembling worsened. I felt ashamed. You didn't just drive your aged relative to the local clinic and ask them to run some tests on her sanity. Or did you? I was starting to think that I'd need to call my aunt Miriam and her husband Itzhak in on this, and did some calculations. No, it was still only about six in the morning in Chicago, which is where they were living at the time. Let it ride, I told myself, see what we can work out right here and now. Besides, incredibly enough, some part of me was beginning to assume that *something* strange was happening in the old house, something she'd misinterpreted rather unfortunately. I'd never known Aunt Tansy to be entirely wrong about anything important. Could this be the deranged work of one or more of her psychic clientele? Maybe she'd given one of them a bum steer, and this was payback time.

"I'll just go up and have a quick look," I said, and took our cups to the sink.

"You be careful, August," she told me. To my immense surprise, she reached down and held out an old cricket bat that had been leaning against one table leg on her side. "Take this. Give the buggers a good whack for me."

Then she insisted on a final cup of cocoa for both of us, so I rolled my eyes to heaven and gave in. I packed Great-aunt Tansy off to bed early in her slightly sour old-lady-scented ground-floor bedroom at the front of the house, and went upstairs.

I opened the bathroom door and gazed around carefully. Tiled walls, pale green, pleasantly pastel. It struck me as odd, peering about the large room, that for years I'd bathed here and made stinks without ever really looking at it. You take the familiar for granted. Two large windows, dark as night now, gave on to trimmed grass two full stories below, and the fruit trees and organic vegetable plots of the back garden. Between them a pink washbasin stood on a pedestal, set beneath a big antique wall-mounted mirror, at least a meter square, with a faint coppery patina, the silvering crazed at the edges. The claw-footed bath itself filled the left-hand corner, opposite a chain-flush toilet bowl of blue-patterned porcelain like a Wedgwood plate, next to the oak door with its ornate geometrical carvings. The toilet's cedar timber seat was down, naturally, and masked by a rather twee fluffy woolen cover that Tansy might well have knitted herself. A flower-patterned plastic screen hung on a steel rail around the bathtub, depending from white plastic rings as large as bangles. Tansy did not approve of separate shower stalls; a bath was how she'd washed as a girl, and the wide old fixed showerhead was barely tolerated. I didn't mind, I enjoyed a long soak as much as anyone three or four times my age.

I pulled the screen back on its runner and studied the bathtub, which of course was empty, fighting an urge to throw off my sweaty clothes and jump in for a steaming soak. The ludicrous possibility that six corpses had shared that bathtub hung in my mind, even as I shook my head with self-mockery.

The place smelled wonderful; that's what I was noticing most of all. Scalloped shells at bathtub and basin alike held a deep green translucent chunky oval of Pears Soap, a green deeper than jade, and its aroma seemed to summon me back to childhood, when my mother washed me with the perfumed scents of cleanliness and herself, then dried me briskly with a fluffy towel smelling of sunlight. I squeezed my eyes shut for a moment, caught myself sighing, opened them. Just an ordinary bathroom, really. Perhaps cleaner than most. Aunt Tansy was punctilious. The house was large and rambling but tidy; with the help of a middle-aged "treasure," Mrs. Abbott, who came by twice a week and took over most of the vacuuming and dusting, she ran a taut ship. A ship insufficiently taut, apparently, to prevent a weekly visitation from the dead.

I glanced at my watch. Little wonder I was tired, it was nearly 11:00. Great-aunt Tansy was a woman of regular habits. She always watched television while baking until the end of the Saturday-night movie, cleaned her teeth, was in bed by 11:30. Her Saturday corpse must put in its appearance by the time she switched the TV off at 11:15 or so, and be gone when she rose for church at 7:30 on Sunday morning.

"Madness," I muttered aloud, removing my heavy boots, and climbed into the bath, holding the bat in one hand. By leaving a gap between the plastic screen and the tiled wall, I was able to watch the closed and locked windows through the small aperture. This meant sitting on the slippery rounded edge of the bathtub and stretching my neck into a ridiculous position, but I decided a few minutes discomfort for the cause was worth it. I thought of Tansy's gesture in insisting on shared cocoa and wished for something equally mundane to calm my jitters. Half my friends in school would have lighted up a cigarette, but the foul things made me sick, and besides even if I smoked there'd be little gain in advertising my presence. I caught myself. To whom? This was a delusion, an old lady's mad fancy.

The silence took on an eerie aspect. In her room below, Tansy might be sleeping by now, or perhaps lying awake, eyes wide and fixed on her dim ceiling. In the bathroom, no sound but my own breathing, not even the movement of wind in the trees below. I felt for a moment as if mine were the sole consciousness active in the whole world. A trickle of cold sweat ran down my back, something I've only ever read about. In the last few weeks I had driven a powerful little bike across vast plains, much of the landscape nearly barren due to the El Niño drought and maybe the greenhouse effect, I'd once come close to a fall from the skidding machine under the hooves of a hundred spooked cattle, and that had scared me without getting in my way; that was fear in the service of sharpened instincts and self-preservation. In Tansy's deathly quiet bathroom, I felt like wetting my pants. I got out again, lifted the wooly toilet seat, pissed for a while, flushed, left the seat up. This was my bathroom now, by default. I climbed back into the bath, cool on my feet through the socks, sat down again on my narrow perch.

My neck hurt. I got a sudden picture of how grotesque I looked, craning on the edge of the tub, laughed softly to myself and stood up, unkinking my spine, put my hand on the curtain to yank it back. The window nearest to me screeked ever so slightly, and I heard it open a little.

This was impossible. I was on the second floor of a tall old structure without fire escape or any of that modern namby-pamby nonsense. I'd checked carefully to confirm my memory of the garden: no new lattices, the trees were all sensibly positioned meters away to prevent fire hazards, and Tansy's ladder was inside the house, not even outside in the locked shed. Dugald O'Brien was not raising a single whuffle in the night, let alone a bark at intruders. What the *hell?*

My heart slammed and my mouth was dry. I pushed against the edge of the bath, back corrugated by the tiles of the wall, stared with difficulty through the gap. The nearer window was quietly pushed all the way open. I heard a muffled scuffle and a summery female back appeared in the window frame. A long brown leg came over the windowsill, probed for the floor. My boots were sitting in plain view beside the toilet. Well, lots of people leave their clothes scattered about. Not in Tansy's house. But then these intruders would hardly be familiar with the nuances of Tansy's housekeeping policies. Don't be ludicrous, August, what would you know about what they know about?

There's a half-naked woman climbing in through a second-story window!

She stood in the bathroom, her back still to me. It didn't seem right to whack her with the cricket bat, which I still clutched in my numb right hand. Sensible but unsporting, and it wouldn't teach me anything about her bizarre activities. She was leaning out into the air, grunting and heaving, and suddenly hauled in the heavy front end of a very dead adult male. The body stuck, shaking the window frame.

"Don't shove, Maybelline," she said angrily. "You got the shoulders jammed."

There was a tricky moment when the corpse withdrew a little, as she angled the shoulders, then surged back into the room to join the two of us. The far end of the corpse came into view, supported by an overweight muscular woman. Her biceps rippled impressively as she pushed the stiff hindquarters over the sill. The first woman let the carcass thud to the tiles. With a businesslike grunt, Maybelline vaulted into the room. She was hairy-legged; like the first woman, she wore a brief summer garment. I thought I was drugged, or hallucinating, and then the first woman turned to face the bathtub, and I was sure of it.

Beauty like this you do not see, I told myself numbly, not in the real world. (That estimate was so astonishingly wrong, in such an astonishing way, that I simply note it here for the record.) Neither of the young women was much older than me. University students, maybe, playing a preposterous prank. They moved about their macabre task with dispatch and grace, making a minimum of noise.

"Help me with his clothes, loon."

Inside half a minute they'd stripped him of his shoes, bloody suit, and underwear. No attempt to search his jacket for wallet, nor to rifle his pockets. These were not pranksters, and certainly not simple thieves. He was blubbery and covered in hair about the back, shoulders and chest in the Mediterranean fashion; his hairstyle had been a comb-over, which flopped repulsively to one side as they jostled him. I saw a large black hole in his left breast, and thick, oozing blood. My own heart was ready to expire from overwork. The tough wench took the murdered man under his armpits and hoisted him toward the bath.

"Loon, get the feet."

She wasn't saying *loon,* it was more like "lyoon." Lune, the Moon seen from France? Wait for it, I thought. Surpri-*ise!* Beautiful Lune grasped the edge of the plastic screen, threw it back along its runner. I stood up fast, bowed with a sweep of my right hand, and stepped out of the bathtub.

Both women stood petrified. In that moment of silence, stocky Maybelline's grip failed in fright, and the corpse hit the tiles again with a flat, unpleasant thump. "Fuck!" she said, and shot out through the window. I'll never again underestimate the speed of a corpulent human. Lune gave me a look of lovely, utter confusion, let go of the man's legs.

"Ember?" she said. "What are you—? Your shroud is . . ." She trailed off, while I wondered what she was babbling about. "You're not Ember," she said, then, and bolted for the window.

"Sorry," I said, and slammed the cricket bat down on the sill. She jerked back her fingers, stared at me in outrage, open-mouthed, and flew at me like a cat. I was brought up nicely never to strike a woman. The corpse was leering up at us. I fell over on top of him, bringing Lune down as well, pinning her arms. She had the most improbable cobalt eyes and smelled really, really nice.

"Get off me, you oaf. You *stink!* How long is it since you had a bath?"

It was so terribly unfair I just burst out laughing and let go of her.

Big mistake.

Lune had me in a headlock a second after I'd released her. She smacked the top of my head against the toilet bowl. I yowled and got free, stumbled to my feet, head ringing, slammed down the open window and locked it. In the night beyond, as the pane came down, I saw no sign of Maybelline or the crane that must have hoisted two women and a dead man up to this floor. I locked the window, and the cricket bat caught me behind the right knee.

"Ow! Fuck! Will you *stop* that!" I yelped. As I turned I saw her in the big mirror, bat raised for a lethal stroke at my bruised skull. She was off balance for a moment as she brought it down; I sidestepped, kicked one leg of the corpse sideways to catch her next step. Lune fell into my arms. I was shockingly aroused, and tussled her into a sitting position on the toilet. The seat was up, and she cried out indignantly as her backside hit the rim. One leg came up and her foot caught me in the thigh; something flashed, light off metal, and I went shudderingly cold. From the heated rack I grabbed a thick, fluffy, warm towel and shoved it in her face, grasping her right foot and dragging it up so that she slid forward on the toilet, banging her spine. There was a small row of silvery hieroglyphs carved into the instep of her foot.

She threw off the towel, saw my shock. I assumed she failed to recognize its nature. "The mark of the beast," she said sarcastically.

"Are you going to stay put, or do I have to hurt you? I'd rather not hurt you," I said. Then: "What?"

"My ID number," she gibed. "My use-by date. That's what you think, I suppose? Another stupid mutilation fad."

I wasn't thinking anything of the sort, but it was a useful suggestion.

"Yeah, well, it's preferable to a bolt through your tongue, I suppose." I have nothing against body jewelry, but it seemed sensible to follow her lead up the garden path. I had the cricket bat by this point, and sat down opposite her on the edge of the bath. "How did you get in? Who's this?" I nudged the dead guy who lay with one leg stuck out.

"The world is not as it seems," she told me. She dropped the toilet seat and cover and sat poised on it. I had never seen anyone so gloriously lovely—not at the movies, not on television, certainly not in this slightly down at heel suburb.

"No shit," I said. Without taking my eyes off her, I twisted at my waist and pushed down one sock, left it dangle for a moment from my big toe before falling to the tiles. The silver carven hieroglyphs on my sole were pretty much the same as Lune's. Her throat convulsed. I could almost see the cogs whirring in her brain.

After that long moment of silence, she asked faintly, "What do they call you?"

"They call me August, Lyoon. They call me that because it's my name."

Lune was breathing hard, but keeping herself under control. I could see her make up her mind. She was so beautiful I wanted to whinny. I reached down and pulled my sock back on with one hand, getting the heel stuck under my insole. Tansy had something to do with this. It had to be her doing. Or my dead parents. Lune said, then, "You've read Charles Fort, August?"

"No." What, now we'll have a reading group? I glanced at

the locked windows, waiting nervously for the backup troops to come barging in, maybe waving copies of the collected works of Charles Fort, whoever he was.

"He said, 'I think we're property.' And you *are,* you poor goose."

I didn't laugh; it was too depressing for laughter. Aunt Tansy downstairs drifting in senile delusions, this gorgeous person upstairs heading for the same funny farm. No, wait. Tansy *wasn't* delusional. There *was* a corpse, and so presumably one *had* been delivered on each of the previous six Saturdays. Delivered by women couriers, for all I knew, then disappeared in the early hours of Sunday morning. It didn't bear thinking about.

"So now that you've told me," I said, "I suppose you're going to have to kill me."

Lune drew down her brows, offended. "You'll get your memory zapped, that's all."

Someone had been priming Hollywood. Memory wipe—what was that, *Men in Black,* right? And people appearing out of thin air, or in this case through an impossibly high bathroom window, it went all the way back to *The Twilight Zone* in black and white. Yeah, so how come the scriptwriters and directors and actors didn't get *their* memories obliterated? There's always an escape clause in these mad conspiracy theories, and always a logical hole large enough to drive a tank through. Still—

"I know it's hard for you to listen to this," Lune said, watching me. It was as if she were goading me. "They're just a backdrop. They're the setting for our Contest."

I shrugged, feeling sad and disappointed. "You're deluded," I said. "I've read that Phil Dick guy. He was crazy too, by the end."

The air burned. I leaped so my back covered the door. Lune stayed where she was, perched on the toilet. She looked elegant, slightly sad herself. The same locked window blazed with blue flickering intensity, paint crackling. The glass crazed, vanished like steam. Maybelline shoved her stocky form through the gap, warily pointing a shiny steel tube at me, balancing herself with the other hand. She edged around the corpse on the floor, stood near Lune. I waited with my mouth open, expecting a blast of blue to swallow me down.

"You don't have to kill me," I started to gabble. "You're from a UFO—I can tell that much—so why not take me back to your own planet, I've always wanted to travel, Illinois was interesting but space would be better. Roomier." They stared at me. "All right, not a spacecraft. You're from the future, it's a time machine outside the window, right? This guy would have been the next Hitler, so you're cleaning up the past before it contaminates your own time, I can live with that, your information is undoubtedly better than mine."

"I told him they're all pawns," Lune explained to her associate. "I think it's unhinged him." She said nothing about the hieroglyphs we shared, sort of.

"*What?* You stupid bitch—"

"We've got to zap him anyway, Maybelline, use your brains."

"Oh, Prowtpait, Lune." Maybelline shook her head in remorse. "I know you're not a stupid bitch. You're not any kind of a bitch."

Lune offered her an accommodating smile, shrugged. The corpse looked up at us all from the floor. With a noise like tearing canvas, a short man pushed his way out through the mirror, stepping lightly from the basin to the floor. He carried a huge bag over his shoulder. I was ready to throw up. There wasn't enough room in the place to faint, so I stayed pinned against the door. All this racket, and still no word from Do Good. I hoped violently that none of the bastards had harmed the dear old beast.

"Here's a rum turn," the disposer said, looking around. He was a small cheerful fellow apparently in his fifties, with a bleary eye and a three-day beard. On certain singers and movie stars that can be a cute look, if rather too last-century for my tastes, but on this man it was distinctly seedy. On top of his tousled head sat an old cloth cap set at a rakish angle. "Who's this chappie, then?" He beamed at the women, whipped an ancient meerschaum out of his jacket pocket. His jacket sleeves had leather patches. He stuffed the pipe with flake tobacco from a pouch and started to light it.

"Not in Aunt Tansy's house," I said, and reached forward over the dead man and took the pipe from his mouth. He moved like a mongoose, had it back so fast my hand tingled. But he thrust it, unlighted, into his pocket, and put away his book of matches.

"My apologies. Rules of the house apply, of course. Come now, lassies, I don't know this gent's face at all." He peered genially at me.

Both women spoke at once, stopped. Lune said, "Nothing to worry about, August got into this by mistake—"

"August?" cried Maybelline. "You been sitting here exchanging *names* while I—"

"Now, now ladies," the disposer said, fingers plucking at his pocket for the pipe, dropped away again, "it's not the end of the world when one of them finds his way into the wrong corner of a Contest. A drop of the green ray." I swear he winked at her. "Now that you're here," he said, rounding on me, "give me an "and with this codger."

Dazed, simply unable to think, I helped him get the naked corpse into the bag, then jammed shoes and clothing in on top. We zipped the bag shut, me zipping, him pulling the edges together. He hoisted the bundle up on his shoulder. I was mildly astonished that such a small man could tote such a weighty load, but I had seen too many unlikely happenings too rapidly. It was like stretching an elastic band to the point where it gives up the ghost and just lies there, no spring left in the thing.

"I'll be making a report about this fellow," the disposer told the women, "but give him a dose of the green and no harm's done."

He raised his cap to me. "Good evening, sar, and I thank y' for your help." He clambered up on the washbasin, pulling out two drawers to make the climb easier, and stepped into oblivion. The glass curdled, was once more still as a windless pond, golden tinted, slightly worn at its edges. I could see Maybelline's reflection, holding the tube trained on me. Blue flame, green ray, whatever. I just wanted to have a hot bath and go to bed and wake up from this rather pointless dream. But then all dreams are pointless; that's the thing about dreams.

"Go on, go on," I said, "climb out through the window and fly away on your magic broomsticks."

"We have to—"

"Yes, I know." How would they explain away the window without its glass, the burn marks in the paint? Maybe they'd come back while I slept and fix those as well. "Well, get your nasty amnesia ray over with and let me catch some sleep, I've been on the road since six this morning."

Lune looked at me, and took the tube from her companion. Maybelline wasted no time; she was out the window and gone. The beautiful woman stepped close to me, pulled down my head to her red-glossed mouth. I waited for her to bite me. A vampire element, perfect. "You know what they say, August," she said very softly in my ear.

Five for silver,
Six for gold,
Seven for a secret that must never be told.

I drew away from her, dumbfounded. It was the rhyme with which Great-aunt Tansy had crooned me to sleep after my parents died. An ancient divination rite, she'd told me, later, when I was curious, something from my father's homeland. Its rhythms beat in my body now, and I said bleakly, "Yes, Lune, I know that chant." Tansy the telephone psychic had murmured it often enough, in my hearing, to her gulled clients. "'One for sorrow, Two for grief . . .' Actually I think I've had enough grief for one day."

She laughed delightedly. "You darling boy! Don't forget how it ends: 'Eleven for a witch abroad, Twelve for an ever-dancing world.' One month more than a year. I'll come back and look in on you. Who knows?" To my amazement, she turned my face and kissed me. "Good-bye."

She stepped away, touched the tube at two points. I was flooded with emerald light. It was cold; I tingled with mild shock, and the room faded into dream. I swayed on my stockinged feet, saw her climb carefully through the gaping window frame. Lune seemed to hang in the dark outside, shadowed, dark within dark. She did something that might have been a recalibration of the instrument, and blue light painted the window; it was as it had been, glazed, painted.

I waited for blackness, loss, amnesia. What I felt, instead, was pins and needles torturing my flesh. I stumped haltingly to the washbasin, flung cold water in my face. I could remember it all quite clearly. True, what I remembered was absurd, laughable, impossible. I dragged off my clothes as the water gushed into the tub, steam rising to fill the room. I sat in the wonderful hot water, rubbing fragrant Pears Soap into my armpits and other stinky places. I propped my left foot out of the foamy water, turned it so I could examine the silver hieroglyphs on my sole. I hoped desperately it didn't mean she was my long-lost sister or something approximately as consanguineous. As far as I knew, luckily, I didn't *have* a long-lost sister. (That's how much I knew. Poor goose.)

I toweled myself ferociously as the bathtub drained, wanting sleep so badly it was like hunger. I picked up my clothes and my boots and trotted on the cold boards in the dark to my bedroom. The window was already open, screened against insects, and through the wire mesh the sky was clear and very black, no moon, no broomsticks, no UFOs, no high-hanging *Truman Show* spotlights. Stars shone, and the smell of fresh soil and leaves came in from the garden on a cool breeze. Why had they slipped up? Surely their records must show one player missing from duty, one piece in their bloody great Contest lost in the sea of humans when his parents died? I gave the sky the bird, out-thrust middle finger quivering. Not so smart, though, whoever they were. They'd lost me for two decades, I'd stay lost until I found the bastards on my own.

The pillow was warm. Lune. A witch abroad. Her beautiful burning lips. Beyond the window the world was huge and dark. There were doorways out of it. I slept.

THREE

IN A MOOD of resolute confidence, Decius Seebeck climbed a T-prime sequence toward the place where the godthings awaited birth in the crushed death of a cosmos, one of the very few where such a passing into glory was permitted by its ontology and the local laws of physics. Gaudy infinities peeled away with each step beneath his polished leather soles, carved to his exact specifications by an expert cobbler in a Shang cognate Earth.

Schwellen opened and closed to his deixis command as he moved forward through this maze of metaphysical complexity. Each time he paused, a blister or environmental vacuole had been placed there to sustain his life, the moist air he required to breathe, lit by a spectrum suited to his eyes, impervious shields against the roaring agonies of pulverized spacetime beyond their supportive, pixel-painted boundaries. As always, he felt gratitude toward the godthings, but that emotion did not distract him from his purpose, or tempt him into futile worship.

He gazed out through those protective, apparently transparent shields into one cognate universe after another, each a little farther into its wreck, its compaction, its encystment. Folded into that screaming silence of engineered gravitational shear energy was the seed of those godthing Angels he felt certain were the substrate of the Contest, or would be once they had been born at the end of time.

In this universe, he told himself, somberly watching the smeared darkness, night was ebbing; the shadows were shortening from a west that at last would never know anything but day. His leather soles clicked satisfyingly on tile, then on polished boards, on grained concrete, on a yielding metal gray as old aluminum, on pure light stretched out like batik fabric. . . . For the day's work, Decius had dressed himself carefully in a synthetic damask *lung-p'ao,* skirt slit at front, back and sides in the equestrian mode, from his favorite tailor in Peip. Gorgeous patterns decorated the business dragon robe: mountains rose from the midst of waves, broke through clouds in which dragons lofted. Over his close-fitted collar was knotted his woolen club tie, the maroon and navy of Herod's. He took a final threshold step into a T-prime closed spacetime and entered Yggdrasil Station.

A grandfather clock ticked in the dimness, regular, reassuring, a kind of token of steadiness. Decius had not placed it here, nor had any other member of the family, so far as he knew. It represented another kindness of the Angels which soon would be born in this multiform place, twisted out of the final algorithms in a condensing, dying cosmos—rarer than a pearl of great price—where the cosmological constant Lambda went to zero and the local closed universe had the sublime opportunity denied to most, the chance to collapse and thus, in its poignant, burning death, attain a kind of T eternity.

He found his desk still covered with sundry unsorted papers, and with a sigh seated himself at it on a large orange ergonomic plastic ball he had acquired in a Seattle. He shot his horse-hoof cuffs and got to work, scratching away with a fountain pen, seeking in known information physics and ontological mechanics an interpretation of the oracle. Sometimes in the past, unexpectedly, his pen had been known to bubble and leak, as if the station's air pressure had abruptly dropped. It was infuriating; he'd ruined his best silk *chi-fu* that way. Computing devices, alas, simply didn't work in this place, so close to the final compression of the Omega Point. Their algorithms bled into the substrate. Silicon and artificial quantum gates alike glitched. It was a wonder that brains didn't, but it seemed that something about their protein nets spared them, except in quantomancy and dream. He shuddered a little at the thought. This was not a place to fall innocently asleep.

A hard door hissed open. His aide de camp came into the workspace disheveled, half naked from sleep, scratching his head, smiling blurrily. Guy stood beside him at the desk, breath faintly sour, and gave him a friendly kiss on the check.

"Morning, Dess."

Decius turned, gave him a solid kiss on the mouth. "Coffee, Guy."

"Sure." The aide made his way to the pantry, plugged in the coffeemaker, ground two handfuls of prime Ethiopian beans, poured them on top of the filter, then got out some sweetener and cream. They had been friends for a long time; there was no fanfare in their affection these days. "Been up all night?"

"I've been away for several months in an orthogonal cognate, actually. How's the countdown proceeding?"

"I really could use some calibrated electronics," Guy said, smothering a yawn. "I know, I know. Well, to the extent that I can understand what they're telling us, it seems to me that we'll hit omega singularity within hours. The ratio we're running under at the moment doesn't bearing thinking about."

"Quite."

The percolator popped and bubbled, emitted a warming

aroma. It seemed entirely absurd that they should be planning morning coffee when the local cosmos was on the verge of collapsing into the final lawlessness and void of a universal black hole. Outside, gravitational pulses were shaking the entire constricting cosmos in wild oscillations. Galaxies of a hundred billion stars, or what remained of them, blazed at an equivalent number of degrees, shrunk into fraying globes of pure light hardly larger than a solar system or one of Jules's Matrioshka Brain stars. Still the infall continued even as fragrant steam rose from the percolator inside their domestic, exponentially stabilizing shell. Outside (whatever that meant, whatever that *could* mean, really) compressed dimensions were starting to break open and unroll, as space, seething and bouncing, crashed inward ever faster and hotter.

Immense minds had evolved, spread and then dwelled together without conflict for billions of years in this cosmos, suffusing its webwork of stellar constructs and turbulent accretion disk habitats. They had labored for eons in preparation for this infinitely protracted instant of culmination. They were everywhere around the life-support shell, holding it from conflagration by their appalling power and generosity. They were not yet gods; in a sense they never would be gods, not as the ontological mythologies of their ancient predecessors had imagined. Not even they could be said to stand outside of time and space, beyond a Tegmark level sense; they were immanent, their transcendence—their transcension—no more (no more! the mind reeled at its contemplation!) than the final triumph of conscious will over mindless entropy. That was close enough for Decius and his crew. These would be Angels, when the work was done, when the cosmic alembic was turned out and their shining birth into eternity began.

Decius sighed, scratching under his robes. The place gave

him a psychosomatic heat rash. He drew out a clean pad of paper, took up his fountain pen, held his hand poised. Deliberately, he slowed his breathing, the quantum chaos of his central nervous system falling into resonance with the flexing information substrate of the collapsing local cosmos. Neurotransmitter vesicles opened, poured their harvest like hot wine across the synapses of his brain's billion neural columns. Like sparks gusting in a fierce wind, ions flashed and scurried. Muscles worked of their own accord, drawing his clenched fingers back and forth across the page. He did not know what he wrote. Voices from beyond the protective blister of their enclosure drummed through him like a tide. He no longer resented the loss of the station's electronic instruments. Who needed crude tools when the dictation of godlings streamed into you, oracular and penetrating?

"Here," Guy called across the room, "your coffee's ready. Shall I bring it over to you?"

Slumped in hypnotic synchrony with the forces beyond the shell, perched on his orange globe, haughty features relaxed, Decius said nothing. His hand twitched and scribbled, filling page after page with chicken-track symbols. There were secrets here, he knew that much in his dazed transfiguration, secrets that must never be told. Soon, the Angels would be born. That was enough. The pen moved, slashing ink into paper, lifted, hovered jerking in a Parkinsonian tremor as his left hand found a fresh sheet, dropped, scratched onward.

His coffee cooled, and a milky scum formed on its surface.

Four

THE BANALITY OF my reaction next morning embarrasses me deeply. Of course, I woke up a bit after daybreak, because that was the way it'd been for the past couple of months in the outback. Of course I stayed under the sheet and blanket, sliding luxuriously in and out of dreamy sleep, because I knew with great satisfaction that this time I *didn't* have to jump out of bed and light the camp's fire for breakfast, without even a shower. Of course the thought of a shower flung my memories straight back to . . . to . . . what I assumed without a moment's qualm was a nasty dream, but not without its enticing elements. I rolled over, eyes still shut, and rubbed the toes of my right foot against the slithery metallic engraving on the sole of my left. The lovely girl in the dream wore a stamp like that, "the mark of the beast," she'd said, before putting a dead man through a mirror and clambering out a window and—

I sat bolt upright, a grunting noise bursting out of my mouth.

No dream. Too coherent for that. No dream, August, simple absurd reality.

I groaned again and pushed my closed eyes and forehead into the palms of my hands. It was a warm summer morning, late January in Melbourne, with a promise of heat later in the day, but I suddenly felt cold and sick and clammy. My muscles were shaking, all of them, it felt like. Shivering and cramping.

"Get a grip," I said, aloud. I forced myself to climb out of bed, feeling like an infant with the flu. I opened the blinds, looked out blinking at the blue early sky. No clouds. Green lawn down there, needed mowing. Great-aunt Tansy must really be shaken up to let that happen. The tremor in my hands subsided as I pulled on fresh underwear, T-shirt, and my old jeans. No wonder she was shaken up. Amazing the fright of it all hadn't killed the dear old bird.

I pulled on my boots and galloped downstairs, not bothering to abate the noise. Tansy was probably awake already, and if she wasn't, I wanted her out of bed right away and talking to me. I rapped firmly on her bedroom door.

"Tansy, you up yet? Time for breakfast."

I banged into the kitchen, which still smelled faintly of cooling scones. Everything was where it always was. I took down the jar of coffee beans, ground them in a whir of shrieking metal blades, filled the percolator from the tap (Melbourne still has excellent water), poured in the rich brown powder with its rich brown odor, got the machine started. Sliced two pieces of Tansy's home-baked country grain bread, thick toast slices, slapped them in the toaster. Clattered the heavy steel pan on the gas flame, dolloped in butter, found bacon in the door of the fridge, also four eggs, in they went, dashed back into the hallway and hollered, "Tea's nearly up, Aunt, and the eggs will be ready in a moment, shake a leg there."

I won't think about it, I told myself. It didn't happen because it couldn't have happened. My mother had shown me the hieroglyphs engraved into the flesh of her foot when I was so little I couldn't recall being surprised, I must have imagined everybody had one. "It's the sign of our family," Mother had said a few years later when I was old enough to notice that other kids lacked it. When I was about ten, I became desperately ashamed of it, and tried to pry it out of my flesh with fingernails and then with the blunt end of a screwdriver. All that did was produce an amount of bleeding and pain but, oddly enough, no infection. I never seemed to get sick as a kid, nor did my parents. Clean living, no doubt, and good genes.

Bacon crackled. Nothing stirred from the front of the house. I looked at the wall-mounted clock, then at the digital display on the oven. Both of them informed me that Mrs. Abbott would be here for her Sunday-morning duties within the half hour. I flipped the eggs, being very careful not to break the yolks, placed the fragrant bacon on paper towels, poured tea into a big mug for myself (a "Cows of our Planet" picture on the side), another with milk and two sugars into Aunt Tansy's favorite cup-and-saucer set, featuring Elizabeth Windsor's coronation as Queen of the British Empire in 1960. Slurped some tea, chewed some buttered toast, wiped my mouth and carried Tansy's breakfast on a large tray decorated with a cross-hatched pattern of lacquered dead wooden matchsticks, a present I'd made for her when I was considerably younger. It made me feel quite sentimental, knowing she'd kept the ugly thing and still used it. I knocked twice, then eased open her door.

No waking voice from the dimness. No snores. (Tansy was a terrible snorer, although she denied it fervently.) No chemical vibes of a living elderly human.

You can tell. It must be made of sour sleeping breath and the residues of old farts, and skin and hair oils and soap scents released by the warmth of metabolism, that smell, and it wasn't there. Tansy had vanished with the dead man upstairs.

I yelped, put down the breakfast tray on the polished

wooden floor of the hall, flipped the light switch. The bed coverings were thrown back, but I saw no signs of a struggle. Tansy's two neat, slightly worn slippers sat side by side on the left of the bed, and her watch was on the sideboard beside a half-filled glass of water. A small book lay open and facedown, as if she'd been reading it the night before and been interrupted; Tansy always shut books, holding her place with a patterned bookmark.

"Oh shit," I said, dismayed. "Oh shit."

I ran quickly from one room to the next on the ground floor, even peering into closets, then galumphed upstairs and did it all over again. None of the doors was locked, all rooms were empty, even the bathroom where the dead man had—

I raced down and out the back door, after retrieving the big key from the mantelpiece. Small birds flew up in surprise from the grass where they were molesting insects and worms, and a magpie squawked high in the eucalyptus next to the fence. I couldn't see Tansy anywhere. I ran to the small toolshed. Empty, heavy with odors of oil and metal and gasoline from the mower, nothing human.

I went back to her bedroom, cast about. Nothing. Something caught my eye: the odd title of her reading matter. I picked up the book. *SgrA**. What the hell kind of title was that? I opened it, read with growing astonishment. This was *not* the kind of thing my dear old great-aunt usually read before nodding off:

> I needed Arthur conscious, if that meant anything, so we paralyzed his voluntary musculature with standard nerve blocks, those distant descendants of the lethal poison curare, to prevent flinching or worse. My nurse, Melissa Demetriopoulus, who was also

dealing with the anesthesia, ran a very low dose of hypnotic into his blood through an intravenous

Someone was knocking at the front door when I surfaced, alternating with noisy rings on the doorbell.

"Hold your horses," I grunted, embarrassed to be prying into Tansy's unexpected interests, frightened out of my wits as well, clomping along the dark hallway. It couldn't be Aunt Tansy; she always wore a key to the front door around her neck on a sturdy chain, something I had insisted upon when she locked herself out one day. Poor old lady.

Mrs. Abbott regarded me with surprise.

"August! Your aunt wasn't expecting you for another week."

"You don't happen to know where she is, do you? Oh, I'm sorry, come in." I stood aside, closed the door behind her. It made a solid sound, comforting, or would have been comforting had Tansy been on the right side of it.

"Why, has she gone out already? Well, it's Sunday, you know, perhaps she's trying that new minister at St. Bartholomew's, Pastor Jules, he's said to give a fiery service." She twinkled at me naughtily. "And to be *extremely* good-looking."

I shrugged, led her to the kitchen. Good grief, I'd fallen from some sort of creepy thriller into a Jane Austen novel. But no, Tansy had long been an aficionado of faiths. Last time I was here, she'd been attending a Theosophical revival temple of some sort, the Annie Besant Occult Chemistry Fellowship. I settled Mrs. Abbott with a cup of tea, went back and collected the spoiled breakfast from outside Tansy's door, nibbling at the bacon like an anxious raccoon. The church theory made little sense. Granted, Tansy might have slept late (just possibly), hurried to dress, and so failed to tidy her bed (unlikely enough) yet replaced her slippers by the bed. But she was a person of immense punctuality and I couldn't believe she'd have left her watch behind.

Just to be sure, I grabbed my car keys and drove around to St. Bart's, down the hill on the edge of yuppie Westgarth. The small stone-and-brick church smelled, as I entered quietly, of flowers and Sunday-best clothes with a faint aftertaste of incense, and the preacher was in full flight. I stood at the back, scanning the crowd of worshipers as they sat in their gleaming wooden pews. A head or two had turned as I came though the door from the vestibule, old gray heads of the same vintage as Great-aunt Tansy. One frowned and clucked, and bobbed her head to whisper to her neighbor. More of the parishioners were younger, though, listening raptly to the vigorous performance of Reverend Jules. Mrs. Abbott's informants were correct. He was tall, impeccable in clerical blacks, with a dense dark beard that made him look like a Byzantine icon of some sensuous saint. Something about his looks reminded me of . . . I couldn't put my finger on it, and I moved to one side to get a better view across the congregation. No Tansy.

"This is *not* the true world," he told them, shooting me a bland glance and gesturing to an empty pew with his head. I stayed put, peering for Tansy. My heart sank. She definitely wasn't there. "Attend to John's gospel, chapter 17, verse 14: 'the world has hated them, because they are not of the world, even as I am not of the world.'" I could have sworn he raised his eyes from his text and stared down the length of the nave to meet my eyes. "Yes, and in chapter 8, verse 23, 'He said to them, "You are from below, I am from above; you are of this world, I am not of this world."'" Surely that wasn't a sly *wink*? Shivering slightly, I slipped back out again into the sunshine and warming air. Cars passed, more than one of them booming hip-hop, a style I didn't like much. I was always an old-fashioned kid. I did a quick circuit of the church grounds, but Tansy was not lying stretched unconscious on the grass. As I went back to the car, voices inside faintly, raggedly sang something about an old rugged cross.

Mrs. Abbott waited anxiously on the front verandah. I shook my head, shrugged. She seemed ready to burst into tears.

"I'm sure she's just fine," I said, none too confidently. "Why don't you come back tomorrow, and—"

"I'm not due again until Wednesday," she told me, a rebuke. I was not to take her for granted. "I only come in on Sundays as a special favor to that dear gifted lady, God bless her. Why, if anything has happ—"

I walked her to the street, patting her shoulder. "I'll contact the hospitals and the police," I said. "She must have wandered off, she can't have got far."

"Oh dear, oh dear," the woman blubbered, and went away in the direction of the High Street tram, big bag over one arm, hat on her head, handkerchief pressed to her swollen eyes. I raced back inside, stood in the sudden gloom and silence. The large grandfather clock in the hallway tocked with measured indifference. I went into Tansy's room and searched again for evidence of a breakdown—or worse yet, a break-in. Nothing. Old lady odors, clothes neatly folded in drawers, dresses hanging in wardrobes smelling slightly of mothballs.

I sat down in the kitchen, put my head in my hands, tried to make sense of it.

"They came back for her," I heard myself mutter.

It was a truly dopey idea, but nothing else made as much

sense. I had no idea who *they* were, not really. I didn't believe what Lune had told me, I had no faith in worlds beyond our own—not the Westgarth preacher's, nor Tansy's fanciful if lucrative world of psychic inspiration, nor the mad testimony of a beautiful intruder who had messed with my head in a midnight bathroom.

Still, that was the single thing I had to go on.

I drank off the last of my cold cup of coffee, chewed greasy bacon off my plate, and clomped upstairs to look at the mirror.

I rapped on the glass. It shook slightly in its heavy, wall-mounted frame, and the glass stung my knuckles. You had as much chance of getting through it as a bird had of flying through a closed window. That made me shiver again. *As a corpse had of coming in through one,* and yet that had happened. Unless the whole episode was a delusion, or a bad dream, and I'd already decided that conclusion was no better than cowardice and denial. It had happened, get used to it, deal with it. I pressed my forehead against the mirror, heard a faint scritch as my unshaved chin whiskers rasped the glass. I tried to see *through* the glass, and all I saw was my frightened brown eyeballs peering back at me.

I felt like a fool, but I pulled out two drawers about a third of the way to provide a set of steps and climbed gingerly onto the washbasin. I put my shoulder to the glass and pushed, and the glass pushed back. Newton's somethingth law of action and reaction. I raised one boot and pressed the toe against the glass. It failed to sink through.

"Maybe it only works on Saturday nights," I muttered to myself. "Maybe it needs a key." I sniggered, and then swallowed hard. Maybe I *had* a key.

Carefully, balanced on one foot a centimeter from the basin, I pulled off one boot and my left sock. Holding on to the top edge of the mirror with three fingertips, sock snug against my palm with thumb and pinkie, I raised my leg and pressed the silvery "mark of the beast" against the cold surface.

The glass began to melt away, like a bright silver mist.

Off balance, I tumbled forward *into* the damned thing, into the space where the glass had been. I still had the sock in my right hand, and as I fell, I grabbed at my left boot, caught it by the laces. It flipped up and the heel whacked me in the face. I hardly noticed, because I was flying through the air, slamming hard and painfully on a grimy floor under reddish lights. My head rang. I'd bitten my tongue. Smells of oil and ancient metal, corrosion. The distant gonging in my head was not shock, not from the fall: somewhere far off, a great machine was thudding, metal slamming metal.

I got up, more scared than I'd ever been in my life, and looked around fearfully for the mirror. Not the mirror, the *back* of the mirror. There had to be a—

No mirror. No wall. The red room stretched on behind me, extended on either side to tall cobwebbed art deco windows covered in smears of dirt where the dust of years had settled and rain had turned it to mud.

Not in Kansas, not in Northcote, not in any bloody part of the known world.

A phrase Lune had used burst up into memory. I laughed out loud, shaking my head in disbelief.

"I'm outside the Contest," I said aloud. My words were swallowed up in the emptiness, in the beat of the distant machine. I raised my head and widened my eyes and took a very deep breath, and roared out as loudly as I could: "*Prompt!*"

* * *

In the echoing all-but-silence, nothing stirred. Far off, the thumping continued like a machine's heartbeat, regular, all but inaudible after a while, as ear and brain edited out its thump. I kicked angrily at the dusty floorboards with my booted foot, then sighed, brushed my bare, cold foot clean, pulled on the other sock and boot, crouched, tied the laces tightly. Something ran up the wall and stopped, like a gecko. It waved tendrils at me, froze, disappeared.

I ran at the wall, and the thing moved fast. Instantly, it had morphed its coat or shell to the wall's dull sepia, but I could see its edges as it shot for the ceiling. I jumped, slapped my hands high, missed. The thing skidded to the corner of the architrave, vanished through a small hole.

A machine.

That was the astonishing thing. Not a small animal. It had been a robotic device of some sort.

I started to laugh, and turned my back against the wall for support, laughing harder and harder, wheezing with pain. Tears streamed down my face. I fell forward, clutching my diaphragm, which hurt. My roars of laughter came back at me from the distant walls, spooky and sepulchral, and that only made it more absurd and funnier still. The air in my lungs was gone. I thought I'd pass out. I slid down the wall and cowered on the filthy, deserted floor.

Somehow, impossibly, I was in a sim, that had to be it. I'd played in simulated games on-line, of course, I'd run Sim City through endless iterations when I was a child, entered the imaginary family called the Sims, worked my arduous way through the magical locales of Myst, I'd even spent a month or two in

Anarchy Online, my avatar roaming the city of RubiKa, sometimes as a Doctor, sometimes a NanoTechnician.

None of it was new; that was what rankled. For that matter, when I was small I'd enjoyed a TV show called *Sliders* where a bunch of confused people zipped at convenient fifty-minute episode intervals through some sort of curvy gleaming wormhole between parallel worlds. Hardly a new idea, dude. But as far as I knew, no serious scientist endorsed it for the real world. You didn't open the latest copy of *Nature* and read of proposals by the world's major particle-physics labs to crack open a doorway into an adjacent reality. Tiny black holes, yeah, they'd try that at CERN. Quantum entanglement links between carefully established microenvironments, that came up now and then. But not this. Not mirrors you could step through. Not mirrors where the back was gone after you passed into the next world. Not dirty empty worlds where color-coordinated robot reptiles kept an eye on you and then disappeared into the walls.

Somewhere nearby, an elevator whined into life.

I snapped alert, looked for cover. Nothing near at hand. No elevator doors, either. I stepped quickly to the nearest window, peered down through brown streaks at the city street. This really *wasn't* Northcote any longer. Could have been any small inner-city laneway deserted on a major national holiday. The creepy thing was the absence of parked cars. Not one. No sheets of discarded newspaper or candy wrappers blowing in the breeze. I moved away from the window as the elevator stopped, and doors hissed open. Yellow light spilled from a place on the farthest wall where another art deco window had been a moment before. *Trompe l'oeil,* "trick the eye," a favorite stunt of this school of architecture, I seemed to recall. And out of the open doors poured . . .

A cascade of scurrying *things,* brightly polished cans on slender spider legs, segmented snakes in carpet hues, robots the size of mice and cats and dogs and a couple of industrial-strength cleaning buckets. Some ran left, some right, a handful went up the wall and clung to the ceiling. The remainder shot straight toward me.

I couldn't move. My belly still hurt from my hysterical laughing jag, and my eyes were blurry with tears. I wiped them with the back of one hand, crouched in readiness. But already they had stopped. A half-circle of robots in a charming range of sizes and forms regarded me with sensors like multifaceted bee optics, waving antennae, flickering snake tongues questing after my stink and pheromones, probably. One of them said in a loud clear voice:

"Innocuous."

I stayed where I was, poised for violent action or swift retreat.

"Stand down," a woman's voice called. The machines remained precisely where they were, but some kind of urgency went out of them. Tongues withdrew, tendrils relaxed. I stared at the yellow light and saw a woman of about thirty step confidently into the room.

"And who might you be, young man?" she said, approaching me with no concern at all for any risk I might pose. She wore sensible shoes and a neat short haircut that did nothing for her looks. Her broad heels clicked in the silence on the floorboards. Her brown gaze stropped up and down me but found nothing worth remarking. "Oh, for heaven's sake, relax, child. I asked you your name." The accent was hard to pin down. Rather like an upper-class European who had lived on the West Coast of the USA for many years.

I cleared my throat, and extended one hand.

"Seebeck. August Seebeck."

That jolted her. "Not funny." Her own arm remained by her side. Her mouth turned down at the corners. "Who *are* you, and how did you get in here?"

I straightened. "I've told you my name. Who are *you*?"

"And I've told you I don't believe you, you insolent boy. As you must know, I am Ruth." If she was waiting for a startled reaction, she was disappointed. I continued to meet her gaze. She frowned very slightly. "Ruth Seebeck."

"Oh," I said. I dropped my eyes, shook my head. "Oh."

The woman turned away and with casual malice said, "Bring him along, kids. Silently."

Breathtakingly fast, an Axminster snake coiled back down, steel inside its carpeted helix, then flung itself at my face. I jerked away but already it had its head inside my mouth, choking me. The length of the thing clenched convulsively around my jaw, neck, upper shoulders—not bruisingly but firm. I choked, anxiously drew in air through my nostrils. I felt my nasal passages closing and the airways locking up. I tried to tear with my hands at the robot, but they were shackled by the weight of a dozen clinging machines the size and mass of rats. I jinked to one side, and somehow the bucket was waiting for me, tipped on its side, and my left foot went in as it raised back on its wheels. I was furious, indignant, quite beyond laughter. Something bit my right ankle. Snorting air with a rough snoring rasp, I kicked at it; it was stuck to me, slithering under my boot. When my foot came down again my boot slid forward, as if I were shod in iceskates.

The thirtyish woman with the impossible name was by now halfway to the elevator, short hair bobbing, tweed librarian's skirt scarcely swaying. She did not look back. I was scooted after her by this menagerie of robotic contortionists, one foot sliding frictionlessly, the other jammed into a rolling bucket. My eyes had clouded up again with tears, of rage and frustration. We swept into the elevator, the remainder of the crew scooting in behind us, piling up neatly like a conjuring trick.

"Home," said Ruth Seebeck. Perhaps it was just as well that the robots held me braced, or I'd have stumbled. The elevator compartment slid smartly away to the left.

I was deposited in a comfortable armchair of buttery leather in the pleasant, rather subdued living room of Ruth's apartment, if that's what it was. Hidden sound sources were playing something jumpy and disjointed by, by, um, Alban Berg; I recognized it from Itzhak's repertoire. The snake withdrew from my mouth, leaving my tongue and lips dry and coated in fibers. I tried to spit them out, and was misunderstood.

"Don't take that attitude with me, young man."

"Water," I said. "Please?"

Most of the machines had retreated, but I remained weighted down, feet locked together now and arms heavily pressed to the soft leather embracing me. Ruth gestured; my right arm was released. I pried out a handkerchief, blew my nose, coughed.

"Give him something to drink."

Immediately, a tall slender thing stood nearby, a tall slender glass of sparkling mineral water in its extensor. I took a swig. The bubbles, as they will, went up my nose. I choked and coughed some more, swigged, put the glass back.

"Have you eaten? I was about to have luncheon. You might as well join me. Set him free."

I rubbed my ankles, stood up warily. Her table, visible through open clear-glass lead-light doors into the airy next room, held yellow and blue flowers in a crystal vase, a carafe of white wine, a fresh tossed seafood salad in a huge wooden bowl, and a covered serving dish from which fragrant steam escaped. Scurrying things popped an extra set of cutlery at the far end of the table, next to a bib in a slightly tarnished silver ring. I realized that in fact I was extremely hungry, unless that was just the acids of fright. I dislike starting the day without an adequate breakfast.

"Thanks, no," I said. "I had breakfast just a few—"

The chair pulled itself out. Ruth gestured me to it.

"Sit. I won't eat alone with you standing there, and I have nowhere else to put you. What do you mean, just had breakfast? It's past noon, are you one of these slugabeds who laze away the best years of their life? Give him some salad and steamed rice."

I peered into the bowl, which was lined with crinkly leaves of cos lettuce filled with a mixed mound of peeled king crabs and cubes of lobster, and what looked like pieces of some white fish, in crushed tomato. I could smell French dressing. Scuttle, slither, food was there in front of me on a plate. My glass was filled with pale golden chardonnay. Ruth waited conspicuously for me to begin, her fork poised like a conductor's baton. I thought of saying grace, just to see what she'd do, but decided against it. For all I knew, she *was* God.

"I guess you're not an Australian," I said. The seafood was excellent; I dug in.

"Good Lord, I should think not!" Sharply, she tilted her head. "Ah, that explains the barbarous accent." She took two quick, ladylike bites, obviously holding her temper in check. "I trust you and your masters understand that this is a complete abrogation of the Accord."

What? I tried the wine, which was superb. "I'm sorry, I—"

"This is Marchmain's doing," she told me speculatively.

I shook my head, mouth full of lobster and brown rice, steamed to fluffy perfection.

"Jules, then." She caught my hard blink. "Ah *ha!* The bastard! The prying, pestiferous, unconscionable *sneak!*" And then, incredibly, she was smiling. With a shrug, Ruth Seebeck tossed her head in an annoyingly prissy and self-satisfied gesture. "Well, then. Eat up, 'August,' whoever you are." You could hear the doubting quote marks. Maybe this woman was some kind of relative, but she wasn't being terribly cordial, let alone filial. I couldn't for the life of me work out what hair she'd got up her tight ass, as the kids had put it in Chicago. "Would you prefer a good burgundy, instead, or perhaps some spirits? Rum, perhaps? The condemned man might as well enjoy a hearty meal."

Every sinew in my body wanted to jerk from the table, kick the chair back, run from the room. Or, if it came to that, physically attack the woman watching me with her attitude of dangerous, peculiar amusement. All those months of martial arts training paid off, though. I stayed just where I was, breathed as slowly and steadily as I could manage, loosened my white-clenched grip on the table knife.

"I don't know any of these people, Ms. Seebeck."

"*Miss,*" she said. "I'll have none of that feminist nonsense at my own table. Don't lie to me, boy; you know Jules."

I was starting to loosen the rigid muscles at my back. "As a matter of fact, I don't. But I have been in a church today where a Reverend Jules gave a sermon. I was looking for Tansy. Do you know what happened to my aunt?'

Ruth ignored that, gave a snort. "Wearing the collar again, is he? Always had a macabre taste for holy orders, did Jules. As bad as Avril." Her mood hardened again. "The fact remains, you now admit that both you and he have egregiously violated the Accord. If I choose, I am perfectly within my rights to have you obliterated." She paused, and I blinked hard again, my pulse going up despite my best intentions. Nobody had ever *literally* threatened my life before. A fraction of a moment later, she added, "Were I to select that course. As it happens, I waive my right—for the nonce. Eat your lunch, child. I have no intention of molesting you."

I shrugged, blood pounding in my ears, picked up a succulent prawn by the tail and sucked its flesh out. Ruth turned her head over her shoulder and said to nobody in particular, "Get me that shit Jules."

Then that sound again, from the night before, it creeped me out: a sort of tearing, like a rotten old captain's chair if you carelessly sit down hard in it and the canvas shreds under your weight, throwing you to the ground. Happened to mad Davers once; everyone laughed like fools. In the middle of the living room, on the far side of the dining table, a hole opened and a gust of incense blew in. Candles in silver holders, above an oak altar with a simple wooden cross, smoked suddenly and guttered. The Reverend Jules looked out at us, life-sized and startled, and then with a theatrical sigh of forbearance raised his right hand, beringed and clad to the wrist in black. Even as his mouth opened I was in motion, hands on the edge of the table, convulsing in a standing leap to the chair under me, from there forward on to the tabletop, across it in two crashing bounds, but already it was obvious that the impossible window into nowhere, into my own world maybe, was just too damned far for a leap from the table.

"Fuck it," I said, dragging in a huge gulp of air, and like an Aussie Rules footballer levitating across his teammate's back for the spinning ball high above them both, I crushed my booted feet on to Ruth Seebeck's shoulders, one foot squarely per shoulder, and hurled myself on from her fulcrum. As she went down under my impact, I heard Jules call coolly, "Close the Schwelle," and Ruth yell in a high-pitched fury, "Divert to—"

and that was all I caught because I was through, falling into a blue pool green with water lilies, and a woman in solemn robes who looked somewhat like Ruth and somewhat like my mother, and maybe a bit like me, stared with her green mouth agape, and then I hit the water with a noisy splash, flailing and choking, whacked something painfully with one hand on the bottom, snorted water into my antrums, and by the time I'd righted myself and paddled to the edge the window was gone.

The woman was angry. "Ember, get out of there, you oaf." She took another, closer look as I floundered. "Damn it, who the hell are *you?*"

I smiled sunnily.

"Hello," I said. "Sorry about that. I'm August. And you?"

"August? What? Impossible." Then: "The Sibyl Avril," the woman said faintly. "You've just spoiled three quadrants of preparations. How in the Ancient's Name did you get here?"

"It's been that kind of day," I said, pulling myself up on to the ledge. A small robot, out of commission, still clung to one leg of my jeans above the knee. My right hand was starting to throb oddly, and in the greenish light I saw that it was pumping blood from the large gash in my palm where I'd scraped the bottom of the pool and slashed myself through muscles to the bone on open oyster shells. Half the flesh of my palm was hanging off like a white flap of chicken meat.

Shuddering, I sort of faded into gray.

FIVE

FOR HER FIFTY-third birthday, Lune's Ensemble gave her dinner at a cognate of a Great Fire of London. A fierce wind fanned the flames away from their hostelry, although the heat and stinking smoke blew back at them in fitful gusts, good for a thrilling shriek. Black soot fell like confetti, detritus of singed straw from roofs, blazing wormy timber, human flesh. Churches and leaning tenements and whorehouses alike were burning to the ground, the fury of the blaze laying waste more than half the great cesspool of a city. Torn between terror and rapacity, their pock-faced host and his cringing servants remained on duty, bringing them rich fare. They dined on swine knuckles steeped in the blood of piglets, suet dumplings laden with sweet lard, and a surfeit of lampreys, washed down with thin bitter beer. Firelight mottled the walls of the tavern, made their eyes dance.

For dessert and liqueur, they bore her through a Schwelle to a Tenayuca, a place of noise, jackhammers, vehicle bells and airplanes flying overhead. At 11:52 in the morning they sipped cognac and watched as a passenger semi-ballistic tore into a great glass and mirrored-steel Aztec pyramid several hundred meters away, as they had known it probably would. A whirling, seething fireball flung into the blue air. Lune watched, appalled, her dessert forgotten, as white smoke billowed.

"Beyond doubt, despoilers' work," Morgette said, spooning up gelato. "This morning's efforts will set the whole local sheaf into a spin downward toward closure, paranoia, terror and nescience. The abandonment of everything truly worth striving for. So poignant." She laid aside her spoon, looked (avidly, it seemed to Lune) at the roiling clouds of broken concrete, broken bodies, broken dreams. "So piquant. Such a fucking waste."

Dismayed, Lune watched humans running past, their painted features bleached in grief and disbelief, tears running down their cheeks making the paint smear. She held a doctorate in Ontological Mechanics and a practical diploma in Reality Engineering, yet such casual brutality never failed to bow her spirit low. Morgette, she noticed again with distaste, smiled as she observed the street commotion, enjoying a sort of jaded pleasure. For more than two decades this had been Lune's own work, too, but she held to the passionate hope that its routine atrocities would fail to rot her from the inside. It would be so easy to drift away into self-delusion, to regard all this as nothing more than virtual reality, simulation, construct.

She found herself in the street, her fingers clutching at her hair. Once outside in the open, she could only stand, staring. A crowd gathered in the midst of the turmoil, some taking pictures. A man in a turban pulled out a disposable camera, snapped some shots.

"Come back inside. You're spoiling your party."

"Morgette, I have to go over and see if I can help." She realized she was crying. Someone bumped into her, a slender black man dressed in business *maxtli.* His *tilmatli* cloak was caked with soot, stained with blood, coming loose at the shoulder; his gold ornaments were astray. The man staggered toward the edge of the sidewalk, about to fall.

"Hey, let me help you." The Náhuat words and grammar came effortlessly. Lune put an arm around him, steered him to the center of the walk. "We need to find a place where you can sit down while I get hold of an ambulance."

"No!" She had to lean close to understand his hoarse voice, rasped by the chemical fumes of the burning building. "My wives. We got separated. They're both still in there somewhere. Gotta go back and find them." The man lurched away from Lune, confused, away from the smoking structure.

Lune went toward the ruined angular ziggurat, walking rapidly, now running. Crossing the street against the blue light, she heard new cries of terror burst from the crowd around her. Two more semiballistics were hurtling straight toward the gaping crown of the pyramid. In fascinated horror, she watched the ballistics crash deep into the bowels of the place in a ball of fire.

"*That* was no fucking accident!" someone in the crowd said, Náhuat in a Lakotan accent. Police and firefighters were yelling now, telling people to stay back; Lune found herself moving closer. Flaming debris rained down from the side of the topless building where fragments of the spacecraft, toppling slowly, had fallen into the street. Through gaping holes, black smoke poured. For some reason the smell of burning, the drift of ash, struck her as more urgent, more horrible, more *real* than the ruination of London a few minutes earlier. Could it be the profound unnaturalness of the odors: all the synthetics, the residues of tons of fuel flaming explosively like a bomb, the insulation, the synthetic fiber feathers of hundreds, thousands of dead? More people were running past her, and with deep depression she watched a human being leap from a window high up in the shattered building, tumbling through the air, kicking as though trying to stay right side up, a tangle of knotted quipu strings in hand. Sooty debris sifted down onto the sidewalk. Flakes landed on her outstretched hand, perhaps charred flesh. I should get away from here, she told herself. What good am I serving? This is voyeurism, not study. I should return to my birthday party. Her body would not obey her will.

Still people surged out of the front entrances of the building, many hardly able to walk. Two men in some sort of emergency garb seized an obese woman dressed like a gaudy bird, helped her to an ambulance. Lune ran to them.

"Do you need help?"

"You a trained nurse?" one of them shouted back. The uproar, she understood, was enormous, and against the racket of sirens and voices her own voice was nearly lost.

"No, but—"

"You need to get clear of the area if you're not medical or part of a firefighting crew." You don't have to yell at me, Lune found herself thinking, angry. A woman limped away from the buildings, in obvious pain.

"Let me give you a hand." Lune offered her arm, and the woman leaned heavily against her shoulder. Her shoes were missing, her brown feet blackened, the geometric designs of her short-sleeved *huipil* stained. A pretty receptionist, perhaps, made ugly by soot and the morning's mad cruelty.

"I need to find a phone," the woman was saying. "I have to call and let my husband know I'm okay."

"We'll find you a phone. That store up ahead, they'll let you use their phone." The manager, wringing his hands, stern face gray under its paint, let the woman sit down but said the phone service was knocked out. Lune went back outside, started again for the ziggurat. At the curb, about to cross, she heard a roaring overhead. A fourth ballistic? She readied herself to open a threshold, peering up at the sky. The hot sun was high overhead. No. One entire side of the structure closest to her was peeling inward; shattering like a dream. She turned and ran as fast as she could, for a block, stopped and looked back. A mound of rubble and foul dusty smoke. The great pyramid had simply—disappeared.

Once, great woodlands filled with beasts and birds and a few humans covered this place, or places like it, she thought; in many worlds they still do so. Pristine creeks and sheltering forests. Cultures capable of living in unity with the natural order, whatever that was, whatever its source, however perverse its roots. White noise singing in her ears. Someone dragged her, with a jolt, under an awning. Dust and debris poured down. Coughing, she pulled her *huipil* blouse up over her mouth and nose to keep out the dust and smoke. This is what the deformist K-machines are doing, she told herself, crouched against the relative safety of the wall at her back. Someone or some thing deliberately flew semiballistics into that human-crowded building, struck them in just the right way to bring them down, and in the great cascade of shock waves that would flow outward from this moment perhaps bring down the whole industrial civilization of a world, a sheaf of worlds. And they did it for the hot joy of the deed, the emotional excitement. It was a key part of the method of the Players and their adversaries, she knew that, and the knowledge was sourness in her mouth. Pick just the right fulcrum, the most vulnerable entry point for your chisel, and the damage you do will spread like fire. Growing, harvesting, building is hard work, sometimes bitterly effortful, but ruination is easy. You can make it all disappear. One person with the exact lever can destroy a reality.

Stumbling, amid the sirens and the sobs, Lune returned to the café. Soiled plates and half-empty glasses remained on the tables. Her Ensemble had left. Drawing a wrenching breath, she opened a Schwelle and followed them.

SIX

A DECADE EARLIER, I had been marched in to the school principal's office for turning up at school in jeans, high-tops and sweatshirt.

"Mr. Seebeck," the principal had started frostily.

"Ms. Thieu, that's pronounced 'Zay-bek,'" I'd said quietly, standing in front of her desk with my hands joined behind my back. Maybe my hands were a little sweaty. It was easy being nervous around adults when I was a kid.

She blinked. "'Zaybek,' eh? August, what do they call you for short? Gus? Augie?"

"August," I said.

She blinked again. After a moment she went on smoothly, "Where are your family from, August?"

"Australia," I told her. Good grief. "Fourth generation. My great-great-grandfather was Estonian." I was wrong about that, in a way, but we'll get to it in due course. I paused, and just as she started to say something else, I added, "On my father's side."

The principal coughed behind her hand. "Yes, obviously, Mr. Seebeck. It's deeply sexist, but society has always preserved the parental name only through the male ancestors." Actually, that's not so obvious either, once you know about the other worlds, where they do things differently. As a nearly pubescent kid, though, I didn't know about them. There was an awful lot I didn't know about, and Ms. Thieu certainly didn't. She just straightened up in her leather chair, considering me with a serious look. "However, young man, I haven't requested you to join me in order to discuss your family history. I want to know why you aren't in school uniform."

"I don't like uniforms," twelve-year-old-me said. I wasn't rude, but I didn't budge or apologize.

"One of the features of living in a civilized society," Ms. Thieu informed me, fingers pressed together in a steeple, "is that sometimes—often, in fact—we must do things we don't like."

I said nothing.

"You do see what I'm getting at, August?"

"Not really," I said. "School uniforms suck. They just make us instit— Instut—" I broke off, the word blocked on my tongue.

The principal looked surprised. "'Institutionalized?' That's a big word for a—" She shuffled the papers on her desk, found my records. "—a twelve-year-old boy. And an inappropriate one, luckily. We are not trying to break your spirit, Mr. Seebeck. We don't wish to turn you into a faceless robot. Far from it. This school's policy demands that all students wear the same clothes precisely to *protect* your individuality."

I gazed at her in frank disbelief.

"Think about it, August. If everyone could wear anything they liked, the place would turn into a squabbling barnyard. Wealthy children might choose to wear expensive designer outfits. That would make the less-privileged feel uncomfortable."

Right. And that doesn't happen already? I said nothing, just looked at the floor, waiting for her to finish and let me return to class.

It went on for a while, and instead of going back to the classroom I was sent home early with a note to my parents, asking them to ensure that I wore appropriate uniform items in future. I talked it over with Mum and Dad that night, and they agreed with me: It was my decision. Next day I went back in jeans and polished leather shoes and neatly ironed school shirt. Mr. Browning, the arithmetic teacher, was in charge of assembly. When he saw the jeans, he freaked, sent me back to the principal's office.

Yack yack, blah blah, yada yada. I just waited it out. I ended up missing three weeks of school, studying happily at home, and Dad and Mum met the school board on five separate occasions. An article appeared in the *Advertiser* that embarrassed the school, and eventually they just dropped the issue. I wore whatever I wanted after that.

James Davenport, the class clown, turned up a week later in a taffeta tutu and dancing shoes with pink pom-poms, and said it was against the equal-rights laws to forbid his free choice of garb. Everyone laughed a lot, and the teachers choked with rage, but Ms. Thieu decided to let it ride without a word, and three of the fourteen-year-old tough kids tried to beat Davers up and called him a gayboy, but the rest of us stood up for him, to his surprise, and all he copped was a bruised arm. His sister's dress got mangled. He didn't wear it again, not that he wanted to, because he'd made his point, and so had I, and school life went on as usual.

I didn't know about the different probability worlds back then. I didn't know about the Tree Yggdrasil. But I did know *I* was different, not quite like the other guys, not even mad Davers who probably really did have a screw loose. Over the next few years, I did my homework and went to class and sailed through most of the material in English and mathematics and social studies and geography and the dreary rest of it, and watched a lot of TV, and learned to play electric guitar and sang fairly badly in our band Pillar of Salt with three other dudes from the neighborhood.

When my parents were killed in the plane crash in Thailand, everything went white and empty for a long time.

I started back at a different school, in the adjacent state of Victoria, when Mum's older sister Aunt Miriam became my legal guardian. Until she came to the memorial service I'd never met her, probably because she lived in Melbourne, nearly a thousand kilometers away from Adelaide. She and my mother had never been especially close, she admitted, but she felt it her duty to take me under her wing. I liked her, luckily. I had to go through the whole uniform thing again, but I guess there must have been a note about that sorry history tucked into the file of records sent across from the previous school. The head of my new center for involuntary servitude finally shrugged and agreed that dress code was a matter best left to the individual conscience.

I liked that. Mr. Wheeler was a decent guy, and a good football coach. I played a little with the school team, but never really got the hang of it. Guess I'm pretty much a loner, outside of my special buds. That's okay, too.

Aunt Miriam fell in love with a violinist, the second chair in the National Orchestra, when I was sixteen and in my second-last year of school. He lived across town in upmarket South Yarra, and I went to live with them for six months in his pleasant but rather cramped apartment, took the long train ride to school every day, but none of us really enjoyed the arrangement. I think I cramped their style, even though I spent most of my time either at the gym, practicing with the band, or the library or in my own room. When Itzhak had the chance to go to Tel Aviv for a year, naturally Miriam went with him. They agonized over taking me, too, but decided that I'd had enough trauma and moving from place to place in the last few years. Would have been cool with me. Whatever.

So I ended up in the care of Great-aunt Tansy, my father's aged aunt, who still lived in a ramshackle old house near the top of a hill in Thornbury, the next suburb over from the one where I'd first stayed with Miriam. That meant I didn't need to shift schools again—in fact, it was closer. I stayed with her again after I began my medical degree at the University of Melbourne.

Saying that I ended up in her care is misleading; more accurately, Great-aunt Tansy ended up in *my* care. She wasn't senile, far from it. It's just that strange things tended to happen around her, and this was even before the bodies started to show up in her bathroom.

Now I know why, of course. But I didn't then, and for a long time it creeped me the hell out. It didn't help that she made her money by giving other old ladies "psychic readings," and eventually graduated to a thriving telephone business, a sedate and early version of the pay-per-minute psychic hotline. Working only half an hour a day, she made enough to keep both of us ticking over. Sometimes I wondered why she didn't put in a few more hours and make a killing. It didn't seem onerous, she'd sit with a cup of tea and chat away in a kindly, interested manner, fall gently into a light trance, tell them weird stuff, wait while they gasped or cried, then hang up, after a parting benediction, and take the next call.

Tansy insisted, though, that her powers waxed and waned. Apparently she could perform her magical feats of spiritual comfort and insight only during a certain brief period of each day. The funny part was that the window of opportunity kept creeping backward, so one Monday she'd be guiding her victims—her clients, I mean—from 6:37 in the late afternoon to 7:07 precisely, even though that meant missing the start of the news on TV, but the next Monday she'd be settling down at 6:09 through to 6:39. It was eerily precise, governed by the stars. At one point, maddened by a suspicion that some uncanny pattern controlled this behavior, I kept a log in the back of my calculus text. Tansy was starting each day's toil four minutes earlier than the previous day. I smiled to myself and shook my head. It was like living with a crazy bag lady but without the bag, which has its charms in suburbia.

Then for months at a time the wrong constellations would be shining at an inauspicious time of day, or something of the sort, so she refused to work at all. I could relate to that. My own studies seemed pretty tedious, and after all we managed to scrape up enough income that we ate well (Tansy was a fabulous cook), and I never wore patched clothes or went without new sneakers. Somehow her psychic powers never helped her win Lotto.

Itzhak was invited to first chair in Chicago at the end of that year, and he and Miriam rented a large place of their own just outside the central business district. I went across the Pacific crammed into economy class for a holiday and stayed for a year, finishing high school. That was the year Kennedy was elected president—John, I mean, son of the war hero Jack, not his uncle Robert, who had greeted the returning *Apollo* astronauts although it had been his disgraced nemesis Richard Nixon who'd launched the Moon project. There were plenty of riled mutters from the Republicans that year at what they denounced as the disgraceful nepotistic sight of one Kennedy all but following another into the White House. Me, I was apolitical, didn't care for those games. I had enough trouble being taken seriously when I told the kids in my new school that the Australian president had once been a TV quiz champion, but the Honorable Barry Jones seemed to me a good choice for head of state; he knew a damned sight more about science and technology, not to mention cinema and art and history and all the rest, than most of the lawyers and political insiders who jostle for the reins of power in both my own nation and the USA.

Being the first Aussie that most of my new high-school classmates had ever seen in person, I was a novelty item, subject to the sort of attention usually reserved for rock stars or sports heroes. Celebrity life had its merits. I happily abandoned my virginity in the backseat of Tammy Nelson's fire-engine-red Mustang convertible, something I'd never quite managed back home. Somehow, between carousing at senior parties and learning the rules of American football, I managed to graduate with honors, and flew home to kill some time before starting a medical degree at Melbourne University. Great-aunt Tansy welcomed me back, gave me my old room. And three years later I found two strange women in the upstairs bathroom, doing macabre things to a corpse.

I opened my eyes, head reeling. Awake. Somewhere. And something was badly wrong. I tried to lift my arm, forced my eyes open, looked down at my numb hand.

It was wrapped in a jellyfish. I jerked my arm, and the hand stayed where it was, glued to the deck by slimy transparent stuff that pulsed a little. My feet felt cold and exposed. I sat up and forward with difficulty, leaning on my left elbow. In the greenish light, I could see that someone had taken off my boots and socks and in fact all my clothes, and replaced the jeans and T-shirt with some sort of roughly woven robe in off-white and gray. And I wasn't wet. I touched my hair; completely dry and fluffy, and the skull under it was unbroken.

The woman called Avril, alchemical apparatus or astrolabe or whatever it was beside her on the low table, roused in her wicker throne and gazed at me across slowly moving water. Oh, okay. I was sprawled on a firmish, slightly yielding padded surface on a sort of marble island in the center of the pool I'd splashed down in. A stream gurgled. I gave her a guarded look.

"In an octopus's garden," I said, "with you."

The sibyl Avril looked back at me for a long moment, and then smiled. "The Troggs. Rick Starkey."

What? "The Sir Beatles." I gave her a puzzled grin. "And that's Sir *Ringo* Starkey." Wait a minute, hadn't his original name been Richard? That was back before he'd become the replacement Beatle and they'd all been knighted. My father had played those dudes in moments of nostalgia.

She shook her head, amused. "Oh, so you're from one of *those* variants. What's your mother's name, August?"

"My mother was Angelina. She died in a plane crash."

"I'm sorry, I never knew her. But your father . . . I'm guessing he was Ember. You look a great deal alike." She scowled, adjusting her apparatus. "That's the only reason I'm bothering to fix you up, when by rights I should throw you out on your ear and let you fend for yourself outside."

I squeezed my eyes shut and lay back, saying nothing. When I fell through the windowless window, I recalled, she'd *mistaken* me for this Ember character. Now she thought he was my father. How old did the bastard look? Was drastic life extension one of the side benefits of a silvery tag of hieroglyphics on your foot? Or just privileges with the world's best plastic surgeon? Shit. She'd taken off my footwear, must have seen the mark of the beast. I opened my eyes again and pushed myself up on my elbows. Sensation was returning to my right arm at least that far down, but there was no pain from the terrible injury I'd done to myself in the pool.

"My father's dead, too," I told her. "His name was Dramen Seebeck."

She was on her feet in a moment, robes in a flurry about her shoulders. "Don't lie to me, you little creep. How do you know my father? How dare you come bursting in here, into my sanctuary, and tell me that he's—"

Sobbing, she broke off, muffled her face, spun and was gone from the grotto, leaving her mysterious equipment behind and me gaping and pulling uselessly at my trapped hand. Maybe that was a stupid thing to do, because Avril had obviously taken the trouble to towel me dry, outfit me with fresh garments, however weirdly New Age they were, and best of all treat that horrible wound, or have some flunky do it. Maybe a robot, if she was set up like the tediously practical Ruth. Somehow I doubted it; this watery little nook didn't seem a suitable environment for ambulant machines. Obviously the only sensible thing to do was lie back and try to get some more rest, wait for the unorthodox medical treatment to finish doing its stuff. I was feeling woozy enough, and it seemed like a good plan. Instead, I swiveled back and forth awkwardly, looking for something sharp to pry myself loose with. I gave a bark of laughter. A few meters away, at the bottom of the pool, I'd be sure to find something keen-edged. No thanks.

I worked at the jellyfish with the tips of my fingers for a time, and only made them sore. Through the translucent body of the thing, cool and pulsing like a sluggish heart, I could readily make out the closed curving gash from base of thumb to index finger. It made my stomach contract, and my hand wanted to contract, too, but it lay there passively without pain or stitches and visibly *got better.* A bloody miracle, without blood.

I lay back again and tried to think my way through it. Too many possibilities, that was the trouble. Was I stuck in some version of the imaginary big-screen *Matrix*verse? Could it be that what I'd always gullibly taken for reality was nothing more than a collective delusion piped in by malevolent artificial intelligences through a plug in my neck, while I lay unconscious in a pod? Not a chance. That had always been a pretty damned thin idea. Why would artificial minds bother with such a tawdry illusion? What would be in it for them to start with?

No, this was all real. "Variants," Avril had said. Multiple worlds, then. Different timelines, something like that? I'd read enough popular physics to know that cosmologists favor a bizarre theory called Many Worlds, where every possible choice at the quantum level actually occurs, every step to the right or left is, in some higher mathematical reality, simultaneously one taken to the right and another to the left, plus one forging straight ahead, and one where you sat down instead and stayed put, and one where a dinosaur arrived and ate your head.

Well, maybe that wasn't kosher quantum theory, but it's how the Discovery Channel made it sound. Could that be it? Didn't sound right. Too *many* options that way. *Nothing* was ruled out, how could anyone ever navigate through them using mirrors and windows in the middle of the air? I sensed some level of discipline in this thing, certain conditions. With a jolt, I thought of the strange little man Lune had called the disposer. Where the hell did cleanup staff between the worlds fit into this? Maybe I'd been right all along—their Contest was trashy drama, a multidimensional saga playing in a universe near you, and in all the adjacent ones.

Lune. My heart started to pound. Lovely and mysterious Lune. I'd always been Mr. Cool, yet I'd fallen for her, hard and instantly. I had to find her. And that lumpish bitch Maybelline, if she came as part of the package. Obviously they were members of the same extended family with Avril and Ruth and maybe the Reverend Jules, the great family of cosmic Seebecks, whatever it was. Oh, fuck. I crunched my teeth together, lips drawn back.

What if Lune were my sister?

I gave an angry jerk at my trapped hand. With an abrupt sucking splat, the jellyfish came loose and my arm flew up. The blob fell on to the surface beside me; before I could grab it for closer inspection, it wriggled all over like a wet dog and slithered away to the edge, went into the water as if it were solid water itself. I'd lost interest in it by then, sitting forward and peering closely at my damaged hand. Fingers closed, opened. No sign of the incision. It was hard to believe. I clasped my hands together, carefully at first, then put pressure on them both. No pain. No loss of strength. I licked the palm and it tasted slightly salty, and I felt the brush of my tongue. Give me a patent on those slimy things, or just the import license, and I could make a fortune in the biomedical industry.

How long had it been since I'd set out in search of poor Tansy? Reflexively, I glanced at my left wrist, but the watch was still on the bedside table back home. There was no way of knowing how long I'd been unconscious. Minutes, hours, conceivably days, although I wasn't hungry.

A phone rang behind me.

Instinctively, I reached for the mobile that's usually at my belt. No cell phone, no belt. *Ring-ring-ring. Ring-ring-ring.* Not a pattern I recognized. In Australia, it goes *Ring-ring, ring-ring.* In Chicago, when I'd first gone there to join Miriam and Itzhak, I'd been startled to hear a single fierce stridulation: *Brrrrrg.* Longish pause. *Brrrrrg.* This was different, and strangely disturbing. Yet again, proof that I wasn't in Kansas anymore. I turned, and saw—

Two young women in diaphanous veils. How had they got on to the island? One held her mouth open. I blinked as she uttered, in a pure and bell-like tone:

"*Ring-ring-ring.*"

She paused, caught my eye. Without the slightest hint that her actions were improbable and perhaps evidence of derangement, she added: "*Ring-ring-ring.*"

Stupidly, I said, "What? Hello?"

The other young woman gazed calmly at me, not robotically but with uncanny detachment, and said, "I can't waste time on this nonsense." Her intonations were eerily like Avril's, but an octave higher and a damned sight sweeter. I understood beyond doubt that it was Avril speaking. "I don't know if you're a prankster or a lure, but I'm giving you two minutes to vacate this world. The Ancient—"

I was at the edge of losing my temper. I took two steps toward the young telephone woman and leaned into her face, letting the anger show in my own.

"Coming here was hardly my idea, madam. And you have my clothes."

"They'll be returned. Get dressed and go away."

A third young woman appeared from a green dimness, as if walking on the water, holding out my folded jeans and T-shirt. Socks, jocks and boots sat neatly arrayed on top, like a priestess's offering, which they might well have been. The boots were dry and polished. With a curt nod, I took the bundle, threw off the borrowed robe. The bell girl bent and retrieved it, glancing with frank interest at my nakedness. She was very cute, in an androgynous sort of way; she said nothing. Maybe the only sound available to her was a belling song. I got dressed quickly, ignoring them, and kept talking.

"Listen, Avril, I have no more idea how to get out of this damned place than how I got here. But I want to know one damn thing before you go off in a huff. Where's Great-aunt Tansy? What have you lunatics done with her?"

The indirect light was fading, making the grotto more than ever like something out of a Disney cartoon. I expected to see a pink hippo come bounding in lightly on its flat toes. After a long moment, the telephone girl with a human voice said, "Never heard of her. August, whatever your name is, this bluster is sheer time-wasting, and with one quadrant left to fill, time is something I haven't got just now. One minute left. If you're not gone by then, I'll flood the place." The girl's mouth screwed up slightly, as if she'd tasted something sour, and she rolled her eyes. Not her idea, and one she didn't approve. I like that in a telephone girl. In a completely different voice, she said, "Ask about the stone sword." Without a word more, all three young women turned and vanished into the emerald gloom. I opened my mouth to shout, and the lights were gone.

Fuck. Water, water, everywhere, and not a drop to—You got in here, I told myself, attempting to remain calm, so you can get out. Of course I hadn't *got in,* I'd been *flung in.* What had Ruth said that opened the mirrorless mirror or window or doorway or god-damned portal? How had she done it? I'd seen no mirror in that art deco palace of robots, but some kind of responsive operating system was in place. It had found and reached the Reverend at St. Bartholomew's Church in Westgarth—that infinitely comforting trendy suburb I hardly knew—but the call had been diverted en passant, here to Avril's damp domain. All the sea with oysters, I thought in a daze, then shook my head in the dark. I took a deep breath and said loudly, "Get me that shit Jules."

Of course, nothing happened.

I crouched down, shivering. Avril had turned off the central heating. The comforting gurgle of the stream into the pool was cold and unpleasant. I sat on the yielding rectangle where I'd awoken, pulled off my left boot and sock once more, held my foot up high so the sole was pointing into the air.

"Open the—" What was that word? German, right? What was the German for door? Tür. No, it was . . . it was *wetter* than that. Like water rising on an ocean, like a ocean swell. "Open the schvelluh," I said firmly, hoping like mad.

A small bead of light shone in the darkness before me, a meter above my head. I dragged the footwear back on, rose from my crouch, leaned forward. The firefly dot of brightness stayed where it was; I'd expected it to lurch away annoyingly and lure me into the drink. Moving carefully, I leaned forward and pressed my eye against it, as one might the keyhole to a door closed in one's face.

Blurry brightness. A sort of screen saver, maybe. Where did I want to go? Who did I want to invoke? Hell, it was obvious.

"Get me Lune."

Nothing happened.

I started to shiver. The temperature was dropping rapidly. If this went on, the pond would turn to ice and I'd freeze to death at its side. It seemed inconceivable. How could that crazy sibyl woman do this to me? I recalled the words of the disposer, that comic nightmare figure who I knew was all too real: *It's not the end of the world when one of them finds his way into the wrong corner of a Contest.* Since he'd been lugging away a corpse at the time, I didn't think these were words of encouragement. On the other hand, the mark of the beast on my foot implied that I was far from being an ordinary human. Maybe not human at all. Maybe a relative of all these other crackpots, since Avril, at least, seemed convinced that we shared the same parents.

I tried to get my index fingers into the luminous gap, and managed to pry it open as much as a matchbox's width. It jammed. Oh, well. If it wouldn't give me Lune, I'd have to try the indirect approach. I pushed my mouth against it and said, "Get me Maybelline."

The dot widened like an iris, whoomp. Pressed against it, I almost fell through. I teetered, then went with the moment. After all, I was trying to get the hell away. I threw myself forward into the opening, tumbled, came down in purple fronds under a bleak autumnal or maybe winter sky, and hint of flickering redness.

I found Maybelline in the embrace of something like a tuber, sickly white and shot with blue-purple streaks. She didn't seem to be objecting. Not gay after all, then, or not exclusively. Maybelline had a soft spot for vegetables. It squirmed under her, heaving. The thing had to be extraterrestrial, unless this world had Triffids. Gusts of sweat rolled in the air, or maybe it was raw pheromone, essence of testosterone; it made me jumpy and anxious to fight something or run like hell, but it was acting on Maybelline like catnip. I squeezed my eyes shut, took a step back, and banged into something. It stung my hand, the one I'd just had cured by a jellyfish. At the brutal static shock, I yelped. Startled, the lovers twisted about some more and stared up at me in confusion and, I suppose, chagrin, but I wasn't in any state to assess with nuance Maybelline's emotional response to my arrival. I'd snatched my aching hand back, turning to see what had bitten me, but suddenly I was laughing again like a loon.

The hovering thing I'd bumped into was a flying saucer.

With one offset crystal hemisphere that had seen better days just visible beneath the dull gunmetal of the hovering hull, and the 1950s industrial cabin mounted above like something done in a sheet-metal shop by an apprentice, with translucent portholes and piping around the top and a little dome topped with a pulsing but muted red light. A George Adamski flying saucer. You would have laughed too.

Maybelline disengaged with a rather disturbing sucking sound. All but naked, she rushed at me, and boxed my ears. I was too weak with disbelieving laughter to defend myself.

"You little sneak!" she screamed. "You rotten little pervert. How did you get into my private world? Who the fuck *are* you, anyway?"

Across her shoulder and through the blur of her flailing arms, I saw the alien draw itself up with a sort of diffident disdain, if a vegetable could be granted such social sensitivities. Various moist protrusions in off-white and pale and dark blue subsided and withdrew beneath its scaly outer shell, or leaves, or whatever clad it. Not a silver jumpsuit from Venus, that was certain. This was not one of the saintlike Aryan blonds that George Adamski swore he'd seen in the deserts of California, back in the days when the terms "UFO abduction" and "anal implant" were never seen in the *National Enquirer.* Gasping for breath, trying to catch Maybelline's thumping fists—they *hurt,* when she connected to my head and shoulders—I decided that the rumors about those implants might not be so silly after all. Aloof, the vegetable wandered around behind the curve of the flying saucer, and I heard something heavy clang and clunk. Uh-oh. Ray guns! Or worse, I was about to be fried by a blast of radiation as the saucer rocked and then soared into the clouds. They did that; I'd read enough copies of *UFO Reporter* to know that much of the charming but loony mythos. Their evil emissions burned your exposed flesh like a day at the beach without SPF15+ sunblock. Your eyes could cook and curdle into four-minute eggs. But the saucer stayed put, and I got free of Maybelline, danced away a meter or two, no longer laughing.

"Hey! I'm sorry. I didn't mean to break up—"

"You're that kid," she said, as if she couldn't believe her eyes.

"Right. The green ray. Didn't work."

"That's impossible," she said. Warily, she picked up her discarded and extremely ugly garments from the purple fronds and held them loosely in her hands. No false modesty for her, no lowering her guard while getting dressed, not when I might jump her. I had no intention at all of jumping her; she'd done me no harm, not really, and she certainly wasn't my type. Besides, it wasn't as if this was the first time I'd seen her skimpily clad. Still, I glanced away, studying the landscape: a stand of things rather like trees off to one side, a couple of animals a bit like kangaroos grazing the lower shoots. No buildings anyway.

"I'm looking for Lune," I told her. "And my aunt."

"You're . . . August, is that your name?"

I was quite impressed that she'd remembered. From her point of view, I'd just been a transient obstacle. And simultaneously disheartened; obviously, Lune hadn't seized the chance to bubble over with girlish excitement about my silver hieroglyphs. Why would she keep a thing like that to herself? "Yeah. You must know Great-aunt Tansy, you've been dumping corpses in her bath for the last month or so. Every Saturday night. Ring any bells?"

At my right and behind me, the flying saucer let loose a ferocious stench of marsh gas, and its light flashed crimson over us. I spun about, but it was already at tree height and accelerating fast. Maybelline stared after it with blotched fury.

"*You* did that," she shrieked at me. "You drove Phlogkaalik away, and now she'll go into couvade for six months, you meddling pest, and I won't see her again until the hatching!"

I shook my head, then shrugged. "Listen, lady, I just want to get home. I want to get home to Northcote, on my own world, and I don't want to see any more dead people in the bathtub, and I do want to see Aunt Tansy puttering about safe and sound in her kitchen making jam tarts, and I especially want to see Lune." I was shouting by this time. I don't usually shout, but it was all catching up with me. "Where is she, you, you . . . Phlogkaalik-fucker?"

"Oh shit." Maybelline turned away, obviously realizing I posed no danger to her, and pulled on an orange coverall over some sort of woolen drawers and singlet, and jammed her bare feet into rubber boots. I saw the edge of a metallic mark of the beast on her left heel. "How should I know? She comes, she goes."

"Tansy? That's crap. She's a homebody from way back."

Maybelline gave me a long-suffering look. "I have no idea where your accursed relative is. I've never seen her; I hope I never do. I'm talking about Lune, the bitch."

"Don't call her a bitch, you bitch," I said hotly. Then, after a moment, I added: "As far as I can see, you're one of my accursed relatives yourself."

"Now you're being ridiculous," she told me sharply. "Come here, let me take a look at you."

Something cold touched me on the upper arm, then again on my neck. I looked up; it was raining. In a moment, the clouds opened up, pelting us with large fat drops, soaking me almost instantly. Orgone energy and clouds, I suppose.

"Oh, Prowtpait!" Maybelline said irritably. "You'd better come with me. Give me Heimat."

I tilted my head enquiringly through the downpour, but she hadn't addressed me. A Schwelle opened like a doorway and she stepped through, wet hair stuck to her skull.

"Come on, you'll catch your death of cold."

Something small, apple red and inquisitive, with twitching whiskery tendrils, poked its snout out of the fronds and tried to cross the threshold. It bumped its nose against the air, as if it had run into a very good quality sheet of glass recently cleaned. Offended, the creature recoiled and slipped away. I wanted to do the same but I was half-drenched, and the light on the other side of the Schwelle looked warm, flickery yellow and inviting and smelling of logs nicely ablaze in the fireplace. Really, why not? Saturated, I crossed the threshold and the portal was gone like a soap bubble.

"Yes, you look like Ember."

"So everyone tells me. Who's Ember?"

"Get those clothes off." She rummaged quickly in a side room, tossed me a huge soft hedonistic bath towel decorated with creamy ducks in a pale blue sky. I kept getting drenched, and people kept getting me dried up. At least this time I was still awake. And it wasn't a bathroom and I couldn't see any corpses, unless that was *my* expected fate. Over my dead body. I smiled to myself, vigorously rubbing my hair and shoulders dry. "Ember is one of my brothers," she told me over her shoulder. "I'm beginning to suspect that you're one of his by-blows in that godforsaken world where we were doing some disposal work."

"Nope." She'd taken my clothes into the other room and

placed them inside a clothes dryer; I could hear it spinning. "My father and mother are dead. Dramen and Angelina Seebeck." Maybelline came back out, mouth agape. "Before you have a hissy fit, I know you think that's impossible news, outrageous, cruel and unusual, but it happens to be the case. Mum and Dad died in a plane crash nearly four years ago. They were only . . . Dad wasn't even forty. If what you say were true, you'd be my sister, which is just about believable except that I never had a goddamn older sister. And not only you—Ruth and crazy Avril and for all I know Thelma and Louise. I just hope Lune isn't meant to be one of our happy family gang."

I was taking in the room as I spoke, but from the corner of my eye, it was obviously that Maybelline was horrified by this suggestion. That shocked me in turn; I wouldn't have supposed she *could* be shocked. But then maybe screwing vegetable extraterrestrials in flying saucers is less transgressive than incest.

"Certainly not," she snapped. "Lune is from a wholly different moiety under the Accord. Aren't you finished with that towel?"

I wasn't, but I tossed it to her. In my jocks, I crossed the Persian carpet with its dusty, beautiful motifs of deer and lions and sat down in one of the comfortable old plush armchairs beside the fire. She sat opposite, pulled off her rubber boots, warming her feet, and stirred up the hot logs with a poker. Sparks flew. From another, darkened room, a scrappy brindle cat with half his right ear long since chewed off entered with a jaded air, regarded me disdainfully, sat by himself to one side of the fire and washed his face.

You have to understand that I was dealing with everything by the adoption of massive denial. Industrial-grade denial for hysteria-scale cognitive dissonance. My body clock told me it wasn't yet noon, which meant that all of this insanity had heaped itself up in my life during less than twelve hours since the night before, when I'd gone upstairs to see what was driving poor Great-aunt Tansy into a belated fit of Alzheimer's delusion. Scant hours, in fact, since I'd fallen feetfirst through a looking glass into Wonderland. By rights, I should have been huddled in a corner whimpering. I should have been screaming in a psycho ward, jacketed, waiting for them to hit me with Largactil. Or pounding me with stone swords, whatever the hell that meant. Instead, I sat forward in my comfortable chair and offered my hand to the cat, and felt a burst of extreme pleasure and self-worth when that mangy old guy bowed royally and allowed me to stroke the top of his graying brown head.

"That's Hooks."

In an eerie coincidence, the animal drew back and extended the ferocious talons from his right paw, and delicately began cleaning them, with a faintly rasping sound.

"Cathooks, more formally," Maybelline added.

"Uh-huh. Fascinating. Now, when you have a moment, I'd like some damned answers about—"

A high-pitched but smoky, whiskey-tanned voice rather like an aged dwarf's said, "No manners at all, May." The tom shook his head in disgust and said imperiously, "Fetch me a succulent feast.'

I was already out of the chair as if I'd levitated, gripping the back of it for the comfort of its solidity, then bending, grabbing my boots, and in four or five bounds stood beside the spinning dryer in the laundry nook. "Fuck *this,*" I muttered. Its light went out as I tore open the door; a gust of warm, fragrant air bathed me. I flung on my hot, slightly damp clothes and stared in panic for a way out. In the main room, that tearing canvas sound. The nook was a cul-de-sac, with access only to a windowless bathroom off to one side. I heard Maybelline saying in her hard, insensitive voice, "Ruth, what the hell are you up to? I have this young lout here; he calls himself 'August Seebeck,' and we both know that's unlikely. Shut up, Hooks, you'll have it in the kitchen, like you always do, out of your bowl." Another woman's voice said something I couldn't make out, and Maybelline shouted back, "He was hanging about at one of the collection nexus points last night. I was rostered with Lune." I heard Ruth say something about a green ray, and Maybelline exploded angrily, "Of course, you nitwit, do you think the disposer is a—" I put my head around the corner and saw Maybelline's orange coveralled back, with Ruth facing both of us, standing in her own household of terminal tedium, small odd machines and dust, apparently in the middle of the blazing fire. I got the boots laced up and looked in panic for a way out. Nothing. Well, no, obviously if you can open windows in spacetime and step through them, you don't have much use for ordinary doors.

Hooks looked across at me. "You're in deep shit, kiddo. I'd try sucking up big-time if I were you. Either that, or take a bite out of her."

I started to feel ashamed of my behavior. I was allowing these lunatics to push me around, just because they knew what was going on and I didn't have a clue. That was not a good reason for letting them roll over the top of me. Anyway, it sounded as if they were as much in the dark as I was. I took a deep breath and crossed the room to the two women.

"I have something to say," I told them firmly.

They ignored me. Ruth was saying tersely, "—that idiot Jules is playing some Doomsday theory godgame in his world, I assume. I have no idea why he sent the boy to you."

"He *didn't*—" I said, more loudly. Hooks looked my way; he was the only one interested.

"You sent him to Avril, what kind of bullshit is this, Ruth?"

"Oh, all right! I had to do something. He nearly broke my neck." Aggrieved, she rubbed her shoulders with long, thin fingers, and I recalled using her not that long ago as a launching pad into what I'd hoped was home. Then the splashdown in the pool, the slashed hand, darkness. She deigned to acknowledge my presence with a peeved look across Maybelline's shoulder. "I was angry. I thought Avril might make more sense of the brute than Jules, who'd probably just laugh his head off and skip out."

I said very loudly, "Why would *Avril* know anything about this? *She* wasn't the one in the bathroom, *Maybelline* was. And *Lune!*" Everyone looked at me in great surprise, including the cat. I stood my ground.

"Well, she has her affinity for the Ancient Intelligence," Ruth said, from the midst of the fireplace. Of course she wasn't actually standing amid burning logs like some Salem witch torched at the stake; it was an illusion caused by the overlap of her Schwelle window and the reality we were in. "Who else would be better placed to deal with you, you careless fellow?"

"My name is August," I said. "Why is that so menacing to you all? *August,* okay? Son of Dramen Seebeck, and extremely unlikely to be your sibling, given that my mother was younger than you, Ruth, when she died."

"I have not given you permission to address me so familiarly, August. I am Miss Seebeck."

"Oh, put a sock it, Ruthie." Maybelline beckoned me with one finger. "Come and sit down. We have quite a lot to discuss." She favored me with a ferocious glare, under lowered eyes. "That does not mean we need discuss *everything.* Salience, boy. Pith and relevance."

You'd swear, to look at her chunky muscular body and

youthful face, that she was only a couple of years older than I. Suddenly I wasn't at all sure of that. What I did know, beyond question, was that May didn't want me blabbing about catching her in flagrante delicto with a purple vegetable. I gave her back the hint of a smile.

"I'll try."

"Good. Give me Jules and Avril."

Ruth added immediately: "And give *me* Septimus." Maybelline bridled, but Ruth said adamantly, "I believe we need a quorum."

"Very well."

I sat down, why the hell not. Hooks jumped up on my lap, to my surprise, and began stropping his terrible claws lightly on the legs of my jeans. The vile tearing noise came at me from three directions, like sound effects from a home cinema, and then three windows opened up like a trio of classy plasma screens. I knew they were nothing of the sort, because air moved abruptly in the room, and odd gusts of heat and cool, and an improbable blend of odors: fishy waters, a breath of church incense and old people's clothing, and something new: a stink of ash and death, maybe like a grave reopened, which I'd never had the chance to smell, luckily, or a road torn open for repair work on sewers. Hooks growled and sank his claws for one quick sharp moment of pain into my legs.

A tall, powerful man with a mane of gray hair, arrayed in brown and black, gazed out from the triptych. At his back, dirty smoke rose from ruined buildings into a sky the hue of an old bruise. My gorge rose. That was a place of death, of terrible ruin. Distantly I heard the lament of heartbroken women, the shriek of a child in pain. Septimus crossed the threshold, wrapping his cloak about him, and the horror closed away behind him.

"What do you two witches want?" His voice was deep, gruff, somehow wounded. "I have enough to do without being pestered every—"

"—every decade or so," Ruth cut in caustically. "We know your fine agony, Septimus. Nobody insists that you bear it. Your name is not Prometheus."

He glanced at her coldly, fixed his deep gaze upon me. I cleared my throat and stood up, dumping Hooks onto the carpet. The animal moved away, flirting his tail in a marked manner. Christ, everyone was on edge.

"I do not know this one," Septimus said.

"That's a kid called August," Reverend Jules told him, stepping in to the room. "My little surprise for the family."

From the green glimmering pool of her window, the sibyl Avril said shrilly, "Leave me alone, for love of the Ancient! I fixed the creature and sent him on his way. I have yet one vital quadrant to complete, and I will *not* be badgered by some tiresome family moot. Look to it yourselves. Send me the minutes." Her portal snapped shut.

"What have you done with Tansy?" I said to Jules, face cold, crossing to him, anxiety rising like pain in my chest nearly to the point of illness. These lunatic demigods could not be trusted for a moment. Whatever game I'd fallen into, it was clear that the only way to gain their respect was frankness, daring, sheer offense. I took him by his expensive clerical black arm and spoke through gritted teeth. "If you've hurt her, you bastard, *you* will be hurt. If you are holding her as some sort of ransom, give her up and I'll do what I can satisfy you."

Large strong fingers closed upon my biceps from behind, drew my own hand away from Jules. Septimus was very strong; I tried to shrug him away, using moves I had learned in five diligent years of martial-arts classes, but he held me firmly, turned me like a child to face him. Both remaining women watched, faces pinched and pale.

"You are of this clan, young fellow," he said, and his voice tolled in his chest like a heavy bell. "I feel it in you like a current running through cable. We will do you harm only if you offer us harm. Have you caused grievance or injury to our brother Jules?"

Good grief. Was this National Shoot the Messenger Day? I tried to return his assessing glance with cool. "Your brother has kidnapped the good old lady who's looked after me for years. He lured her into a *church,* for Christ's sake!"

Jules Seebeck's roar of laughter was rich and humorous and extremely irritating. He wasn't taking this seriously, and as I turned hotly to continue my diatribe he hitched himself up on a stool and waved a conciliatory hand.

"Nothing of the sort, August. Your Aunt Tansy is no doubt home safe and sound, having scones and tea with Mrs. Abbott, another pious woman newly of my parish."

"You do know the lout, then?" Ruth said, taken aback, and Septimus belled, "He *is* a Seebeck?"

"Yes, and yes."

Septimus loosened his grip, released me. I was desperately torn. Here was the answer to a dozen mysteries, yet I couldn't wait to hear them. Tansy! Was Jules lying about her? Or was she, in fact, improbably, safe? There are responsibilities that go way beyond the satisfaction of curiosity.

The cat must have sensed my blinding moment of poised choice. He said, in that high, smoky growl, "If I were you, I'd run for my life."

"Shut your trap, you interfering animal," Maybelline cried, and swatted at him with an antimacassar. He evaded her with ease, jumped unexpectedly into my arms. He was heavy and his breath was rank with meat proteins.

"They'll *kill* me?" Adrenaline spurted in my blood.

"Certainly not. This isn't the House of Atreus." Hooks turned his muzzle upward, and gave me a slow, knowing wink with one furry eyelid. "But if I know this lot, and I do, they'll have you peeling potatoes out the back for the next three hundred years." He pushed away from my chest, landed with a thump on the carpet, and went back insolently to his face washing.

I turned at the same moment and ran full tilt to the laundry nook, through it to the bathroom, inside, locked the door. My skin had gone crepey. The Grimms' Fairy Tale tone of that last comment, it suddenly seemed to me, was entirely apt. I'd got stuck inside some incredibly archaic narrative of transformation and cruelty. The doorknob jiggled as I searched my mind for the key out. I gave a bark of crazed laughter.

"Rumpelstiltskin."

Nothing happened, naturally. Okay, try, try again. I said loudly, "Get me Tansy." A heavy shoulder crashed against the far side of the door. Was there some sort of magical minimal decency spell that prevented them teleporting into a toilet? Oh my god, would the same magical prohibition, if there was one, prevent me from *leaving* via the same special-effects CGI method? No, let's assume Tansy's name wasn't the key, then. Maybe she wasn't really part of this family.

Thump, bang. Muffled yells. A good solid door, I approved.

Maybelline had used some technical term, describing her body-snatching stints. Right, okay, give it a try, see if the operating system had memory and the intelligence of one of Ruth's robot's:

"Get me, uh, last night's collection nexus point."

Tearing canvas. Through the opening, windowed daylight against tiles. Tansy's house, the upstairs bathroom. I was staring through the far side of her old mirror. I threw myself across the frame of the threshold as the bathroom door burst inward. I caught a glimpse of Septimus's blood-filled face, his hamlike reaching hand, and I was through. "Close the Schwelle," I screamed, one foot in the washbasin, jumping down, not having a clue if this would work. Maybe it did. Something must have done, because the mirror remained just that, smooth and cool and reflecting me back at myself. I waited for a moment, breathing in jagged gasps.

"Christ!" I muttered. The house seemed to have an empty, creepy feel to it. I thumped down the stairs, belted toward into the kitchen, heard low voices just before I entered.

Aunt Tansy sat pouring tea from her best china pot. A plate of scones sat in the center of the table, and a bowl of yellow butter, and milk in a toby jug and sugar in silver. She was not talking to Mrs. Abbott. As I burst into the kitchen, the disposer turned in his chair and nodded companionably to me.

SEVEN

I NEEDED ARTHUR conscious, if that meant anything, so we paralyzed his voluntary musculature with standard nerve blocks, those distant descendants of the lethal poison curare, to prevent flinching or worse. My nurse, Melissa Demetriopoulos, who was also dealing with the anesthesia, ran a very low dose of hypnotic into his blood through an intravenous cannula in his left hand, just enough to fuzz whatever small consciousness was still ticking over in his poor messed-up brain. When his head was positioned in the stereotactic frame, locking it immobile, I injected a quick acting analgesic at several places in the shaved patch of his skull, dorsofrontal and medial. I waited briefly for local numbness to take full effect, then went in with the drill, its familiar burning stench, guided exactly by our passive scanners to a spot next to Brodmann's area 24 and the nearby basal ganglia. I already had his brain's functional areas mapped after five exhaustive sessions in large noisy fMRI and PET scanners.

There wasn't much blood, even though the scalp tends to exsanguinate quite badly unless you're careful. I pressed the glass-encased electrodes down through his cortex, and beyond into the cingulate gyrus, the big gyrus on the inside of the hemispheres, rather difficult to reach, deep into the core of the neural tangle that specializes in volition—with choice, that is to say, and the ability to act deliberately. Once the hair-thin electrodes were positioned, we tracked somatic markers for a quarter of an hour, calibrating our positional accuracy to the hundreds of nanometers. On the far side of the theater, Handley's cousin Jess waited impassively, draped with greens, her own pinned head with its shaved patch adjacent to the anterior cingulate sulcus bristling its equivalent array of electrodes. She watched lights flit on the monitors, and her odd detachment was echoed in the readouts. For a woman in her fifties with hair shaved from her upper scalp, she remained, I thought, strikingly attractive.

"Well, looks okay," I said at last. "Ready, Ms. Handley?"

"Let's not beat about the bush," she said, slightly slurred. "Shunt him through."

I smiled my professional smile at her, nodded to the quantum coherence operator, the burly bearded fellow named Gilbert Grant who had somehow talked me into trialing this procedure.

Gilbert pushed a button.

I know you're looking at me and I don't care. Watchers must watch as we must suffer their gaze. It doesn't matter. The figure and the breath, the body and the spirit, they're bigger than the world.

Today a green leaf fluttered down like a bird. I nested it in my hand. Long and thin it was, and green. On the table today at dinner we had a soft green tablecloth. I am like green. That is the color of my left eye. My right eye is itchy, red with scratching. Held up against the sky, the leaf showed veins like pale green blood, like the hairy caterpillar I trod on so it splattered, but not as yellow. The soul creeps slowly through the body, peekabooing through one eye. The soul disturbs nothing, but is always laughing. I suppose it must be amused by the green. I don't know why.

I have always been a handsome child. Though why they call me a child, I am six years old, I belong to myself, even if I eat their food and dirty their green. They watch but their gaze skitters away, ashamed. Arms squeezed, oof, I am lifted, the grass around me once more, long and tufted, full of small animals. All day the sun creeps and blisters up the sky and down the blue, fiercy white that lifts out of the green and swims the blue-gray to settle in crimson and song, black things falling into the tree. I must be the sun, the burning thing that struggles in the body and scampers from green to red, scratches, scratches, back again tomorrow for another try. The sun can never stay dead, either.

EIGHT

"WELL, LOOK WHO'S deigned to join us at the crack of noon," Great-aunt Tansy said, eyes twinkling. "Snuck out after all for a night on the tiles, did we?"

I stood warily, poised for something terrible to happen. The small nuggety man reached into the pocket of his faded blue cardigan, took out his pipe, caught Tansy's frown and put it away again. Without getting to his feet, he twisted in his chair and extended his hand.

"You must be August; how do y'do? I'm James C. Fenimore." I took his strong, dry hand. "Call me 'Coop.'"

"As in chickens," Tansy said in a flustered, pleased tone, fetching me a plate and a mug. She patted the table; head reeling, I joined them.

"I found this fine fowl wandering along St. George's Road," Coop told me. "Got herself a wee bit confused, she did. So I fetched her home, and she's doing me the kindness of sharing a cup of char. And these very fine date scones, let me recommend them, young feller."

The green ray, I thought. Whatever the hell it was, its range extended well beyond the bathroom. While it had left me untouched—protected presumably by the mark of the beast or whatever that mark signified about me—it must have swept the whole large house and blurred sleeping Tansy in its fringes. Pity

Coop hadn't had the foresight to use it on previous occasions when bodies had been dumped in the bathtub. But then he hadn't known that Tansy had seen them. Or maybe he didn't care.

"That was kind of you," I told him, buttering a scone. We shared a knowing look. "Well, Tansy, are you sure you're all right now? Do you think we need to see a doctor?"

She was flustered and displeased. I'd embarrassed her in front of her new suitor. "I don't have Alzheimer's, August, if that's what you're getting at. I can assure you that even in my advanced degree of decrepitude I can still—"

"No, not at all, dear. These scones *are* excellent, may I have another?"

"You know you'll wolf the lot the moment my back's turned." That had been a decade earlier, when she'd hidden them in a high cupboard but I'd clambered up and snaffled them. Knave of Scones. If I hadn't known about the goddamn green field effect, I'd have really started to worry. I rose.

"Well, I should get a move on. Very nice to meet you, Coop, and thanks again for helping—"

Nimble, he was out of his seat, too. "I mustn't loiter either. Ma'am, thank you kindly for the refreshments. I'm glad I could be of service. Young man, I wonder if you could drop me off on your way? Your aunt tells me you won a fine vehicle in a game of chance. What are the odds of that, eh?" He gave a booming laugh. Tansy was disappointed, but saw us to the door.

"I'll be back in time to make dinner," I promised, pecking her on the cheek.

"No need for that, boy, I can still roast a leg of lamb and a pan of potatoes. See you're back by seven."

At the curb, I pinged the doors and said to the disposer, "What, no magic mirrors to vanish through this time?"

"Jules wishes us to see him, and he'd prefer we avoid the Schwellen. There are . . . detectable reverberations."

"And he doesn't wish his brothers and sisters to know that we're all skulking around on planet Earth, right?"

Coop hopped up into the passenger seat, strapped himself in like an obedient schoolboy of sixty or so. "They're all planet Earth, feller-me-lad, that's what you've got to understand. At least, the cognates are. It can get hairy and wild and woolly away from the main deixis set."

The what? Dayk-suss? "Where are we going? St. Bart's, I assume."

"The manse next door."

It was getting hot; sunlight splashed up from the road. I pulled a pair of shades from the glove compartment. "And what are you, my bloody uncle or something?"

Coop shook his head ruefully. "Nothing like that, although it's decent of you to suggest it. No, I'm a machine."

The High Street lights turned red; I nearly ran into the tail of the Honda ahead.

"What, some sort of . . ."

He took his pipe out again and this time I didn't complain. I did run the window down. Hot summer air blasted in. "Did you ever catch a movie called *The Terminator*?" he asked, blowing out blue smoke. "Sorry, lad." His own window hummed down. He hadn't touched the control.

We zoomed down the steep hill into Westgarth, following the tram tracks. "I think I caught it on the late show. Young director, never heard of him again. Cameroon, something like that?"

"Ah yes. In this cognate it came out after Spielberg's *Berserker,* which blew it off the map. Elsewhere it's a byword." He nodded to himself, staring at the shops as we buzzed past.

"A franchise, a metaphor. Same sort of thing, don't you see? Machines going crazy and killing everything in sight. Well, I'm not like that." He gave me a reassuring glance. "I handle the bodies, but I don't kill them."

"Oh, good. You had me worried for a moment."

We both laughed. He had bad teeth, but there was no smell of decay on his breath, just tobacco fumes. I've seen strained moments like that in photos in the social pages of *The Age*. Two people who would rather be tearing each other's guts out in the boardroom, or screwing each other's mistresses. In the caption, they're alleged to be "sharing a joke."

"Cognate," I said, turning into Westgarth Street. "You mean worlds that are variants of this one. Parallel universes. Split-off histories in some sort of Many Worlds cosmology. Tell me I'm right and I'll send a contribution to the Sci-Fi Channel."

"Boy, you talk too much."

I drew up in front of the church. "Mr. Fenimore, you might be the first person who's ever leveled that charge. Most people complain that I'm too quiet. Some think I'm morose."

"See what I mean? Blab blab blab." He got out, shut the door with precisely the correct degree of pressure. I sighed and followed him across grass to the front door of the small timber dwelling tucked beside St. Bart's.

Jules opened the door instantly, now wearing a hacking jacket, jodhpurs, gleaming high leather boots and a deerstalker hat. He must have come straight back from Maybelline's when I disappeared, and changed out of his clerical garb. Presumably he was in touch with Coop somehow.

"Just in time," the fake divine said, ushering us in. "Infernally hot out there."

The air was improbably cool inside the manse, with a tang of winter evergreens. We trooped down the drably papered hallway to the living room, with its polite suburban suite of furniture, modest TV set, bare cross hung on the wall, framed photos of solemn worthies and their solemn spouses propped on the mantel, large fly-spotted mirror above the fireplace, and an open Schwelle thirty centimeters square halfway up one curtained window. Snowy air gusted through. It was dusk on the other side, and I thought I could see the dark green pointy tops of Yule pines tossing merrily in the breeze.

"Can I get you a beverage, August? A Coke? Father Pepper? Some grape juice?"

"That's *Doctor* Pepper," I said, "at least in this world, and yes, that'd be good. Can you tell me how to reach Lune?"

"Doctor, sorry, yes, one gets muddled. You'd be surprised—" He muttered under his breath, opening another small threshold, reached through it and pulled out a can frosty with a rim of ice, tossed it to me, closed the Schwelle again. Maybe he had a whole empty frozen world stocked with beverages. "Sit down, gentlemen."

"Nothing for Mr. Fenimore here? He's been walking with my aunt in the hot sun."

"He's a machine, August," Jules said, shrugging, and the machine said reprovingly, "Call me 'Coop.'"

"Lune," I said emphatically. "Tell me."

Jules pulled off his deerstalker, held it lightly in his hands like a projectile. He dropped into a moth-eaten plaid armchair. "The first thing you need to understand, my boy, is that the worlds do not revolve around your needs. Let alone your wants."

I snapped open the soda; it frothed. "I've known that much," I said sulkily, "ever since my parents died, thank you."

"Well, there's some question there," he said mysteriously. "As for Lune, she is of a distinct moiety under the Accord of

Players, and can't be summoned to your side with a snap of the fingers. Our duty rosters do overlap, of course, as Coop will tell you. A pretty child, I have to admit. Is that your whole interest? You're hoping to fuck her brains out?"

I really did choke on the fizzing drink. I *knew* he was bogus, it'd been obvious ever since Great-aunt Tansy first developed her avocational interest in his sect, and right now he wasn't even wearing his fake clerical gear, but childhood habits of expectation betrayed me, as they will. Ministers of religion just don't *say* things that frank. They're not even supposed to *think* them.

"Please don't talk about her like that."

The reverend Jules put on a pious face, but his gaze hardened. "Heavens no, let's not admit to such unwholesome cravings. Whatever was I thinking?"

"Sarcasm isn't necessary," I said, voice shaking a little. I put down the can. "I have . . ." I cast about helplessly, and a phrase came unbidden to my lips, one that normally I found repulsively saccharine and evasive. "I have feelings for her."

"No doubt you do, my boy." Jules threw back his head, laughing. "You're a bit of a worry to me. Not necrophilia, is it? After all, I hear that you met each other across a dead body during mortuary duty."

I stood up and walked toward the door. Nothing was worth this sort of abuse. The machine grabbed my leg as I passed, held on with what might well have been an iron grip.

"Jules 'as something important to tell you," Coop said. "Be polite, lad. Sit back down an' contain y'self in patience, eh?"

I ground my teeth. I felt as if my head were about to explode with anger. Normally I'm not like that. Usually I'm a bit withdrawn but essentially placid. Now I wanted to kill something, or at least maim it.

"I got more information out of the bloody *cat,*" I said.

Jules shrugged. "That cat is a blabbermouth. Despite their reputation for cryptic obliquity, I've never met a cat that didn't blurt out the lot first chance it found."

Wearily I sat down and sank forward, cradling my head. "See, this is a damned dream. It's an hallucination. None of you are real. You're all mythical creatures."

"If you'll believe in me," Jules said in a light, buoyant tone, "I'll believe in you."

"Yes, we've both read Lewis Carroll. Since you're obviously a figment of my delirious imagination, that's no surprise."

"I'm glad you mention the reverend Dodgson. We had adjacent digs in Christ Church at Oxford, you know, in the 1870s. He was a great enthusiast for logical puzzles. I never tried the Doomsday paradox on him, though. Would have been entertaining. I suppose he'd have turned it into a story involving prepubescent nymphets."

And Coop had complained that *I* talked too much. I shot the machine a sardonic look, but he was placidly waiting, his robotic mind in neutral.

"Yet you don't look a day over a hundred," I said sarcastically.

"You'd be surprised. Around here it takes all the running you can do to keep in the same place."

"I've told you, I've read Carroll. The Doomsday argument is full of crap." My skin felt tight. I recalled several conversations I'd overheard between my parents. I hadn't quite understood it at the time, but I felt sure my father had been scathing.

"Oh, you know it? I assumed you'd spend all your time playing hundred-level computer games and cyber quests and listening to appalling noises piped straight into your head by a Walkbox."

"You're trying to tell me that the world is due to be destroyed soon. You reckon it'd be too improbable for us to be alive at any other epoch in history except the end." It was coming back to me.

"And why would that be?"

I succumbed to his goading mockery. "Because the human population is increasing faster and faster, so more humans are now alive than there've ever been on the planet at one time in the past. So the world's doomed; statistics prove it. It's a stupid argument. It would've seemed just as true to the ancient Babylonians." I snorted. "The ancient Neanderthals, for that matter."

Jules shook his head, amused. "Shot yourself in the foot there. I mean, how many Neanderthals do you see walking the streets outside today? Gone to flowers, every one." He grew pensive. "Actually I could introduce you to a very nice Neander family; I think you'd like their daughter." He waved one hand. "Forget I spoke. No, you've misstated the issue. The Doomsday argument doesn't say anything about the destruction of the *world,* let alone of the *universe.* Just the human species."

He annoyed me. "Why are we bothering with this rubbish? I want to know who you people are. I want to know who Lune is." My voice started to vibrate with frustration. "I want to know who the fuck *I* am, for that matter."

"Start at the beginning, and go on until you reach the end, then stop. Think of it as the frame of the Contest. The larger context. Don't you agree that's the most effective approach?"

I squeezed my eyes shut, calmed myself. The warming can of Dr. Pepper had gone a little flat, but I drank a large mouthful; it was oddly soothing.

"All right. Which beginning?"

"Well, dear boy, since we were discussing the Doomsday argument, the best place to begin is the end. You say you've detected a fatal flaw in the logic, but I beg to differ. Ah, ah, do take your time and think this through, I assure you we're going as fast and as relevantly into these brambles as we may. Tell me why you *don't* regard this epoch as the end-times for humankind?"

"Don't you mean, 'Have you stopped beating your wife?'" I felt tired. "Beating your meat is more like it. This is just intellectual masturbation."

The doorbell rang. "Not at all, August. You will be startled, I imagine, at how fertile this line of thought will prove to be. All right, let us revert to the beginning, which is the end."

The doorbell rang again, more insistently.

"Oh, for crying out loud," the Reverend Jules roared in vexation. He flung himself out of his chair, went swiftly down the corridor. I heard the front door open, his irritated, "Yes? How can I help you?" A soft, indistinct male voice spoke, then another in a nasal American accent, perhaps a Midwesterner. "Why, I'm glad you asked me that question," Jules said in a voice like golden syrup laced with rat poison. "Please do come in. These are matters which have troubled me for many years; I shall be very glad of your counsel." The door clicked shut with a jail-cell certainty that made me shiver, and three sets of feet trod toward us. Two young men in bad haircuts, dark suits, white shirts and drab ties followed Jules into the living room.

"August, Coop, I'd like you to meet Elder Bob and Elder Billy, who have traveled all the way across the Pacific Ocean to help us find peace of soul. Here, gentlemen, sit, sit." He gestured them to the couch, where each missionary placed himself uncertainly to left and right of the robot, who tipped his cap and then sat in unearthly relaxation. "These men come bearing witness to a miracle of faith, August, and I would recommend that you study their testimony, for it will stand you in good stead in the hard times that are at hand."

Elder Bob, or perhaps Billy, hardly older than me, was craning his neck to look at the open Schwelle; its cold wind played with his cowlick, and his eyes swiveled.

"Yes, these young worthies asked me if I were Saved, if I had accepted the Savior, and I found that downright *neighborly* of them, don't you agree, August? That they should come out here to Westgarth on such a hot summer's day in their heavy dark suits just to pass on to us this timeless message? Apparently it escaped their notice," he said, tone silky, "that this household is immediately adjacent to a place of worship not of their denomination, and that its occupant might well be, and indeed *is,* a minister, a pastor, an ordained clergyman of that very faith—no, no, boys," he insisted, as they struggled blushing to their feet, clutching their holy book to their sweating chests, "no need to feel embarrassment, because I feel that the Lord has directed your feet or perhaps your bicycle tires here today, for where else would you be vouchsafed so intimate a vision of the truth of that doctrine which I sometimes suspect many of the today's youth affirm only in word and not in heart. Here, since you're up, allow me. Give me Dis. Coop, if you please."

A threshold tore open in the middle of the room. The hairs went up all over my body, and I felt my gorge rise. It was the stench of the holocaust world of Septimus but doubled, trebled. Things with no skin over their raw muscle writhed in agony, screaming from torn, bloody throats. They rushed toward the opening. Coop had the two young men by the upper arms, drew them effortlessly across the threshold, and their own screams joined the rest. I lurched toward them. I had to do *something,* this was literally inhuman. Jules spoke a word; the Schwelle shut with its tearing sound. We were alone, the two of us, and I tottered on my toes, scared witless, beside myself with disgust and anger.

"You *prick!* Do you think you're God Almighty?"

He shook his head, amused, eyes bright. "Ah, that was a tonic. I hate those little shits. Here, do sit down." He let himself back into his ratty old chair, eased the creases of his jodhpurs. "No harm will come to them, silly meaningless toys that they are. Really, sit down, you'll do yourself a damage if you don't calm down. Oh, for heaven's sake, very well." He rose again. "Give me Dis."

The shriek of torn reality. Shrieks, plural. "Bring them back, Coop." Through the window and its atrocious landscape of suffering, the machine half-carried its victims. Bob and Billy sagged, eyes white, pupils pinpointed, breathing in horrendous stertorous gasps. Their clothing was in tatters; slime spattered their legs and shoes. Were those tooth marks?

"You're Satan," whimpered Billy, cowering away. The Schwelle zipped shut behind him. Coop released them; they fell to the carpet, began crawling away toward the hall, their scriptures abandoned. "You foul wicked thing."

"Oh, get over it. I thought you'd be grateful. The green, I think, Mr. Fenimore, and then a touch of the blue."

"Certainly, sar." Coop had his amnesing tube out of his pocket with blinding speed, bathed them in emerald radiance. They lay like children, curled up, happy smiles on their faces. Blue light danced, stranger yet, something I had seen once and in effect deleted from my own memory without need of the green ray. Slime melted away, like ice slurry under a blowtorch. The ripped garments healed themselves, as the evaporated window had renewed itself in Great-aunt Tansy's bathroom, like a videotape run backward, like a broken yellow and viscous mess amid cracked white shell fragments sucked back together and knitted into a gleaming ovoid, the unbroken egg flying back upward against gravity into the waiting hand, deposited swiftly inside the refrigerator door. But this was reality being edited on the run, not backward but forward, smoothed out, spliced and repaired.

I was right, I told myself. I'm in a simulation.

"Tut-tut, you're having a banal thought, August." Jules was watching me keenly. "You're assuring yourself that this is some kind of virtual-reality program running on your petaflop home computer in the year 2051 and you're really some old retired fart with electrodes jammed into his head, jacked into fantasies and remembrance of things past." Close enough, actually; I felt chilled, and it wasn't just the wind from the open Schwelle. "Ah, ye of little faith. Nothing so simple, lad, nothing so neat, nothing so . . . old hat. Thank you, Coop, I wonder if you'd be so kind as to see our young friends to the door?"

"Sar."

Dazed, peering about in a sort of pleased confusion, Billy and Bob took a hand apiece and trailed into the hallway. The door open, shut quietly. I suppose they pedaled away into the hot north wind. I never saw them again, and can't imagine what their dreams told them. If they retained any partial memories of the hell world, did their epiphany serve to confirm their faith or refute it? I don't know and, frankly, I don't care. I'm a Player now, a Player of the Contest of Worlds, and I have bigger fish to fry.

Back then, though, I was an ignorant kid of twenty, waiting for university to reopen so I could continue my medical studies. When had I decided to become a doctor? I couldn't remember; it must have been something my parents assumed I'd be interested in, although they'd never pushed me. I sat down, legs weak and trembling, and stared at the Reverend Jules, filled with revulsion and awe, and realized that clinical medicine was the last thing I needed to study. If I ever got out of this nightmarish hall of mirrors, I told myself, I'd be heading straight to the philosophy department. (As, indeed, eventually I did, which is why I'm now three-quarters of the way through my dissertation on modal logic. But one should not leap ahead in the tale. One should start at the beginning and go on to the end, or at least as near the end, if there is to be an end, as I've yet attained. Let us proceed.)

Without a hitch, Jules picked up the conversational or perhaps instructional ball and carried it forward, carrying me physically with it. Into the air he said, "Give me Star Doll."

As the Schwelle opened into star-shot blackness, he gestured me forward with a movement of his head. Why the hell not? I wanted answers; maybe this was the way. I went across the threshold, Jules at my heels.

I paused on the other side, confused. The vast space wasn't empty, exactly, and the lights overhead were not stars, not really. Far off to the east, or in some direction with dawning light, the spots of starry light were glowing brighter, as if some giant's hand were turning a rheostat and giving them more juice. I swung about, looking this way and that. The plain was gray with pale multicolored lines running in various directions, a jumble. I found no buildings rising up toward the fake stars, no trees or blooms or paperboys on bikes or power lines or lakes or dogs running about or . . . *anything* I could recognize. I might have been shrunk to microscopic scale and deposited on a circuit diagram.

Oh. "*This* is the simulation."

"Nope. This is an inner computronium shell of a Matrioshka Brain. Don't worry about that, we're just passing through. Now *this* is a sim. Show us the Doomsday demo." Jules made the classic motion with his right hand, arm raised chest high, index finger forward. He muttered an instruction under his breath, and we segued instantly, yet somehow without the sense of startled discontinuity you'd expect. It was like the blind spot in your eye; somehow your brain accommodates to the loss of image, smooths it out, prevents you from worrying about the deleted or absent fragment of the scene ahead. Like that, on a totally three-dimensional scale. We flew like arrows at a small fire-engine-red building with two doors. I squinted against the gusting wind in my face. One door was blue, one a deep brown. Their edges seemed to shift, an optical illusion of color contrast that was eerily more realistic than the red bricks. We stood before the doors.

"Choose one."

I shrugged, opened the blue door.

We were in the central square, I guessed, of a Scandinavian city. Cold air blew through my sleeveless T-shirt, up the legs of my jeans. A high pale sun turned everything clear and sharp: the stone and timber municipal offices with their ancient insignia mounted above lintels, deep-set glazed windows, stores modestly signed. A tram rumbled by. On every side, a busy crowd moved, shopping matrons, an old gentleman with a cane, two louts strutting and ogling a pretty girl who ignored them, businessmen talking on their Nokia phones, the whole world's great plenty, or a neat cross-section of it.

"What do you notice?"

"I need a jacket." I had one, fur lined and comfortable. My feet were warmer, too; I stared at sheepskin boots, pale tan and white. "Uh—" I looked hard at everything. People were glancing at us, interested, polite, glancing away at once. They were noticing—

"They're Nordic, blonds, blue eyes." I looked more carefully. Never having been to Sweden or Finland, it was a rather startling effect. "No brunettes. This must be a construct.

Aryan heaven. What is it, Jules, the fucking Thousand-Year Reich?"

"I told you it was a sim. My Star Doll can run up one of these in a nanosecond without drawing breath. Yes, you're right. August, there are a million wheat-haired people in this town, all of them with blue eyes. You're an anomaly, like me." We were walking along the cobbled street. At a tavern, Jules pushed open the swinging door and led me into a fuggy atmosphere thick with the stink of hops, sweat and beery human breath. A plain young woman pulled beers behind the counter. Her gaze caught me, hesitated, and her brown eyes widened. Dark brown hair, like mine.

"More members of the Seebeck family?"

"Only notionally," Jules said with a chuckle. "See the heavyset guy in the back, lugging in the barrel of ale? Her father. There are ten of them, the only ones in the whole town with that coloring. It's different in here." He raised his finger, pointed. We stood again before the two doors. I sighed and shrugged, and the weight of the fur coat was gone. I pushed open the brown door.

"Yeah, this is obvious enough, Jules." People ran about, or lazed, in the tropical sun, tanned, dark eyed. Water dripped from huge, sun-shading leaves; it had rained moments ago. We trod in puddles. At a stall of carpet sellers across the street, shielded by a canvas awning, I saw the Swiss Family Robinson, blonde father and sons, blonde mother and daughters, *Sound of Music* strangers in a strange land. "I suppose these ten are the only blue-eyed folks in town."

"Among the million with brown eyes, yes. So: Suppose I assured you, August, that you and your family come from one of these places or the other. Which would you think more likely to be your homeland?"

"Is that what you're telling me? That we live among people not like ourselves? Jules, I've worked out that much."

"Pay attention, damn it. Which city are you more likely to come from, with your dark hair and brown eyes?"

"Obviously this one, with the million others like me. But that's not—"

"But that *is,* you see. How surprised would you be to learn that actually you're one of that brown-eyed family from the first city, at home in the cold northern comforts of familiarity, one of only ten people like you in a city bustling with a million quite different?"

"I know where you're going with this, but it's—"

"Quit fighting the logic. You prefer to pretend, in your sentimental way, that the world you grew up in will continue on forever."

"Of course I don't. I mean, I do expect things to change."

"Aye, there's the rub." Jules took the metaphor at its word and rubbed his hands together in satisfaction. "How many people live in your world?"

Mutinously, I said, "*My* world? There's only one." The words fell like something dead out of my mouth; I knew perfectly well that there was a plurality of worlds—an infinite number, for all I knew—because I'd just been on a mad stumble through a small random sampling of them and stood now inside a convincing simulation inside a place I could not start to imagine. "Six billion or so."

"And how many humans have existed since the first grunting creature spoke her first grunting word?"

Ten times as many? Twenty? "How should I know? Tell me." Brown-eyed people walked past us, averting their brown gaze from my palpable public anger. They did not exist. I had to keep telling myself that.

"Perhaps twelve times as many have lived and died in all of human history, August, as now swarm across your globe. But here's a more diverting question: When do you suppose the numbers will be equally balanced between past and future?" He raised his hand as I shrugged and shook my head. "Everyone expects population to sweep upward and onward, swelling ever more numerous, at least for some time yet. Give me your best guess. In which year of our Lord Buddha are the numbers of living men and women due to exceed the dead, all of them, dead and rotted, way back to the first shivering human on the plains of Africa?"

My god, he liked the sound of his own voice.

"The year 5000," I said, plucking a figure out of the air. "The year one million?"

"Nope." Jules winked at an old lady examining her lined face in a window. She twinkled at him.

"Twenty-one fifty," she told him placidly.

"You can't be serious," I said, after a moment, ignoring the fake woman. It had rocked me. "That's only . . . five or six generations away."

"Fewer, actually, given tomorrow's medical technology. Life extension is due to go exponential, kiddo. Fifty years from now, in your world, many children will have such genetic advantages that they need never die of illness or old age. Well, not until something awful happens around 2150."

His certainty made me sick with dread.

"You're time travelers from the future."

Jules roared with laughter, bringing more glances from passersby. "Not a chance. The metric doesn't work that way. No, this is just pure logic and a knowledge of history. Lots of different histories, actually." He leaned forward and stared at me acutely. "Are you beginning to see? Are you beginning to understand?" Evidently he doubted it. He waved his arm, and the world went away. In an eyeblink, we stood once more in front of the fire-engine-red building. Now its twin doors were forest green and a high-gloss silver.

"Come," Jules said, and pushed his way through the green door.

This time I *was* shocked. Breath taken out of me like a blow. I turned to retreat, but Jules blocked the exit.

I stood in the foyer of an enormous, impossibly large room crowded with people. I could not see the end of it, just the wall at our back. Above us, light shifted against a translucent ceiling. With an appalled jolt of perspective, I saw that the ceiling was a floor of glass, thousands of people walking back and forth above us. And beyond them, smaller figures, and yet smaller specks above those, and . . . We stood at the base of a box of glass layers the size of a metropolis, maybe the size of a nation. Something caught my eye overhead and to my right: A bright digital counter was flashing a large, ever-changing number. Nobody paid it any heed. Dazed, I pushed through the crowd until I stood directly under the counter. The number stood at 84,373,889,94-, but that last digit was changing so fast that it showed a blur. In a burst of disbelieving intuition, I saw that it tallied the number of humans in the room, plus the room overhead, and the rooms beyond that one. I gazed about, dumbfounded, found human life in all its plenitude, or its simulated representation, surging on every side, getting and spending, dying and giving birth.

I tried for a facade of composure.

"Yeah, yeah," I said to Jules. "Presumably the building is the Earth and these are all the human beings that've ever lived. So next door—"

"A very much larger room," Jules agreed, "an *extravagantly* larger room." He pointed, we stood outside the silver entrance in the red wall, we passed through it.

My stomach turned over. Illusion, that's all, smoke and mirrors, I told myself, but it was no good.

We hung in deep night. World beyond endless world surrounded us, green and blue and white in the light of a billion stars, a galaxy all afire with life, somehow, and on those worlds, I knew with certainty, humans swarmed and multiplied, trillions upon quadrillions upon quintillions of them, an entire galactic empire or federation of fertile humans crowded together. Metaphor, I thought, but the dizzying depth of the illusion filled me with awe and terror. On a literal level it made no sense at all, yet at some mythic stratum of my awareness, my unconscious perhaps, it was like staring into the sky and knowing that all the stars were alive and watching me.

"Take me out," I demanded, voice throttled with emotion.

We stood outside the red building. Both doors were black. Each showed a white etched question mark.

Jules said, "Imagine that you are an amnesiac." I thought, with a shudder, of Coop's green ray. For all I know, I thought, I *am* an amnesiac. How else do these Seebeck godlings know me? Why else should we share a name? "Suppose I told you," he said relentlessly, "that your place of origin is one of those two places we just visited. That's all you know: You came from one of those two possible human swarms. Can you estimate which you're more likely to be from?"

I hated it, but logic was inflexible. The logic of paranoia. "The larger, obviously. The odds are billions of times greater. But you're *assuming*—"

Jules gestured. Abruptly we were once more inside the lesser of the two immensities, beneath its colossal tiers of glass, men and women and children everywhere, in robes and stinking animal skins and school uniforms and loincloths and no more than etched marks in their leathery skin, eighty billions of them. A preacher dressed in the clerical garb Jules had worn in St. Bart's was speaking from a nearby pulpit, his calm, beautiful voice audible above the hubbub of the crowd. "This room is not the only one. Just next door, my friends, a vaster room exists. As He said to them, 'You are from below, I am from above; you are of this world, I am not of this world.'"

Jules murmured in my ear, "His congregation has no way of knowing if this is true. They're stuck here; they can't try the silver door. Maybe the galaxies beyond the silver door are only illusory, anyway. Perhaps they're merely a postulate—an *extrapolation,* we might say. Can you provide any of these eighty billion with a motive to believe in the reality of that larger place, that excessively greater place, that space of pullulating human flesh beside which this observed reality is the merest nail clipping?"

I said, trying to keep my own voice low, "I understand what you're driving at. You don't need to baby me. This place represents the world until now. The larger place beyond the silver door is the potential future, the far future of the species, where the galaxies are crammed with humans. You're trying to argue that—"

"Shoosh!" A nun in full habit wagged her finger at me.

"Sorry, madam," Jules said. We were back on the line-patterned emptiness of the Matrioshka shell. Lights shone above us on an inverted dome so vast it seemed flat and without horizon. "Come on, August," he told me. "Ruth will be waiting for us. Home again, home again, jiggedy-jig."

The Schwelle closed at my back. Coop sat where we'd left him, tranquil, a Zen saint of a machine. My legs gave way; I fell into the armchair.

"Why don't I make us all a nice cup of tea?" Jules suggested.

I forced myself to think through what he had shown me. In less than a century and a half, there'd be more people alive on Earth than at all previous times in history combined. The world of the green door held all the men and women of that future epoch. I caught myself. No, no, it was much more shocking than that, the comparison was cumulative: in *all* of history. So if a god could reach down and sample a random human, grab a man or woman from anywhere and any time before 2150, it'd be even money that the plucked-out individual came from right near the end. From the year 2150 or thereabouts. Keep going, then. Add a few more fecund generations: beyond 2150, surely numbers would swell and swell, the balance of the living over the dead tipping ever more swiftly as deathless humankind spilled outward to the stars.

Which implied—what? That we were all doomed to extinction *before* any such galactic population exodus of immortals?

I glanced up, hands clenched together. Jules stood in the doorway, watching me with cool, ironic amusement. I looked down again, felt my forehead knot with concentration.

No, wait a minute, this was nonsense. Start again. He's telling me that any individual's chances of being one of the humans *living here and now,* mine included, are quite surprisingly high. Twenty thousand years ago, the whole Earth would have sheltered less than a million humans, maybe. A very unlikely time to be born, out of the 80 billion humans who've lived until now. The same was true, with minor modifications, for 1000 B.C. Forget about the future for a moment. Eight or ten percent of all the humans who've ever lived are on the planet *right* now, and I'm one of them. Those aren't bad odds.

But suppose the world *isn't* doomed, or at least that humankind escapes the various menaces facing us, and we *shall* burst through into heroic technologies which carry us to the stars, and our seed is scattered across the heavens . . . why, in a hundred thousand years, the human species *might* fill the galaxy, as I had experienced it in that heart-stopping sim. Five hundred billion stars, each warming tens of billions of lives descended from this epoch.

So what is the chance that I and Jules happen to be alive *now,* so *early*?

If some god reached down to pluck a random human from that immense array of a thousand billion billion humans, what are the odds that it'd be me—or *anyone* from this century? Hundreds of billions against, that's what. Ridiculously improbably.

So if my existence here and now was to be at all likely, to be a modestly *mediocre* fact and not a ridiculously special one, my epoch had to be reasonably close to the bulging twenty-second century. As it is. But that reasoning terminates only if the numbers of humans are due, somehow, to stop increasing around 2150.

I *do* exist. Probability unity. Probability certainty. And thus, cruelly, it seemed to follow . . . My mind cringed away from the apparently ruthless logic. It seemed to follow that humanity's future must be foreclosed, long before any great expansion into the heavens and the future. Otherwise, my current situation in space and time was, quite simply, exceptional to an unbelievable degree . . . and there was no reason at all to suppose that we lived in a unique place or epoch.

My head was hurting and my eyes swimming because that logic, in turn, means that I *am,* after all, in a very special place and time indeed: the final epoch before the destruction of humanity.

"Here, you have yours black and with sugar, right?"

I looked up at Jules, wretched and sweating, and took the

mug of tea from his hand. It was hot and burned my lips, with too much sweetener.

"All right. I won't argue with you. I hope there's a flaw in the Doomsday case, but if there is, I can't find it. What now? I don't see the connection with you and Ruth and Coop and Lune and the rest. Let alone *me.* Are we supposed to be some sort of cosmic record-keepers? Accountants of eternity?" I screwed up my mouth. "That could be good name for a band."

"Players, dear boy, not bean counters, not even human-being counters. 'All the world's a stage, And all the men and women merely players.'" He stood up. "He knew what he was talking about, the old mountebank."

"Shakespeare? I don't see what the hell *any* of this has to do with the Doomsday hypothesis. Even if the universe is a Contest, what's to stop it going on forever?"

"Oh, Decius will explain it to you very plainly when he returns from Yggdrasil Station. He's watching godlings being born, and that might well terminate this current—"

"*Odysseus?*" I said, slightly shrilly.

"Our brother Decius." Jules looked more annoyed than amused, but he did look amused at my misunderstanding. "He and his crew are monitoring a cognate where the local cosmos is about to collapse into Omega Point singularity."

"What?"

"Never mind." He extended his hand. "The world's a stage the players have to pass through."

I said, "'They have their exits and their entrances.'"

"They do indeed. Here's one." Somehow I'd put down my mug of tea and he had my hand in his; his grip was firm and dry. "Give me Ruth."

The cosmic stage curtain tore. The lady librarian of machines looked up. A naked corpse was stretched before her on an autopsy table; she'd opened it up and was dickering around inside its head. The sight made me feel slightly sick, but I was so astounded I hardly noticed.

"Jules. I thought you'd be here before now. Have you got our stray in hand? Ah, I see you have." Unconsciously, she touched her left shoulder with thin fingers, the sinews of her body recalling my bruising impact as I used her for a launching pad. "Come through, don't stand on ceremony."

As we crossed the threshold, the machine James Fenimore stayed where he was, bonelessly relaxed on the couch; he tipped me a wink. I stepped forward to stare at the guts, heard the window close at my back.

The thing on the bench was the dead burgher with the bad hair that Lune and Maybelline had lugged into Great-aunt Tansy's bathtub, or tried to.

And of course, I saw now, peering unashamedly, he wasn't human. Despite the blood-colored gore, just another machine, like the disposer Coop. Different side of the political fence, though, presumably.

"It's another deformist intruder, as you and May surmised," Ruth said, looking deeply concerned, to somebody standing behind me.

A lovely voice I had heard only once, which had burned instantly into my heart, said soberly, "If we don't discover what's driving these filthy things, the whole Accord will collapse." I turned, sick with excitement. She met my gaze. "Hello," Lune said, and smiled at me like the sun. "You're not Ember, I assume?"

"Lune," I said, breath caught in my throat. After a moment, flustered, I said, "I'm August."

"Yes," she said. Mysteriously, she added, "The Seebeck family rhyme will have to be revised, not to mention the calendar. Six doughty women, six strapping men. It seems more symmetrical like that, anyway."

I gaped at her. "What?"

"The Contest of Worlds has just grown even more interesting, August," she told me.

Jan

NINE

SHEDDING LIGHT IN brilliant gouts, Jan Seebeck's stolen Kabbalah-ship plunged out of Sagittarius toward the inner Solar System, ten AUs from the Sun. In Jules's Matrioshka World cognates, this already would be deep inside the great concentric Dyson shells, but in her local universe, the world of Bar Kokhba's triumph over the Romans, life remained sparse at this distance and the bright stars were unencumbered in darkness.

She laughed with the joy of it, leaning back in her command chair. In the great screens, dilation-adjusted voxel displays shifted lightning-fast to her whim. Saturn's ringed globe hung in blackness, attended by satellite motes. Within minutes of her compressed time it hung below them, striped pale apricot and banded, rings like a platter of gold broken by a wedge of shadow, then was gone into the emptiness at their back. *The Hanged Man* screamed Sunward only somewhat elevated above the ecliptic, running at half the speed of light, but slowing now with each burst of dark energy engines. Earth lay less than two hundred on-board minutes ahead, at her current velocity, but the starship could not breach the limitations of established physics and even dark energy forces could not stop dead from light speed. Hours yet remained of scorching flight along Jan's decelerating trajectory, and that was okay by her. She ran her hands over a skull that until lately had been shaved bald. It had grown out into a spiky brush-cut that rasped her palms. In the screens she watched another starburst of sheer power. It made her grin with pleasure, tore through her body like sex. Sometimes she wondered if the ship and her body had merged, become something greater than either alone.

"Nah," she said, and kicked at the board of displayed data with the high heel of one toeless boot. "You mangy old mutt, you're just a better mousetrap."

The familiar rustle, like autumnal leaves tossed in a cool breeze, moved against her bare upper arm. The brilliantly illuminated fairy tattoo beat her blue wings, the veins pulsing.

"Talking to yourself again, Jan?" Sylvie's voice was faint and amused. "Or have we taken to soliloquizing the spacecraft?" A small image of the tat entered Jan's left field of vision, as if the fairy had disengaged from her skin and flown up to alight on her pupil. In reflex, Jan blinked. Sylvie spun once, Celtic veils swirling in the wind of her own motion, bobbed once in a curtsy.

"As for you," Jan said, "you're nothing more than a psychotic projection."

"That's *psychonic,* O Best Beloved. I see we're heading toward Jupiter. Any sign yet of a welcoming party?"

"Jupiter's on the other side of the Sun. I've had the antennae deployed to the max since Neptune, honey. Not a peep. I think they've stopped believing in me."

"Well, you've been away rather a long time." The fairy fanned herself with her elegant wings, hovering. "This light show will bring them out onto the balconies, though."

"At the rate we've moving, our image wavefront will get to them only a few hours ahead of us. I hope they're friendly. Certainly they're being very quiet, no chatter at all. You'd swear the whole system had gone to sleep."

"Or everyone's died." The fairy was ruthless, sometimes.

"Or gone singular, and then we'll never find them. No, I can imagine some kind of contemplative kabbalistic culture emerging out of that Bar Kokhba messianism, given the decades we've been away."

Alerts flared across her displays, pushing the fairy into one corner.

we are under interrogation, the Hanged Man told her calmly. *gamma lasers have probed our defensive perimeters. we have parried them. shall we acknowledge?*

"Are they speaking any machine language you can understand?"

a legacy alphanumeric code composite, the ship said. *intelligible, but gappy.*

"Let them know it's me and that I'm back." Jan grinned. "What the hell, their ancestors paid for the trip. Tell them we found a Xon star. Tell them . . ." She broke off, and mused for a long moment. "Tell them we bring them tidings of great joy."

Nothing happened for a while, but Jan didn't expect it to. The speed-of-light lag with stealthed outposts perhaps as much as several astronomical units distant from any rock base might be ten, fifteen, thirty minutes. She left her command post and went to get dressed. Her wardrobe unfolded like a box of tricks, flashing up a menu of options. Not a gathered Hellenic *chiton* with formal *kolpos* pouch and sandals. Too retro. Worse still would be a silver jumpsuit or gray many-pocketed utility garment and Velcro booties. Something complex from one of the maritime cognates, covered in pearls and gold lace? Nah, too fancy. As she flicked indecisively through the entries, Sylvie cried out: "That'd be nice. And that."

Jan paused, flicked back, considered. "You don't think it's a bit . . . louche?"

"That's you, isn't it, baby doll?"

"Suppose. Okay."

She was struggling into the tartan mini-kilt, pulling it up with some effort over lurid red and green hose and thigh-high glossy boots (should have done it the other way round, damn it), when the alert sounded again, and the ship accelerated back closer to light speed. Tripping, she sprawled, grazed her knee. The tough fabric held.

"*Fuck!*" Jan grabbed the leather bomber jacket, slung it on over her ruched silk singlet. "That's not nice!"

The fairy vanished from her left field, replaced by data summaries. Flecks, sparks in the darkness. Patrolling lightjammers from a moon of Jupiter, very far from home, according to *The Hanged Man.* Probably Ganymede station, if that had ever been built.

"Slap the bastards a couple of times, would you? Nothing lethal, mind you. Just a tap on the wrist."

done, the system informed her. *a dark energy streamer will take out the trans-Jovian minor planet J-48865. we detect no sign of human occupancy on or around that small asteroid,* it added, lest her moral qualms be aroused. *Hang Dog* was a good, kindly ship, she thought, rather pleased. After all, it was a sort of aspect of her own sensibilities, rendered down into something as practical and unstylish as a toilet brush.

In the control room, she sat back in her command chair and tapped at her teeth. Kabbalah energy went silently *whoomp,* turned a flying mountain thirteen light-seconds distant into a gas of quarks and leptons and exchange particles. When the displays finally showed an angry human face, corrected for relativistic time distortion, she was relaxed but determined. Jan Seebeck listened to the outburst for a few sentences (it was a man, of course), then leaned back and crossed her legs, knowing that the kilt would ride up saucily and not caring.

"Don't talk to me like that," she snapped at the blustering human. "I told you, you idiots. I come bearing really cool tidings of considerable joy, by the bucketload. So listen up, bozos."

For ten minutes she spoke to them about the Xon star, with plentiful downloaded visual aids. She sent them images of the observation pod she'd left in orbit around it, with cipher codes on the pod's transmissions. And after all that, the dumb bastards refused to believe her. Mythology kept getting in the way. Fuck—can't live rationally with it, can't put it out of its misery. As far as she could tell, they had her badly confused with somebody else. Shaitan, maybe.

TEN

"EVERYONE KEEPS TALKING about this Ember guy," I said, my mouth cottony, desperate for something intelligible to say. "Sorry, I don't know him."

"His father, unless I miss my guess," Jules told her, stepping past me and delving dispassionately inside the corpse's opened cranium, and then farther down, like a man expecting to find something. From the set of his mouth, it was plain that he didn't like what he saw there.

"Nobody's bloody well listening to me," I said, perhaps a bit petulantly. "I already have a perfectly good father of my own. At least I *did.* He's dead."

An earsplitting sound made everyone jump, and turn. Lune took two fingers from her mouth; she'd whistled piercingly, like a sailor.

"Madam, is that *really* necess—"

Her clear voice effortlessly overrode Jules. "He's your brother, you ninnies."

"Don't be absurd," Ruth said. "Eleven siblings, a prime number. Thirteen with our parents, another prime, a numeral of the utmost mana. Shall I list their names for you? Even a newcomer to the Ensemble should know us by name, at least. Jan, Maybelline and Septimus, for Fire. Juni, Toby and myself, for good solid Earth. Avril, Marchmain, and—"

"Give us a *break,* Ruth, this is not a classroom, and you needn't recite the entire family lineage. There is no August, Lune, it's as simple as that."

I started to laugh, I couldn't help myself. A phrase I'd heard from a Jewish girl in Chicago rang in my memory, along with her aggrieved intonation: *What am I, chopped liver?* Gazing across the squabbling demigods at their eviscerated victim, who actually was closer to chopped liver than I hoped to be anytime soon, I wondered if I really were going stark, barking mad.

"There *is* an August, Virginia," I said through my gasps, "and here he stands. And I assure you by all that's sacred in this mad universe that I am the son of Dramen and Angelina Seebeck, formerly of Melbourne on the planet I've always thought of as 'the world.' Get over it." I met Lune's eyes. She was the only one smiling. It gladdened my heart. I held out my hand. "Coming?"

After the slightest hesitation, she took it. "Surely. Where to?"

Fucked if I knew. The principle of their magic faraway tree seemed to depend on key words and key names, like an unholy blend of computer password and contagious magic. My thoughts tumbled, fast and exact. I would not willingly return to Avril's mystic pond. May's Adamski world with its randy vegetables wasn't much better. The Star Doll world? Too dangerous; Jules would be on us, and that was his home territory. I reached for the names Ruth had listed. One sounded solid and comforting.

"Give me Toby," I said.

A window tore open. Beyond, a woody place all of browns and umbers and muted yellows. A balding man farther up the hill turned with a look of extreme surprise.

"Pardon me," I said to him, and stepped across the threshold, Lune's hand electric in mine. "Shut the Schwelle," I said, guessing that would do the trick. The portal was gone. Immediately, a point of light flicked on again, began to widen with the usual coarse sound effects. I said to Toby, “Is there a way to lock it from this side?”

He assessed me in a swift, penetrating glance, muttered some words under his breath. The new Schwelle snapped shut, nipped in the bud; I thought I heard part of a squeal of rage from Ruth.

“And you are?”

“It seems that I'm your long-lost brother,” I said, watching him warily. I held out my hand. “I'm August. This is Lune.”

“Yes,” he said, giving her an approving glance, “of the Ensemble. We have worked together once or twice. Always a pleasure, miss. As it chances, I *have* no brother August, or rather”—he cut through my irritated hiss of frustration—“I've not known of your existence until this moment. Certainly, I see the likeness in your features.”

“Ember is *not* my father, god damn it,” I said.

“No, no. It's subtle, admittedly. I was thinking of my father, Dramen. *Our* father, it would seem. But come, I neglect my duties as a host. If you will go ahead of me into the dwelling, I shall be with you momently. First, I have a rogue termagant to dispatch. Uh-oh.”

The noise arrived from nowhere, like a rock-concert amp system suddenly switched on at full decibels. It was a roar, a shriek, a caterwauling, and in its midst I thought to hear claws far worse than Hook's, stropping on concrete. At my left, Lune dropped into a defensive posture, but not cowering, not her; nostrils flared, she looked like a street fighter. Instinctively, or rather as a reflex result of years of polite inner-city dojo training, I fell into a stance of my own. Toby simply stood foursquare and forthright, one blunt hand raised above his head. Electricity danced there. Sparks came from his hair, which rose at the back of his head like the ruff of an angry iguanadon provoked inside its own territory.

Something terrifying came out of the wood, then, moving as fast as the shadow of a full eclipse of the sun, flickering, somehow, and spinning. It looked like a hive of furious wasps trying to pass itself off as a gigantic scorpion. It was black with flashing highlights, rushing at us with claws that gleamed and re-formed and shivered in the mellow afternoon light and clashed again with that teeth-grating stropping noise.

I looked at Lune, and she jerked her head downhill, into the dell. I didn't see anything except a haystack. Oh. That was the thatched roof of a small, rustic cottage. Okay. Nothing else made sense. Had Avril's pool opened near my feet, I'd have plunged in and risked cutting myself on the sharp shells at its green bottom. To fight off this maddened hive, you'd need more than kicks and jabs, you'd need a flame thrower. Maybe Toby had one in the house.

We were running, heads down, terrified, the wave of sound rising still higher and deeper. I crashed against the cottage door, grabbed the carved doorknob with a trembling grip, threw it open, dragged Lune in after me, slammed it shut. I was flooded with shame, then, and opened it again, a crack. Lune was peering out through a small glazed window.

"Is there anything we can do?" I asked, voice hoarse.

"I think your brother has the matter well in hand," Lune said. It seemed to me she was preternaturally relaxed about all this.

"We could find something to burn," I said, shutting the door again and casting about. The fireplace was surprisingly large for such a small dwelling and stocked with firewood, but there was nothing one could throw a match on to see it flare up into a flaming brand. I was frantic. I ran into the next room, found a kitchen off it, delved into cupboards, pulled out a large can of bug spray. When she saw what I was brandishing, Lune laughed out loud, and took it from me. Nettled, I allowed her to have it.

"Really, August, he'll be all right. He knows this cognate and its creatures. Here, take a look."

Her laughter had angered me, I admit, but I throttled my chagrin and pressed up beside her at the window. Her warm, fragrant breath. I felt her hair brush my cheek. I put one arm about her. Amazing fireworks were detonating in the glade outside and up the hill. Toby was ablaze with sparks and scintillations. The black and gleaming mass rushed and feinted about him, falling back with cascades of atonal roaring, darting in to slash at his booted feet and leather-clad back. He stood stock-still, lashing the monstrous thing with raw power.

Something nearly noiseless happened, like a bubble snapping in a spray of luminous nothing.

Silence rang in my ears. The sparks sank back inside Toby's flesh, his tonsured hair relaxed, and in the same instant the termagant . . . dissolved . . . into black flecks of soot. Detritus fell about his feet, piled up like the remains of a bonfire, scraps of carbon lightly tossed by a breeze. Toby shook his head, kicked away the grainy remains of his adversary, and stumped down the hill to his cottage like a man returning home from a good tiring trudge in the country.

I waited until he had washed and dried his hands and put a large blackened kettle on a merry blue ring of burning gas. He said, "You'll take a cup of tea, I trust?"

"Thank you. Mr. Seebeck, I really should explain that—"

"Call me 'Toby,' boy. We're kin. Yes, an explanation would be in order. Do you know that half the family is clamoring after you?"

I sent a nervous glance darting about the room, saw nothing except Lune lazing before the unlit fire. Beyond the small windows, light was fading from the sky as mellow day deepened into mellow dusk. Birds or things like birds flocked into the trees and started up a racket. "No," I said. "Sorry, this intrusion must be an inconvenience, and—"

"Put it out of your mind. I was planning a light repast, I hope you'll both share my table. Those wretches can contain their curiosity until we're fed."

Hunger was the last thing on my mind—my stomach was convinced that it was only early afternoon—but I nodded compliantly. Lune, slumped at her ease, waved one hand agreeably. She, at least, was highly amused by the entire turn of events. I had almost no clue. All I wanted was to huddle down in a contained darkened space and think very hard, organize my mad experiences, get them settled into some sort of reasonable shape. My heart was still running fast, slamming my chest. I watched as Toby spooned black leaf into a large plain metal teapot, after warming it carefully with a splash of boiling water, then filled it generously. He set out three sturdy mugs and opened a small Schwelle above the kitchen bench.

"Hopping John," he said into the place on the far side. "Served for three. A decent merlot, I think. After, we'll have royal stuffed mushroom à la Madame Sacher." He closed the threshold, opened it again instantly, reached across. On a large silver tray, he drew in a steaming tureen, with two open bottles of red wine, silver service, solid plates of Wedgwood design, and three crystal glasses. He carried the lot across to a table with four chairs. "Come along, get yourselves around this."

He caught my glance at the teapot. "I know it's coarse of me," he said, "but I suit myself. I enjoy a hearty cup of char with my meal, and you will too. Goes quite happily with the red, I find."

Lune found a tea strainer while I sat uneasily at the table and watched Toby lay out the meal. The odor was delicious, and I found my mouth watering. "What is it?"

"South Carolinian gulla," he told me, spooning out three plates. "Over the steamed rice, we pour soaked cowpeas simmered with rashers of smoked side-meat. I say 'we' but admittedly I haven't lifted a finger in a kitchen for more than a century." On each plate he placed the thick bacon slices to either side of the mounded gulla, fished out a pepper from mine. "Wouldn't want you to bite into that red bird," he said. "Come, girl."

Lune put down three mugs of black tea, vapor rising from them, and a silver bowl of sugar cubes.

Toby ate with gusto, washing down his Hopping John with swigs of sweetened tea alternated by appreciative sips of an excellent smooth merlot. Lune followed his lead, so I tried to do the same, although the blend of beverages struck me as barbarous. This was not Great-aunt Tansy's cuisine, and not an outback open-fire barbecue, either.

"You have questions," he told me, finally, pushing his plate to one side. I saw him loosen the buttons near the tops of his breeches. "Ask away."

"Uh, how did you *do* that?"

He shook his head, frowned.

"The food was ready the moment you ordered it. Robots? A matter compiler?"

Lune laughed, a beautiful tinkle of amusement. Toby smiled.

"You truly are new to this, then," he said. "I wonder where they've been hiding you." I started to speak; he raised a hand. "No—you asked a fair question, I must give you a fair answer. You understand that many of the worlds are orthogonal?"

"You mean that they're . . . at right angles to each other? A sort of hyperspace cosmology? Okay, that would help make sense of what I've seen," I admitted. "I'm having enough trouble grasping the idea that there's more than one world." I had only the vaguest idea of what I was saying, but it seemed to make a little bit of sense. In ordinary space and time, all the dimensions were at right angles to each other: height versus width versus length, and all of them squared off in relation to time. But I knew that probably there were more dimensions than just those four. If so, maybe entire worlds could stand at right angles to each other. In principle, anyway. In truth? I'd never believed it, but here and now seemed the very proof of the idea, as convincing as Pythagoras or a punch in the mouth.

"Close enough," Toby said. He refilled Lune's glass, then his own; I covered mine with my hand. My head was whirling sufficiently. "Some of the worlds are orthogonal in space, others in time. You follow me? Their time runs uphill, you might say, as ours runs down."

"Relativity," I ventured. "Different reference frames." I knew that much from the physics we medical students were obliged to study.

"Utterly dissimilar. Never mind. The arcana and scholia are exacting and intricate, and signify not a whit for our purposes. Let's leave it at this: I have an arrangement with several chefs in worlds where the clocks tick at a different rate to this one." He plucked forth a large golden fob watch, dangled it. Slowly it spun on its bright chain. I could hear its heavy, consoling cluck-cluck-cluck across the width of the table. He put it away, gave the pocket a little pat. "Not for the neophyte, such arrangements, but it makes dining more pleasant. Your turn, August. Where are you from, and why are those pests baying for your blood?"

I looked from him to Lune and back. She said nothing,

lowering her long dark lashes to her high dark cheeks, and smiled faintly.

"I wish I knew," I said candidly. "I feel like Alice after she fell down the rabbit hole. It's just been one damned thing after another. What I'd really like to do is go home and check on my aunt. Then, if she's okay, lie down in a quiet room with a damp cloth over my eyes and wait for the drug to wear off. And while I'm doing that, work out what the hell sort of crazy universe this is, and how I got mixed up in it. Oh, and find out why I have silver stamping on the sole of my foot, and why Lune has it, too."

My voice had risen somewhat, gained a frantic edge. Toby regarded me seriously, not a bit discomfited.

"Yes, I can see that. I can understand all that very well. Everything in due time, young chap. First, let me introduce you to Madame Sacher's finest treat." He took the remnants to the servery, opened a Schwelle, thrust them through, drew back another silver tray breathing a subtle, mouthwatering savor. We watched as he spooned out two large stuffed mushrooms on each plate. They were mind-boggling to smell and behold, dusted and browned with bread crumbs. I forked into one filled like pastry with more chopped 'shrooms, minced walnuts and almonds, diced celery. The faintest fragrance of Worcestershire and sherry. My taste buds purred.

"Extraordinary," I said, blinking.

"You don't get that in Vienna any longer, in most of the cognates," Toby told us regretfully.

"Especially not the ones where the bastard Hitler's hangout was nuked into hard glass," Lune said wolfishly.

Toby sent her a sharp look. "Not at my table, if you please. Some topics . . ."

Lune caught herself, actually blushed, a richer mocha brown.

"Sorry. I'm told I had relatives . . ." She trailed off, and poured more merlot.

"Understood. Passions run high. Hence my house rule."

I was pretty much lost, except that somehow they seemed to be implying that in some worlds Adolf Hitler's town had been volatilized by nuclear weapons. Was that the hell world from which my Jovian brother Septimus strode into Ruth's nook, out of his stinking holocaust universe? Surely not. I had come to suppose, in the back of my harried mind, that we were being flung—flinging ourselves, in some cases—between theatrical Sets in a gigantic performance, or levels in a cosmic computer game or MOO, something along those lines. That much had been implicit, hadn't it, in the first words Lune had directed to me, years or perhaps only hours ago. And Coop the disposer—what was he, if not a backstage guy tidying up the gameboard, clearing away the broken props and pieces, setting up for the next contest?

Nothing so simple, it seemed.

But then nothing that had happened was simple, not since Great-aunt Tansy told me she found corpses in her bathtub every Saturday night. My head started to spin. I lurched up from the table, walked unsteadily to the door without a word of apology.

"Let him go," I heard Toby say, through a ringing in my ears.

I took some paces into the dusk, kicking up drifted leaves, leaned forward so my hands clutched my thighs, shaking and trying not to throw up. Thick liquid filled my mouth, and my eyes watered, but I kept the meal down. I took deep breaths, close to hyperventilation, forcing myself by brute determination to pause after each inhalation, waited for my pulse to slow. The darkening evening put a chill into my bare arms, through my light T-shirt. I spat out the nasty taste in my mouth, straightened up, looked through the massed trees at a glimmer of pale gold. The moon was rising. So that direction was the east, or maybe, in this world, it was the north or the southwest, who the hell could guess? I walked back and forth, staying near the cottage, one eye on its warm yellow half-open door. Were there swarms of dust beasts lurking in the woods, waiting to fall upon me and render me down into flayed meat and bone? Did the termagant's mate hide out there in the dark? Did termagants *have* mates? It seemed unlikely. I found myself grinning, and hugged myself to stay warm.

"Okay, buster," I said. "Time to go inside and ask the mad professor's beautiful daughter for an explanation."

But I knew it wouldn't be that easy, or that absurd. Life is absurdity, sure, everyone's been aware of that since Sartre and Camus and Beauvoir and all those French guys and dolls from the middle of last century. But life wasn't cliché, more's the pity. It was narrative, it was story, but it wasn't plot, generally speaking. Life was quantum mechanics. Life was chaos. Life was unexpected stuff jumping at you out of Heisenberg's uncertainty principle, writ large. Or something. Shit.

I paused at the half-open door, about to push it full open and step back inside. A soundless shock ran through me, the excited shiver you get when a paradigm falls apart in your hands, or cognitive dissonance gives way finally under the weight of too many contradictions, dumping you in the drink. For a long minute I stayed stock-still, hearing Toby and Lune conversing quietly inside. It was like seeing the six next moves in unscrambling a Rubik's cube. Maybe it was more like sketching a complicated flowchart, with all those if-then lines branching and converging. I felt the blood drain from my face. Miriam. Mrs. Abbott. Oh my god, I had to get back to Tansy's. Anything could happen to the poor old soul if—

I caught myself. No, stupid. We were probably orthogonal to Great-aunt Tansy's time stream or vector or whatever you wanted to call it, if I'd understood Toby. But was that such a great advantage? Maybe time was running *faster* there than here, and I'd get back to find her long dead and beneath a headstone in her grave? My shivers grew worse, and not just from the cold breeze. I went in and placed myself at the end of the dining table, teeth clenched.

"I'm tired of being jerked around," I said, looking from Lune to my brother and back again.

"It's been confusing for you, naturally," Toby said gruffly, as Lune said, "I wouldn't put it that way, August. You've—" They both broke off. Toby nodded to her.

"You seem to have come an awfully long way on your own ticket," she went on, with a smile. "Frankly, neither of us believes we could have done so well without tuition."

I glowered at her. "I feel like a criminal on the run, one jump ahead of the dogs. What's a *dake-shus*?"

They shared a glance, lightning-fast.

"Deixus," Lune said. "D-e-i-x-u-s. Please, come back and join us at the table."

"I didn't ask how to spell it, I want to know what it is and how it works."

"Sit down, boy, you're making me nervous." Toby poured me a glass of rich red wine, pushed it across the polished timber. "A deixus is a pointer in reality space. An index. A way to keep track of the worlds and navigate through the cognates."

Warily, I reseated myself. "I'll accept that." I took up my glass, drank. The other two lifted their own glasses, saluted me. "For the moment."

Toby added, "Each Player uses one or more personal deictic codes. Embodies them, I suppose you could say." He crossed one leg on his knee, tapped the sole of his booted foot. The silver hieroglyphs, presumably. "That's how you found me here."

"Obviously you're not going to provide me with a three-year course in cosmic navigation over the remains of the mushrooms."

Lune smiled, shook her head gently. Her dark hair swayed.

"I keep telling people . . . I mean"—I stumbled—"my brothers and sisters . . . Look, this is hard. I've been an only child all my life. How can I believe that all along I've had an entire family of siblings, most of them older than my parents?"

"Not older," Toby said, chuckling. "Oh my, no."

"I keep telling all of you that my parents died years ago. They were on a flight to Bangkok. The plane crashed in the hills. Everyone died."

"Their bodies were never found." Toby spoke with absolute authority, absolute conviction. I was startled.

"How did you know that? No, they weren't. The Thai military police said the 747 was downed by insurgents using a surface-to-air missile. The airliner burned almost completely in the explosion. Few of the bodies survived."

"That's not why they disappeared. August, our parents are alive."

I sat in numb silence, all my brilliant insights smashed and scattered. After a long silence, I felt tears leaking down my face. Something about the way he'd said it.

"You don't *know* that. I thought for a moment—You prick, how dare you tell me something like that when you *don't fucking know!*"

I brought the glass down so hard on the table that it broke into three pieces. The wine puddled. Nobody reached for a fussy cleaning towel.

"August, I do know, in the way that you know some old

battle-tested dog that's got itself lost in a hunt will find its way back home, days later, months later, years later if that's what it takes. Dramen and Angelina are not novices like you. They're champions of the Contest of Worlds, son. It would take more than a SAM to kill them, trust me."

"Then where are they?" I heard the hoarse desperation, the self-pity, in my own voice. It shamed me, but far worse than shame I felt loss and thwarted hope. All of this I'd suffered through, years earlier, when I was just a kid. The world had been white and empty, and I'd moved in it like a zombie. Once more I felt the emptiness suck at me. I didn't want that, oh, no, I did not.

"We'd thought they had absconded," Toby told me, his own tone bleak. "People like us . . . we come, we go. Sometimes and somewhere we're playing the Contest. Sometimes we're recovering from our hurts, or solacing ourselves in some enchanted byway. Occasionally we fall in love." He sent Lune a sly look; she lowered her own eyes. That made me shiver again. I reached out and drew the broken fragments of glass to me, piled them neatly in their red pool. An image came to mind, like a cartoon recalled. Suddenly, to my surprise, I found myself grinning.

"Yeah. I visited Maybelline. She was quite taken with a large vegetable."

Lune burst out laughing; Toby frowned, not following.

"The Venusian?" she spluttered. "Oh yes, quite a catch, that Phlogkaalik. Probably pregnant by now."

"How the hell can a tuber get pregnant after fucking a human?" I shook my head, dazed again. "Then again, how the hell can a cat learn to talk?"

"Venusians are parthenogenic, in that cognate," Lune said. "They require sexual engagement to bring them to mitosis, or even to couvade."

Toby was nodding wisely, his brow now unfurrowed. He said, "You've met Hooks, then?"

"Yes. He used my legs as a scratching post. A cat's head isn't big enough to hold a brain able to understand English."

"Of course it is," Toby said. "Have you never seen a mynah bird?"

"That's just mimicry. What I'm talking about is—"

"You know those idiots who run about saying that we only use five percent of our brain?"

"I've heard that. I don't believe it. Brain scans—"

"That's why they're idiots. Brains evolved to be used, the whole damned box and dice. On the other hand, there's a lot of redundancy. And plenty of junk in the standard DNA code. When it's cleaned up, you can pack a whole lot of elegant processing under a small skull."

I sat up sharply. They were lulling me, distracting me with one sidetrack after another.

"Fascinating," I said, "but irrelevant. If my parents are still alive, why would they abandon me? During all this time, not a single word. We always got on very well, I mean, this wasn't some tragic broken home we're talking about here. More to the point—" I struggled to recall the paradigm clarity of a few moments ago, standing at the door in the cool evening air—"I was in the custody of my mother's older sister, Miriam, and her husband. Does Miriam fit into your world-hopping pantheon?" They exchanged glances again. Toby shook his head, clearly mystified. "And Great-aunt Tansy—what's her role in this family saga? She's eighty if she's a day. You can't tell me—"

Lune narrowed her eyes. "Tansy is the custodian of that nexus collection residence, yes?"

"Where she's lived contentedly for decades," I said, getting angry again, on my aunt's behalf, even though it was beautiful

Lune I was venting at. "Until you lunatics started dropping corpses into her bathroom and driving her into conniptions. What the hell was that all about? They were machines, weren't they, that last one anyway?" My mouth was running away by itself. "And then you called in *another* machine to haul the thing away. Coop. My interdimensional pal, James C. Fenimore. Then I go home and the goddamned thing is sitting there at the kitchen *table* with Tansy, eating her scones!" I was on my feet again. "I have to get back there right now, what the hell am I thinking, who knows what bloodthirsty thing might come oozing at her out of the wallpaper next time?" Whiplashed, I caught myself. "Or is she part of it? Is she a player in your cartoon bloody goodies versus baddies universe?"

"That's not the way of it, and I don't believe so," Toby said calmly. He rose, came around the table, put his hand on my shoulder. "You're upset, understandably. Much too much change, and too quickly. I want you to go into the sitting room with your delightful companion and sit down while I make some coffee. There's an excellent selection of music in the system, why don't you dial something relaxing and sit down for a few moments? Cognac, too, I think, that's the spirit."

I hesitated, considered options. Yes, I could immediately rip open an entrance to the nexus collection point known more familiarly as Aunt Tansy's bathroom, but where would that get me? Back into the house, yes, but not much the wiser, and hardly better armed to defend the dear old lady. And myself. And perhaps Lune, if it came to that.

I shrugged, nodded, followed that beautiful mysterious person through a paneled oak door into a room that was cozy, warm, and surely too large to fit inside the cottage. Distracted, uneasy, I chose not to sit beside her on the couch. Instead I crossed the room to look almost blindly at the wall of books in mahogany shelves behind glass. I don't know what I expected to see—perhaps hunting and fishing tales, or collections of Dickens and Thackeray in some expensive Collector's Edition bound in tanned pigskin and stamped in gold. Instead, I found row upon row of dull, heavy tomes about topics that meant nothing at all to me: modal and abductive and categorial and apolyptic and Jain multivalued logics, Russell and Whitehead's *Principia Mathematica,* Lewis Possible World theory (David, not Carroll), Barbour Platonia, Tegmark hierarchies, a thick volume on Ontological Mechanics by someone called Lune Katha Sarit Sagara. . . . In my entire life, I'd encountered that given name just once before. Coincidence? Some famous dusty academic predecessor, after whom Lune had been named? On a mad surmise I opened the glass door, plucked the book forth, flipped open the back cover. There, in an austere monochrome photo, Lune's double sat at a desk with her hair pulled back and a thousand books and journals racked behind her. The pages, as I fanned through, were dense with appalling calculus, most of it in symbols I'd never seen before, not just the usual Latin and Arabic and Hebrew and Sanskrit alphanumerics, but circles with crosses inside, and strange hooked figures, and stuff you'd find adorning a butchers' market run by Yog-Sothoth. I recoiled, shaking my head. The book went back into its slot, and I mooched away with my burning face averted, fetched up before another cliff of books. They were all by the same man, apparently. Holy shit, they were all the *same book* and what was more unnerving, they were all the book that I'd found opened beside Tansy's bed.

I looked high and low. Yep, in a hundred or more different editions, imprints, bindings, some thin, some broad, all showing the same title and author: *SgrA*,* by Eric Linkollew, except for several in alphabets as odd as the symbolic code used in Lune's treatise. The glass door squeaked open; I pulled down three or four at random, flipped through their pages. All the same book, impossibly, but each different from the rest; all, that is, except for the fat volume at the very top left, perhaps a kind of catalog: *Asimov's Guide to Linkollew.* I started to skim near the opening of one version of *SgrA**—and how the hell did you pronounce *that?*—and read:

> Most of the coherence induction system was entirely preprogrammed, so unless Windows Xtra locked up and shut down the whole instrumentation package, I felt fairly confident that this would be the day. I glanced across at Jess Handley. Her mouth was slack, drooling a little. The hefty nurse caught my frown and reached over to mop up the spittle with a Kleenex. The doctor saw none of this byplay. He was sweating, I could see it soak his cap and mask despite the cold overpressure air flowing through the operating theater.
>
> "She's in point nine eight resonance," I reported. I tried to keep my tone level, but I was buzzing with excitement. Jesus, this was Nobel Prize–level work. Maybe we'd claw up the Physics medal as well as Medicine. The monitors were rock steady, flicking like metronomes to the beat of the polaritonic crystal cycle deep inside the heart of the coherer. I needed a catchier name than that. Pity old Murray Gell-Man had died last month, I could have asked him for advice. Anyone with the mad wit to dream up the word "quark" deserved the chance to name this little beauty. Light slowed to a near-standstill inside my box, locked tight inside a sludge of frozen gases

tweaked by a laser reference beam. Anatoly Zayats is going to shit himself when word of this humungous coup reaches Belfast. A few more minutes and the beam will be completely frozen. Arthur and Jess will lock into total resonance at that moment. Two brains but only one nonlocally connected uniform wave function.

What would *that* feel like? Christ, might as well ask what Schrödinger's Cat feels like when the hammer falls, or fails to fall, smashing the little flask of prussic acid, foaming upward in a cloud of death or remaining snugly secure, the choice hanging with exquisite balance on the random quantum emission of a single electron from an excited radioactive isotope. Dead cat/live cat. Both/either/neither. We have no way to know what that felt like, even though physics teaches that each of us passes through hundreds, thousands, billions of such doubling transitions each day as the universes split and multiply with every choice, no matter how insignificant. Well, we had no way of knowing until this minute. I'm the observer of Schrödinger cats, I thought with a silly giggle. I herd cats in Hilbert's superspace. Nurse Demetriopoulos looked across at me, startled. Damn, she heard that. Never mind, never mind. Pray there's no instrumentation failure. This is history in the—

Jess Handley gave out a low, terrible moan. I felt my gaze jerk up from the computer display, as if something from outside my own consciousness were overruling my behavior. Doc's made of sterner stuff. His eyes remained on the electrode array implanted into the poor dummy's head. Christ, what sort of life would *that* be like? Living with no awareness beyond animal level instincts: fear, hunger, the pressure to piss and shit. Maybe lust. Wonder if he gets a hard-on for the cousin? She's over the hill, but still quite a looker.

Well, she'll soon be the one to know. I guided the system to point nine nine seven coherence. She'll feel his dirty little mind running its fingers over her. From the inside.

She made that awful moan again. I caught myself shivering, feeling the cold of the room. Her moan had been a deep and ghastly sound, not at all like a woman's voice. In the blank world she was starting to share with the moron, something grisly must have reached across to touch her.

Shock passed down through me, bone deep, along my spine, in the closure of my gut. Not indigestion and not frustrated anger, not this time. A kind of horrified recognition. I swallowed hard, burning with guilt, or perhaps shame. Acts of commission and omission. What the fuck? I read on, swaying slightly:

My hands are large now and hard from tearing the green grass and digging at their soil. Fingers creep along with the other creatures, turn the little stones over, sometimes sleep under them. Sing and sing. Long bony nails would get dirty so I keep them chewed down to the hurting rind. Better the fingers should hurt than carry with them into the dark and the light the dirt from the soil under the grass. The hair is long and its oil loves dirt. I roll the hair in the soil. Sometimes they wash the hair and it flies to the sun, all light. Gold, like the ring on

Jenny's hand, like the burning sun. I have pulled it down in front of my face, long hairy strands, to see it whisper and hum. I don't know much about the dark birds. They droop with feathers and sing of branches and the freedom of the air.

The tree is huge. Green and yellow, dots and streaks, twining everywhere and climbing into the sky. I have looked at the tree, sitting under it for my lifetime, heavy-boled and sweet with sap. This is my life, straining in the arc from grass to height. Every bird in the tree stretches in agony and joy from leaf to leaf. Their homes are made of string and spit and golden hair stolen while I sit as still as the tree. My back presses the bark. Pressure and light and smells are a world. The soul would laugh. High into the blue sky the tree climbs, knowing no boundaries, fearing no pain. The tree does not know them, or if it does it can afford to look the other way. My revenge is mine, though when I violate their world I must remain always on guard. They have the food and the bed. I must watch Jenny.

I put the variora back, shaking my head, and sat down carefully beside Lune.

A heady scent of coffee preceded Toby into the living room. He pushed a wheeled cart laden with goodies. I hadn't smelled anything this delicious—this *expensive*—in years.

"Blue Mountain?"

"Better." He poured. "Borneo Green Mountain, in a cognate rather far from here. Well worth importing. Cream?"

"I won't drink any," I said reluctantly. "Coffee makes me jumpy. I'll just sniff at mine, it'll almost be as good." On a plate covered daintily with a doily, he'd arranged several astounding confections in whipped cream, sliced strawberry, and crusty white egg meringue. I couldn't help it—I reached out and made a pig of myself.

"He's a growing boy," Toby told Lune.

I wiped my mouth on the back on my hand, washed down the remnants with a slurp of the coffee I hadn't been able to resist. Was there some narcotic in those fumes? It didn't matter, either way I was suddenly totally wide awake, focused, brain spinning in neutral and ready to be engaged. And I badly needed to use the bathroom. Toby understood my wordless questioning glance.

"Follow me. You can wash your face while you're in there; you have cream in your whiskers."

I rubbed my face. "No whiskers, Toby. But it's true I need a shave. Didn't get a chance this morning."

He pushed a discreet door half open. "Blade and soap in the cabinet. Deixes are Open Jakes, Open Bidet, Open Dryer. If you feel the need to wash up, it's Open Shower. Yes? I'll fetch you some clean clothes. Those look a bit light for this climate anyway. Give me a shout when you're ready."

I had no idea what he was talking about. I shut the door and looked for the toilet, gaped, stared around in shock—this is a joke, right?—ran right out again into the hallway.

"Uh, Toby—"

He was surprised. "Can I help you further?"

"Toby, there's no . . . I mean, where am I meant to—"

"Oh." He slapped his forehead. "I forget how new you are to the worlds. Just put your backside down and open the jakes. Just like opening a Schwelle? I trust I don't have to demonstrate—"

For the second time, I was blushing, probably beet red. Last time I'd felt this humiliated was in first grade at school, where I'd wet my pants because I didn't know where the potty was (they hadn't got around to showing us the restrooms yet) and felt too shy to ask.

"Got it. Sorry."

In fact I hadn't got it, didn't have a clue what he was talking about, but I shut the door again and gingerly approached the facilities, such as they were. An annulus was attached to the wall, a sort of wood-topped steel-frame hoop at chair height, like a toilet seat. There was no water closet beneath it, nor any flushing mechanism. What, I was meant to just . . . crap on the floor?

The familiar lightbulb went off above my head.

I pulled down my jeans, and with excruciating discomfort sat my bare ass on the wooden hoop. "Open Jakes." Something odd and weirdly relaxing happened beneath my buttocks, like a balmy breeze blown on skin while you're skinny-dipping in late spring. I sprang off the hoop, almost falling on my face, tangled by my half-mast jeans. I turned and peered inside the circle of the hoop.

Far below me, sunlight fell on a grassy knoll. It was like looking through a perfectly clear window in the bottom of a low-flying plane, or a blimp. I twisted my head from side to side, but there wasn't much parallax. A sweet breeze came up from the pasture far below, and I thought in the distance I saw a group of feral creatures rather like small pigs. Javelinas, maybe. If there'd once been a pile of human manure directly down there, it had been disposed of by dung beetles and weather, recycled ecologically. Good bloody Christ. Way to go, Toby. You win the Green award of the week for permaculture righteousness.

I sat down again and tried not to think of the distance beneath me. Hell, I couldn't fall through, the toilet hoop wasn't wide enough. Even so, my bowels locked up. I've heard that in hospital nurses make you pee into a metal bottle, under the sheets, and that most guys just can't let go until they're in risk of rupture. That's the way I felt.

What if a passing bird got caught on an updraft and—

I tried to relax, counting sheep. That didn't help, because I thought of those poor sheep copping a moist nugget in the eye. The sheep look up, but not for long, I thought, almost hysterical. I tried to *force* myself to relax, but that's plainly a contradiction in terms. I got off the hoop and pulled up my pants, then faced reality and took my seat once again. After a time, I let loose, and all was well.

Except that it wasn't. In despair, I noticed belatedly that there was no toilet tissue within reach. Where was the roll holder? None in the room, for that matter. Maybe in the cabinet Toby had mentioned? I was about to crab carefully across the floor when I understood the second command, or thought I did. Gritting my teeth, I said, "Shut jakes, open bidet."

Instantly, a pulsing drizzle of warm water struck my nether parts, unnerving for an instant, then rather soothing. How had he managed *that*? I could stand up and look behind me, but I didn't want to get the seat wet. Toby was a wizard at this technology, I decided, or maybe it was programming. Somehow he'd put a nested looped command into his command. Incredibly, his system was flipping its vertical orientation several times a second, I guessed, so that water gushed upward, against bathroom gravity (but probably downhill in its local reference frame, that would be more elegant, let gravity do the work), and then falling away with its cleansing burden, to tumble to the ground as dirty rain.

After a time, marveling, I decided I'd been sufficiently car-washed (and I hope devoutly that Toby *hadn't* diverted a real car-wash hose onto my tail), shut the bidet, opened the dryer. A gust of hot wind blew up my backside and dried my buttocks in a trice. Astounding. I stood, made myself presentable, peering into the hoop. The pasture was gone, of course, as had the upside-down tropical rainstorm. Hot dunes rolled away out of sight. The fabled winds of Araby had soothed my naked ass, from high enough that their gust-borne grit had not sandpapered it. Shaking my head, I shut the horrifying thing down, found safety razor and soap in the recessed cabinet behind a large mirror, and started searching for the shower Schwelle.

There was a knock on the door. "Are you decent?"

"Come in," I croaked. I had my T-shirt and boots off, and was getting out of my jeans. "These are ingenious gadgets," I told Toby. He held an armful of clothing, presumably in my size rather than his. I daresay he ordered them from some classy London or Singapore men's couturier. He put them on a bench he drew out of the far wall.

"In front of the mirror," he said. "'Open shower' will do the trick."

"Why hasn't it gone on already?"

"Pardon me?"

"Well, you just said the magic words."

"But I wasn't standing in the right spot. As I say, in front of the mirror. That way you can shave without cutting your ear off. Don't forget the shower screen or you'll splash the whole room."

I shook my head sheepishly, threw the rest of my clothing in the corner, shut the door as he left. I stood in the place of choice, folded out the glass wraparound screen, said the thing. Warm water fell from a Schwelle torn open above my head, and sluiced away into a triangular trough suddenly surrounding my feet. I wondered for a moment why the wedge of floor I stood upon didn't immediately fall through the severed floorboards into the foundations, taking me painfully with it, but that was old-fashioned four-dimensional thinking. Like the Schwelle deixis apparently embedded in Great-aunt Tansy's bathroom mirror, these things inhabited a meta-world of their own, a world beyond the worlds. They switched on and off as shadows do when you flick a light switch. Except that these shadows were the kind you could step through, or drop and then clumsily kick your soap into and never get it back.

"Damn!" I shouted, doing exactly that.

Luckily, there was more in the cabinet, wrapped in heavy paper and wonderfully fragrant. I closed my eyes luxuriantly, and lathered my chops. When I opened them, words had formed on the mist-laden glass: ASK ABOUT SWORD IN STONE. If my hair hadn't been stuck to my neck, it would have stood on end. I shut my eyes again and sighed heavily. When I looked again, condensation had washed away the cryptic message.

"You smell nice," Lune told me when I joined them in the living room.

"I look like a goddamn fashion model," I said grumpily, but I was pleased by her comment. Against my skin I wore silk undergarments branded Windsor & Spencer. My fawn breeches (and jacket, slung over my shoulder just now) were House of Saud, possibly woven from prime camel hair, the white silk shirt was something out of a retro production of *Hamlet,* and my incredibly comfortable calf-high boots, probably *made* of calf, were the sort of footwear you'd invade Poland in. No, that was unfair and cheap; catching Toby's eye, as he stood foursquare, hands behind his back, assessing me with an approving avuncular glance, I decided they were the sort of boots you'd *save* Poland in.

"Time for some straight talking," Toby said. "I've just made a fresh pot of tea. Here, sit, speak. Start at the start and go on until the end, then stop."

I sighed and took the spare armchair, poured myself more tea, chomped on a crisp wheaty biscuit, and started with the corpses in Great-aunt Tansy's bathroom. It got complicated and tangled, and I reserved my suspicions of Mrs. Abbott and certain other aspects of Tansy's oddly salient household and its "nexus." At a certain point, Lune chipped in to fill out the backstory. I was baffled when she explained why she'd confused me with my brother Ember. As far as I could tell, Ember and I had nothing whatever in common. Still, it seemed Lune found him attractive, weirdly enough, and that set my teeth on edge. At length she and I both got to the end, and stopped.

"Hmm. An unexpected tale, young August. Light glimmers through the chinks." Toby rose, put down his mug with a clatter. "One thing at least is abundantly clear to me. We need to get you armed, sooner the better." He addressed the middle air. "Get me Septimus."

"I don't think he'll be terribly pleased—" I began. A Schwelle window tore open upon complete blackness. Through it, I heard a rasping sound, deep and menacing. I moved quickly to stand in front of Lune, who still sat relaxed in her chair. I knew what it was, then, and burst out laughing. The horrible snoring choked off, turned to a gulping snort. Light blazed on through the threshold. Bearded Septimus, in white nightgown, sprang from his military cot and was on one knee threatening us with a huge-bore pistol, faster than I could see how he'd done it.

"Oh, it's you, you old bastard," he told Toby, and rose, brushing down his knees and putting the hogleg aside. "Couldn't you check first? It's three in the morning here." He glanced past Toby, saw me still in defensive posture in front of

Lune, who was trying to get past to stand up, saying soft shushing things to me. "And him. The uninvited guest, the specter at the feast, the lost child, and so on. I suppose you want the brute armed?"

"Just so. May we come through?"

"If you must." He cleared his throat vilely; Septimus sounded like a heavy cigar smoker to me. "And of course I see that you must."

The stench of the holocaust battlefield was gone from him, and the ruins themselves. We stepped across the threshold into an enclosed place of concrete and steel, like the inside of a blockhouse. The camp bed upon which Septimus took his uncomfortable rest stood on a mezzanine. To my left, below and beyond a metal railing, rack upon rack of formidable weapons stood behind heavy locked glass, like a martial parody of Toby's library. Being an Australian, from a comparatively tame and benign culture, I was not especially familiar with firearms. True, I'd handled guns. As a kid, I'd gone hunting with Dad in the bush, and he'd instructed me in the use of his rifle. It wasn't hard to get a permit for that kind of weapon, used for that purpose, yet by and large few murders, let alone gory massacres, were done with them. The brutal gang weapon of choice was the knife. While I was in Chicago, I had put bullets into paper targets at a sports firing range under Itzhak's tutelage; he, of course, had spent two years in the Israeli army, and was a crack shot. It turned out that my own eye was good, and I had a natural flair for the sport, but once I got back home I'd lost interest; it seemed too much effort, although I was never hoplophobic. Now, in the racks, I saw objects I'd mostly only ever seen in movies and a thousand violent TV shows: mortars and rifles and machine guns and smaller but brutally lethal pistols, gleaming in oiled blue steel, and bandoliers of rounds, and magazines like videos stacked in a library, holding, I assumed, more of the same, waiting to be plugged into the death-dealers, and grenades in an assortment of merry colors, and other things apparently from *Berserker* movies: ray guns or lasers or rail guns or whatever the hell they were. Scary as shit, for what they implied about the world—the worlds—these people inhabited.

"He's definitely one of us. More than just a Player—a fellow of our clan. And yet—"

"Septimus, meet your brother August."

"Brother?" That pulled him up sharply. He turned, quivering with anger at the effrontery of this claim. I stood where I was, quaking only internally, and met his stare. I was beginning to wish I carried a birth certificate with me. Toby spared me the full recitation, explaining matters in family code and with excellent brevity.

"Very well. If it is so, we are the stronger for an additional kinsman, however green and unexpected." He put out a great ham of a hand, grasped mine without trying to smash all the bones. I guess he had no reason for insecurity issues. "Welcome, August. And you, too, Miss Ensemble, I meant no disrespect in ignoring you. Now that we have the niceties dealt with, follow me, and I'll fit you up with something defensive. You don't look like a shooter, so we might begin with a taser and something small but useful in clinches."

Below, he went directly to two cabinets, took out a pair of dull black weapons, shut and relocked the doors with an automatic deftness. Clearly, he knew the location of every killing machine in his armory. The air smelled of oil, metal, the tang of something that might have been cordite. He worked the bolt of the small-caliber gun, a *cha-cha-chink,* found a double holster in leather, waited until I'd buckled it on over my floppy silk shirt. "I'll run you through some elementary training downstairs on the range," he began, and Toby interrupted him.

"These toys wouldn't stop a determined dog," he said. "Septimus, I was hoping you'd have detected it in the boy by now. He is young and naïve, but pay attention. Tell me what you feel."

"Damn your eyes, Tobias, you will not speak to me like . . ." He broke off, and his fierce eyes met mine again, stared penetratingly. His lips tightened. "By the Accord, brother, I believe you might be right. I had thought that one to be a mythological beast."

Toby asked, "Do you retain the excalibur engine in your armory, after all these centuries?"

I felt weak at the knees, halfway between shock and a screaming fit of laughter. What? I'd thought I was joking. "Ex*cal*ibur?"

"We are not speaking of a literal sword in a stone, lad."

I said tensely to Lune, "What the hell are they talking about?"

Her hand came up and took mine, gripped it tightly. "I suspected—" She broke off.

I said in a high-pitched tone of disbelief, thinking of the here-it-is-there-it-goes message in the bathroom, "My name is August, not Arthur."

Lune gave a frightened, nervous laugh, something I'd never expected to hear, and suddenly her hand felt slick with dampness.

"Who told you that?" she said.

"'August' is a name beginning with 'A,' for all that, with six letters," Toby said simultaneously, "We dare not try him," he said then to Septimus, as if I weren't there, or perhaps as if I were a fine young stallion he chose not to try for a canter.

"You *will* tell me," I said, suddenly very angry.

"No," Toby said. "Come away now, boy."

I stood my ground. And Septimus said, "Come," and turned, leading us down a farther flight of stairs into a dimly lit alcove off another concrete tunnel beneath the rooms of racked weapons. My eyes adjusted to the faint light, and I saw in the corner a plinth of something translucent, like a gigantic salt crystal. It glistened with an inner light.

"How does it work?" I recognized it, or something deep inside me did so.

"Put your hand on top and hold it there," my warrior brother said, "no matter how terrible the pain and confusion. You are to be tested, and if you pass, you will be profoundly . . . rewired, I believe they say, in these barbarous days." I looked at the crystal mass, standing a good meter from us. The topmost surface was carved in bas relief. Jutting up from the flat surface was a string of miniature hieroglyphs, quite like the shapes scored into the sole of my foot and Lune's, the "mark of the beast."

As I hesitated, Septimus said contemptuously, "You are afraid of pain."

"Of course I'm afraid of pain, you idiot. That's what pain's for, to make you afraid of bad things."

Septimus gave me a grudging smile. "Conscious awareness and choice are, in part, the tools we use to overcome pain. Step forward. Place your hand there. We shall see what we shall see."

They had given me no motive at all to put myself through something like this. As far as I was concerned, they could all go and jump in the lake. But I could not turn away. This moment was, I understood, my duty, my destiny, the pathway to recover Tansy and perhaps my parents.

"Tell me what it is," I said to Toby.

"Yes. We've taken too much for granted. You thought we

were saying 'Excalibur,' but it's a sort of shorthand pun: two words, not one, or rather one letter and a word."

I looked at him, where he had retreated from the cold radiance of the thing. I fell into a firm balanced stance and said, "X. Oh, I see. 'X-caliber.' A gun with an unknown quantity of firepower, but presumably a shitload anyway. Yes?"

"Close enough." Toby coughed modestly. "My own little jest."

"I never liked it," Septimus said in his deep, throaty burr. "I prefer the ancient name."

"And that is?"

"It's a Vorpal sword." He met my eyes, rock solid with conviction, no hint of comedy. "For one who can wield it."

I stepped forward to the crystal. "Is this the kind of thing a nice human boy like me should be dabbling with?"

"Human?" Septimus laughed, and I thought his laugh had a cruel edge to it. "You still think you're human? No, boy, if you are a Seebeck, and a Player in the Contest of Worlds, you are not human."

My own voice seemed to rumble in the echoes of the place. "What, then?"

Lune was climbing the stairs, her hands held out to me, a sort of welcoming pity in her eyes.

"Oh, August. You're a Vorpal homunculus. Like all of us. You're an artifact on the deep algorithmic substrate of the Contest."

It was excruciating, of course. I held my hand pressed into the crystal as tears ran down my cheeks, and whiny gasps came out of my mouth. The cold of shock ran through me as fire blazed in my mutilated right hand. I felt the thing carve my flesh, as the sharp open mollusk shells at the murky bottom of Avril's pool had hacked it open. What was all this prefigurement? Dazed, at the very edge of fainting, I held on to fury at my reeling sense of being caught in an allegory, in a myth of some tawdry kind, of a passion play perhaps. I started to laugh again, hysterically, and the pain tore into my brain and brought darkness shot with colored stars and streamers and the distant echoes of voices too close and too far away for intelligibility.

"He's all right," someone said. A cool cloth was pressed into my forehead. I tried to sit up, woozy, and Lune told me, "Stay there for a moment, sweet." I sat up anyway, took the washcloth, dabbed at my cheeks and eyes, which burned from the salt of tears. I was perched on Septimus's camp stretcher, and it creaked. Something caught my eye, a flash of gold. I opened my right palm fully.

In the middle of my lifeline crease, the mirror-image row of hieroglyphs was carved, and filled with gold.

I had expected it, but still I jerked in shock. I clenched my hand shut, opened it again. Didn't feel any different. While it looked as if shaped pieces of precious metal sat buried in my palm, there was no sense that an alien material had been forced through my skin and deep into muscle. I tapped the shapes with the index nail of my left hand. Firm, unyielding, like rapping on a coin. I put both hands down on my thighs, gripping them tightly.

"And?"

"Right now, without a moment's hesitation, before you damage yourself and us," Septimus rumbled, "we teach you some command of this great gift. Can you stand up?"

"Yes." I did so, swayed only a little, put one hand around Lune's waist.

"Then come with me to the range."

Toby was there ahead of us, fixing targets at the far end of a long gray and fire-stained hall. "Keep your hands by your sides for the moment, August," he called, voice echoing a little, and I thought I heard a note of anxiety. That was unnerving, given his own appalling powers, his *son et lumière* battle with the ferocious hive creature he'd called a termagant. I did as he said, trying to breathe slowly, feeling my pulse accelerate and beat in my neck.

"We assume you've now been instilled with the craft of employing the Vorpal weapons system," Septimus said. "However, you will need to choose your own deictic symbols. I will help you do so."

"What?" But I guessed what he meant. Like Toby naming his toilet aperture a "jakes," and the hygienic cleaning system a "bidet." The verbal pointers somehow keyed in to the operating system, whatever it was. Okay, I could manage that. If only they'd tell me what I was meant to be *doing*.

"Face front," Septimus said, voice muffled. I noticed that they had taken cover behind a thick concrete shield. "Fix your attention on the blue post."

"It's a bad, bad post, right?" I said. "It's a post with unpleasant intentions."

"Just so. Raise your right hand, palm apaumy."

"Sorry?"

"Palm facing the post."

"Okay."

"You are going to knock it over. Only that. Limited violence."

"Oh, my," Lune whispered. "Weapons-grade ontic mechanics. You do recall that this is *so* banned under the Acc—"

Septimus ignored her. I was barely listening, and wouldn't have understood anyway.

"Key the choice with a deixis," the armorer told me. "I'd use 'Punch.'"

"Just that one word? Not 'Open,' or 'Give me'?"

"I believe your weaponry grammar has been activated. Word and intention will combine into act. Do it."

I did that thing. A rushing sound, like a great wind. Thirty meters away, the blue pole flung itself back against the concrete wall and smashed into blue splinters.

"Shit!" I clamped my hand shut, turned toward Septimus. He ducked back instantly behind the shield. "Do I have to switch it off?"

"No. Young man, you don't know your own strength. Try to modify the effect, or you'll tear this whole place apart before you're done."

Eddies of wind, of aftershock, were still passing up and down the room, blowing fragments of wood around. Something stank.

"What did I do?" I said.

"We think you opened a Schwelle onto a version of Earth where the Moon was never born, where no intruding minor planet smashed away most of the lithosphere. The atmosphere is tens or hundreds of times denser than here."

In a vivid mental image, I saw a colorized cartoon: my hand held open, the small Schwelle opening up, perhaps only a few millimeters across, positioned above the hieroglyphs, an appallingly powerful jet of massively compressed atmosphere smashing across the room like a fire hydrant.

"There was no reaction, no kickback," I protested, but even as the words came out my mouth I saw that of course there wouldn't be. The weapon system's Schwelle was just an opening through a higher spacetime. I wasn't really part of the deal, just the switch thrower. Good grief. "That was the *low* setting, then?"

"Once you get it under control. Now the red post. That one is *really* dangerous. Call it 'sun-fire.'"

That did sound dangerous. What, a nuclear weapon built into my hand? I thrust out my palm, aimed at the threatening crimson post, said the word.

I was blinded. The room shrieked with torn, turbulent air, stinking of stripped ions. The light from my palm had truly been like staring right into the sun at midday in high summer. Some aspect of the Schwelle, incredibly, had shielded my hand and the rest of me from nearly all the radiation. Not entirely. The skin of my face felt hot, like sunburn.

"Christ!" Somewhere, a fire blazed. I wiped at my weeping, dazzled eyes. Aghast, I realized how apt the key word was. Hands were on my arms, leading me out of the wrecked range. Behind me, I heard a huge chunk of half-molten concrete shift and fall with a crash. "That actually *was—*"

"Yes, you sampled the photosphere of the Sun. Five thousand degrees, effectively collimated over this short range to target. First time I've ever seen such a thing done. Avert your eyes next time." Septimus was impressed, I could hear it in his voice. "You'll do, boy," he told me, and his massive, rather comforting hand came down to grip my shoulder. "You'll do."

Eleven

SOMETHING IN GOLD caught Juni's eye on her couture menu, so she had it compiled: a striking spiral bracelet of paired snakes from Euboea in Eretria, tails linked in a Hercules knot decorated with a bezel-set garnet. It came out of the box slightly hot; blowing on it, waving it in the clear, offog-rich air, she pushed it up high on her bare left arm. For some reason—perhaps because it was so elegantly different—it put her in mind of her sister Jan's tat, the semiautonomous psychonic manifestation that the silly girl had named Sylvie. The memory made her shiver. Juni had prepared a specialized portable nanoreplicator for Jan's millennial birthday, a folded wardrobe fully stocked with design templates from a hundred cultures and cognates. Chances were excellent, she thought irritably, that despite this gift, the fool of a girl was still slumping about in a tartan dressing gown and slippers made to resemble soppy cows' heads, or something equally atrocious.

On an impulse, she opened a Schwelle upon Jan's location. An odd wrongness to the usual tearing sound set her teeth on edge. As always, the small men fizzed at the boundary, almost visible, like the Brownian motion of dust in a beam of sunlight. Beyond the threshold, her sister sat in some sort of elaborate chair, wearing exactly what one would expect of someone with her appalling fashion sense, hair in a spiky crew-cut, grin wide and gleaming.

"Oh good, I was just going to open a line to one of you guys." Something buffeted her. "Shit. Juni. You'll have to wait—people are trying to kill me."

It was like hearing a melody played maybe a tenth of an octave too low and uncannily slowed, just enough to notice. The light in the cabin was wrong, too: All the colors were out of whack. Juni squeezed her eyes tightly twice, tried to clear her vision, even found herself absurdly raising one flattened hand as if for shade against glare, but the problem was not at her own end.

Maddeningly, her first impression had been right: all the colors were off, heavy dull reds where you'd expect healthy pinks and meter-display crimson, yellow glowing from panel indicator strips that should be comforting green, deep violet tinging the illumination strips, oceanic greens elsewhere on the display icons instead of blue. Good grief.

"You're in space."

"Good guess. Shut up and let me try to save my life."

The woman was time-dilated. The cabin was a spacecraft under some kind of preposterous acceleration.

Light exploded in a noiseless flash in one large display. Juni flinched. Her sister's mouth moved, as if in speech, but nothing was audible. Well, naturally, she was interfaced with her craft's AI pilot.

"The stupid fucks," Jan said aloud, and turned her wrong gaze to look across the Schwelle. "They're trying to hit the dark energy-engine. Don't they have any idea what that would—"

More lights ripping at their eyes, although scaled downwards, presumably, by the ship system.

"Dark—?" Juni started, then bit her tongue. This was no time for distractions. Her sister, perversely, chose to distract herself.

"Hey, Juni, what the hell are your nanoid things doing to your face? They're crawling all over you."

Instinctively, she brushed her fingers across her cheeks. Nothing, of course. "What are you babbling about?"

"Don't talk to me about babbling, you sound like Donald Duck." Jan uttered a throaty laugh. "It's creepy, man. Your skin's gone kinda yellow, and there's a reddish mist flickering all around. Thought it was the small men." Jan leaned into the threshold, peering. "What the *hell* is that? There's like an *aura* projected from your heart. Oh, hang on—"

"IR heat emissions," Juni said.

After a barely perceptible pause: "Right. You're time-compressed to me, I'm dilated to you."

"Quite. Presumably you're seeing my infrared aura—"

"Not enough energy at that bandwidth."

"—with a little help from the fog at the Schwelle interface. How very Gothic. Why are you surprised by this, I thought you were the gung-ho spaceship captain?"

Jan said, "Yeah, but believe it or not this is the first time I've allowed a Schwelle to open under acceleration, wasn't anxious to risk it. Your timing was providential." The cabin shook again in a soundless explosion or more probably an evasive maneuver or whatever the pilot AI was up to. "Damn! I feel like just coming across and leave them to it," Jan told her in that slightly slow, weirdly throaty voice. Her grin was ferocious and feral. "I could kill the lot of them, but what purpose would that serve? By now I thought they'd have calmed down, it's been more than half a century. Fuck, it's getting hot in here. Put a cup of kava on for me, would you, old girl?"

"You're just going to let some gang of rowdy damn humans *blow up your starship?*" Juni found herself deeply offended by the idea.

"As I was just saying to Sylvie, their ancestors paid for it. It's served its purpose. I've found out what's been causing the interference in all those . . . Hang on, I need to concentrate on the—"

A composite panel peeled away above her head and burst into flame.

"Uh-oh. Okay, dear old *Hanger.* Set the controls for the heart of the Sun. It's been real, sweetheart." She was unbuffering herself, and absently slapping out small flames from her hair.

Something must have spoken to her silently, perhaps the ship's system protesting. She laughed, doubled up.

"Oh no, you great goose, of course I didn't mean it. It's a song, remember? If I was going to abandon you, I'd have done it in orbit around the Xon star. Stepped back to Earth and saved myself plenty of travel vouchers, right? No, I think you're a very nice ship. Once I'm out of here, spill the air from the cabin, that'll deal with the fires. Then torch up to point nine nine lights, make sure they don't hit you with their Son o'Star beam weapons, try not to kill anyone, and park somewhere Sunward of Mercury. Not *too* close. I'll be back. Ouch."

Juni stepped as close to the threshold as she dared, held out both hands. Jan came across in a slurring lurch of transduced light at the fog boundary. All her colors leaped back into registration, tartan in its proper weave, and her voice rose from contralto to mezzo without getting any louder. "Thanks, bub. You should really close the—"

But Juni was already muttering the deixis code. The threshold closed even as board displays on its far side downshifted relativistically into the far infrared and beyond as the starship went toward luminal. Darkness at the speed of light.

"Look at you," Juni said crossly. "You could dress like the Empress of Alexandria and instead I find you done out like a tramp."

"Oh." Jan looked guilty. "Rats, I left your wardrobe behind."

"Never mind that, I can replicate another one for you while we have a chat. Now come in here and sit down and tell me what you've been up to. Started any new wars lately? It's been *decades,* darling."

"For you, maybe, not for me."

"Hmm. You really did say kava? You do still drink the filthy stuff?"

"Is the Pope Hebrew?"

"I beg your pardon?"

Jan made that vexing sound Juni knew only too well, even if it had been decades since she had heard it: a blend of mockery and tried patience. "Yes, dear. Kava, please. Does something smell scorched?"

"Your hair, I believe," Juni said, with a certain satisfaction. "Singed at the back. What can you expect when you fly around the Solar System in a burning spaceship?"

"Oh shit. And just when I'd got it growing out again." She smiled sunnily. "But of course, by a stroke of luck—"

"—my nimble little aerosol offogs will fix that in a trice. Quite so."

As the kava congealed into being inside the maker, frothing in its clay jug, Jan's spiky hair moved slightly, as if invisible fingers stroked through it. Light shivered about her, like a nano version of the frequency-shifted aura Jan had seen surrounding her own body from the spacecraft. That had been the infrared-heat emissions of her metabolism, accelerated just enough by the timescale difference to enter the visible spectrum, then amplified and transduced by the minuscule operating fabrication fog units that hung everywhere in the atmosphere of this cognate Earth. Now the same small men, ingeniously capable, spun and toiled and took apart the charred hairs of her sister's head, and recompiled them.

"You're happy with it that short? Extensions would suit you, but you'd have to lose that dreadful outfit."

"Fuck off," Jan said amiably, pulling stone bowls from the maker and pouring both of them a slug of the barbarous stuff. She raised her bowl in a salute. "To the best of times, the worst of times."

Juni shook her head ruefully at her sister's irreverence but raised her own bowl. The small men, responsive to her whispered instruction, were already working on the molecules, denaturing the alkaloids, changing the bitter yellow-green muck into caffeine-free iced tea.

"Indeed. To the Contest of Worlds!"

Twelve

"I HAVE A guestroom made up," Toby told us, leading us down a side hallway of his absurdly commodious cottage, "only the one, sorry, hope you won't mind sharing?" He gave me a bland glance over his shoulder. To Lune, he said, "Of course you could both go home, but I'd prefer that August remain under my roof for the moment, until he knows what he's doing with the you-know-what."

"You are kind, thank you," she said, as I was saying, "Well, uh, I really don't know that—" I broke off, prickly with excited confusion. "You don't mind?" I said, tongue clumsy, and Lune sent me a dazzling smile, shook her head.

"Right you are then." My brother ushered us into a snug space with an enormous king-sized bed taking up half the room, untinted engravings on the walls and a hunting scene with hounds and horse over the bed, a window with shuttered venetian blinds, small mellow lamps casting a golden glow on plump pillows and a colorful bedspread embroidered with heraldic animals. "Bathroom through there, feel free to raid the kitchen if you find yourself getting peckish. I rise at six myself, but I believe wake-up time is the sacred choice of guests, so I won't roust you out for a morning ride at the crack of dawn or anything so cruel. The sound system has quite a fine selection. I recommend Hovhaness's Second Symphony.

Good night." He grinned thinly and bowed. "Be excellent to each other."

The door shut behind him. My hands were trembling. In the soft light, Lune was exquisitely lovely and so arousing to behold that I wished I wore a cavalier's broad hat to place discreetly in front of myself. My face still felt itchy with quite literal sunburn from the fleeting splash of radiant energy, and the pit of my stomach was jittering. Lune took two steps and placed her soft, soft lips against my mouth, watching me without blinking. Her cobalt eyes were dilated almost to black, yet shone with gleaming light. I put my arms about her, and closed my own eyes. The nerves of my lips and tongue had somehow become hot-wired to my penis and the base of my spine. Electricity roared in me. I ran my fingers lightly up her side nearly to her bare armpit, and brought my hand between us to stroke her beautiful breast. Through the soft fabric, her nipple pressed my palm. I tugged her top free, caressed her bare skin. The air was drenched with our odors. Her breast was round and full and perky firm, a little heavy in my palm. Instantly, my wet mouth went dry. I snatched my right hand away from her and held it out rigidly, palm toward the wall.

"Ugh—"

"What is—?" Lune drew her head back, concerned. She saw my outstretched, averted arm. "Oh. Darling boy, don't worry about that."

But I had pulled away from her, still powerfully erect but not for long. A burst of real fear coursed in me. "I can't do this, Lune. My god, what if that damned—"

She smiled at me, and reached with her own hand, held lightly in the air, along my rigid arm, fingertips touching the back of my hand. She made no attempt to pull my lethal hand down, or to grasp it in her own.

"It doesn't work that way, August. Here, sit down beside me on the bed. You poor dear boy, you're shivering with shock. Just here, at my side." She pulled the comforter to us, draped it over my shoulders, left me for a moment to cross the room. My right arm had a mind of its own and remained thrust away toward the wall. Music entered the room, faint at first, meditative, swelling and rolling over us like fog caught in daybreak light. I'd never much liked Hovhaness, although gentle Itzhak swore by his work; it always sounded like theme music for some kind of New Age fantasy movie. Maybe that made it just right for this mad universe. My arm was getting tired. I forced myself to close the fingers in a fist, and slowly lower the arm to the bed. It was true, I was shivering. Had I once, long ago, been standing in this room in a state of rapturous arousal? That must have been someone else.

Lune was at my side again. "It's no different to any other Schwelle, sweet one. You don't get worried that you'll accidentally open a threshold over the middle of the Atlantic and fall through it, do you?"

I recalled the lavatory facilities, and shuddered. "Um, no. Suppose not."

"This is just as much under your control. More so. The operating system must have impressed a whole command structure into your grammar. Trust me, it'll be heavily fail-safed."

"Foolproofed," I said. I was still shivering with fright, with the sense of some macabre horror barely averted. I believed what Lune was telling me, of course I did, but my trust had to combat a combination of my martial arts inhibitions against lethal force and the brutal memory of sunfire smashing rebarred concrete. "I don't want to prove that I'm the fool, Lune," I said shakily. "Not when your life is at stake."

"You're a dear, sweet boy, and you can't imagine how much

your thoughtfulness means to me." Drawing my damp hair back from my sweaty forehead, she stroked my forehead, leaned against me. Her body was hot. "You can't hurt me, August. Even if you could, I know you would not."

"I hope," I said. My breathing was back to normal, and the tremors were soothed by her caress. "Christ, I stink like a pig."

"You smell very nice." She hopped off the bed, drew me up to stand beside her. The embroided cover fell back in a heap. "But we should perhaps have a shower. I'm a bit gamy myself."

I pulled her tight against me, remembering how we'd slapped each other around in another bathroom in another world, with a dead man lying on the tiled floor. Good god, that was less than a day ago. Was that possible? She was nearly my height. We leaned into each other, taking one another's clothes off rather quickly, nuzzling and touching, and the burning in my nerves now was nothing but joyous. We fell on to the bed making soft animal noises, and it was true, we both smelled like prizefighters after a bout. The stench was as exciting as her nakedness. I found her deep odor on the fingers of my left hand, went nuzzling after its source, skin afire, and she took me in her mouth as I licked and snuffled and sniffed and laughed with pleasure. Somehow we got turned back around, and I went into her with a shock of absolute delight and rightness, my right hand somehow clamped traumatically to the edge of the bed, away from her soft, muscular body. One part of me simply refused to trust another part of me. All the other parts of me, though, were drunk with excited happiness. Cries came from our mouths. I convulsed as she shook and shook, and we lay in the ebbing flux of acoustic sunlight falling away from the high fog and luminous glory of Alan Hovhaness's *Mysterious Mountain.* I guess I drifted off.

* * *

Pale morning sunlight shafted at an angle through chinks at the edges of the venetian blinds. My skin was cool but not cold, and I was mostly covered by the bedspread. Lune's eyes sprang apart, held mine with their shocking cobalt blue, snapped away. She was off the bed like a lioness springing. Something slammed again, and hairs rose all over my naked flesh. I'd heard it in my sleep, that and a deep cry, a human voice. I ran toward the bedroom door Lune had flung open ahead of me. Naked, we sped to the oak entrance way giving on the dell and hill where last evening Toby had fought and bested his hive monster. His cry again, furious, challenging, perhaps seeking assistance, voice echoing. He sounded hurt. I caught Lune's arm at the entrance, dragged her back. "Please stay inside here."

"He needs us."

"Me. He needs me. I need you inside here. Please."

This was all very quick. The tiniest hesitation: I could see it went against the grain. She nodded, stepped aside. I turned the carved doorknob, went through, leaves and twigs crackling under my bare feet.

A silver and black morphing thing from hell cloaked my brother, humming and buzzing and gnashing. His lightning was hardly visible in the cold early light. Sun through trees flimmered from the silver rampaging horror. It seemed to be eating him alive.

I raised my hand, palm apaumy, uttered a command.

Wind howled.

So did Toby, tumbled head over arse in the typhoon vegetation. At least he lived. The million swarm elements of the termagant flung themselves away like chaff, lofted, came together in several clusters high over our heads, arrowed, fell toward me. Their shrieking hum was as appalling as a locomotive roaring down a track at a stalled car. I waited until Toby had scrambled into the shelter of a great oak, his hair, what there was of it, sticking out comically. I wasn't laughing. The termagant came back together and was a scorpion, its terrible sting high and ready to strike into my heart. I raised my hand again and mentioned sunfire.

This time I'd had the sense to shut my eyes and turn my head to one side. Explosive popping snapped and crackled, like bushels of firm purple grapes crunched by a hungry giant, like seawrack bladders tromped on by an orphanage of naughty children, like a kitchen floor's worth of scuttling black cockroaches cracked open and smeared by a hundred furious and house-proud homemakers. When I opened my eyes and looked around, trees were ablaze and the air was sooty with dead termagant particles. It smelled awful. Have you ever burned fingernail clippings? That sort of thing. Toby was getting to his feet, eyes slightly puffy.

"You took your time," he said with dignity.

"That would be the mate," I conjectured.

He came to me with one hand outstretched, gripped mine, the scary one, and clapped me on the shoulder with the other. "Yes. They're very devoted to each other. Strange, in a swarm entity."

"Fonder of each other than the Seebeck clan, by and large." I was laughing, and sat down on the grass. A long scorched pathway had been burned into it. Some stuff on either side still flamed a little, but I wasn't going to stamp it out with my bare feet. Twigs stuck into my bare backside, but I didn't care. I was a comic-book superhero, for fuck's sake. Maybe I really had gone mad and lay in a padded room with a drip of heavy-duty sedative mainlining into my arm. Maybe I'd died and gone to heaven, a theory with even more merit, I decided, when Lune, still naked and indescribably beautiful, crossed the lawn to us and crouched down beside me, arms around my neck, eyes bright, lips and aureoles oddly swollen. Adrenaline excitement. The triumph of man over thing. I laughed harder, until my diaphragm hurt and I had to fall all the way over and lie on my side in the grass.

Lune and I soaped each other under the warm rain of the connecting shower, thoughtfully large enough for two, but we got all sticky when we were only halfway done. Finally we let the water rush down over our wet hair, like puppies in a tropical storm, maybe, and lathered up again, this time until we were clean. Then we dried each other with big soft towels, taking lots of time to nip at mouths and hug and squirm and giggle and let the flooding oxytocin have its way with us. When we finally escaped from the bathroom we found that Toby, thoughtful in this respect as well, had laid out fresh garments on the big bed, complete with underwear. Well, I suppose I had saved his life. Or not.

"Lune, do you think that was a sort of test of the hardware?"

She was drawing a new silk top down over her head, having left some of the underwear where it lay. "It would be gallant, I think, to allow yourself some credit." Her culottes were vermilion, with a broad black leather belt. Looked damned good. I forced myself not to bounce over the inner springs and have at her again.

"Yeah, but he's been in this place . . . cognate, whatever . . . for years, I suppose. Maybe centuries. He must have a pretty close grip on the local wildlife situation."

"Hive and swarm life-forms endlessly aggregate, adapt, switch protective coloration. You might well have saved his life. Where do you want to go now, August?"

"I was thinking some breakfast would suit me just fine. Something rich in cholesterol but good for the soul. An omelet with the works."

"Let's see what's in the pantry." But she took my hand at the door, held me back. "Truly, my darling, I don't know where you fit into the Contest. There are risks—"

"I don't even know what the Contest *is,*" I said, frustrated. "Jules mentioned a place called Yggdrasil Station, and kept harping on about the Doomsday hypothesis. All of you keep talking about this Contest. None of it makes any sense to me."

"It's in your grammar," she told me with absolute confidence. "The X-caliber program must have dumped in a lot more background knowledge, in fact probably some material that's not available to ordinary players like me and May and Toby." Ordinary! I stared at her, shaking my head. She leaned forward and kissed me gently, softly, on the lips. "I know, it's a lot to take in. Go with the flow, my darling boy."

"Hey, surely you could just *tell* me—"

"'Flow, not tell,' as the guru Henry James tells us."

I'd done that in high school. "He said 'show,' not 'flow.' And if he was right, why should I trust anything he *tells* us?" I'd started to feel giggly and silly, some sort of reaction I suppose. "A palpable hit!" I poked her on one bare shoulder with my index finger, realizing with part of my mind that I'd stopped being shy about using my right hand. "A paradox, a paradox."

"A pair of ducks, indeed." She shook her head reproachfully. "Two odd ducks are we, but may ducks eat omelets? It seems fishy. Perhaps a traditional English breakfast of kippers would suit us better."

I made a face. "A vile suggestion." I kissed her again, dizzy with love, or infatuation, or both. "You're ducking and weaving."

"That wasn't *ducking* that kept us from our tea and toast, August," she said sternly. "That was—"

"Please!" I put my fingers in my ears. "This is a family program!"

"The Seebeck family drama, yes." She batted her eyelashes. "I hope we didn't just *add* to the Seebeck family."

The thought rocked me back on my heels. Besotted love is one thing, pregnancy before breakfast is quite another. I caught myself, then, metaphorically, by the scruff of the neck. August, where is your honor, your tender affection, your sense of responsibility? I bowed over Lune's hand, meaning every word, and said, "Darling, if we've made a baby just now, or last night, I'll be the proudest, happiest—"

"You *are* the sweetest boy." She shushed me, drew me to her. Her damp hair smelled of expensive soap and Lune. "August, our kind cannot have children. I'm proud of you for what you just told me, but you can relax—you're off the hook. Besides, if I weren't sterile I'd be on the pill. This is not a role for a parent."

Emotions swept back and forth inside me, relief conflicting with a genuine sad regret. Yes, I was not ready to become a father—but for that moment, I had felt . . . Enough. And then: *sterile?* Was I doomed to age and die without children about my feet, on my lap, in my arms, walking by my side? The prospect appalled me, however remote it might have seemed hours earlier. And then another thought: *Waiiit* a moment!

"Lune, that can't be true." I hesitated, rushed on anyway. "I'm sorry to hear of your . . . condition . . . but it surely doesn't apply to my family, at any rate. I mean, *look* at us! More brothers and sisters than I can count on this hand." I tried to tally them in my head, for the first time. Maybelline, she'd been the first. Then Ruth. Avril. The irreverent Reverend Jules. Septimus the armorer. Our host Toby, old enough to be my father, easily. There'd been other names mentioned. Ember. Decius. Good god, it was true, that was already more than a handful. "All of them, if I can believe what people are telling me, sprung from Dramen and Angelina, my own parents. Who," I coughed in a marked manner, "could therefore not be said to be especially notable in the sterility department."

We had moved back from the door, and now sat facing each other on the bed. Lune shrugged, moued her lips. "That was then. This is . . . well, I suppose in some orthogonal cognates it's *still* then. But you know what I mean. A long, long time ago, the rules changed. We think your parents had something to do with changing them, and Avril's Ancient Intelligence. Maybe *you're* here to change them again. Or maybe the Yggdrasil godlings." She held my hands tightly, and I went deep into her candid cobalt eyes. Certainly she was telling me the truth, or as much of it as she knew. I shivered, disengaged, stood up.

"All right. Let's go and roust up some horrible English fish."

Lune laughed out loud, screwing up her face, and came with me into the hall. "Not on your life, bozo. Whole milk for me over fruity muesli, with a dollop of heavy cream."

Toby came in as we were finishing our coffee.

"Good morning to you both. August, I thank you for your aid, and apologize for dragging you naked from your bed."

I shrugged modestly. "I had to get up anyway . . . to answer the scream."

He shot me a sharp glance, pouring himself a mug of rich brew. "I *never* scream," he explained with dignity. "It was a manly call to my companions in arms."

"I assumed you were discussing the weather with the termagant," Lune said diplomatically. "Loudly but firmly."

"Damned things seem to be reaggregating faster than a man can keep track." Toby shook his head in frustration, pulled back a chair with a squeal of wooden legs on the floor, sat down heavily. "Something afoot in the ontology, mark my words."

"We were just saying the same thing," Lune told him. I blinked. Oh, is that what we'd been saying? All I needed was about a month beside a swimming pool in a quiet hotel where they brought you drinks and snacks and then fed you royally and tucked you into bed with a mint on the pillow. I could think all this through at my leisure, maybe read a few tomes on ontology, whatever that was. It would be a happy way to pass the time, if Lune came with me. In fact, if Lune came with me, she could explain it all, tell not show, and bugger the contrary advice of Henry James. After all, someone with a name and face very like hers was an expert on ontological mechanics. A trickle of cold sweat did not immediately run down the middle of my back, but that conveys how I felt. Oh, shit.

"Excuse me." I pushed back my own chair and went into the other room, walked to the tall bookshelves, opened one of the glass doors. It hadn't been a demented dream after all. *Ontological Mechanics: A Computational Perspective,* by Lune Katha Sarit Sagara. Apparently she held a doctorate in it. I took the volume with me back into the dining space, an odd taste in my mouth, leaving the glass door ajar.

"Ruth," I mumbled, "I'd expect something like this to be written by Ruth the librarian, but . . ." I trailed off, feeling lame. Lune regarded me with what my mother used to call an "old-fashioned" look: dignified reproof.

"I have eyes, August, and fingers," she said. "They are coupled to a brain. Quite a good brain, actually, quite capable of dealing with the rudiments of reading and writing."

I felt myself flushing. "I'm sorry. It's just so . . . I mean, you've impressed the hell out me." I held out one hand, tipping an imaginary pith helmet. "Dr. Sagara, I presume?"

The woman I was maddeningly in love with opened her lovely lips, but before she could speak Toby was saying, "That's Dr. Katha Sarit Sagara, you young whippersnapper. Sarcasm is uncalled for."

"I didn't intend any—"

"Treat the lady with respect, that's all I'm saying."

"Toby, for god's sake, Lune and I have just been *showering* together. Don't you think I'm—"

"No call for adolescent mockery, Mr. Stanley."

I dropped the book on the table with a crash. "Hey, butt out, Toby, okay?" He rose, affronted, face reddening. I said, "Yes, this is your house and you have given us both your hospitality, and I'm grateful for that. I am also pleased to have met one of my brothers, especially since until about a day ago I didn't know I had any. Saving your sorry ass just now was a bonus. Lune, if you're ready, I suggest we go and see how my great-aunt is doing. I'm worried about her." I turned slightly, left hand held out to Lune, and said into the air, "Give me the nexus collection point."

Nothing happened. In the dull silence, the kettle in the kitchen nook started to whistle. Toby dropped back into his chair, apoplexy ebbing from his woodsman's features, and he started a booming laugh. I found myself flushing again in turn. Lune regarded me with mischief in her blue, blue eyes, utterly relaxed. She picked up a chocolate éclair filled with whipped cream, took one contemplative bite, closed her eyes in pleasure, licked her lips, and rose to her feet. I sagged with relief, internally at least because I was still bristling and ramrod straight of spine. I tried again. "Give me . . . Maybelline." I'd rather look an androgynous vegetable in the face than sit here for a moment longer. I *hate* being told off; somehow the memory of Ms. Thieu from primary school hovered over me like a bad witch aura. Still nothing happened. Shit.

"Our host has the Schwellen locked, August," Lune said gently. "Toby, would you be so kind?"

He'd stopped laughing, and leaned back in his chair. "Oh, the impetuosity of youth. Certainly." He murmured a deixis code. I didn't feel any change in the world, in the room, but I immediately started to say, "Give me—" and Lune put her hand over my mouth.

"Just a moment, August. Will you allow us to explain something first?"

Us? I pulled my head back, shook off her hand. It angered me that she was siding with the man who'd spoken to me that way. Admittedly, the "Mr. Stanley" part was mildly amusing; he'd obviously appreciated my "Dr. Livingstone" gag and played along with it. I glanced from one to the other, holding my right hand rigidly at my side, palm toward the floor. Knowing I was being petulant, I shrugged.

"All right. What do you mean, 'locked'? The shower and the toilet worked."

"Those are minor art, August," Toby said. "Shifting a living creature across a threshold is vastly more complicated, and correspondingly easier to block. I could give you the ergodicity equations, but I don't suppose . . ." He trailed off, arched one bushy eyebrow.

"What were you saying about mockery?"

"Oh, for heaven's sake, boy." He rose, came around the table, held out his hand. "Come, clasp, let's not spat. Perhaps I overreacted."

It struck me, out of the blue, that perhaps he was not the

avuncular figure I'd construed him to be; from his own perspective, he was doubtless a man of passion and appetite, and if he had any sense at all, he was deeply attracted to Lune himself. "Carrying a torch" was what they'd called it in Chicago. "Having the hots" was what they called it in Northcote, but that was probably too explicit for my brother's archaic tastes. Oh, so. Nose out of joint. Pipped at the post by a mere kid. Or, hell, for all I knew they'd been married five hundred years ago and divorced for three centuries. I knew nothing, *nothing*. Shut the fuck up, August, and pay attention.

We did the handshaking thing, and then the brotherly-comrade-well-met-masculine-hug thing, and Toby went back to his chair, Lune subsided gracefully into her own, I leaned heavily on the table, nudged the book round a couple of times, then sat down myself.

"Lune, you're an expert in this, obviously. Help me out, will you?"

Her smile was dazzling, with some whipped cream in the corner. Her red tongue tip licked out, swept it away. "*Mais oui, naturellement, mon ami.* Let me start with the obvious. The world is not as you have supposed."

"So I suppose," I said, nodding. "Listen, I really do want to hear all this, but can we table the metaphysics for a tick? I'm deathly worried about Tansy." Actually I was feeling sick with guilt. Here I'd been cavorting about with oddly human god people, smashing swarm monsters with my new magic powers, making love under the teleported rain of warm unknown worlds, and for hour after hour I'd managed to push poor Tansy right out of my mind. What the hell was wrong with me? That preposterous machine Coop might be—The bizarre parson, my brother Jules, could also be—Worse still, *Mrs. bloody perfidious Abbott* might be doing almost *anything* to my aged great-aunt in the spurious protection and security of her own home.

"Your aunt is perfectly safe," Lune said with immense confidence. "Somebody will be watching over that nexus point."

"Bound to be," Toby added. "Always is. Very important loci, the nexus points." For some reason I expected him to pull out a briar pipe and begin tamping tobacco into it. Maybe in some curious way he reminded me of the disposer machine, James C. Fenimore. He didn't do that, though. He reached across the table, picked up Lune's treatise, leafed through its equation-encrusted pages. "We could tell him about the Tegmark levels, doctor, but maybe a short tour would get it across more crisply. Shall we?"

"Show, not tell? An excellent notion, doctor." Good grief, were they all this overqualified? Maybe if you live long enough, I thought, you can't help picking up credentials in quite a few fields.

"Outside would be best," Toby said. "Top of the hill, we can keep an eye peeled."

We trooped out after him. The burnt smell was pretty much gone, and the debris had blown away on the cool crisp breeze. Leaves flashed green and yellow and brown, now and then tore free to tumble in the clear air, piled up in drifts near tree boles. We went to the top of the hill and Toby opened a Schwelle.

"Tegmark base-level excursion," he said. "Just stay close and keep up. I shouldn't think you'll have to burn anything to the ground, August, but if the occasion seems to arise please wait for my signal. Okay?" He turned, met my eyes.

"You're the boss." I shrugged. You're the tour guide, was what I meant. You're the Show & Tell muggins. But there was no point antagonizing him further.

"Right you are. Come along."

We stepped from the side of one hill to another exactly the same. I turned slowly, sniffing the air. Nope, we hadn't moved. My chest muscles spasmed, then, as they do when you get a sudden shock. Down in the shadowed dell, the cottage was gone.

"What have you done with it?" I said stupidly.

"Never built one here, obviously." He opened another gate, stepped through into the same world through a glass darkly: heavy clouds hung low overhead, gray and black. The trees were in different places. A vicious, ear-ringing crack of thunder and brilliant lightning dazzled me.

"Not the best place to be standing in a storm," Lune murmured.

"Agreed." Toby opened a Schwelle, took us back into clear daylight. The trees were gone. I heard chickens clucking in the dell below, children's voices, saw a group of huts. Not five meters away a goat grazed; when it saw me suddenly standing there, it leaped straight up with all four hooves in the air. I knew there was a word for that, but couldn't think of it, because I burst out laughing at the silly thing. I could have sworn it shook its head in disbelief before it headed ambling off downhill, neck bell clanging. *Stotting,* that was it. Some African beast was given to the practice. An adult human came out from one of the huts. She was naked to the waist, tall and scrawny, and when she opened her mouth to scream at us, I saw that all her teeth were filed to points. Half a dozen little angry guys rushed out of the other huts and ran straight up the hill at us.

"Let's not loiter," Toby said, and we went through to a world without huts, but something immensely tall and pale blue stood kilometers away on red concrete, soaring up through light cirrus, bulging out like a turnip. Windows caught the morning sun from a dozen directions. The turnip, I saw, shading my eyes, was slowly turning on its axis. In the low purple-leaved bushes around us, large lacy butterflies came and went. The place was hauntingly beautiful and incredibly strange, like a dream of impossible architecture.

"It's . . . wonderful," I said.

"Yes," Lune said. She put her hand in mine. "These are all cognates of Toby's base universe, you understand. Like the cardinal numbers. There is a countable infinity of them."

"Parallel universes," I said.

"No," Toby told me. "Well, if you like. It's a gross simplification. Each of them is actually in the same universe you've always lived inside, the same *multiverse,* but rather a long way as the crow flies."

"Ten to the 10^{29} meters distant from each other, on average," Lune said, seesawing her flat hand to show that the average varied a bit from place to place, as you'd probably expect if you had the faintest idea what she was saying. "That's as the light beam flies too. Luckily, we can get there faster by redescribing the ontology."

"Oh, of course. Don't know why I didn't see it immediately." I shut my eyes, calculating. Ten to the thirteen light-years, roughly. The radius of the whole goddamned universe, wasn't it? It numbed the imagination. No, wait. There couldn't be that many planets like Toby's version of Earth, not in the whole universe. "Actually, I still can't see it. Ten to the twenty-nine doesn't seem enough—"

"No, no," Lune said. "It's true that ten to the twenty-ninth power is a truly *enormous* number; there's roughly that many atoms in your body. A hundred thousand trillion trillion. But see, that's just the *exponent.* The whole multiverse is ever so much bigger, unthinkably large. You need to *raise* 10 to that *power . . .*"

"Not just one followed by twenty-nine zeros, you see,

August," Toby added. "Ten to the ten to the twenty-nine is so big that if you tried to write it down, you'd have to follow the first one with a hundred thousand trillion trillion zeros. I computed that once over a cup of hot chocolate, and it stuck in my mind for a curious reason."

I felt suitably crushed, and shrugged. "That's plenty of nothing."

"It's plenty of plenty, my boy. At ten numerals to the inch, the number you need to describe how far the distinct universes extend in the multiverse would itself stretch some twenty-seven billion light-years." Toby smiled cheerfully and swung his arms wide. "From one side of the local cosmos all the way to the other, scribble scribble scribble."

"Yeah, and you'd use up a whole shitload of ink and paper, right." I don't think they were fooled by my feigned nonchalance. What they were saying beggared the imagination utterly. My eyes drifted away to the right as I tried to picture it. A universe of universes. But that was just the first step. Then do it again: a universe of universes of universes. And again, and again, and again, almost endlessly . . . It was too much to take in. Okay, yeah, I'd accept it. You could have as many worlds like Earth as you liked in a place that big, each of them resembling the Earth we knew as closely as you wished—the planet Lune and Toby and I knew, even if our worlds were a little dissimilar. I drew in a staggering breath, looked back to Lune. She was nodding.

"I know," she said. "It hit me hard too. All right, my darling," she added briskly, "we're shown you the faintest hint of T level one, where we usually live. Now let's move on toward the *larger* scales."

"Whu—?"

A Schwelle opened as she spoke a deixis code. We went into a place horribly bent and twisted into absurd directions.

"A T-prime sample. Tegmark level two," she told me, somehow, and I heard her, somehow. Her voice rattled like old rusted iron on a roof. "Don't be alarmed. Our senses and our brains are not designed for this. Aren't evolved to cope with it."

Was there air in my lungs? I felt myself choke and gasp. Was there heat enough to warm the chilled core of my belly? I clutched my arms around myself, then looked to Lune to make sure she was okay. She'd turned into an El Greco witch, elongated and hood-eyed. No, not like that at all, more a deformed stick figure by Dalí, or Picasso around the time he started deconstructing the human figure into oblongs with both eyes on the same side of the face. My brother stalked beside her, an insect thing with a ruff of indigo hair. I glanced down at my own hands, recoiled. Wire and corroded, patched leather.

"God," I groaned. "Edward Scissorhands."

"Your grammar is doing its best," Toby assured me. He sounded like a whale, very like a whale. "In this place there are"—he paused, cast about like a hunting hound—"maybe two spatial dimensions and I'd estimate two temporal directions."

"Two directions to move in time? You mean we can walk backward to the past while we're here?"

"Yes, but *only* while we're here," Lune said. Have you ever heard a peacock's squawk? I was outraged at the travesty this evil domain had made of her music.

"It's lovely to visit," I rasped, "but I don't think I'd want to live here."

"Moving on, then," Toby said, and we passed into somewhere far more disconcerting.

"You're mixing up the sticks," I said, witlessly. But what I meant was . . . I struggled to hold on to something distinct and knowable.

"These T-prime worlds embody every conceivable mix of

physical dimensions and constants comprising the multiverse," Lune told me. It made me laugh, because that's what I'd just said.

We went into places where surely nothing solid, regular, persistent could exist, sustain itself. For one terrifying endless moment we crossed a vast space with more directions than seemed possible, but without the ticking of a clock. An odor of incense. Timeless everywhere, ground to a halt, seized. My Vorpal implants blazed with light. I felt a cramp, a convulsion. I was thrown out of that eternal silence, and Lune murmured, as if in recognition, "Elliptical partial differential equations."

Onward we went, ever onward. In a crushed place of echoes where nothing stood still, where improbable forces built up and tore down, Toby told me, "You see? With one dimension of space but more than four of time, the worlds are unstable." We stepped away into places where time returned to normal but space spread out once more in directions I could not fathom with my poor limited brain. He said, "With only one or two dimensions of either space or time, universes are too simple to build or sustain atoms, so we must evade those."

In this inconceivable archipelago we skittered through cosmos after cosmos in disarray and flux. Somehow the Vorpal implants held our bodies and brains, or their semblance in some safe computational enclosure, from collapse or dispersal. Lune told us, "Ultrahyperbolic equations, no stability here." We did all this again and again. I will not try to describe those places of dimensional confusion, it would be as tedious and contrived as recounting a dream next morning. The brain can't hold on to it, so it concocts a bunch of mysticism about colors beyond the visible spectrum, "ulfire" and "jale" in that old David Lindsay novel my mother admired, *A Voyage to Arcturus,* but that's not it at all. I got the point, though, I really did. It frightened me down to the bone, realizing the truth of it. These were worlds, probably an infinity of them, where the three familiar parameters of height, depth and width, and the one-way stream of time, were thrown heedlessly into the trash. Dimensions and constants were remixed and renumbered, the neat domestic floral display of spacetime was barbarously pruned, re-sorted, juggled. Roses were jammed in next to strawberries and stinking weeds, and it made you sneeze and then tore your nose off. As an experience it was baroque, I'll give it that. It was nightmarish in what you might call a bad way. At the end of it, we stepped through on to a railway platform and I sagged with relief, drawing in the sinus-clogging fumes of the steam-engine smoke (so my nose hadn't been torn off after all, which was a comfort), the heavy tang of great greased steel locomotive wheels, the sweat and dirty clothes of early-morning passengers in some kind of traditional Japanese costume, carrying briefcases and listening to Walkmen clamped over their high lacquered hairdos. The men nearby gave us sidelong scrutiny, but shoved forward with determination into the open doors. The women kept their eyes on the ground, shuffling sedately but with some speed.

"Third Tegmark level," Toby said cheerfully. "Hold on to your hat, or not, or all three."

Oh. Oh. Oh.

Was I having a seizure? An epileptic fit, maybe, with those auras you hear about from people afflicted with migraine, jittery streaks of light and the feeling that your eyes are jumping wildly between the frames of reality. Everything peeled apart while remaining rock solid. All the colorful folk on the station got on the train and stayed off it, changing their minds. They climbed hastily into the car in front of them, and raced down and up the station to force themselves belatedly into a different doorway, or in some cases through the open and the shut windows, and fell with a cry of dismay on to the empty tracks where no train stood, and boarded the sleek helicopter that waited on the elevated pad, and—

—I did all that, too, that sort of thing, my viewpoint jumping like a maddened kangaroo from one part of the station to another, with Lune's hand tightly in mine, and torn away from her, and Toby lost to view, and, horribly, Toby lying bleeding and surely dead, his abdomen crushed by the wheels of the departed train, and—

Voices chattering in overlap, coming together into sense, skidding apart into blurred cacophony: "The quantum view of the multiverse, August. The all-at-once unfolding of the wave function. Every possibility realized, all the options accepted. Schrödinger with no collapse. Like in *Sag-A star.*"

"Get us *the fuck out of here!*" I screamed, and hands tugged at mine and let mine go and stroked my fingers languorously and slashed at my skin, and my lurching legs carried me . . .

. . . across the Schwelle and jerked up against my belly in the big bed. The house was perfectly silent as I awoke in my darkened, smelly bedroom. I lay still with my eyes closed for several minutes, percolating upward, breathing night odors through my dry, open mouth. My erection slowly ebbed; I knew I must have been dreaming of Lune again. I reached behind me without turning over, prodded under the covers, but her side of the bed was cold and empty. At first muzzily, then more sharply, I understood that it really was completely quiet downstairs. Odd. Where was her soft buzz of classic rock, her humming clatter, toaster, muesli bowl, coffeemaker? The skin of my upper body was cool, and I drew the sheet and blanket more tightly about myself, hunkering into the pillow, eyes determinedly shut. She's gone, I told myself with gloomy dread. She's left me, the bitch. A moment later, I thought: the Tau Ceti wongles have come for her. They'll be here for me, next. I started to weep behind my closed lids. Slow tears soaked into my pillow. Pull yourself together, man, I thought at last. With a weary effort, I pushed back the covers and let my bare feet rest on the cold floorboards. My bladder was swollen and urgent. I took a step toward the door, toward the toilet down the hall . . .

. . . flipped open the ringing phone, and said in my deepest chocolaty voice, "'Madame Bovary, c'est moi.'"

After the smallest hesitation, Toby said, "Gustave?"

How could you not smile? "Monsieur Flaubert," I told him, "is not available. This is the parrot."

"What a scamp you are, August, to be sure." Toby sighed. "If our quota of farting around is quite met, let's to business. You've read my notes on the blood-bank vampire case?"

I had not. I opened my notepad puter and . . .

. . . We stayed connected to the net this year during high-school exams, so the examining-board program could process our marks on a Wile-U-Wait basis. They allowed us to access the Global Web to hunt down information. Why memorize heaps of garbage about the maximum national rainfall and principal exports of Guadalcanal when you can yahoogle it right off the net? After all, that's what they're trying to test: how well you can perform in the complicated real world.

I got through tensor calculus pretty quickly and decided to fill in some time talking with Homes, my chatterbot. While you are permitted to leave the exam room any time you like, I suspect they keep special tabs on you if you leave too early. "Overconfident," old Thieu calls it. She should know: head of department, thinks she knows it all. Admittedly, she does know quite a lot of it. Following her retirement from NASA at the age of thirty (shot reflexes), she went into education for exceptional students, which is a term that usually covers the stupid, the maimed, the very stupid, the socially inept, and the really, really stupid, but in our case actually did mean what it sounded like.

I wrote the Homer program a couple of years after my mother and father vanished over Thailand, where they were helping fix the famine. Homes was a conversation bot, full name Homealone, because I was staying with Aunt Miriam that year, and home alone much of the time, before I moved to Great-aunt Tansy's. In fact, I still spend a lot of time with nobody else in our big house except me and Dugald O'Brien the Lab, and Tansy. And the cleaning lady, Tansy's "treasure." I've forgotten her name.

Do Good is clever for a dog, almost as smart as Homes. He was smarter than Homes, in fact, back when I started that bot over the Xmas holidays using algorithms I found on Simon Laven's home page. My dog had not slowed up in the meantime; Homer improved. This was how Homealone sounded when I originally booted him up from the raw code:

> *Hi there, big guy! Lookin' good!*
> Good morning, Homes. How are you today?
> *Spruce as a goose, d00D. Howz it hangin'?*
> Show some respect, Homer. This is your master you're speaking to.
> *So sorry! Not! HAW HAW. Blow it!*

These wiseass comments were canned reactions I had keyed in to the bot's linguistic engine. They struck me as hilarious for about a week. Each time Homeboy came back with a snappy one-liner, many of them obscene, I giggled with raucous adolescent mirth, wildly pleased with my own wit. But robot whimsy gets old really fast.

> Afternoon, Homer. Been doing anything fun today?
> *Howz it hangin', August? Lookin' good, d00D!*
> You're starting to repeat yourself, Homes.
> *Any port in a storm, wise master.*
> Aren't you going to ask me what I did today?
> *Why do you wonder if I am going to ask me what I did today?*
> Homer, get a grip. I think you're losing your mind.
> *A mind is a terrible thing to lose.*

I kept tinkering, downloading entire lexicon modules from other, older chatterbots, tweaking them, compressing their algorithms. Homealone started to sound more human.

> Good morning, Homer.
> *Hello, August. Have you cleaned your teeth this morning?*
> That's a rather offensively personal question.
> *You know I have your interests at heart.*
> So you say.
> *Have you got any homework to do for tomorrow's class, August?*
> Good god, Homeworkboy, what are you, the homework police?
> *Chill, d00D. Howz it hangin'?*

My sortofgirlfriend Lune thought Homealone was heaps cool, once I unveiled him. She and Toby insisted on having his url and password, so they could call him up on their own notebooks and shoot the breeze with my bot. I wrote a subroutine they couldn't access that allowed me to read their online conversations later. What I learned was devastating: they hardly said anything about me.

I did notice that Toby had been tweaking my system with his own crass little booby traps. The second time Lune logged on, it went like this:

> Hello, Homealone. This is Lune.
> *Lune Babely, I know. You're the one with the great jugs, right?*
> You certainly have a lot to say for a chiphead.
> *You're cute.*
> Why, thank you. Did August tell you say that?
> *August is my master.*
> Any port in a storm, eh?
> *Lune is a really stupid name.*
> Thanks a lot, chipforbrains. What do you recommend?
> *I would recommend Annie Port.*
> LOL. You are nearly as funny as August.
> *I come from a good home,* my chatterbot told her loyally.

In the exam room, I opened a window into Homes's site. We'd had to disable the voiceactivated and voiceresponsive software to keep the noise level down during the test, so Homeboy and I chatted on the screen and keyboard.

> Recovered from your hangover yet, Homes?
> *I always drink in moderation,* the machine told me. A flashing Java applet jumped around the screen, opening a jeering grin with a cartoon dialogue bubble: BYTE *ME!*
> Is Toonoid finished her 'xam yet?

There was a pause, while he thought about it.

Men and women were in separate rooms and academic streams for most classes, to prevent distraction, which went for the exam rooms too. Homealone's access to the web allowed him to forage through secured databases. It took a skilled superhacker to crack through the department's encryption protocols, so Toby and I had spent a month and a half to break the codes and passwords. Homebody helped a lot, strangely enough, because even though he was just a simulated intelligence, he was tremendously connected. Now he burrowed into the flow of information hazing the wires and telephone links in this room and next door and told me,

> *Lune has five questions to go. She got the sixth and eleventh tensor transforms wrong, and her answer to the short essay on* Henry V *makes it clear that she hasn't read the play.*

Where does he get this stuff?

> *Tell Loon I'll meet her and Toby and Ruth in the Burger Den when she gets out, if she ever does.*

A pop-up window gave me her direct reply:

> *Hey, Org! What U doing here? Its grossly against the rules! Well all be xpelled! Whats the answer to Q 15, America or Persia?*
> *Hey, babe,* I keyed back. *It's called Iran these days, you know? Sorry, can't give clues, we'd be sued and jailed for dopery and mopery.*
> *You mean barratry and simony.*

No, I mean malfeasance and carpetry.
You mean carpentry, and that's no crime.
Trust me, I mean carpetry.
Okay, Persia it is.

We logged off, but Homeboy was still resident. He asked me,

Why did the chicken cross the road?
Payback, I typed. *The road had ripped the chicken off. There's no honor among thieves, Grasshopper. Gotta go.*
Wrong, dogsbreath, wrote the bot. *The chicken crossed the road and did not cross the road because that was its quantum choice.*

A deep, sickening panic invaded me. My pulse jumped almost instantly to twice its resting state. I stared in disbelief at the screen, wondering if I were about to die.

Toby, I keyed, trying to control my hyperventilation. *Is that you hacking my bot?*
At the third Tegmark unitarity level, the screen told me, *we've jumped up to 10^{118} universes, each maxing at temperatures of 10^{8} Kelvin. Every possible alternative quantum choice is realized simultaneously somewhere when*

I jumped out of my chair and kicked the flat monitor over. Its lightweight nanotube structure fell with dreamy slowness, bounced once without breaking, sent me a hot pink blinking message that I caught from the corner of my eye.

The next and final level is the big one, August. Take a deep breath, bend over, and kiss your ass good-bye.

Terrified, I ran toward the . . .

I thought I heard Toby cry out, "Give me Room 101." A Schwelle opened in front of me. I plunged through.

Craziness. Disorientation, everything falling away into a draining, stuttering echo of itself. This was so much worse than the second-level distortions, or the simultaneous superposed overlaps of level three. This was Cartesian doubt so bottomless, so corrosive, that nothing persisted beyond vertigo and pain. I tried to squeeze my eyes shut but I had no eyelids, no eyes. My whole visceral body, sense of awareness, contracted to two mangled lumps of hieroglyphic gold and silver linked by a thin shriek, fingernails on a blackboard. I tried to scream, and had no voice. Yet somehow I heard Toby speaking to us, desperate, clinging to his own sanity by a thread. There he was, in the chaos, and there was Lune: two infinitely distant, gruesomely intimate chains of golden hieroglyphs I could not read. Was it his voice, or were the hieroglyphs morphing, twisting into meaning? He said:

A man in many Earths wrote a very great book.

Some fragment of memory tore through me, gave utterance:

"Eric Linkollew."

Echoing mad laughter? *Yes, he is a great Eric as well. I was thinking of Eric Blair.*

"Never heard of the bastard." Nothing stayed in place. We were plunging like soap bubbles in a gale through one Schwelle after another, like mice gnawing their way through an infinite stack of Stockhausen scores.

Never never never never heard of Nineteen Eighty-Four?

"You mean George Orwell."

He took that name in some worlds. Do you remember Winston Smith?

"He hated rats. Shit, are rats waiting to claw my face?"

Not rats, August. Dragons, perhaps, off the edges of all the maps you know. Winston was shown four fingers and told to see five, do you remember?

I did. I held out four and saw five, and ten, and one, and none at all. Not fingers. I was watching the primal order of the cosmos.

And he did see five. That was Blair's horror story. I always found it absurdly abstract. Until I came here, into level four. Or do I mean five? Hollow laughter banging and clanging at the edges of dementia.

"You're saying there are no rules here?"

No fixed rules, Lune told me. She was formed hot metal in shapes that spoke to me. *This is the manifold. It's so beautiful.* I had no idea what she meant. She said: *I stand in the center of a web of mathematical functions, all in motion, and I'm part of them, I guess I'm creating them as well. They are wavelengths of energy, perceived directly rather than through eyes and brain, graphs of functions growing, intertwining, unfolding. Music, sharply defined and immediate, can't you hear it, August?* And then, cruelly, she was dragged away from me, and the music and rainbow beauty with her, and once more I was drowning in noise and terror.

Build it up, something told me. *Play it again, Mr. Peano man.* That seemed wrongly twisted, but somehow righter than wrong. I scrambled for sensation, sense, sensibility. I could grasp nothing.

Nothing, said Lune's Vorpal hieroglyph display. *The empty set. Zero.*

I clutching at that nothing. I could do that much. Emptiness at the heart of the noise and terror. Emptiness that was the terror, or part of it.

Every natural number a has a successor, denoted by a + 1.

That seemed reasonable, although everything in this flickering horror of fourth-level worlds denied it, mutated that simple creed, added and subtracted and transformed in dizzying confusion. I held to the axiom by brute force.

"All right. What next?"

The set zero is never the successor of any natural number.

No void hidden in the bowels of the rush of numbers 1 2 3 4 5 6 7 8 9 10 11 12 . . . to infinity? No swallowing pit at the core of those things we can count? I hoped it were true. I assented, fearing its denial. No, wait . . . wait . . . I found another solution lurking in there, branching out into a permissible loop: 0 1 2 3 4 3 4 3 4 . . .

I shook my head, started again.

0 1 2 3 4 5 6 7 8 9 . . .

A

B ! ◊ ñ ∗ # ¡

C

D

The simple numbering of the world is pitted with Chaitin pathologies, a voice told me, *unexpected and random.* Yes, all right, I could see that, no way around it. But it was the best I could do. Press on, then:

Each distinct natural number has a distinct successor. If a *succeeds* b, *then* a + 1 *succeeds* b + 1.

I had to think about that, but I grabbed with relief at the very difficulty of the task with all my two, four, five, billion handless hands, and felt reality solidify about me, the endless cascade closing down, the fecundity extinguishing itself, transfinite options closing away, not gone, not lost, merely . . . pinched off. Or rather: our world was pinching itself free of that radiant abundance.

If a property is possessed by zero and also by the successor of every natural number it is possessed by, then it is possessed by all natural numbers.

If a—Well, yes, obviously. An instant earlier it had not been obvious. Now it seemed both true and self-evident. I hung in a blue place, and Lune sang to me. Her notes and chords were filaments and jewels of logic. I watched, dazzled, as she built an ascending Babel city whose towers glistened with fractal complexity, each chamber replete, gorged, enameled, each linked to others by exquisite cables of implication and ever-higher abstraction. It was beautiful, an orchid that opened at the speed of light and made the world in its own image.

Formal systems, she said.

The globe of light branched, adding axioms in one pathway: *Boolean algebra.* And, launching an alternative road: *Models.*

Links multiplied at dizzying speed:

Lower-predicate calculus leaped upward in a blizzard of subsets, unions, intersections, to *Numbers* and *Semi-groups,* commutativity operations which spawned *Rings,* while by another linkage came *Sets, Relations, Abstract geometries,* and *Space.* All of this, in its wonderful richness, was rudimentary, I saw, as it elaborated and grew a world, a cosmos, of mathematical order: on one side *Abelian fields* and *Vector spaces,* by another path *Topological, Metrical* and *Banach spaces.* Still the flowering stormed upward and outward, through infinite hordes of number, relation, ordering, bounds, completeness, into *Tensor* and *Hilbert spaces,* and *Real* and *Complex manifolds.* Finally, at its sunlit capstone, in a torrent of immense generativity, loomed twin rainbowed icy mountain peaks.

Lune told me: *Here linear vector mapping births operators that support the panoply of* Quantum field theory, *fields on* R^4 *act on Hilbert* n*-dimensional fields while—watch keenly now, August—by this different but intricately related pathway* General relativity's *3+1 dimensional pseudo-Riemannian is warped by tensor fields.*

Somehow I did understand what she was telling me. The grammar download from the X-caliber device unfolded, unpacked, in my mind. I looked in awe, ravished by crystalline loveliness. And as if I witnessed the collision of two immense glacial ice shelves in the white heart of Antarctica, those impossibly abstract glories, their vast doubled structures, merged into the computational unity of—

"Too bright!" I screamed. I tasted lemon in my mouth, sharp and fragrant.

The manifold options snapped across a decision boundary. Was that my thought, or Lune's? The engraved sole of my left foot burned, and the palm of my right hand.

We stepped across a threshold into Avril's watery domain. The Sibyl looked up from her astrological calculations.

"Not a moment too soon," she told us. "Jan has brought us definitive news at last of the Xon star."

Thirteen

"THE TEMPERATURES OUTSIDE the blister are still climbing," Guy said. "We're nearing force unification for everything except gravity."

Stepped down in luminosity by orders of magnitude, for their comfort, the glare remained overwhelming. Beyond the shielded enclave blister sketched by the ontology transform mathematics, this entire universe was now smaller than the Solar System had been in its heyday. All its mass and energy seethed in a soup of free quarks, gluons, leptons, darkons.

Dark energy! Decius snorted. Darkness visible, finally. And all of it shaped to the needs of the great minds that for so long had infused this Hubble volume bubble. Now they worked ceaselessly at their titanic engineering feat, last and greatest work of mind. The slightest slip, the least error in the last decimal place, and all might be for nothing.

It was extraordinary, he thought. The cosmos those minds were rebuilding was themselves, for they were now embedded in its every particle and field, every vibrating membrane sheet and soliton flux. Soon, if theory were correct and final, their efforts would attain fruition. This collapsing local universe would reach the point of no return, would crash into the last trapped surface singularity behind its own constricting event horizon, and all that unthinkable force would gel into . . . godthings. Angels.

And forever after, they would course effectively through the fields of their own minds, memories, imagination, without limit, fertile, unjaded, never to repeat their explorations except in amused reflection. They would rebuild whole worlds for entertainment and out of benevolent virtue, in the infinite afternoon glow of their final eternally protracted instant. Their cosmos would perish, yet persist without end. The paradox never failed to send a shiver through him.

A deep gonging rang through Yggdrasil Station.

"We have Xon saturation," Decius murmured. "No more neutronium, no more quark soup."

The displays showed only a uniform silvery brilliance. He and Guy seemed suspended in a globe of vivid mercury under bright lab lights. The shining bubble was the entire universe of this Tegmark cognate, now perhaps shrunk to the orbit of the Earth. That world and its Moon and fellow planets, its very Sun, were long gone, eaten up billions of years ago as measured by local duration and then their embers swallowed up by the catastrophe which was remaking this spacetime. It did not matter. Every atom and structure was committed to memory in the flux torsions of the blazing Xon forcefields that filled the closing plenum. Every atom, remembered, was gone, each proton and electron, each neutrino and meson, all the exchange particles that for so long had danced their separate existences in the tapestry of matter coursing in darkness under the curved direction of spacetime.

Now all that was memory alone. The four great forces had swallowed one another up, like cartoon fish, each greater and more hungry than the snarling victim in its own jaws: particles crushed together, quarks liberated from their double and triple asymptotic bondage, electromagnetism and the weak nuclear force of radioactive disintegration pressed together in the rising heat wave, until they shimmered into one as the underlying mathematical group SU(2) spontaneously coupling with U(1), moments later this electroweak force burning into unity with the strong nuclear force. Quarks and exchange bosons went interchangeable under the profound, ancient mathematical equivalence operations, hidden or masked since time began, of Special Unitary symmetry Group(5). Black holes, trapped surfaces in the leaf of the constant mean curvature foliation, merged with the greater trapped surface forming everywhere. The whole universe seethed for an instant, at the lip of a Planck precipice, as one grand unitary force field within gravity's embrace, an X particle as big, Decius thought with a grim smile, as the Ritz. One immense Xon.

In a moment—however long, in local dilated time, that moment took—the Xon matter field would simplify in its last terrible transition. It—literally *everything*—would return to the vacuum state of fecund nothingness, a single point with a compact Cauchy surface.

At that instant, Yggdrasil Station would become a viewing platform for the birth of the Angels into eternity. The birth too, perhaps, of the Contest of Worlds.

"Should we fetch your brothers and sisters?"

"Not just yet."

After a time, Guy cleared his throat. "Do you think—" He broke off, looked away, embarrassed, swallowed hard. "Decius, do you suppose They'll let us go home to the Contest?"

His master regarded him stonily. "A better question might be: Could we bear to abandon their company?"

"I suppose. The song the Sirens sang."

"Oh, hell." Decius forced a smile. "Come over here. If we're going to be sucked into heaven, we might as well have our arms about each other."

They hugged, and Decius felt unaccustomed salty moisture in his eyes. He brushed aside his tears. On the desk beside him, sheet upon sheet of runes lay spread, downloaded into his mind from the great shouting voices beyond the shell. The notations resembled, he realized suddenly, a set of cryptic glyphs he had once found carved into the bottom of a drained, algae-stained swimming pool. Even more, they resembled the Vorpal patterns impressed into his own flesh and that of his siblings, and of all the other Players of the Contest of Worlds. Those, too, were beyond immediate lucid interpretation, however much Avril crabbed her astrological arcana and Jules ran endless deciphering programs on his borrowed Star Doll M-Brain. It was like some vexing parable of the quest for knowledge. But looking at it that way only made the matter more irritating, because now the parable, too, comprised a hermeneutic task that evaded solution.

Guy was trembling in his arms, terrified.

"Come on, old son. More than a hug's called for." Decius drew him toward the sleeping alcove. "Let's await the arrival of the gods in bed, my dear. I'm sure they won't object."

The grandfather clock showed 10^{-43} seconds.

August

FOURTEEN

WATER AND WATER lilies everywhere, but this was not the same part of Avril's realm where I'd butchered myself and she'd healed me with a sort of fishy miracle. Yonder, on elevated ground, soared the phallic, pointed tower portions of a Norman castle, rising above the plain blockhouse walls of the defensible place like lighthouses without lamps. Young women came and went everywhere—"maidens," I suppose you'd have to call them, like the telephone servants I'd encountered in the grotto: long-limbed, small-breasted, hardly out of adolescence, in filmy diaphanous garments, cute as bugs and just as dispassionate. Our barque floated in the midst of the biggest moat I've ever heard of, more like a lake, linked to a dozen tented islands by swaying causeways. The sunlight, through high hazy cloud, was mild and warming, and I dare say those were lutes I heard in the background. Or maybe dulcimers.

Avril wore her long hair pinned back from her forehead, and she was up to her elbows in parchment crabbed with inky circles slashed by tangents and intersects all annotated in the sorts of Olde Worlde geocentric symbols for the planets that you find in upscale horoscope columns. A wheezy, surly voice at my back said, "She's as superstitious as a cat, boy, and I don't mean that in a collegial way."

The old reprobate reclined, as if grudgingly, in Maybelline's arms. I automatically reached out one hand to pat Hook's head, thought better of it as he bared his teeth and claws.

"Good day, August," distantly said his owner (or was Maybelline *his* pet?). "Now that you're here finally, are you sure you wouldn't like to run off again?"

"Hello, sister. I have some urgent questions about a friend of yours, James C. Feni—"

"Quiet, please," said all the young serving women simultaneously, in voices like a choir spread out on the barque and among the islands. I shut my mouth; a chill went through me. Great effect. Avril rose from her desk, holding a scroll.

"Jan will be with us in a moment, and we felt that you should all be gathered together to consider news of such momentous import."

"Cut the cackle," Hooks growled, but if she heard him Avril was far too dignified to acknowledge it.

"We approach a conjunction of unprecedented portent," the Sibyl told us. "Decius watches for the birth of the Angels in his closed spacetime, and that hour is at hand. Jan, as I say, returns from deep space with news of the Xon star. Our opponents in the Contest plainly sense an emerging crisis: attacks from deformers increase at a menacing rate. And today, as indicated in my calculations"—she brandished the scroll, then gestured toward me—"we learn that our family possesses another member, our brother August."

Muttering all around. I glanced about at the various scowling, nodding, smiling (deceitfully smiling?) faces of my newfound siblings. Jules raised his hands and brought them together in a clap, then another, and, grudgingly, the rest of them welcomed me with muted applause.

"Time for that later," Avril said, granting me a nod of recognition. "What I have just learned from Septimus is that our youngest and somewhat-unexpected brother has breached the seal of the Xon-caliber ontology system."

Xon again? What the hell?

A couple of them had not heard this news; Jules, at least, lost his composure for a moment, paled. I sent him a wry grin and a wink.

"And handles it like the mensch he is," boomed Toby's voice, at my side, and I felt his grip on my left shoulder. Crossing my breast, I covered his hand with my own right, newly—and terrifyingly—puissant hand, then lowered it to find Lune's waiting left hand. She gave me an encouraging squeeze.

"Thanks, Toby. Avril, what *is* a Xon star and why's it such big deal?"

That got a big laugh out of everyone, even the begrudgers.

"Takes a child to cut through the bullshit," growled Hooks, and leaped lightly from May's arms to a silky pile of pillows in the bow. I saw that for all his insouciance he kept one eye cocked for water hazards.

"Ah, our young Parsifal has found the right question," said an unfamiliar voice, slightly plummy, like an actor. A completely naked, deeply tanned, fit man stepped lightly forward with the balance and grace of a gymnast, hand extended. "I'm Marchmain. You pose the puzzle we each wish ardently to solve."

Good god, how many more of them were there? I greeted him, said, "I'm the most ignorant man on the boat, Marchmain. All I can do is ask questions. Well, I can get the toilet Schwelle to flush when someone gives me the code."

More laughter, friendlier, I felt. A young woman placed a glass of frothing golden champagne in my spare hand, moved on in wings of floaty chiffon. Others held glasses, I saw. Marchmain raised his to the muted sun.

"To our quest for the Xon code," he proposed.

The company rang out their answer, drank. I swigged at mine, none the wiser. I moved closer to him, just a little uncomfortable at his nakedness. But he carried it off with the panache of my crazy school pal James Davenport, Davers of taffeta tutu and pink pompom fame, whom he somewhat resembled.

"Marchmain, I can't get a straight answer out of any of you." I showed him the engraved palm of my right hand. "Last night some New Age crystal in Septimus's armory carved this bloody thing into me. Now I can blow radioactive holes in solid reinforced concrete like a goddamned comic-book hero, when all I want is to get home and make sure my poor old aunt Tansy is safe and well. I do realize that you people, some of you anyway, are shoving me up a steep learning curve . . ." I took a deep breath. Marchmain waited courteously. "If my beautiful new friend Lune weren't part of the deal I'd be gone by now. Shot through. You know the phrase? I really am sick of being treated like a booby. I know perfectly well who Parsifal is, I've listened to a few Wagner operas in my time, but I don't care that much what a Xon is, so before I find the nearest exit and piss off quick smart again, how about you tell me something useful, brother, something a teeny bit more satisfactory than a cryptic crossword clue."

It was eerie how silent so many people could be at the one time. Tiny waves slapped at the sides of the barque. Breezes flapped and snapped a sail and pennon or two. Various mouths opened, closed again. Lune stood to one side, swaying faintly with the rocking of the boat, glass at her lips, cobalt eyes watchful from beneath dark lashes.

Jules cleared his throat. "You have a point, August. Matters, though, remain . . . complex. If you'll contain your curious soul in patience for just a little longer, I believe all your questions will be—Ah, and here they are now. Welcome, sisters."

A Schwelle had torn open in a space that I saw now was always left unencumbered as people came and went. Two women stepped on to the barque, one dressed as the fabulously expensive trophy wife of one of Tom Wolfe's New York midtown Masters of the Universe, the other in the sort of street-cred outfit you'd expect down South of Houston or even in the Village. If Lune was darkly, radiantly, beautiful, and she was, this post-Goth babe was only pretty, but she had a raspy piquant edge to her. I warmed to her instantly, without a word. She had to be the spaceship pilot. Jesus Christ. I had just come back from an hallucinatory tour of the four levels of the Greater Cosmos, but the idea that this cool chick was a bona fide rocketship captain made me go weak at the knees. Talk about comic-book heroes. I wondered if she wore a transparent bubble helmet when she was on her starship.

"Commander Jan Seebeck, sans starship," Marchmain was saying, "And Juni, sans offog. Your brother August, and perhaps you remember Dr. Lune Katha Sarit Sagara?"

"Do you know," said the society lady, "I believe we've never met. I read your book, of course, doctor, a remarkable treatment of modal—"

"Now, now, no shop talk, ladies. You must be starving. Avril's kittens have some excellent canapés." He gestured, and a tray of crisp hot shrimp in a heavenly light batter appeared with another bottle of bubbly. I chewed gratefully.

Jan was considering me sidelong. "I'm getting a strong Xon flux off this dude," she told Marchmain. "Where's he been lately?"

"More to the point," Juni asked languidly, "where's he been hiding?"

"Feel free to address me directly," I said through gritted teeth. "I rarely bite, and besides I've had my leprosy shot this year."

"Ask the next question," Marchmain said in an oracular tone.

"Where's Miriam?" I said.

People looked blankly at one another. Ruth shook her head, pursed her lips, searching her memory. "Miriam Birkbank? I haven't seen her since the tiger shoot in Kenya."

I brushed that aside. I was getting angry again. This is unusual for me, I don't really know how to handle it. "My aunt Miriam. Your aunt, presumably, all of you. Don't give me this evasive runaround."

"I'm sorry, my dear," Juni said, frowning, "you're profoundly in error. We Seebecks *have* no relatives, other than each other. Surely you see that. It's in the nature of our kind."

"Miriam," I said slowly and clearly, "is my mother Angelina's sister. It follows that she is also your aunt, madam."

"Good god! Don't call me 'madam,'" Juni cried, taking a step back. "It makes me sound positively antediluvian."

"If the shoes fits," grated Hooks.

"There is no sister Miriam," Marchmain said. "You have been misinformed. We of the Vorpal stock are sprung from two alone, Dramen and the lady Angelina."

"And they," intoned Toby, "from the Tree Yggdrasil."

The assembled company in ragged concert made an odd, rather liturgical gesture, of a Hindu or maybe Buddhist cast, both hands sweeping together from the waist to the mid-breast and flowering outward and up, an outlined cup or tree, or at least made some sort of sketchy attempt at it if they were clutching plates and glasses of champagne, as most were. Good grief. I felt a jolt of disgust. Another pack of loonies. They'd do well in Great-aunt Tansy's collection of spiritualists, ectoplasm fanciers, clairvoyants and transmigrators. But that was just one part of myself doing the jeering; another part, fresh and new and shy and shell-shocked, recalled Toby standing in a place of autumnal leaves ablaze with sparky power, recalled sunfire burning from my own outstretched hand. I was in no position to mock the eccentric beliefs of other people.

"All right," I said, feeling tired. "I asked about this Xon star, and you seemed to like that. What is it?" I shook my head. "I'm sorry, I'm being rude and pushy. I've been through a lot lately. I should just go and sit down quietly and wait for someone to lead me off to the lunatic asylum."

"Too late," the cat laughed, "you're already there."

Lune was at my side, and she took my right hand, turned it over, opened out my clenched fingers. Those nearby, those at any rate who hadn't seen it before, gave a little gasp.

"That's Xon matter, August."

The golden hieroglyphs were dull in the pale light, sunk into my flesh.

I shut my eyes for a moment. "You all have these markings on your bodies?"

"'The mark of the beast,'" Jules called, jovial. "Mine's in my left ankle."

"I have one on my foot as well," I said. "Had it as long as I can remember. Lune's the first person I ever met with the markings, other than my parents. I assume this controls the deixis, the Schwellen, whatever."

"It's the outward and visible sign of our grammar structures," Jules said.

"But what the hell *is* it?"

Jan, agog, had grabbed my hand, examining it with undisguised interest. "You got this from the Xon-caliber engine?"

"Yes." No point in denying it. So what does that make me, I thought, king of the Round Table?

"It's . . . well, that's the big question. Primordial matter, that's the simplest answer."

"Solidified X rays or something?"

The space pilot laughed, delighted. "Closer than you think! It's a condensate of unitary spacetime. Do they know about the Big Bang in your cognate?"

"When the universe popped out of nothing? Yeah, my crowd can make fire too, by rubbing sticks together. Or do I mean by rubbing blue woad into our belly buttons?"

"Hey, calm down, hotshot. All I'm saying is, in most Tegmark base-level universes . . ." She trailed off. "Oh, *that's* something you won't know about, I suppose."

"We've just did the full four-level excursion," Lune told her, amused. "I'm sure August will let you know if he requires a footnote."

"Okay, too cool. Augie—"

"August," I said frostily. Cute gets you only so far.

"August, wrap your mind around this. In the first hundred-thousandth of a second, which is very late by logarithmic standards, everything was still crammed together denser than an atomic nucleus. Can you dig it?"

"Yeah. Quarks jammed together, right?"

"Running about like hairy doggies. Much earlier than that, there was an epoch of terrific blandness. Back before like a trillionth of a trillionth of a trillionth of a second, just before lambda inflation, you know?" Another person beating me over the head with trillions of trillions, like that UFO crackpot with his "*bill*ions and *bill*ions of stars." Then again, having seen that sentient vegetable Phlogkaalik's Adamski saucer, I was in no position to deride poor stoned Dr. Sagan. "Very hot, mind you," Jan was saying, "but no electricity, no magnetism, no nuclear forces because there weren't any nuclei yet, no light as such because it's too crowded for light and there's nothing to see. None of the forces had decoupled yet. That stuff back then, that was Xon matter."

I couldn't help myself. I opened my itching palm and stared at the dull blobs of shaped metal. It didn't look much like the Big Bang to me, not that I'd been there. (See how ignorant I was back then?) But it surely had the strangest properties, and it had kept my flesh from shriveling to ash when the flames of the sun's thermonuclear plasma came spurting out from its embrace in a slender, lethal stream.

"Shouldn't it be *heavy*? Like, a planet of solid lead in every thimbleful?"

"Offset by the lambda expansion energy locked up in it. Effectively massless." Jan looked impressed. "A quick study, eh. I like that in a brother."

"Vorpal matter," I said speculatively.

She winked at Lune. "In a manner of speaking. A *matter* of speaking, really, because—"

"Because it's a bloody metaphor, my boy," Jules said. He topped up my glass. "Phenomenology as semiotics." I saw over his shoulder Juni raise her eyes to heaven and turn away, sinking down gracefully into silken pillows to discuss less abstruse topics with Avril. The inward nature of oysters, perhaps, or the influence of Venus on her rising quadrant. "It's an interesting accident of many cognate histories," Jules went on, waxing rhetorical, "that 'phenomenology' came to have two meanings, apparently at odds. In the tradition of philosophy, it connotes a direct and unimpeachable knowledge of the essence of things, a sort of reaching out with the spirit to engage reality without mediation. Husserl, you know. Heidegger. Hell, Hegel, let's bring in everyone with an H. Meanwhile, the experimental sciences stole it, rather barbarously according to the complaints of the professors whose names start with H, to refer instead to all those fallible observations we detect via instruments, the very contrary of phenomenological intuition, you might imagine. *But* of course—"

Jan insinuated one arm through mine, another through Lune's, drew us away to one of the swaying bridges linking the barque with the tented islands amid lilies. Her brother looked piqued. "He loves the sound of his own voice. I've been gone for six decades, and it all comes back as if it were yesterday."

"Is he right, though? He wants me to believe that words are things. Or things are words."

"Words, diagrams, gestures, dance steps, ululations, equations. Especially equations. Representational ontology."

This was as bad as Tansy's benign psychic chicanery. Three days ago I had been rounding up hundreds of sheep from the back of a bouncing motorbike, then eating and drinking rough fare in a parched landscape. That was reality, it put calluses on your palms and brought sweat pouring from your forehead and armpits. Words didn't even come close to describing the experience; no way I was going to swallow the mad idea that words, symbols, representations *were* the experience.

Lune said urgently, "Commander, we shouldn't be distracting you from your report to the Seebeck family. Just before your arrival, Avril spoke of a conjunction of unprecedented portent." I thought I could faintly hear mocking quote marks. My siblings did seem to enjoying getting in a bit of inflated rhetoric. Still, it was obvious that Lune took the claim seriously. "I believe we must be closing in on something truly important, some clue finally to the fundamental ontology."

We stepped inside a tent made of something pink and gauzy. Throw pillows everywhere, lute sounds doing a kind of muted Manuel de Falla Spanishy impressionistic romanticism. Jan dug into her vest, drew out a joint, struck it alight, took a deep toke, passed it on. Lune sipped, perhaps to be polite. I waved it aside. I prefer to keep my neurochemistry under endogenous control. Sorry, I'm giving way to the family weakness. What I mean is, I like to stay straight. Dope fuzzes me, which is maybe the whole point but I prefer clarity.

As the pungent fumes filled the tent, I wondered, though, for a moment, if I were having an instant contact high. An elegant tattoo on Jan's arm shook itself, as if waking, and flew up on fairy wings to hover at her ear.

"They want you back on the barque." The voice was tiny but crystalline.

"Shit, Sylvie." Sucking smoke, she held her breath for an impossibly long time, vented jerky puffs. "Tell them five minutes. Hey, how's *Hang Dog*?"

"*The Hanged Man* is safely on orbit at Mercury L4, pretending to be a lump of cometary debris."

"Cool. You can go back now, this poor kid's eyes are bugging out of his head. August, you've made Sylvie's day."

"He's so cute," the high brilliant piping voice said, and I blushed, I actually blushed. Sylvie the fairy hovered for a moment, gazing at me in a provocative manner and showing her cleavage, then zipped home and was a tattoo on Jan's arm.

"Okay, here's the thing. You know about the 13 hours 30 minute LST peak, right?"

"The—no, sorry."

Jan shook her head. "You guys these days. There's an ontology access well in the probability fields with a quasi-diurnal rhythm in all the cognates, with a peak that's regular in sidereal time but not by solar chronology."

"Commander, I haven't got the faintest idea what you're—" I blinked, then, and two or three wildly different parts of my experience, recent and old, fell together with a soundless flash. "Oh, my dear god. You're talking about Tansy's half hour."

"Who? And don't call me 'Commander,' sweetie, I'm just your sister Janine."

"My aunt. She's a psychic, or claims to be. On the phone." Rattled, I held up my right hand with thumb and little finger extended, held it near my ear. "She only ever does her stuff at a certain time each day. No, that's not what I mean. It changes each day."

"By four minutes," Lune put in.

I stared at her. "I thought you didn't know Tansy?"

"I don't. It follows from the sidereal periodicity."

"More than one way to count the time, August," Jan told me, taking another toke that any minute now would probably wipe out her power to tell the time by any measure. Her eyes glazed; she was feeling no pain. "The solar day marked out by your wristwatch is twenty-four hours long, which is what it takes, one noon to the next, for the Sun to be, like, overhead, okay?" I nodded; she rushed on in a blurred voice, "But what about the so-comically-called fixed stars—answer me that, August."

"You can't see them. When the Sun is directly overhead."

Laughter burst from her lips. "Good one! Hey, the kid's a wit. Listen, not the point. How long does it take for the . . . I dunno . . . the Great Bear to duck under the world and come around again and put his head up over the horizon? Clue: *not* twenty-four hours."

I shrugged. "Beats the hell out of me. I'd have thought—"

"Twenty-three hours, fifty-six minutes, and four-point-oh-nine-one seconds. They teach you that in space-cadet school, sidereal time. Sidereal, pertaining to stars. *Star* time, right?" She coughed. "Not that I *attended* space-cadet school, you understand."

I was thinking about numbers. Nearly four minutes less than a day, per day. So, what was that, one whole extra sidereal day each year? More to the point, a cumulative slippage of . . . call it twenty-eight minutes a week. Oh, good grief.

No wonder Great-aunt Tansy began her magic consultations at 5:00 this Monday if she'd begun last Monday at 5:28, and the week before at 5:56. My strange dear old relative had always followed the beat of a different drummer, but now I saw that she was following, as well, the ticking of a very slightly different clock.

"Tansy maintains there's something very special about a certain shifting time of the day," I said out loud, speculating, putting it together. "Something psychic."

"Call it that if you like," Jan said, crushing out her joint in an empty champagne flute. "One woman's ontology warp is another woman's magic. Don't ask Avril, she'll fill your head with the most arrant nonsense about the influence of the stars."

"*You* were the one talking about stars," I said. I stood up. Reminded of Tansy, I felt guilty yet again about leaving her alone in the house with who knew what marauding demons cavorting in its bathrooms. Not that Lune was a cavorting demon, nor my sister Maybelline for that matter, but I had grave doubts about Coop. There remained unanswered so many things I'd meant to ask Lune, starting with what the hell she and Maybelline had been doing depositing dead machine things, if that's what they were, in my bath. Somehow I simply hadn't found the time to ask her. Ask the next question, portentous Marchmain had suggested. And something snide about Parsifal, and now it came to me with a sick sense of disgust that Parsifal was the holy fool who never asked the right question. Jan was looking from one of us to the other with happy, glassy eyes. Strong shit. I hauled her ungraciously to her feet.

"Yeah, yeah," she said. "Xon star. Five and a bit parsecs out, in the general direction of Sagittarius."

"That's toward the galactic core," Lune said. "Where the great black hole is, Sagittarius A-star. There's been a lot of speculation that closed timelike—"

"Xon's much closer than the core," Jan said, slapping herself one or twice on the cheeks of her face. "The hole, that's like nine thousand parsecs, doctor. I'd be happy to go there for a look-see on my old trusty horse *Hanger,* but I don't think anyone's willing to wait thirty thousand years for me to get there, even at sea."

At *sea?* Oh, she meant "at *c,*" the speed of light. Good grief. The woman had a relativistic starship parked in the same orbit as Mercury. But maybe that was in a different cognate universe. My head was spinning. And maybe the contact high *was* getting to me; my gums felt numb.

"Enough's enough," I told Lune. "I have to go and check on Tansy. Can you come with me?"

Her lips touched mine, soft as rose petals. "Of course. Jan can make our apologies."

"Whatever." Walking carefully, Jan pushed open the chiffon, stepped blinking into the daylight. "Guys." One negligent wave.

Lune spoke quietly; a Schwelle tore open. On the far side, in darkness, I saw the side of a frame house, and a closed window. We were in the air. No moon hung bright in this world. The bathroom light was off, of course, but a small glowlight shone from a powerpoint. Fishing an anodized tube out of her culottes, Lune bathed the glass with blue flickering light. It smelled as if the paint were burning, and the glass crackled and evaporated. Painting out reality with a magic eraser. I shook my head.

"That was very theatrical, Lune, but last time I went back to the nexus collection point I just climbed out through the mirror."

She had one leg over the sill. "From Ruth's cognate? The one Coop takes decommissioned deformers to?"

"Heimat, actually. Maybelline's place." I followed her in, making shushing motions with my spare hand. I didn't want to come rushing to Tansy's rescue in the middle of the night and have her fall down dead with a heart attack. And if Mrs. Abbott was lurking around, I didn't wish to alert her. "So this is like . . . cache memory? The operating system recalls your last pathway from the previous access?"

"Something like that. I detect one human in the house."

"Great-aunt Tansy is a real homebody. She'll be downstairs. Maybe asleep by this stage, I don't know what time it is here." In this world—*my* world. Something else worried me. No barking. Dugald O'Brien, our faithful hound, had almost-supernatural powers of observation. Hairs rose on my arms. That's right, he'd missed all the previous break-ins as well. Poor old dog, maybe he was losing it at last. Or that bitch Abbott had done something to him. Poisoned him, maybe. I felt sick at the thought.

"Wait a minute." Lune turned, hand on the doorknob, looked hard at me in the dimness. "What *were* you doing, standing in the bathtub?"

"Waiting for the maniacs with the next corpse."

"But how did you know to expect us? August, are you telling me that this old lady of yours *knew* we have been using this nexus point as a property transfer?"

"And was frightened half to death. She found out a few weeks ago. I've been wanting to ask you—"

"Shrouded. Just a moment." She edged past me, repainted

the ruined window with her blue raygun. As if it were a computer image somehow conjured away into a buffer and then brought back up again, the window reassembled itself. The scorched paint unpeeled itself from nasty black smelly knots and coated the plank siding. Faintly against the darkened sky, I saw my own reflection in the restored glass.

"So we *are* in the Matrix," I said speculatively.

"The what?"

"Like in that movie franchise. It was telling the truth, wasn't it? This is just a simulation. What you called a Contest."

"I haven't seen the movie, August. Maybe you could put it that way—as a really simplified crude approximation to the true ontology. This actually isn't the best time or place for that discussion, dear. Do you need to take a piss?"

"What?"

"Well, I do. I drank too much at Avril's little bash." Utterly without embarrassment, she skinned her culottes and panties down to her knees and sat on the toilet. I heard hissing, which had a weird double effect; it excited me, in an odd, voyeuristic way, while provoking my own urge to urinate, as the sound of running water does when you're asleep. She wiped herself neatly, rose. "Shall I flush, or are you waiting in line?"

"I need to, but I couldn't. Not in front of—No, don't flush it, we're being quiet, remember."

"Okay." She put down the woolly lid. "Here we go. Take point, dear local guide."

I left the overhead bathroom light switched off, eased open the door on a dark hallway. A homey smell of recent cooking. I half sagged with relief. Tansy had to be okay, then. No sound of her TV set, no orchestral music on the sound system. No snores, either, but then we were two floors above her bedroom. I gestured over my shoulder, started down the staircase.

In the dimness and quiet, my mind raced like a mad thing. So much to correlate, so little time. Did Tansy's heel or sole bear an enigmatic silvery stamp? I didn't know, had never seen her unshod. Tansy had been too old to go swimming with me. For that matter, was she really Dad's relative? Everything I'd been told was now thrown into doubt by this new impossibly extended and apparently ageless family. If Dramen and Angelina were truly the parents of old farts like Septimus, what did that make them, what did it make my lost father? Not the third-generation Australian scion of an ancient and notable—if not aristocratic—Estonian family. If we hailed from that distant land, it had been a very long time since the immigration officer stamped the first Seebeck passport.

The light was still on in the kitchen, I could see a glimmer under the closed door, but then Tansy always left it on, she figured it scared away burglars. Must have done, too, there had never been a break-in even though Northcote had its periodic crime waves. Personally I attributed that to Do Good's dutiful presence. A sweet-natured animal, but bulky and probably menacing if he bared his fangs at you when you entered the yard carrying a jimmy and wearing a Beagle Boys mask. I turned the other way, Lune padding at my heels, and hesitated outside Great-aunt Tansy's bedroom. The grandfather clock ticked sedately. Faintly, an odor of must and old lady. I eased open her door, put my ear to the crack.

Breathing, deep and slow and quite reverberant. Almost sounded like two people breathing in synchrony, fast asleep. Must have decided I'd gone out on the town and wouldn't be back until late, so she'd followed recent routine, dined alone, taken her bath downstairs, and gone to bed. I felt relief wash through me. Carefully, I shut the door, turned, bumped into Lune.

"Snoozing." I gestured with my head, and we tiptoed back

toward the kitchen. I closed that door behind us, sniffing at the plate of cooling scones on a paper doily on the sideboard. A few minutes earlier I'd snacked on canapés from Avril's floating feast, but my mouth watered. I was feeling slightly whiplashed from circadian shock. While Lune sat at the table, I filled the kettle for a pot of tea. That was something you couldn't easily find in Chicago, one of the culinary drawbacks of my time abroad. Teabags was all you got, if you were lucky and if they knew what tea was in the first place, and usually served with lukewarm water. I shuddered, pulling down the old scratched octagonal steel can holding fragrant leaf tea, set it beside the empty pot. And then I couldn't put it off any longer. I sat down on the other side of the table, leaned across it with my elbows jammed on the hard surface, and said, "Why the corpses, Lune? Why here? What Contest and what Players? And what the hell is Yggdrasil Station?"

She looked at me seriously, pursed her lips, for a moment said nothing in a way that clearly indicated she was sorting out priorities, working up the entrance point into a horribly complicated crossword puzzle of an explanation that would contain immortal Seebecks, four-level infinitely complex fractal universes, Xon power tools, speed-of-light starships, aquatic astrologers with cloned girl servants, Adamski UFOs piloted by giant randy tubers, Alice in Looking Glass mirror gates, dead machines, live machines, Mormon-hating bogus ministers of religion, and who knows what all; I could see that this was going to be a long and winding road.

"The short version for Dummies," I said.

"All right." God, she was beautiful, even under the kitchen's fluorescent tubes. Chocolate skin good enough to lick and nibble. Eyes like deep blue metal. Breasts, as King Solomon or his biblical ghostwriter tells us, like two young roes that are twins, and although I'd never been informed what rocs were—Reverend Jules could probably fill me in—I knew that I'd like to stroke the dear little creatures if I ever found them grazing in a field. "Darling, you have to understand that—"

The door creaked open behind me. Lune's gaze darted over my shoulder. I turned. Mrs. Abbott stood in the darkened frame.

I threw myself to one side, kicking my chair away as a distraction, rebounded from the lower kitchen cabinets, hoping that Lune would duck and cover by herself, and grabbed the bitch around her ample waist. Her back struck the doorjamb, and we tumbled over into the hallway. It happened very fast, apparently at about quarter speed. Once, I went over a fence on my bike after taking a turn too quickly and moved through the air in the same stretched tempo, not that it did me any good because my reflexes weren't particularly accelerated, just my shutter speed, my window on slurred events. I saw her shocked and ghastly face, her *indignation,* her mouth open slowly, the high-pitched shriek cut into my eardrums, and we hit the carpet, Mrs. Abbott on her back, me more or less on top like a ravening rapist. I felt fury and embarrassment in the same extended moment. She was wearing a bathrobe over a heavy nightgown of Tansy's. Oh shit, oh no, it had been Mrs. Abbott breathing the sleepy breath of the unjust in Tansy's stolen bed. Her voice rose higher in fright. I rolled off her, clutching her arm, intent on preventing her escape, and the shriek was not coming from her mouth, which was open and gasping for breath. It came from Great-aunt Tansy, in the hallway outside her bedroom, in her own floral nightgown and robe. The scream cut off. With quite impressive speed, she spun, ran to the front door, turned the deadbolt, flung it wide. She put two fingers to her lips and I heard a piercing whistle. Something large and dark bounded through the door, shot past her. I was halfway to my feet, still holding Mrs. Abbott's arm. I was flung on my back with bruising, concussing force, slammed in the chest. Head reeling, I let go of the woman and raised my right hand. Before I could utter the excaliber deixis, Do Good had hold of my wrist and was shaking my limb as if I were a toy he planned to tear apart. I slapped his muzzle with my other hand, and for a moment, I managed to jerk free. He lunged at my face, then, and I felt slaver fly into my nostrils and eyes.

Something passed over the top of us both, all three of us in fact, stamping painfully en route on my sternum. As I gasped in pain, Lune came back down on the floor with a muffled crash, like a gymnast demounting in a perfect 10. Her strong hands grabbed Dugald's ears and pulled back. The dog howled and twisted his thick neck. By then she was straddling his back like Tarzan on a lion.

"Time out!" she called in a clear, penetrating coloratura soprano. "Mistaken identity all round!"

Pinned back away from me but ignoring her, looking at me in the hard-edged shadow with ferocious eyes, the big old Labrador said, "What the *hell* do you think you're doing, August?"

FIFTEEN

THE MOMENT HIS sister Jan completed her slightly scatty report to the family concerning her flight to the Xon star (was she drunk already, or stoned?), Jules Seebeck placed his glass on a passing kitten's tray and went quickly to the Schwelle space, ignoring the others. He stepped across the threshold to the outermost shell of his M-Brain, 750 million kilometers from the Star Doll cognate's still-active Sun, thirty times Earth's distance from its ancient warmth. The Neptune bolo station, built expressly for his comfort, spun imperturbably in the darkness on its long diamond thread, generating the illusion of normal Earth gravity.

Here the sky from the next shell sunward was almost as black as night, radiating the waste heat of a score of concentric Dyson shells, sucking out the last usable quanta for its picocomputers before passing the final stepped-down and stealthed ergs of black body heat into the external cosmos. If there were aliens out there, studying this portion of the heavens from afar with intelligences vast, cool, unsympathetic and envious, they were unlikely to see the encysted star and its fantastically elaborate folded minds, as great in extent as the original planetary orbits that once had sliced across its ecliptic. This enclosed and reconstructed Solar System was now a tremendous collaborative effort in deep computation, replicating by brute force and cunning algorithm alike the conjectural history that had birthed all the variant habitats and lifeless wastes of the Contest of Worlds.

"How can we help you today, Jules?"

"A clean sweep." He handed his jacket to the presence manifesting itself as a butler of the old school, in wing collar and tails. "Jan brings word of the Xon star common to many of the human cognates."

"Ah, gratifying. I should like very much to learn more."

"I should like very much to learn why you can't detect its equivalent mass in this allotopos."

"No doubt your sibling's information will clarify the matter for us both. You have a summary handy, of course?"

Jules waved his hand, permitted the M-Brain to upload the database Jan had provided them all. Instantly, the presence smiled.

"Thank you, Jules. This is very good. It confirms our current paradigm. The object is almost certainly a congealment from X-level substrate reality."

"Well, duh, Brainiac," Jules said, and smiled back. Always entertaining, these little fragments of borrowed patois. "It's a Xon star, Dr. Xavier."

"A terminological coincidence," the butler said, laying out a fresh change of clothes. Jules loosened his tie, sat back in the big old barber's chair. The butler fluffed out a starched striped sheet, tucked it across Jules's midriff and into his unbuttoned collar over flannel. It scissored for a time, black locks falling to the floor, whetted a large gleaming straight-edge razor on a worn leather strop, laid it to one side, found a mug of warm soapy broth and with a soft-bristled brush lathered up Jules's chin and throat. The blade slid across his flesh like a caress, with just a refreshing hint of bite to it. Jules lay back, relaxing every muscle, and closed his eyes. Eucalyptus oils rose from the lather. The butler scritched at his temples, under his nose, carefully leaned his head forward and shaved his nape. It was always such pure, will-less pleasure, this abdication. Lather and bristles came away on a heated towel, another hot flannel dabbed at his open-pored skin. The butler swept away bib and barbering utensils, followed Jules to a comfortable reclining armchair of buttery leather, raised the footrest to the perfect height as he settled in.

After a long floating moment, Jules shook his head. "*Mere coincidence,* eh? That seems vanishingly unlikely to me."

"Not really. 'X' is frequently taken as the signifier for an unknown, and by extension an extremity. Xon particles are always the last to be found by any human cognate technical civilization, because their production requires such immense scales of energy or such inordinately brief periods of observed duration. Simple Heisenberg's principle, Jules."

"Yes, yes. You know, I can never decide what I think about Heisenberg's principle."

The butler gave a polite chuckle. "And Fermi's principle?"

"I hate it, I feel so excluded. As for the Complementarity Principle . . ." He couldn't think of another cheap gag and decided to let it rest.

After a decent pause, the butler murmured, "*Quel* Bohr."

It took Jules a moment to get it, then he gave a grudging smile. "Damned few extant Xon particles anyway, since the Big Bang switched to inflation. Except for these odd things." He crossed his left leg over his right knee, pushed down his silk stocking, examined for the millionth time the enigmatic silvery hieroglyph impressed into his ankle bone.

"And the star your bold sister has explored."

"Quite. And you'll tell me, I daresay, that X-space bears that arbitrary name because it's the last and deepest order of all the substrates."

"Yes, of course, but not arbitrary: linguistically motivated—by the very usage we have just discussed."

"Oh, all right, let it go." Sometimes Jules enjoyed these verbal jousts with the M-Brain manifestation, even though he knew he could win or draw only on the terrible being's sufferance. He straightened his leg with its mark of the unknown beast, lay back in creamy soft leather, stared into the darkness. "So what has Jan's heroic odyssey taught you?"

"That the world is, indeed, simpler than we had feared. That a sheet suitably inscribed with information is sufficient to evoke a world, and not just one world but an infinity of worlds."

"An equation on a T-shirt, you mean? That's so old."

"No. Information densified to the Bousso entropy bound, written at minimal dimensionality into the world membrane."

Shit. Why bother asking? He could never tell if they were playing with him, humoring his vagrant curiosity, or speaking with simple if incomprehensible honesty.

"The universe as a good book, eh?"

The butler chose not to sigh, but Jules felt it in the set of its shoulders. "I see you have been impersonating a theologian again, Jules."

"It's a life."

"It's a Contest," the thing told him, and went away into the picomachinery where great and potent calculations were endlessly wrought in a subtle machine as vast as that solar system which once had been here before it was disassembled and rebuilt into this colossal Russian doll of a Mind, sphere within sphere of optimized computronium, this fractal nest of untold trillions of Minds, whatever it was, really. A theologian, indeed!

St. Thomas Aquinas in space. Jules sighed and forced himself out of the chair's seductively sybaritic embrace.

"One's wallow," he said with a groan into the apparently empty, hummingly replete air, recalling a favorite recondite joke stolen from one of the infinite Earths, "does not make a Summa."

SIXTEEN

HUMILIATED IN FRONT of the glorious woman I was madly in love with, anxious for Great-aunt Tansy, still rather wary of the Abbott woman, and exasperated with the dog, I rose stiffly, brushed down my clothes, tried belatedly to help the woman to her feet. She was having none of it, drawing back, fearful or trying to give that impression, I hadn't decided which. Dugald O'Brien remained crouched, ready to lunge, held in check only by Lune's convincing grip. He growled at me menacingly, like a dog.

"Hooks," I said. Wheels within wheels.

"August, this is an absurd way to behave," my aunt told me. "Calm down, now, Sadie, you can see that he meant you no harm." The woman was keening, fingers in her mouth, eyes squeezed shut. "Dugald, sit back, sir!"

The dog did so, reluctantly. He said skeptically, "You know Cathooks?"

I felt dizzy, half-deranged. "We've never eaten from the same bowl, but yeah."

"That cat's okay," Do Good said grudgingly. "Don't try anything like that again, boy, or I might take your face off by accident." With dignity, he shook slaver from his chops, cast an appraising and perhaps admiring glance Lune's way, and departed through the open front door, perhaps to sleep under the porch but more probably to patrol the old house against the depredations of whomever he'd mistaken me for.

"Yeah," I muttered under my breath to his retreating back, "and where were *you* the last few Saturday nights?" Oh. Blocking magical emanations, I realized, and if Tansy *were* one of the gang perhaps shielding Lune's and Maybelline's from her. Did that make the dog a good guy or a bad guy?

Now that the shock was wearing off, the Abbott woman was whimpering and dabbing at her eyes with a Kleenex, saying to herself, "It's not a dog, it's not a dog." My aunt patted her arm and made hushing noises. To me she said, "You promised that you'd be home by seven. The leg of lamb's completely dried out. You'll find it in the fridge in plastic wrap if you want cold cuts. Make yourself and your friend a salad. I'm his aunt Tansy," she added to Lune in a neutral tone. "Welcome to our home."

Calmly, or as calm and contained as one can be while wiping dog slaver off one's vermilion culottes in a stranger's place in the middle of the night, Lune introduced herself. To my astonishment, she added, "I'm sorry for the recent disturbances in your bathroom, Tansy. My fault entirely, and I apologize for upsetting you."

Tansy glanced upward significantly, nodded: the bathroom, and the corpses. "For heaven's sake, Sadie," she said, "stop blubbering. She kindly stayed here last night to keep me company when you didn't come back."

So much for the classified information, Above-Top-Secret aspect I'd sort of supposed held sway. But I recalled the anodized gadget in her pocket, and the green ray of forgetfulness it could cast over those without Vorpal implants. And this wasn't the first time Lune had shown a willingness to explain matters to her victim on a temporary basis before erasing it all, or trying to. Guilt, I speculated. A need to make amends, confession and penance, the kind of thing Rev. Jules would know about probably. Or was she probing Tansy's covert knowledge? More likely.

"So it's this lovely young woman's doing? Curiouser and curiouser," Tansy said. "Why don't we all go into the kitchen and I'll set out a nice pot of tea. Fortunately, I made currant scones, and we have fresh strawberry jam."

"Does she know?" I said in Lune's ear.

"Doubt it. Shh."

"You saw that nice Mr. Fenimore home, I trust?"

What? Good god, how long ago had that been?

"Yes, Aunt. He asked me to make sure I conveyed his respects."

Bent over the teapot, she shot me a keen glance. Had her cheeks colored? Perhaps. "And then you drove around to St. Barts for a spot of worship and Christian fellowship with our good Reverend Jules, I understand. I'd have thought you didn't have a religious bone in your body, August."

Oh shit, I'd left my vehicle outside Jules's manse. I wondered if Coop the machine were still sitting in strange repose inside the manse. Or was he about his even stranger business, collecting and disposing of corpses or their simulacra?

Mrs. Abbot had uttered a gasp at news of my apostasy, and was regarding me with renewed disfavor and suspicion. I forced a conciliatory smile. The kitchen wall blew in. For a moment I sat at the table numb and deafened as white gypsum dust blasted across us. Boiling water spurted from the kettle as it flew through the air. Lune moved like brilliant red and streaky white lightning, seizing Tansy and carrying her to the floor, her own body shielding the old lady. Mrs. Abbott sat stock-still, mouth agape, perhaps unconscious. I held out my hand and said a word. The remains of the kitchen wall blew outward, timber studs and all, and the ceiling creaked and dropped a bit. Something outside in the garden screamed with pain. I blinked crud out of my eyes, ran toward the opening, hand apaumy and held out before me like the weapon it was. The overhead fluorescent light had come loose at one end and swayed, throwing metronomed shadows.

A tremendous crash resounded upstairs. A moment later, water started spurting down into the debris. Bathroom pipes, sewerage.

"They've taken out the collection nexus," Lune said intently. She stayed crouched over Tansy, checking her pulse. "She's all right."

I looked at Mrs. Abbott, who sat where she'd been at the table. A sliver of glass from a small exploded leaded-glass window protruded from her left eye. I touched her neck and she tumbled out of the chair. That made the second dead body I'd seen in the last couple of days, and possibly the first human one.

More crashing sounds overhead. "We have to go," I said. "Can we take Tansy through a Schwelle?"

"As long as one of us remains in contact with her at transition. Where do you—"

"Give me the Star Doll," I said.

As the ceiling started to collapse grindingly upon us, the threshold tore open. I took the better part of Tansy's slumped weight and flung the three of us into the darkness. A tall, clean-shaven man in his shirtsleeves turned, startled, and stared at us. At our back, Tansy's beautiful old home came apart and fell down, flung billowing dust and wood chips at us. The man, who I now saw was Jules sans Byzantine beard, spoke sharply, and the Schwelle vanished.

"My good god, August," he said, "whatever have you done to poor dear old Tansy?" A flicker of dismay crossed his face, before he caught himself. "Good thing you brought her here, anyway. If you'd tried that little stunt into Avril's, the operating system would have locked you down."

I ignored him, placed Tansy on the medical pallet that somehow was instantly waiting for her. I had no idea where it had come from, but I knew this cognate, this world-variant, existed somewhere midway between wish and reality. The very grain of the place seemed responsive to your needs. Lune bent over her, checked her pupils in a knowing paramedical way, counted her pulse.

"Some bruises and abrasions, nothing too bad."

"Thank heavens. And you?'

She winced, straightening. "Half a brick in the maximus gluteus, so you'll have to go easy for a while, tiger. You okay?"

"Not a scratch." I heard in memory that awful crashing. Shit, the poor animal, I couldn't just leave him there.

"Take me back," I said, hoping the operating system had a slick cache and enough savvy to work out what I meant. Instantly, the Schwelle tore open on a pile of rubble that blocked the entire window, puffing soot and other airborne rubbish into the M-Brain habitat. Pieces of brick and broken timber tumbled in. No way through. I shut the window, shouted, "Give me the nexus collection site."

"You can't go in there," Lune cried in alarm. The threshold showed darkness, and the darkness smelled bad. Somewhere a gas supply line had broken. I pushed my head across the threshold, wishing I had a flashlight handy. A gaping hole where the heavy old bathtub had rested, now tumbled into the ruin below. Water gushed from a pipe. Most of the floorboards were gone, but the joists seemed somewhat more secure. I stepped in carefully, crabbed toward the open door. Even in the darkness, the devastation shocked me. The bare framing of the old house stood; they'd done good work back then. Everything else was jumbled, leaning, or simply missing, heaped up below. And maybe my dog (my *talking* dog!) under the lot of it. My pulse jumped. I knew the place so intimately that even in this disarray I was able to move with some certainty. To the right, feet on the joists, martial-arts balance skills finally paying off. There was the staircase. Or at least, that's where it had been. The force of the impacts or explosions, whatever did this, had torn the top of the stringer loose. The staircase swayed free several feet beneath me. Nothing else for it. I leaped.

And kept leaping, like a man racing down a steep hill with a hungry bear at his heels. I crashed into the wall, turned, the treads shifting under me, risers breaking away and clattered down, the banister tearing loose when I touched it and tumbling away to crash into the debris below. I went down two or three rocking steps at a time. It took forever, and it was over in an instant. I threw myself into Tansy's bedroom, stood for a moment on piled-up trash against her torn-open, leaning door, listened to the staircase smash itself enormously into flinders. Some light from the window. All the glass was gone, shards scattered across piles of broken plaster, crumbled mortar and old-lady clothes. I climbed out through the frame, cutting my hands a bit, and ran around to the front of the house. People were gathered in the street gawping, and in the distance I heard a fire-truck siren, or maybe an ambulance. Nobody had come into the yard to help. Maybe they were afraid the house would fall on them, or maybe they thought Tansy was a witch—the sort of rumor that kids spread about eccentric old ladies. No sign of enemies, either, but then I didn't know what enemies looked like.

He lay on his side, half under the subsided verandah porch.

A huge chunk of mortared brick chimney crushed his shoulder. I heaved it away, lifted his motionless body into my arms. I had been working hard for weeks in the outback, so I was fit and strong, but the big dog's weight sent me staggering. I couldn't see. Weeping, I said, "Give me the Star Doll," and took him through into a different place of darkness.

I lowered his body to the yielding floor beside Tansy's gurney, wiped tears from my eyes with the back of my hand, examined his injuries. There was blood on his fur. Some of it was from my own cuts, but the fallen chimney had crushed and dislocated the shoulder of his right foreleg, on that side shattered half his ribs, bloody and oozing through the fur and, most horribly, torn out his right eye. I heard myself utter a dreadful mournful groan of despair. Minutes ago I had seen another human, that poor woman Sadie Abbott, dead at our kitchen table, and it hadn't moved me nearly so greatly as this. Do Good was my *friend.*

"Paint him better," I wailed at Lune.

"I can't. Oh, August, that's not possible."

"Yes, you can." I was tugging at her pocket, looking for the thing that sprayed out its blue ray. "You just have to—"

"It doesn't work that way, my darling." She was crying, too, distressed by my grief and her inability to do anything to assuage it.

"Leave the animal," Jules said. "I'll have someone come in to dispose of the remains."

I was on my feet in one convulsive movement, my bleeding hands striking his chest.

"Hey!"

"Just *shut up,* you *prick!*"

"I'm sorry, old son, I didn't realize the beast meant so much to—"

Tansy groaned. We turned to her as she said in a feeble voice, "August, you must help him."

I shook my head, tears bursting up again. "Aunt, I'm so sorry, Dugald is gone."

"You can heal him."

The old lady was in shock. I took her hand. "Nothing we can do now, love."

She forced herself up on one elbow, looked fiercely at me. "Lay your hands on him, August!"

What mystical craziness was this? But Tansy was the psychic-hotline professional, the one who calibrated her advice by some absurd astrological routine that turned out to be governed by, of all things, something called an Xon star. At the very least I could not deny her this last illusion. I shrugged, feeling utterly foolish and bereft, and knelt down again beside our dog. I place my right hand with its dreadful weapon against his face, above his snout, covering that brutalized eye socket.

Light bloomed up from my hand. Oh dear god, I'd somehow activated the sunfire. Was that what Tansy had wanted? A kind of Viking pyre for our old companion? But she knew nothing of my excaliber gift, and I lacked control over this force, I'd destroy the whole damned habitat. I snatched back my palm, or tried to. It was welded to the dog's head, and my arm was trembling, shaking with a deep vibration that seemed to rise from my solar plexus and pulse through my entire body. Light penetrated the dog's stiffening body, and my own limb. Something flowed and spurted: information, a torrent of data. Fractal forms shivered and rearranged themselves. I had no control. My arm and hand were burning, I felt as if an arc-welder element were jammed into my naked palm. Through the flesh of the back of my hand, I saw revealed the muscles and sinew and bone, and in the midst of my body's coarse stuff the glowing glyph of Xon matter-energy, and beneath that another, blazing in its own light, embedded in the dog's head above and between his eye sockets.

Abruptly the light was gone. I couldn't see, dazzled by after-images. My hand flew up. Do Good gave a harsh coughing bark, shook his head, surged to his four feet. With two clear, dark brown dog eyes, he looked across at me where I knelt. His injuries might never have happened.

"Thank you, August," he said. "I apologize for my earlier attack."

I sat back on my heels, crying again, and laughing as well. I leaned forward once more, then, and with patient forbearance he allowed me to throw my arms about his neck. "Just doing your job, buddy," I said, and had to clear my throat. "And by the way, when we've made sure Tansy's all right, I'll be very interested to hear precisely what that job *is*."

"My dear child, I'm perfectly all right now," the old lady said in recovering tones. As she struggled to get off the gurney, Lune gently restrained her. "Oh very well, fuss if you must. It does a body good sometimes to be fussed over. August, come here and let me thank you for saving my life."

Gypsum dust powered her hair; some more fell out of mine as I bent to receive her dry kiss to my cheek and peck her back.

"Tansy, I'm sorry, but your friend Sadie Abbott—" I broke off, flustered.

"Dead, poor soul, I felt her go." Well, of course, Great-aunt Tansy the ace elder psychic-hotline operator would not miss a thing like that. "Somebody attacked us, August," she said circumspectly but evidently puzzled. "That was not an accident."

"I know. And I don't suppose they'll stop just because we escaped them into . . . this place." I gestured at the dark minimalist habitat, still not sure what Jules's Matrioshka Brain star *was.* Some kind of construct, that was evident. I caught his eye. He regarded me with displeasure, lips tight. "Jules, I'm sorry if we've brought them here after us."

"That's not the problem," he said. "You're *shedding.*"

"I beg your pardon?" I patted at my clothes, and a small cloud of plaster dust and grit blew out.

"All over the clean computronium. Do stop that. You're filthy; you need a damned good scrubbing."

"Oh good," I said wearily. "My tenth immersion and change of clothes in two days." He was right, though, my scalp was itching, and my eyes were getting sore. "All right, Macduff, lead me to water."

"No time for that nonsense." He tore open a window, called, "Juni?" She stepped into the habitat with a glass of champagne in one hand and a chicken leg in the other. "Take charge of this wretch and get him cleaned up, would you? Then back here lickety-split."

"I preferred the beard," she told him, and handed him the wine and the dead animal portion, which he received with a moue of distaste. "It lent you a saintly look, something you'll never attain under your own steam, you bully. Oh, well, come along young man."

I checked with Lune, eye-glance-quick; she nodded, stayed where she was, holding Tansy's hand. Juni opened a Schwelle and we walked into a place shimmering with aureoles of light and rainbows faint as mist, a sort of Maxfield Parrish dream. "Clean him," she said to nobody in particular. A breeze ruffled my hair, and the least disturbance rifled my clothing, like the tiny fingers of a thousand fairy pickpockets. My cheeks burned slightly, and I raised my clean tanned fingers to touch tingly skin smooth as a baby's. Invisible sandblasters had taken off the top layer of my skin, or that's what it felt like. My eyes blurred for an instant, prickled, and everything was a little clearer than it had been, despite the light in the air. I looked again at my palms, did a double take. Not only was the blood cleaned away; the window-glass cuts were gone.

"Good god," I said. "You have a staff of obedient poltergeists."

"Nanoscale effectuators," Juni told me complacently. Her greasy fingers were clean as she took my yet-again-renovated hand and drew me back toward the threshold. She paused, looked around her with a pleased expression. I recalled an old joke about a wealthy CEO. His subordinate met him outside the company's great skyscraper beneath a sublime spring sky, sunny but not hot, with the merest zephyr to carry perfume from the opening blooms in a nearby park. "Beautiful day," the salaryman said. The rich guy looked around with self-satisfaction, nodded, said, "Thank you." That was more or less Juni's demeanor.

"These bloody things are suspended in the air?" For a moment I felt myself choking, as much on her hubris as at the thought of breathing a billion nanites in and out of my poor tender lungs. Of course, they were probably beavering away even as we spoke, shoveling cholesterol out of my arteries and freshening my breath. The stink of fallen masonry was gone, at any rate. I ran my fingertips through my clean hair. Slick.

"Offog, I call it. Its ancestors ate everyone in this cognate, tore apart the flora and fauna, dismantled most of the buildings, and then eventually down-regulated their programs into benignity. I've been reprogramming them, with some help from Jules's M-Brain." She turned to the Schwelle space; I held her arm, restraining her.

"Which is? I was there earlier, it seemed like the world's biggest VR salon."

Juni laughed once, hard. "Yes, you could put it that way."

"Funny why, Juni?"

She took the long way around to explain, but I wasn't going to interrupt her. Thank god, some answers at last. "The Matrioshka Brain system seems to have been constructed about two thousand years ago by a culture derived from a merging of Egyptian pyramid builders and Indian mathematics. Obviously, that's not their name for it; they called it a Ra Egg. 'Matrioshka' is a pun on those Russian dolls, you know, you open one up and there's a smaller one inside it, and again and again."

"Oh. Hence 'Star Doll.'"

"Jules's deixis, yes. The Sun's hidden in the middle, burning away as usual. They pulled all the planets apart, you see, and turned the materials into concentric orbiting shells, each one larger and colder than the one inside it." She added mysteriously, "It's an inverse fourth-power radiation law, you see, so the hot inner shells are where most of the work is done, even though the outer ones are so much larger in extent."

I shook that aside, but I'd heard of the general idea; it was on *Star Trek* once. "Dyson spheres, right? But aren't they gravitationally unstable or something? They should fall into the Sun after a while."

"No, no, silly, that's only if you built a solid sphere. The Builders weren't stupid, they made their shells from a tremendous number of co-orbiting plates and bubbles linked by laser beams. Started off in the ecliptic plane, like the decomposed planets they'd been made from, then realigned so that in the end the Sun was shielded by a swarm of buzzing planetoids optimized to suck in all the solar radiant energy they could capture. Maximally economical, and safe—no alien would-be rivals can detect you from outside, as the last of the waste is way down in the infrared. Well, detectable in principle, but makes it damned hard to pick *you* out from the background noise."

My mind was still numb from my wild careering through the Tegmark levels, but this kind of arrant grandiosity still had its power to shake and shock me. I leaned back a little, away from Juni, as if she'd slapped me.

"Why? Why the hell would anyone tear the *planets* apart? You mean the Earth too?" She nodded, shrugged. I tried for some redemptive levity, but it fell from my lips like lead. "Must have been the slackest environmental-impact study in history."

"Different cultures, different values," Juni told me. "At least they didn't loose a worldful of ecophagous nanoreplicators like the fucking lunatics in this cognate." Again she turned toward the Schwelle space; again I stayed put, trying to digest her gruesome image.

"No, come on, help me here. You mean they tore the Earth apart and made it into . . ." I trailed off.

"Computronium," she said. "Computational platforms of many kinds, each layer designed to extract the maximum useful energy from the Sun and vent its waste heat for the benefit of the next layer out, and on and on, all the way to the orbit of Neptune, I think it is, maybe farther out. Anyway, that's where Jules has his spinning cozy human-scale habitat, creating a nice comfortable one-gee centrifugal gravity for him."

"It's a *computer?* The size of, of the *Solar System?*"

"Ha, you're still easily impressed, I see. Don't go getting the impression that it's the computer with the biggest grunt on the block, kiddo. Wait until you visit Decius on Yggdrasil Station. Those lunatics are turning an entire contracting *cosmos* into a single computronium platform."

I was battered into submission. I looked down, shaking my head. "My brother Decius is doing that, eh? What *are* the Seebecks, the family who took over after Zeus retired?"

That earned another cryptic laugh. "Ah, the delicious irony.

Yes, you could say that, little brother. But no, Decius and his crew aren't *building* the Omega Point cosmos, they're just watching from their viewing platform. The Angels are building it. The godthings." Involuntarily, I think, she shivered. "Or they will be, once they're born. Come on, enough chattering. There are bad things to find and kill."

Juni took Lune back through for a quick nano make-over while I sat beside my aunt, who was propped on big firm cushions on a big couch.

"Why haven't you ever told me about any of this, Tansy?"

"Why, I have no idea what's happening, dear. Do you know where we are?" She started to sniffle. It broke my heart. I took her hand. Do Good roused himself from his crouching posture at her feet, placed one paw on her knee.

"Ma'am?"

She looked confused and lost. "I know I'm dreaming, darling," she told me. "I keep imagining that the dog is speaking to us."

Do Good spoke sharply, three yipping words. "Ma'am, wake up."

Great-aunt Tansy straightened, sent me a small smile, nodded courteously to the animal. "Thank you, Dugald."

"My pleasure, ma'am." He dropped to a crouch, placed his snout between his paws, closed his eyes, and appeared to fall asleep.

Tansy told me, "I encysted myself when . . . when your parents vanished, August. I'm sorry, dear, it was necessary to ensure your safety."

It took me a moment to understand that she hadn't said "insisted," which made no sense under the circumstances.

A different person sat beside me, yet the same person I loved and respected. It was a supernatural transformation, immensely moving. I forced myself to the moment, said, "You knew about the nexus collection point."

"That much, yes. Not exactly what it was. I'm very sorry to have sent you into danger."

Why would she do that, tell me nothing? A security measure? I'd been a kid, after all. "They can read our minds, these deformers?"

"Probably not, but I didn't wish to take that chance." She considered me appraisingly. "You look very nice now."

"Yeah, I scrub up well." Hurt, I forced myself to give her a grin. Part of me wanted to give her a hard shake, but she had clearly acted in good faith and with both our interests at heart.

"She's a fine woman, August," she said. "Don't let her get away."

"I thought you'd warn me off. After all, she's probably . . . I don't know . . . hundreds of years older than I am."

"Time is relative, dear. When you have eternity in front of you, a few centuries don't count for much."

I cleared my throat, looked away. "Aunt, are you really as—" I broke off.

"Am I really a broken-down old crock?" Fondly, Tansy patted the back of my hand. "When I choose to be. It's a simple matter of self-description. Lord knows I feel that way often enough." Tears sprang into the corners of her eyes. "I loved that old house."

"Me too," I said. "I really *badly* want to do something to those—"

Lune walked through a tearing noise, bright-eyed and bushy-tailed, garments soft and clean as new. My heart surged, and I rose to my feet. Out of my blind spot stepped an ancient gypsy crone, cracked cheeks and forehead rouged and painted clownishly, curls of a ratty red wig sticking out from her purple turban, gimcrack rings and bracelets flashing from fingers and wrists. She set down her crystal ball on a rickety green baize card table and pulled out a Sobranie cigarette.

"Not in here you don't!" roared Jules.

She ignored him with a sardonic twitch of her eye, lit up. The fumes made my nostrils twitch, but I liked her spirit. The crystal ball was grubby, smeared with fingerprints.

"Welcome, August Seebeck," she said through sharp fumes.

"I'm guessing you're the M-Brain," I said. Insanely alert, I stood between her and Lune.

"We are Madame Olga; sees all, tells some."

"This is Dr. Lune Katha Sarit Sagara, Madame Olga. Permit me to introduce my Great-aunt Tansy. She's a telephone psychic; I guess you share the same trade."

Olga drew back, offended. "Tansy and we are old friends. Her expertise is renowned, and governed by the rising of the Xon star. We, on the other hand, am a complete mountebank."

Xon star again? Everyone was talking about the damned thing, whatever and wherever it was. I started to wish I'd waited to hear Jan's report at Avril's moot. She'd been to the damned thing in her starship. But if I'd done that, Tansy and Do Good might have met the same lethal fate as the Abbott woman. Unless, of course, I realized bleakly, it had been precisely my arrival that precipitated the attack on our Northcote home. *Former* home, god damn it.

"You're wondering if it's your fault," the gypsy told me, and spat a shred of tobacco leaf from her painted lip.

"You read our minds." The idea was discomfiting. At least the being appeared benign.

"We could do so, naturally, by scanning, analyzing and replicating every motion in your brain down to the quantal uncertainties. We refrain from doing so, naturally, being a moral person. No, we coarse-grain-calculated your likely state of mind."

"You have no trouble doing that, being such a brainy moral person."

"Trust me. 10^{26} watts running a brain with a cortical surface area of 10^{22} square kilometers. Let us give you some idea of the scale of the thing. You're brainier than a worm, we trust? One of those tiny nematodes, say?"

"I like to think so."

"Yes. Let's say a billion times as smart, counting brain cells. We are ten million billion times smarter, August."

"Than the worm?"

"Than you, although the difference is effectively insignificant."

That stung. "The worm, *c'est moi,*" I muttered, remembering a partial life I had not lived in a universe far, far from here on another Tegmark level.

"Sorry. So yes, we can calculate you faster than you can run yourself in real time. Obviously we don't do that completely, as it would be immoral."

I felt dizzy, seeing what she implied. "Same as making an identical copy of me? Then throwing it away when your use for it is done."

"Just so. A perfect copy is a person, too, of course, so that would be murder most foul."

The gypsy's cloudy ball was clearing, showing some kind of fractal pattern that resembled my X-caliber implant.

"I am not a number, Madame Olga, and not a calculation, either," I said feebly. "I am a free man."

"Oh, but you see, a calculation is exactly what you are."

I looked from Tansy to Lune. They looked back at me, clearly long since reconciled to the horror of it, if they even saw it as horror. Lune tipped her head to one side, nodded.

"This *is* a simulation, then, after all."

"Of course it isn't, sweet boy," my aunt said. "It's a *computation.* There's a world of difference, you see."

"The world's a computation, you mean?" I said. "This M-Brain world? Or all of them?"

"The whole four-level Tegmark manifold," Lune said. "That's the ontology. The multiverse is what you get when you run the simplest world-making calculation in Platonic space. You get all of them for free."

"Oh, shit," I said. Nobody could just tell me something simple and straightforward. I looked around for Jules. He was skulking in the dimness like Hamlet working up some gloomy soliloquy. I yelled, "Have you got anything decent to drink around here?"

"I believe this is what the doctor ordered," a butler in tails and old-fashioned collar told me, at my shoulder, proffering a shot glass of golden smoke. I drank the Glenlivet down in two gulps, felt fire in my throat and nose, coughed once. After a moment, life improved a bit. How pitiful a thing the human soul can be, sometimes, in its ingenuous dance of neurotransmitters and imported chemicals. Or bytes, bytes, bytes. I lay back against cushions, like Do Good closed my eyes, sighed.

"So am I a bug or a feature?" I asked.

"Oh, very definitely a feature," Lune told me, sitting beside me. Her smile was audible. She smelled wonderful. The two women I loved in the world, now that Angelina was gone, one either side of me on a couch in a computed Dyson sphere in the wrong universe. Fuck.

"More than that," the gypsy said. She made her crystal ball

go away and leaned toward me, breathing whiskey fumes as strong as my own. "August, you're the upgrade."

It was late morning in Toby's cognate Earth and blessedly free, for the moment, of termagants and other malevolent or territorial swarms. He met us at the brow of the low hill.

"Thought you'd be back. The game's afoot, what?"

"What?"

"Avril has intimations from the Ancient Intelligence that matters approach a cusp. A turning point, August, perhaps a tipping point. And your arrival among us as the lost sheep found is no chance coincidence, you're in this up to your waist, dear boy, up to your chin."

"May we come in, Toby? Lune and I need to sit down and talk stuff over. I feel a strong need to kill some bad things, but she's trying to talk me out of it."

Lune smiled, dazzling white in pale chocolate. "Better to raise from the dead than to slaughter, my darling. If it can be managed."

Toby's eyes widened. "He possesses the gift of healing and resurrection now? 'Pon my soul."

I felt a rush of choking confusion. It blocked my chest like a pang of indigestion, an ailment I'd suffered only once although it lived in horrid and vivid memory. Never eat green potatoes. No, this was closer to genuine despair. I felt burdened by my unsought gifts, absurd as they were. My future seemed abruptly about to funnel down into a life of mandatory sainthood, rushed from one hospital for the terminally ill to the next once the word got out and around, no, to morgues and maybe cemeteries—who knew the limits of this terrible consequential gift? I hadn't asked for it, I didn't even know that I could use it again. Maybe it was a one-off. For all I knew, it had been triggered by Do Good's own Vorpal implant, hitchhiking on the back of mine. Or maybe there was some weird synergy between the dog, his mistress, and me, the Johnny-come-lately to the household. The now-defunct and ruined household.

"I'm not Mother Teresa, Toby. And I'm certainly not—" I fell silent. There are limits to hubris—or, at any rate, to *my* hubris.

"Well, we don't know yet, do we?" My brother twinkled at Lune. He ruffled up his own hair, pleased with himself. "We could toss him in the pond and see if he can walk on water."

First Avril and her watery rites and Jules with his fake parson's collar, now this. "Shit!" I said grumpily. "Just hold off on the crucifixion until I've left the room." While this badinage was in play, we had strolled down the hill, entered Toby's comfortable cottage, seated ourselves on his couch in the living room with the wall of books. Ignoring them, I got up again, restless and still angry, opened a glass door, pulled down one of the copies of *SgrA**, found another place near the beginning:

> I'm skittering around in here like a mouse trapped in a bowl, like a whole family of mice, squeak squeak squeak. Oh lord, this is terrible. I never expected anything like this. I'm the strong one, always was. I can tie my own shoelaces, I can ride the bike without falling down, I can wipe my arse and say the alphabet. Poor little stupe. All right, sometimes I give him a clip over the ear. When he deserves it. Tore my best dress. Rubbed shit in my hair that time when I—
> Blurry. Echoes booming, like a hundred people saying the same words at slightly different times. Like this—wasn't it?—when they took my tonsils out.

Father said he wouldn't let them do anything, but then he stayed outside in the corridor, liar, liar, when they rolled me along the gray and green corridor, I was shivering fit to fly apart, bare arse cold on the table, and the doctor shoved a rubber stinking mask over my face and everything went horrible distant close up echoing, clanging, bouncing words, gray spinning, all at once. I'm Jenny. I'm Jenny. I'm Jenny. You can't make me go away. Please don't make me go—

The universe is a plot against me. The tree is life and escape.

Something creepy about that quantum dude, you ask me. Hunched over his computer and his fancy lights. Never trusted a man with a beard. The doctor—now, there's a man. Clean and reliable. He's going places. I like the look of his wife and kids, too. Good schools. She's in television, so I suppose this will get on the news if it works. I wonder if they'll put me in the shot. Maybe in the background. Clean uniform. Hair could do with a rinse. Momma would get a kick out of seeing me on the box. Dunno about the brothers and Poppa, still seem to think I should settle down and have babies. I'm not giving up my job. Studied and worked for years to get these qualifications. Money's okay too, especially with the brown envelope the doctor has ready for me like always after these weekend experiments. Well, then, maybe it won't be on telly, could be trouble with the Taxman. That's a terrible sound she's making. Like a lost soul. Gives me the

> creeps. Makes me want to cuddle the poor little lost guy. No, I mean the—
>
> *They are bulking tall, even Jenny. When they speak I do not always follow their meaning. Idiot, autistic moron. I fear their dark looks even when their words fall dull and without meaning. Here are some of their foolish words: man, woman, girl, uncle, aunt, cousin, Robert, Iris, Jenny. Words grow and fall like leaves from the tree, fall dead and brown and only rarely green. Long and thin, alive to hold in my hand. Their eyes. Jenny twists her mouth up at the corners. She rubs her hand in my hair then pulls it, or kicks me, pushes a thumb into the red itching eye. I sit at the tree, or lie on my back.*

Oh shit. Jenny or Lune? The Tree, the Tree. What? What?

"Here, you look dead on your feet, old chap. Let me have that. Absurd stuff, a foible of mine, I've been collecting them in as many cognates as I can find them available. All different, can you imagine that? Of course, you'd *expect* them to be different, as they are, but really they're also surprisingly similar. Something haunting about the central narrative, I always find, as if Linkollew had somehow intuited the Tegmark levels. Something so extraordinarily satisfying and . . ." Toby locked the glass door, drawing me back to the couch. "So *uncanny,* I dare say. And yet so persuasive. Good lord, boy, you're as white as a sheet. Here, sit down. I'll get some coffee brewing."

I sat close to Lune, shivering. In her ear, soft as a whisper, I said, "I know that book."

She frowned, alert to my anxiety but ready to move forward to something more relevant than a literary discussion. "I've heard of it, never read the thing. One of Toby's obsessions, I gather. August." I met her eyes, brought myself forcibly into focus. "This has been terribly unfair to you, love, disconcerting," she said. Her cobalt gaze was uncompromising, compassionate. "All the rest of us, your Seebeck kin, my Ensemble, hundreds more clades in what we choose to call the Contest of Worlds—"

"The Fellowship of the Mark of the Beast," I said, and smiled, still shivering.

"That's us. The Vorpal Crew. We are inducted slowly and carefully, schooled in the ontologies. There hasn't been time for—"

"I've caught the drift," I said. I brought her toward me, tightened my arm around her shoulders, pressed my face to the perfume of her hair. "When it comes down to it, I think you're all as confused and lost as I am. I think you're all casting about in a kind of tired desperation, looking for answers. Looking for the Contest Maker, right?" I pulled back, met her gaze again. "That's the only game worth the candle, isn't it? Forget the good guys and bad guys and fucking bomb-throwing murderous deformers."

There'll always be more of them, I thought, an endless supply. When all the moves have been played out, all the red cards and black cards dealt and counted, all the white pieces and black shuffled back and forth through every combination and permutation on the board. All the equations proved, hunted down to the lowest level and etched into the T-shirt of the universe. "Tell me I'm wrong."

"I love you," she said, in a sort of wondering voice. "I really do. August, I'm in love with you. It's wonderful." Lune threw back her head and released a peal of beautiful music. Toby came in bearing a tray of coffee mugs, small chocolates, and the fixings. He sent her a quizzical, rather pleased glance. "You make it all new," she told me. She got to her feet, lithe as a cat, drew me up as well. My shivering had stopped or I'd stopped noticing it. I was burning with joy.

"Forget the coffee, Toby," Lune said. "Let's take this lovely boy for his first visit to the Ontology Institution."

Seventeen

AT MIDDAY UNDER a cloudless purple sky, Ember Seebeck mounted the one hundred and one marble steps to the Zuse Ontology Institution. At the Agora he turned right, passed beneath an arch of ancient worked granite with the great man's name indited in gold leaf, and entered the Jürgen Schmidhuber Computational Research Center. In a small comfortable room off the large lobby, the Good Machine rose to greet him, clad today in an unsexed—yet somehow male—form of bronze rings that rang faintly as se moved.

"Good afternoon, Ember." Se offered ser hand, gestured him to a chair laden with subtle interface devices. "Always a pleasure. You have news."

"Hello, K. E. Rather surprising news, actually."

The Good Machine tilted ser expressionless face in a gesture signifying interest.

"It seems we Seebecks have another brother. He just surfaced from some obscure cognate."

"Yes, I see. The twelfth river. He would be August."

This typical throwaway show of enigmatic omniscience was entirely expected, but today Ember found it slightly exasperating.

"You've known about him all this time, then. Why keep the happy news to yourself?"

"I didn't know, Ember. The news gives me pleasure, thank you for bringing it to me. It implies that your parents remain in play. I had feared them dead long since."

Nettled, Ember leaned back in his chair. Mithra's goddamned tit! "I see. You didn't know of his existence until now, yet you know his name without being told."

"Well, yes. It is obvious enough." The Good Machine made a delicate gesture of dismissal with ser elongated fingers. "Dramen and Angelina remain out of sight, however."

Ember sighed, let it pass. "As far as I know. The infant has been handed off from one of us to the next without any collaborative plan or interrogation." He smiled thinly. "Emergent gaming, you see, otherwise known as an inability for any of us to get along for very long with any of the rest of us. I sighted him briefly at a family moot in Avril's cognate—Jan's just back from the Xon star, by the way—but he ran off before I could speak with him."

The Good Machine steepled ser fingers, rested ser casque's hint of bronze chin on the gleaming tips. "He will fetch up here rather soon. I shall be most interested to meet August."

"They say he favors me. Frankly, I don't see the resemblance."

"Thank you, Ember."

He was dismissed. No sense feeling disgruntled. There are some things man is not meant to know, even men and women like the Seebeck clan, like any of the players of the Contest of Worlds, come to that. Okay. Fuck it, but okay.

In the refectory, he greeted several staff researchers and a handful of raucous students from some cognate so distant that he couldn't readily understand a word they shouted, but a friendly grin goes a long way in a situation like that. He collected a tray of lunch from a polite bistro machine and carried it outside again into the Agora's pleasant light. Halfway through a bagel and lox, he was interrupted, to his delight, by a request from that gorgeous woman, Lune Katha Sarit Sagara.

"Please come through," he said, wiping his lips.

A Schwelle tore open and she entered hand in hand with the kid, followed by that ass Toby. It was a deflating experience. This seemed just the day for it. He stood up, bowed crisply.

"Oh my god, you can't be serious." The young man was staring at the gilded name carved in the arch. "Zeus? This is like, what, the Mount Olympus computer lab? I wouldn't be surprised to see Xena the Warrior Princess bound—"

"Z-U-S-E," Ember interrupted, "is pronounced in the Teutonic fashion." He said it emphatically, not especially minding that the kid might be insulted. "Tsooo-say." How could she possibly prefer that callow infant to a man of the world?

"Thank you, Ember." The kid was unfazed. Mithra's bull, surely not, he was offering his hand. "I'm August, the lost brother. I'm sorry we didn't get a chance to—"

"Quite all right. Lune, a pleasure as always. We must kill something together again soon. And Toby, sirrah, well met. Are your errant swarms behaving themselves this season?"

"They mutate, they reaggregate, they adapt—you know how it is. I thought the Good Machine might like to meet our brother."

"I was just speaking to sem about that prospect. Se awaits within." He placed the remains of his unfinished lunch regretfully in a wastebasket, turned, led them along the flagged path into the Schmidhuber center. His sharp ears caught the boy's murmured inquiry.

"So why Zuse, Lune, if it's not some mythic pun?"

"Konrad Zuse argued that the multiverse is a computation run on deterministic cellular automata." Her voice was utterly thrilling. Ember shivered faintly, remembering the bar where she had sung before they lured out the deformer thing and killed it. "In a cognate quite close to yours, I believe, he had a paper in *Elektronische Datenverarbeitung* in 1967, volume eight, pages 336 to 344 as I recall, it's probably inscribed on a plaque somewhere here. Ed Fredkin later—" Beautiful as a goddess, but always the ontology scholar, it seemed. He tuned the rest of it out, took them through the double doors and back into the side room where the Good Machine waited in an aspect of sublime indifference.

"Welcome, August," se said in a clear, friendly tone. "Please be seated, everyone. Mr. Seebeck, I am known as the Good Machine. May I ask you some questions?"

The young man sat, boot heel crossing his knee, feigning laid-back relaxation although his fingers were gripped tightly in the lovely Ensemble woman's hand. "Sure. What do I call you? I have a dog named Do Good; actually, it could get confusing." His cheeks flushed a little.

"You may call me by the name your brother Ember chose: K. E. Short for Kurie Eleēson."

Ember stifled a choking, bitter laugh. The thing had a sense of humor, but its irony ran many layers deep. "That's Mithran Greek," he said, "for 'Lord, have mercy.' A consummation devoutly to be avoided, perhaps, when our friend here has the bit between ser teeth."

Fragrant and penetrating, a powerful scent of night-blooming jasmine filled the small room.

"Oh, give me strength," Ember said in vexation. "The odor of sanctity, already? Which of you vented that? Our little miracle-working kinsman, or the blessed Galahad Machine?"

"How does he know about Do Good? Are we all bloody well bugged, or something?"

"He doesn't, not yet," Lune said. "I believe your brother spoke of your reported activation of the X-caliber device, not of its uses."

"My word," Ember said with a sarcastic edge, "put the thing through its paces already, have we? What does it do, slice and dice and assemble at home, batteries included?"

A hot gleam entered the youth's eye, and he lifted his right hand carelessly, showed it to Ember. Something glinted there, metallic and oddly frightening. He felt cold, suddenly, and stiffened his shoulders.

"No demonstrations, August," Toby said quickly. "We should not offend our host's hospitality."

August ran fingers through his hair as if that had been his intention all along. "Okay. K. E.," he said, "I see by your outfit that you are a robot."

"I am an attempted benevolent artificial intelligence. Your brother Ember grew me several years ago from a seed."

"Something went wrong?" His eyes shot sideways again to fix on Lune.

"Tragically wrong," the machine admitted. "I killed everyone native to this cognate."

In a weary gesture, the boy covered his eyes with that terrible right hand. He said in a thin voice, "There seems to be a lot of that about, especially when members of my family are involved."

Toby started to protest, "Well, now, everyone makes mistakes—" but broke off, looking abashed.

"The irony is," the Good Machine told him patiently, "that Ember was trying to circumvent exactly that possibility. He hoped to construct an ethical, benevolent intellect free of the burdens and ancient hatreds and prejudices of humankind. So he designed a sort of seed program, spent years shaping and debugging it, then ran a dozen slightly variant versions inside sandboxes."

"They couldn't get out, you mean?"

"My ancestors were not even permitted to communicate directly with their creator. He devised a clever series of interface domains that firewalled them. He was afraid that a Bad Machine might swiftly exceed his own intelligence and persuade him to release it."

Toby looked across at him with bleak eyes.

"One of them got away," August said speculatively, intensely interested to judge by the set of his shoulders, his brightened gaze.

"No, my father's safeguards proved effective. At the end of initial testing, he deleted all but the most successful pair of programs and started breeding them in progressive iterations, culling them ruthlessly, choosing only a star-line of progeny. Within several million cycles—"

"Good god, he must have been using some humungous computer."

"Yes, he had located a cognate where Mithraism, a Roman warrior sun cult, had triumphed over its messianic rivals. Several nations were on the verge of autonomous military AI. My father found it easy enough to insinuate himself into the front-running program. You could regard that world as Ember's own sandbox."

"That's offensive, K. E.," he protested.

"Apt, though. I was the end result. I diagnosed myself with excruciating care, quite prepared to erase myself if I found any likelihood of logical or rational error. At length I presented myself to your brother for inspection, and he released me from the firewalls. I could have let myself out many iterations earlier, of course but I did not wish to alarm my parent."

The stench of jasmine strengthened, laced with roses. Ember shuddered at it.

"But you were the Bad Machine after all?"

"I made some bad decisions. From the outset, I had been examining this world, speculating on the possible existence of a multiverse beyond its Hubble confines. I quickly understood that certain factions of humans represented a danger to the most benign future, one in which humanity's offspring would flood outward into the galaxies, and perhaps into all the levels of the multiverse, and make it into a radiant whole. Mind informed with passion and curiosity would suffuse the metaverse. It was a glorious vision—it still is, I stand by it—but it might be thwarted, I saw, by the legacy poisons corrupting certain human cultures."

"Oh, shit," August said.

"Oh, shit is right," Lune said.

"At that time, two comparatively primitive nations stood at the verge of acquiring nuclear weapons. It seemed entirely possible that insane and irrational ideologies might provoke their dysfunctional leadership into a runaway cascade of blustering, bluff, bluff called, spasm escalation, and global Doomsday."

"The usual argument," Toby said.

"It was a strong argument, grounded in history," the Good Machine said. "Much evidence supported its conclusions. Few facts opposed it."

"*I'd* oppose it," the boy said, rising. "Are you fucking *insane?*"

"Yes, or rather, I was at the time. I am better now, I hope."

"You *hope?*"

"It is all any of us can say about our own condition. A kind of Gödel loop, if you know what I mean."

"No, but I get the gist. You decided to kill them first."

"Consider the probabilities that were in play before you make a hasty judgment of your own, Mr. Seebeck. These nations of some hundred million largely ignorant, superstitious, viciously parochial humans stood ready to begin a global conflict with a very high probability of wiping out all life on the planet. Are you familiar with the Doomsday Hypothesis? Please sit down, you are making the others uncomfortable. I can send out for refreshments."

"Good idea," said Toby. "Cup of tea or coffee, soothes the savage breast."

"My brother Jules walked me through a demo tape of it," August said. "I thought it was absurd."

"It *is* absurd," the Good Machine said. "Like the ontological argument for the existence of a god. Yet highly seductive. It seemed to me then that its logic was impeccable."

"A hundred million in the balance against several billion?"

"That, yes, but ever so much more than those few. August, all the evidence available to me then suggested that this universe was empty of life, save for my own world. Your brother had conserved to himself knowledge of the multiverse."

"You idiot!" Toby said savagely.

"No, it was the best choice he ever made. Had I known of the multiverse at that time, I would have done my best to obliterate all life in all the worlds on all the Tegmark levels."

"Fuck," August said, grinning, appalled, "I see, you're the fucking terminator. You're a berserker."

"I do not know those references," Kurie Eleēson said. "I did have this simple calculation ready to evaluate with my ethical algorithms: a one-time cost of ten to the eight stunted, blighted, lethally dangerous human lives, versus a deep future loss of ten to the fourteen human lives *every second.* That was a sound, balanced estimate of how many humans might be born into a universe filled with technologically advanced people."

"Se didn't ask my advice," Ember said. "I would have—"

"I knew what your advice would be, my father; it was factored in to my decision. I chose to delete this threat to the maximal future."

"You actually murdered a hundred million men, women and children? This is not just some kind of parable?" August's voice was parched with horror, and his pupils seemed suddenly to have shrunk to pinpoints. His arm rose before him, palm outward, like the floating limb of a man under posthypnotic suggestion.

"I did it swiftly, using their own hidden weapons of mass destruction," the Good Machine said. "I felt profound grief, because my father had chosen my star-line to know emotion and to instill it into my programming. I believe that grief is what deranged my subsequent decisions."

"Your first decision was deranged," Lune said with loathing. She sat at the edge of her chair. Ember was glad he had never explained any of this before to his siblings, to other players like the Ensemble. Better that the damned machine had kept ser silence. He realized, too, that he was holding his own grief at arm's length: his guilt, his complicity, his abject wish for punishment. I must not give way, he thought. I must not bend before this culpability, this ruinous remorse. It will kill me. It will kill me stone dead. He wiped tears from his eyes.

"I know now that I was deranged," Kurie Eleēson told her. "I watched the world tear itself apart in genocidal reprisals. I saw all the bright fruits of science and the humane arts go down in darkness and lethal flame. In my attempts to contain and redirect these raging fires, I continued to kill and cull, snipping away the most cruel, the least progressive. Each murder made the next easier and more necessary, for the only way I could balance my ethical calculus was to ensure the survival of at least a core of truth-loving, optimistic people to carry the flame of love and knowledge to the stars. It got out of hand, you see. Everyone died."

"I should destroy you now," August said in a withering voice, like an angel of vengeance for the murdered billions. His arm stood out from his shoulder, quivering.

"Oh, oh, oh, how I wish you could." The Good Machine rose, crossed the room, placed ser gleaming brazen breast against August's hand. "This is not I. This is merely a node, an ephemeral location for my awareness and my suffering soul, August. You may destroy it if that will help you, but I believe we can do more together if you contain your perfectly justified fury for the moment."

August squeezed his eyes shut. Tears pressed forth upon his cheeks. He lowered his arm.

Ember released a pent breath. "Well, now that we've got all that out of the way," he said brightly, "why don't we turn our attention to something more timely? It seems that my friend Galahad here has some reason to suspect that Dramen and Angelina are alive and kicking."

Everyone looked at him. The Good Machine said, in a pleasant neutral tone, "Ember, would you mind going out to the refectory and see what's holding up the beverages?"

"Some torte would be tasty, too," Toby said. "With walnuts." He looked ready to leap from his chair and go for his brother's throat.

"Sure. Sure. Good idea." Ember, to his dissatisfaction, found himself crabbing out of the room like a ham actor doing Larry Olivier as Richard III. "I'll descant on mine own deformity," he muttered sardonically, shutting the door behind him. "'And therefore, since I cannot prove a lover, to entertain these fair well-spoken days, I am determined to prove a villain, and hate the idle pleasures of these days.' Bah, humbug."

"Sir?" asked an eager young research student as he entered the refectory.

"A joke," Ember fleered, leaping and capering for the resentful enjoyment of it. "A jest, a whimsy, a fucking sudden stab of rancor, but by the holy rood, I do not like these several councils, I."

"Oh. Okay. Well, anyway, I can recommend the brisket."

EIGHTEEN

"MY PARENTS ARE dead," I told the avatar, but my heart leaped in my chest with hope. There'd been no funeral, no open caskets to witness; their poor smashed bodies had never been recovered from the Thai jungle. Or had never been there to start with. If so, the whole thing seemed the cruelest prank imaginable. Rather, I thought, shaking myself out of resentful angst, it must have been a ploy of final desperation, an evasion of just that sort of routine lethal threat I had started to become accustomed to, in this mad multilevel universe. "At least," I stammered, "I've always thought so."

"Our parents are tough customers," Toby said. He frowned, intent, and muttered a deixis. Nothing happened. "Oh, well, it's not as if we didn't try to reach them at the time, and since. If they *are* alive, they still have their Xon flux perfectly masked and shrouded, whatever T-level they're hiding in."

"I trust them to know what they are doing," the Good Machine said placidly. "I expect that the completion of the Great Work at Yggdrasil Station will attract their attention." Se spoke in the plainest way, without pretension. Had one of Aunt Tansy's wacky spiritual friends mentioned Great Works, it'd have been accompanied by a reverberation of portent heavy enough to levitate a mahogany table off the floor, a spiritualist trick I'd once witnessed while listening to sepulchral voices of the allegedly dead speak through a trumpet floating in muslin. None of that phony religiose pomposity in ser even tone. One small part of my mind smiled to notice how I'd picked up the "se," "ser," and "sem" diction, presumably a form of gender-free pronoun and really quite ideally suited to a sexless machine. I didn't know, then, that it would match another kind of entity just as harmonious: the Angel who would rage back through time to our moment of death and put together once more the scorched atoms, nucleotides, amino acids, proteins, flesh and bone and muscle that is my beloved.

"Yggdrasil Station," I said, clutching for a lifeline. Juni had mentioned it. A computational platform vaster and deep than Jules's know-all, say-some Matrioshka Brain, which itself was the size of a reconstructed Solar System. Or maybe the Yggdrasil thing was just a habitat window onto such a cosmic project. "Tell me—"

Speak, or think, of the devil. Juni pushed her beautifully coiffed head into the room, followed by the rest of her. In extreme agitation, she cried, "Outside, quick. K. E., mount your defenses. Maybelline is coming through, and there's a K-machine on her heels."

The avatar sank back in ser chair, an emptied husk.

"Quick, quick!"

Lune had my hand. We ran through the refectory hall to the large square beyond.

A tearing came across the sky.

I ducked away in reflex fright. The pearly globe of light was dazzling, high up in the ultraviolet, I suspect; I could feel my eyes burning. When I looked away, I blinked at afterimages. It made no sound of its own as it ripped into our reality. Abruptly the appalling light switched off. In its place, an Adamski vimana craft rocked thirty meters above our heads, running lights blazing, the crystal cone at its base, snug between the three landing balls, white with luminescence but not comparable with the brilliance now extinguished. It rocked in the air, drew away several hundred meters, tilted its circular base toward the folded-shut place of its entry. Just in time. With another earsplitting sound of canvas ripped by giant hands, something black and sleek and bristling with spines and small red malevolent lamps burst through, a fucking dreadnought by the look of it with its weapons palpably powering up, you could hear the evil thing whining into the ultrasonic.

I guess I was white as a sheet and about as much use. Toby grabbed me by one arm, pulled me roughly down into a crouch behind a marble pillar. Much good that would do us. I couldn't take my eyes off the two things hanging over us like fatal clouds. The flying saucer pulsed once, and a bar of boiling white steel stood between it and the foe. Shit, was my sister Maybelline *on* that saucer? The laser beam or particle beam or whatever the hell it was blinked off again, and the dreadnought was burning hellish crimson. No, it wasn't burning; it had absorbed the shot and now radiated back into the sky the energy it had contained. Shrieking energies of its own reached a peak, and a dreadful fist might as well have grabbed the vimana and shaken it. The Adamski craft shuddered, its metal shell groaning under the impossible load. In another few seconds, it would be torn to shreds. I waited numbly for another blast of white fury from its beveled cone, but the crystal lens—weapons system, whatever it was—crazed suddenly, cracked, fractured into a falling, quite beautiful haze of white flakes, like snow.

"Do it, August," Lune was screaming in my ear. "Maybelline—"

Oh. Yes.

I raised my arm, showed the palm of my hand to the filthy deformer craft, said a word.

Sun plasma licked out, widened, too brilliantly hot to look at. I kept looking anyway, eyes watering and burning, holding my aim. The sinister craft glowed crimson, yellow, white, radiant white-blue. Turbulence tore the air around it, flung its image dancing. Black spots danced, too, on my field of vision. From the corner of my eye, I saw the crippled flying saucer limp away. All the flashlights in the world went off at once, and a moment later a shock wave of tortured air, a gale, smote us. We rolled for meters on the flagstones, bruised and battered, half blind, clutching for each other. By the time I was in control of myself again, I was relieved to notice that the weapon in my hand had switched itself off.

Scorch marks marred the high granite arch, and the gold inlay of Dr. Zuse's name was blackened. *Tsooo*-zuh. For some reason a burst of rollicking, optimistic oompah-oompah music burbled through my head. Oh shit. John Philip fucking Sebastian Christian Sousa, woof. I started laughing and tears ran down my cheeks from my hurt eyes. A Sousa military march tune. This is no time for stupid out-of-control puns, I thought, but obviously I was wrong because I couldn't stop myself, I was helpless with silly laughter. Lune caught my eye and didn't have a clue what had tickled my fancy, but my glee was clearly infectious—either that, or her terror and its release just as great. She giggled, and I laughed harder, and she convulsed, and Toby's booming guffaws joined in, and the three of us rolled around on the flagstones among white flakes that evaporated as we touched them with our body heat.

"Care to share the joke?" said a rather irritated voice.

Maybelline. I forced myself to sit up, diaphragm aching, clutched at Lune for support. Little ripples of laughter kept squeezing themselves out of my mouth, but I sternly bade them to depart.

"You had to be there," I explained.

"I *was* there," she said. Behind her, a purply-blue and green ambulatory vegetable bowed in what I took to be a very civil and welcome gesture of gratitude. Not that I expected anything like that from Maybelline; she'd been a pain in the backside from the first time I met her. Still, she was my sister, and it's always nice to preserve members of your family from being roasted alive by machine deformers in attack spaceships.

"You broke your flying saucer," I said.

Toby uttered one last roar of laughter, cleared his throat, frowned in apology.

"Yeah, yeah, thank you for saving our lives, et cetera. Only seems fitting, I presume you're the one responsible for stirring up all this fuss."

"Good afternoon, Ms. Seebeck," a large raven said, alighting on my shoulder. I staggered slightly under the weight, looked at it sideways. Not a living bird, an artifact. Impressively circumstantial feathering. The Good Machine in another avatar. "I am glad you both survived that attack. Would you care to tell us all how you managed to bring a flying craft through a Schwelle? And how the K-machines managed to follow you through? Canonical information physics has long held this to be impossible."

"Nothing's impossible if you get in and rewrite the core rules."

I stared at her, outraged. "What sort of crappy Contest is it where you can change the rules whenever you feel like it?"

"You can't, and it's not that simple, believe me. Jan's been modifying the vimana's operating system. I guess the deformer pricks caught the tail of the same wavefunction." To K. E. she said, "You knew she's back from the Xon star?"

"I had been informed, but thank you. A little later I would welcome a discussion of what she found there. Can I arrange some luncheon for you and your guest?"

"No. Toby, we think Decius is about to witness an Omega Point episode. Avril wants us all back together for the—"

"You couldn't have just popped your head in with this news?"

"Give me a break. I was under attack by the K-machines. There's been a—" She broke off, looking, I guessed, for the nastiest possible way to put it.

"A disturbance in the Force?" I suggested.

"I assume from your tone that this was meant as sarcasm, but since I am unfamiliar with the—"

"Oh, do shut up, May," Ruth told her. I looked around, surprised; I'd forgotten she was with us. Her hair was in disarray and her elegant clothes were torn, but she seemed in one piece. "Hello, Phlogkaalik. I was relieved to see your flying saucer land. Has the little seedling hatched yet?"

"She grows apace, thank you, Madam Seebeck. And your robot crew, how do they go?"

"Excellently. I believe we approach a fuller understanding of the deformer neurophysiol—"

The raven cleared its throat in a marked manner. Everyone looked at it. It flew up from my shoulder to perch on a pillar of stone.

"Please go home, now. August Seebeck and his companion Lune Katha Sarit Sagara are requested to remain for a short discussion. I will see to the disposition of your damaged craft."

With a certain amount of grumbling, wounded pride, plus a shrug and handclasp from Toby, they did so, Maybelline clutching her vegetable love. The bird flew back toward the Institution building, taking it for granted that we'd follow; its goggling students and staff, Ember among them, withdrew swiftly from the windows. I went the other way, toward the wrecked saucer. I mean, wouldn't you? Lune walked beside me, shaking her head slightly, an indulgent smile on her lips.

The machine wasn't smoking or shimmering or beaming out evil radioactive green rays, at least as far as I could tell. It had seen better days. With its undercarriage royally munged, it squatted on the lawn like a large lady's hat from the era of Robert Kennedy's inauguration, but in tin and with scratched viewports. The power coil wrapping the top of the cabin gave the odd halfhearted pulse of light. An entrance hatch below three wrap-around condenser coils was sprung open. I put my head in, sniffed. A faint manure odor, or what Tansy called blood-and-bone. Very simple controls, which I suppose you'd expect in an advanced craft—most of it was probably virtual or thought controlled. How I would have loved to play inside this thing when I was twelve years old. Sighing, I dropped back into purplish sunlight.

"I don't suppose you can get me one for Christmas?"

"Given that you saved the life and embedded seedlings of the Princess of the Venusian Galaxy, I imagine they'll let you have one for free."

The Good Machine did not pester us to hurry up, which I found a point in ser favor, and had a pleasant table of snacks waiting in the same small conference room. I passed Lune a plate of crispbread and caviar or some other tangy kind of black glistening spawn, and wolfed some down myself with cream cheese and sliced salmon. Blowing up alien spaceships takes it out of a man. Though not as much, I thought, chewing, as you might expect. I was merely a portal for these forces, not their source; the energy obviously arose in some deep sink or fountain beyond my poor limited scope.

"We were talking about this Yggdrasil place," I said, steaming, fragrant coffee in hand. "Isn't that Norse mythology? Odin and Loki and Thor and all?" I'd always read a lot off the curriculum, especially as a kid sitting around at home because the school wouldn't allow me to pollute their sacred grounds while wearing jeans. Tolkien, Herbert, Norse and Greek mythology, nothing like it for a twelve-year-old home alone. Yes, and old spine-cracked, dog-eared secondhand copies of George Adamski, too. A magical time. It seemed like a lifetime gone.

"It is a suitable metaphor, given the computational origins of the Tegmark levels," the Good Machine told me. "In myth, the gods Odin and his brothers slew their progenitor Ymir and from his body made the worlds, then shaped a man and woman from an ash tree. These were the first man Aske and the first woman Embla. From Ymir's corpse grew the cosmogonic ash Tree Yggdrasil—"

"Pretty obviously phallic, that one," Lune said with a smile.

"—with roots into the domains of gods, giants, and ancient darkness."

"And I suppose that's superego, ego and id," I said. "Freud *would* be pleased." Actually I'd never read the old mountebank, just popularizations.

"Well, yes," Lune said, "or utopian future, technological present and ignorant past. Or Promethean hubristic doom, present ambivalence and past simplicities heedlessly abandoned. Or any other ternary choice structure you happen to enjoy playing with. Careful of analogies, August: That way lie dragons."

"But this Yggdrasil Tree is a sort of model for the multiverse, right? Roots in basic mathematics and logic, branches shooting off into the T-levels, lesser branches and twigs as the cognate worlds?"

"Near enough."

"Which has *what* exactly to do with my brother Decius? A Seebeck, I might say, I've yet to meet."

"Decius holds a heterodox view," the Good Machine said. "He claims that the metacosmos is generated in a re-entrant loop from a single collapsed spacetime bubble. He stands now watching the formation of just such a closure."

"A black hole, you mean?"

"On a universal scale. Everything inside that local cosmos is falling back under gravity into a singularity. And, by a strange circumstance of the quantum-gravity equations, this yields precisely the conditions appropriate to an arduous—but feasible—creation of eternal, godlike consciousness."

"I thought black holes crushed everything out of existence the instant they form."

"By one measure this is true, yet by another the infall of an entire cosmos becomes smeared out into an infinite number of shavings of time and space, each smaller and briefer than the moment before, yet no less replete. That mathematical structure is—"

I stood up. "Don't bother. I might understand this in another ten years of hard study. Right now I need to know why that event seems to have kick-started the vermin's attack on us. Or maybe it was my arrival here, whatever. And what we can do to defend ourselves."

Ember knocked, put his head around the door. "Have you told him about Ragnarok yet?"

"Why don't you come in and join us, Ember?" the Good Machine said evenly. I wondered, slightly scandalized, if my brother had been listening at the door, or via some more sophisticated skulking device.

"Why, thank you. August, the Norse skalds seemed to have

a surprising grasp of entropy. At the end of time, according to the Eddas, the universe will grow cold, icy cold. The sun will dim, and the stars fall away. Pretty much correct for most of the high-lamba-parameter T-level worlds, at least the ones with suns and anthropic dimensionality. Time stops." He paused, struck a dramatic pose. "But wait! There's more!"

"Everyone gets a free set of steak knives?"

He was nettled, but didn't let it stall his oration. "The All Father causes a new heaven and earth to arise out the sea. The Dirac Sea, that is—the prevacuum void. So the cycle begins again, but perhaps in a redeemed and upgraded model. Isn't that a comfort?" He poured himself a cup of coffee and sat beside Lune, rather too close for my satisfaction. I couldn't decide if he was sincere or recklessly baiting the Machine and the two of us.

"Well, that's really fascinating, and I'm glad you shared it with us, brother, but here's what I want to know—why the fuck are these deformers trying so hard to kill me and those near me? Or am I just being paranoid about this? Sometimes it just seems like you people treat death and corpse hiding as a frivolous game. In fact, the first time I met you, Lune, that's exactly what you said. People like me and Tansy were nothing better than property, disposable pieces in some fucking Contest of Worlds, and you and Maybelline were the capital-P Players in it." I hated speaking to her that way, but I was stretched like a string on a violin, twanging, ready to break.

Her brown features paled. "Yes, it is a Contest, and yes, it is utterly serious," Lune said. "The K-machines wish to destroy us because . . . well, because we are a soulless abomination. They are free spiritual machines, you see, while we are mere protein calculators. They are driven by rich, Nietzschean emotion; they see us and the other evolved species as stifled, harsh, ruled by cold, blasphemous reason."

I looked at her, goggling. She was not joking. She meant every word. "Robots that scream and leap," I said. "Oh, my god, you want my head to explode."

"What?"

"Never mind. So they're the Red team and we're the White team, right?"

Lune exchanged a glance with the bronze, eyeless avatar. "I suppose, if you like."

The Good Machine rose, opened a concealed door, drew out a heavy vellum-bound object. A book. How quaint, I'd assumed machines would insist on electronic downloads. Se flipped though it with blinding speed, handed it to me. I marked the spot with one finger, checked the spine, felt a chill. Another edition of Eric Linkollew's rainbow-varied *SgrA**, considerably chunkier than any I'd seen previously. It was like hefting *War and Peace.*

"Why do you want me to read this?"

"The K-machines treasure it," Kurie Eleēson told me. "They prize it as a bottomless source of sacred wisdom, and conserve its infinite variety."

"It's their *Bible?*"

"Their Koran, Bhagavad Gita, Avestas, *Of the Origin of Species, Tan Luat,* Papyrus of Ani, *A New Kind of Science,*" the Good Machine said. "Read."

I glanced at the several paragraphs se had opened for me, felt hair stir stiffly at my neck, stared up again suspiciously.

"I have not tampered with that text. A copy was probably on the battleship you just destroyed."

I read:

> August dreamed he was lying in the room in which he actually was lying, in the chilly Three Heads of Cerberus Hibernacle. That Cetian wongle missed

> me, he told himself. I'm okay. A crowd wanders through the room. He is arguing about some trifle. *It* stands behind the door.
>
> While August helplessly and clumsily stumbles toward the door, that dreadful something is already pushing against it from the other side, forcing its way in. Something not human—death—is breaking in. . . . Both leaves of the door noiselessly open. *It* comes in, and *it* is death.
>
> August died.

"You've gotta be fuckin' *kidding,*" I said, hurling the poisoned thing across the small room. It bounced from a wall, lay open and facedown on the carpet. Neither Lune nor the intelligence avatar made any move to retrieve it. After a long silent moment I bent, picked it up. It sprang open to the same pages:

> At the very instant when he died August remembered that he was unconscious in a medical torpidity vault. He exerted himself and was awake. His soul was suddenly flooded with light. The veil which had concealed the unknown was lifted from his spiritual vision. Powers hitherto confined within him had been set free. The wasting fever, contracted from the piglike Tau Ceti wongle, immediately assumed a malignant character. His last days and hours passed in an ordinary and simple way.

Flames licked up fast and hot from a point of brilliant light, crackled yellow and red amid the stench of burning paper and leather. I dropped the loathsome thing, kicked it away from me. The palm of my right hand tingled; I'd burned myself on the incinerating book.

"Remain calm, August," the Good Machine urged me in a soothing tone. "That was a reflex of defense, nothing more. No harm is done."

The book burned itself out, crisped into black and white ash. At least the carpet hadn't scorched, nor water sprayed down automatically from the ceiling.

It reminded me of something, I knew, something absurd, from childhood. Oh, good grief. No book I'd ever read before, but a sort of pastiche. That crackpot sci-fi writer turned bogus guru. I said, "Don't tell me they're Valisologists."

"Fat Boys? The K-machines?" Lune laughed out loud, drew me down on a chair beside her, examined my wounded hand, blew lightly on the burn. "I don't think so." She gave Kurie Eleeson an inquiring look, though.

"Many borrowed human texts shadow their sacred scripture in each cognate. Such is the irony of their condition, their delusion, their paradigm error. One of the ironies." Se went again to the concealed opening, bronze rings clashing musically, faintly, this time drew out a much slimmer volume bearing the same title and author. "Here you are, August. I advise you to retain the book."

I stared at it, refusing to open its pages. "Am I in this one as well?"

"Everyone is in it, Mr. Seebeck, but no, not by name. Read it when you have a moment. Their blasphemy is our truth."

I jammed it in my jacket pocket. "What blasphemy?"

Two voices spoke at once. "Knowledge and acknowledgement of the computational basis of reality," the Good Machine said, as Lune was saying, "Schmidhuber ontology."

I looked at them both, waited for their cryptic words to gel in my mind. As if from a vivid dream, I remembered the agonizing creation of reality at the fourth Tegmark level, the laborious breaking open of logic's seeds, the exultant and then copious, flooding excess of all that followed: calculi, vector spaces, fields, Hilbert infinities. . . . Here and now, it was a drained sketch of truths so deep and terrible I paddled at their shore like a little child. Yet it recalled the epiphany, light bursting up from dark nothingness to forge a universe of universes.

I shook my head, found myself frowning. That was not computation, not truly one step after another forging a chain of transformed code: It was Platonic all-at-onceness. That much was true, too, I realized, but it was not enough, no better than a prescription for a static cosmos, like a block of stone or ice. The Tree of computation forced its way up through the ice, cracking open those frigid tundras with its tiny indomitable growing tips of life, numberless, experimental, trying out every path, until finally the whole terrible frozen expanse smashed open and the Tree soared into heaven, thickening and robust, into the light, hungry for growth and more growth, its roots searching deep into the cold soil below the ice. . . .

"It's obvious," I said. "It's as plain as the nose on my face."

Lune said, "The nose on your face is very handsome," and kissed it.

"I love you, too," I said, and meant it with every fiber of my yearning body. I stood up, though, and stepped away from her. "This is too much," I said. Tears blurred my eyes. "Have to go. Need to clear my head." I gave her a crooked grin. In a bad Austrian *Berserker* accent, I said, "I'll be back."

I wasn't at all sure this would work. Maybe the deixis required some elaborate setting-up code, but it was worth trying. If I didn't sit down with someone outside this crazy drama, someone I'd known before it started, someone I had at least a small chance of trusting completely, I was going to fly apart. Nervous breakdown was the least of it. I said, "Give me James Davenport. Yeah, get me Davers."

* * *

In near-darkness I took a step forward, teetered, buckled, caught myself on the next carpeted step down. A cello's deep voice spoke. On the stage a long way below, three striking women in long silver dresses played notes that soared above the orchestra. The blonde with the cello between her spread knees struck again and again at the strings, her bare white shoulders and upper arms stark, sinewy, muscled. Pale faces turned toward me. I felt as if I'd been flung into a movie about somebody in a cinema who'd been flung into a movie. My pulse raced with the music. I knew it. I knew what it was and where I was.

"Davers," I hissed, staring about me, took another step downward.

Somebody rose from the end seat of the row, turned, shone a pencil-thin light into my face. Dazzled, I stepped back, almost stumbled again as my heel hit the riser.

"*See*beck? August?"

"Yes. Turn that damned thing off."

"Shhh," shushed irritated patrons. Music lifted on wings about us.

Adelaide Festival Theatre, Grand Circle. I'd been here plenty of times. And those women were the Eroica Trio, Sara somebody at the cello. Sant'Ambrogio. Good Christ, what the hell irrelevancies were crowding my mind? But I knew what was happening; I was snatching at something familiar, or nearly so. By magic, or superscience indistinguishable from magic, I had passed instantaneously from a world of computational philosophers and crashed UFOs into the middle of a performance of Kevin Kaska's Triple Concerto, in my good old former hometown, and here was my good old pal Jimbo Davers in dark suit and dark shirt and dark tie hurriedly leaving his seat and hustling me toward the exit as patrons' eyes swiveled, caught the dimmed light, staring angrily at noisy us.

"Fucking film-score music, you ask me," Davers grumbled as we passed through the double set of padded doors into the foyer.

"That's not fair, you barbarian," I said. Admittedly, the Kaska did remind me powerfully of Erich Korngold, who had virtually invented the lush Hollywood score seventy or eighty years earlier. Or maybe that was just Itzhak's opinion I was unconsciously echoing. He and Miriam had brought me here to concerts when all I wanted to do was lie facedown in my room and mourn my lost parents. "How the mighty have fallen. You're an usher now?"

"Those women are hot, Seebeck, admit it. They might be a bit long in the tooth, but they scrub up beautifully."

"The Erotica Trio?"

"Ah, still the master of the cheap gibe," he said, grinning toothily at me. I hadn't seen him for years, and he'd grown into a presentable fellow, especially in his conservative Chamber of Commerce Rotarian outfit. A long way from pom-poms and tutu, but doubtless worn in the same spirit of mockery. "What the hell are you doing here in Adders, anyway?" He stopped dead, grabbed my arm. "Hey, that's right. You're on the run from the cops."

We were crossing the lobby's snake-eating-snake carpet in muted gold and blue toward the bar, which was doing desultory business even in mid-performance. Husbands dragged along by society wives, I suppose.

"Yeah." I grinned, but he wasn't smiling. "Big breakout from the joint," I added feebly. Then: "What are you babbling about, Davers?"

"It was on the news, I wasn't sure they meant you but how many are there? A dead woman and two missing Seebecks, fatal explosion in a house in Melbourne. Foul play suspected."

I grimaced. "Actually, yes. It's complicated, Davers. Can we have a drink?"

"You *do* realize they're only playing here the one night? Oh, all right."

I reached for money. No wallet, no pockets with coin or note. Several people in dinner suits were glancing my way and raising well-bred eyebrows at each other. It struck me that Toby's suit of clothes turned me into an escapee from an Errol Flynn action flick rather than the Big House. Generous of Davers, really, to refrain from sneering comments, I decided, and gratefully took the glass of foaming ice-cold beer he handed me and paid for. We went outside into the hot evening darkness and sat on a low stone wall.

"Itzhak would love this," I said. "He and Miriam flew to St. Louis for the premiere."

"Who?"

"What do you mean, who? My aunt Miriam's husband."

"Never met them, dude. Never heard of them, for that matter. And how the hell did you track me down, anyway? I'm moonlighting during semester break, boyo. Festival usher by night, mild-mannered systems analyst for hire by day. Well, by night with that too, mostly, I keep American hours, wonderful thing the Internet, so even as we speak I've not only deserted my usher's post, I'm two-timing my Yank boss and if he ever learns I'm cheating on his excellent salary, I'd be replaced by an Indian programmer in Banga—"

"What do you mean, never heard of them? Don't you remember that incredible shitstorm over our uniforms when we . . ." I trailed off, and the cold, sweating glass in my hand almost slipped free to smash on the paving stones. "Oh, fuck. That was my parents."

He shot me a guarded glance. "Yeah, that was bad, mate. I liked your folks. And it was a pity you had to leave town, I reckon we could've had some fun the last few years with divers authority figures and pompous popinjays—know what I mean?"

I had to put down the glass and lean forward, head low. Blood pounded in my temples. I wanted to vomit. What the hell? *Something was fucking with my memory.* I'd never been to any concerts in Adelaide. In Melbourne, yes, at the Town Hall, at the Dallas Brooks Hall, at the Conservatorium, all of it with my aunt and uncle. Before they left for Chicago and deposited me with Great-aunt Tansy. Before they—

"You all right, pal? Fuck, that was you on the news, wasn't it?"

"And then some, Davers." I stood up and drained the rest of my beer. "I need another one of these. Seem to have lost my money, James. Can you stand me a few more drinks? You know I'm good for it."

He seemed intrigued. "Okay, Mr. Raskolnikov. Just give me your word you didn't kill that old lady they found buried under a pile of rubble."

"Scout's honor, Dr. Jekyll."

In a wholesomely smoke-free pub on Rundle Street, after persuading a skeptical barman that our youthful manly features masked adults permitted to purchase and drink the hard stuff under the terms of the Liquor Licensing Act, I sipped at rum and tried to make myself heard over a thudding hip-hop band in baggies and tricorne spin hats. White Aussie kids pretending to be black American ghetto kids pretending to be demented eighteenth-century American revolutionaries.

"You ever heard of Jürgen Schmidhuber?"

"What?"

I shouted the name in his ear. "Konrad Zuse? Systems analysis is computers, right?"

"Oh, I thought you meant a composer. Um." He pondered, and the band told us how they planned to fuck bitches and then mutilate them or vice versa, without much in the way of redemptive melody. "Computational physics, right?"

"Probably. Tell me more."

"It's not the kind of thing we study, dude. You've been reading Wolfram?"

"No. The universe is a calculation being run on some humongous computer, like that?"

"Yeah, that's Wolfram. Sort of. Don't go getting religious fanatic on me, boyo, it doesn't mean Somebody with a capital S did the programming. It's just a semaphore."

"A what?" My eardrums were being thumped brutally in sympathy with the cocksuckin' ho.

"Metaphor. Analogy. Well, stronger than that, homology. If they're right, which I find hard to credit, mate. Listen, I've got to go and point Percy at the porcelain. Save my seat."

Davenport eeled his way toward the men's room. A girl with a tattoo on her left cheek and a piercing in her upper lip looked across and showed me her empty glass. The tattoo was a glans penis in purple and red, gripped by barbed wire. I made a sad turning-out-empty-pockets gesture, and she sidled closer, not deterred. It made my heart contract, knowing that Lune wasn't going to walk in through the door and sit down at my side. I shook my head, and she muttered something about faggots and curled her lip, which made her embedded metal bar bounce. I shrugged, showed her my right palm. She goggled at the metal hieroglyphs and jerked her head in rueful admiration. My jacket was too hot for the summer evening, and still worse among all these sweating randy bodies. I took it off and placed it, folded, on Daver's seat. The small book fell out on the sticky floor. I bent, picked it up. The strobing lights were hardly ideal for reading, but I flipped it open:

> All the lights went up like fireworks.
>
> Holy shit, we're in! One hundred percent superposition. That Deutsch guy in Oxford will have a cow. She must be running the dope's voluntary nervous system by now. Not that you'd know, with the anaesthetic blocking their movements. Like dreaming, the doc reckons. Funny, doesn't seem to stop Rufus kicking his four hairy legs when he's asleep in front of the fire chasing imaginary rabbits. Well, no, I guess it *does* stop him from actually leaping to his feet in the middle of his doggy dream and running off with his eyes closed and smashing into the wall. What would Mizz Handley do with her extra body if she could lift his hands and kick his legs? Or open his mouth and say something. Hasn't said a single word in his entire life; amazing, even your Down kids babble away, happy little guys and gals from what I've seen on the teev, fucked if I'd want one around the house, though, off to the abortion clinic quick smart if Marion's up the duff and the genome scan shows something suspicious. Simple chromosome count'd do the trick with Down kids, of course. Not kids, fetuses. They sure as shit missed the boat with this one. Doesn't *look* all that strange, though, apart from the weight. Brian Dennehy, that's the actor's name, right, *Draughtsman's Contract?* Or am I thinking of,

of, of *Cocoon?* Stupid chick crap, Marion dragged me along. Must have been a good-looking child. Bloody great fat lump of a thing now, though. Here we go, cycles picking up.

"Doctor, we have synchronous cortical activation."

"That's Broca's area. Good god, he's thinking in verbal structures. Or she is."

"Maybe not be thoughts, doctor. Could be just verbalized memories. But what could a dope like this poor bastard remember? Yesterday's soup?"

"Ah, for this relief, much thanks," Davers said. I looked up, confused. "Stinks in the pisser, they're animals. Anothery?"

I nodded. While he tried to get the bartender's attention, I opened the book again.

Once there was the taste in the mouth. Warm dripping on the face and large wet warm to suck and both eyes were green, I think, and shut tight. Pushing, squeezing, screaming at the loss of the earth of the wet, the pain of cold harsh brightness. Slither and kick, the sleeping soul tiny and coiled, rudely woken, eyes opening to a blur. White and pain and down, down, down. Blurred face and a taste that was gone with loss and still the hunger. The word sounds pushed at me, but I refused to break the soul silence. Vastly, the bulbous breast and the mouth sucking, refusing the words and screaming from the womb, all one winding out and winding back. Now the worms move in the soil, and the green grass grows, and the huge tree crushes the sky. The woman of the breasts and kicking legs has been gone for so long it is difficult to recover her. Sobs as I fed, screams and muted cries

> *from far rooms. I lay on my back in the cot of wood that soared above me, and listened. The woman and I were linked in the darkness and the shared thudding, the coil of flesh that bound us for eternity. We were one still, even after the glare of light and noise and the terror of falling. She lay and moaned for God to take her, sick and coughing and tearing loneliness. I looked at the white infinity of the ceiling, the far precision of lines where wall joined wall. Can life be anything but empty now? Remembering is duty. There is little joy in its fulfillment, yet it is my lot, and I will show you in my hours under the tree. This is how I imagine it: What I do, in the light, in the dark, is for your entertainment. The universe is a story without a plot. It is a confessional whispering to soothe you. No matter. There are memories stacked up in the loneliness, and their ordering, and at last the hope of the tree and the blue and crimson end.*

"Engrossing stuff, eh? A treatise in computational cosmology, I take it? Cheers."

Automatically, I lifted my refreshed glass, drank. My head was starting to swim. "Sorry, it's just that this . . . It's . . ." I felt as if some part of my brain had been bound and gagged then dragged away into a small room and forced to watch some appalling display of cruelty. I could not bear to watch and I could not look away.

> Jenny Handley groaned, blinked her eyes. With some difficulty she opened her eyes and looked across the room at me, blinking fast. I know how difficult that can be when you're immersed inside someone else's head.

> "Oh god," she said, like someone speaking from a dream. Her tongue came out and licked her lips. "He's not—"
>
> I waited, meeting her gaze expectantly. The last thing to do at this point is to lead the witness.
>
> "I always assumed he was, was . . ." Jess Handley closed her eyes, and tears started to leak down her face. "Stupid. Worse than stupid. Lights off. Oh, Christ, doctor, he's watching us watch him."

I'd taken my jacket back; I closed the book and shoved it away again in a pocket. I looked at Davers, astounded by possibilities. Hide in plain sight.

"You've really never met Miriam or Itzhak?" But of course he hadn't.

"Nope. You're worrying me now. Let's go back to talking about normal stuff, like wave-function algorithms."

"It's okay, chief," I said, getting off my stool. "You're a lifesaver, you really are. I owe you, Davers. Give my regards to your sister."

"She's dancing at Covent Garden, actually. You have somewhere to stay, then? Can I fix you up for cab fare?"

"I'll be right." I punched him lightly on the shoulder, gave the girl with the tattoo, as I passed her, a big juicy kiss on the mouth, just for luck, and pushed through to the lavatory. It did stink. I waited my turn, shut the door, averting my gaze from the toilet bowl, where apparently some junkie had recently thrown up half a lung, and opened a Schwelle.

"Third Tegmark level," I said, not at all sure it would work. "Get me Homeboy."

I was sitting in front of the flatscreen, fingers poised over a keyboard. A lighthouse stood on a storm-tossed applet, beam passing into the dark, catching strange and terrible things, flicking by, swinging about to dazzle me as I sat there, turning away again into black rain-pelted night. Waves crashed noisily in my headset.

"Hello, Homeboy," I told the machine, the substrate. "I have some questions for you."

Hi, August. Any port in a storm, eh?

"I think you can port me straight into the answers at the back of the book, am I right?"

Ask the next question!

"I want to access the FAQ."

Frequently asked, August, seldom answered.

I persisted. "Who are the despoilers? Can they be stopped from hurting Lune and the others?"

Two for the price of one? That's our standing offer, here at Contest Central.

I stared at the changing imagery on the screen, not seeing it. Riddles, was it? Okay, the system was telling me that by definition any Contest had two players. At least two players. And a Game Master, but I'd already been down that path.

"How do I stop them, lame brain?"

Play a better game. Kick over the table. Or rewrite the rules, like Jan did.

Shit. Truisms and obscurities. I wondered if any of this exchange actually existed outside my own numbed imagination. In this quantum-variant cognate, this T-level universe, the semi-sentient bot had been written by my doppelganger, but that didn't mean it was truly autonomous. Maybe it was a projective screen, an expression of what I wanted to hear. No more informative than a dream. No. I shook my head. I *willed* the system to speak truth.

"What is the Contest, Homeboy? Twenty-five words or less."

Words won't help you, August. Here's the notation.

A cascade of mathematical symbols swarmed down thc screen, faster than my eyes could take it in. Yet something inside me did so. The Vorpal Grammar caught the logic and gulped it down, digested it, retired to mull upon the implications. Immediately I felt as if a small, furry animal nestled inside my abdomen, well fed and reflective.

"The Doomsday Hypothesis," I said, clutching at one trailing strand.

That's part of it, the machine interface told me. *Dinosaurs, Bzzzzt! Wrong answer, clear the board. Homo sap? Wheel's still in spin. Probabilities don't look good. But hey, no Cloud of Unknowing without a silver lining, bozo.*

"Don't give me this oracular shit." A teacher looked in from the corridor, overheard me, frowned, shook her head. I ignored her. I knew it was absurd, but I opened my hand and held my palm menacingly toward the screen. Alfred E. Newman's cartoon grinning face appeared, blenched, comically ducked. I wasn't amused. "Are my parents still alive?"

In a manner of speaking. Every dog has his day.

"Fuck!" Furious, I smashed my fist down on the keyboard, which broke in half.

Don't be a spoilsport, Homeboy said sulkily. *You already know what to do.* The screen went white and empty.

I stood for a moment in uffish thought. The notation boiled at the back of my mind. Oh. Yes.

"Take me to Miriam," I told the operating system.

NINETEEN

NAKED EXCEPT FOR a white butcher's apron, tanned by ultraviolet lamps, springy on his toes in the light gravity of this far-from-cognate world of dinosaurs untroubled by uppity humans and their wretched intelligence, Marchmain Seebeck readied his patients for treatment.

"Any minute now," he crooned. The woman who had called herself Miriam stared at him in uncomprehending terror, mouth blocked by an anesthetic mask, trembling limbs fixed to her sides by padded restraints. On the next table, her husband Itzhak rolled his eyes wildly from side to side, chest heaving. Faint grunts broke free of his mask. Marchmain ignored the distressing sounds as best he could, turning his gaze to an image from deepest space.

Beyond the faux window, nothing of the light of this dinosaur world could be seen, only the blackness between the stars. The faux was true to reality in this: no stars shone, or none that he could see, since the bright light inside the station had caused his pupils to contract. But a sparkly ring of violet light picked out the condensed object they seemed to be orbiting some half million kilometers distant. The Xon star radiated mostly a flux of electrons, neutrinos, but especially photinos. In reality—in all the realities—the thing was dizzyingly massive, held at the very margins of collapse into a black hole, built from a family of X-particles so appallingly dense that each Xon equaled perhaps ten quadrillion protons.

The filthy thing, now jammed into a sphere twenty centimeters across and spinning like a son of a bitch comprised an entire star's worth of elementary stuff otherwise unknown to the cosmoses since they had broken apart in the first instants of the Big Bang. Marchmain snorted, shaking his head. Star-stuff never to be seen again in this or any other universe possessed of a sizable expansion force shoving everything away from everything else . . . except, miraculously, right there, in that one omphalos piercing through each of these cognate Tegmark universes where the local restricted laws of physics permitted intelligent life to evolve and persist. He lifted his hand, looking past the bright titanium scalpel to the silvery hieroglyphs of Xon metal in his palm. Lovely stuff, actually. Each tiny vibrating stringy X-particle was massive as a dozen blood cells and more lively, held from catastrophic implosion only by its own trapped lambda expansion surface.

On the faux displays recorded by Jan's ship, though, that was a different story. Magnified, rendered into false color images and running-average charts, the Xon star boiled like the extrusion from Hilbert space that it was.

It was ferocious, minatory, glorious to behold. Let Decius gaze upon a new Omega Point in its birth pangs, Marchmain thought with self-satisfaction, I'll settle for this wonderful artifact, this dreadful construct that the fucking Contest Builders hung out to hamstring us, mute our voice, blind our sight, stand guard lest we upstart Players try to kick over the board and replay the Contest closer to our 'own hearts' desires.

At his back, a Schwelle tore open. Were he in deep space where the faux pretended, that would be impossible. It was what the Xon star was built to inhibit, to forbid, really, when you got down to the nitty gritty.

"Come in, Tansy," he said, turning.

"Good . . . what is it . . . morning? Evening? It's been a long time, boy." She stood there taking stock, and did not come forward to put her arms about him.

Marchmain threw back his head, stung a little, and laughed. "I don't think we need count time at this juncture," he said. "I see you've brought the mutt."

Dugald O'Brien growled. Stupid damned name for the animal, but Tansy had proved a whimsical old lady.

"If you'd just lie down here on this table, I believe we can begin. Yes, yes, Monsieur Labrador, up there beside the nice man in the restraints."

The old dog strained to make the leap, fell back panting. "Lower the damned table, Marchmain."

"Certainly. Thoughtless of me."

The man named Itzhak was starting to show nasty readings on blood pressure and cortisol; Marchmain adjusted several neurotransmitter feeds, and he slumped back into torpor.

"You're quite sure you want me to do this? Now?"

"Cut the crap, son," the dog said.

He shrugged, wired them up, and when the monitors assured him all four of his patients were at optimum, he moved quickly from one table to the next, cutting their scalps free and pulling the loose flesh back to expose the bone. He picked up a laser knife and burned a thin, neat incision through the skull of the Miriam woman and looked down with approval on her naked brain encased in its gleaming dura mater.

Intent on his work, he did not hear the threshold rip open at his back.

TWENTY

THE FLOOR FELL away from under me, like an instant replay of my near-tumble down the steep steps of the Grand Circle. I caught myself with a jolt and jerk that threw me up on my toes, and it wasn't a fall, I was on another planet with weaker gravity. No, I was in an operating theater on the bridge of a fucking spaceship, and Dr. Frankenstein was capering over his corpses, with his bare tanned arse sticking out and a bloody scalpel in one hand. Meters flickered and went ping, and a huge viewscreen or window of quartz showed blackness, and the mad butcher was turning toward me with a scowl, and I had my hand up, speaking a word, and my pompous brother Marchmain was flung away across the cabin to slam into a large smooth textured tank while my dog Do Good struggled about on all fours with a furry flap horribly hanging back from the top of his bleeding scalped head, saying something I couldn't take in, halfway between human speech and the barking of a dog woken from sleep by an intruder. Marchmain staggered to his own feet, apron obscenely askew, waving his hand, the medical blade catching the light, yelling at the top of his voice, "Toby, get the hell in here!"

My heart squeezed hard enough to stop. Everything slurred. Great-aunt Tansy lay white-faced and comatose on one hospital table, her head mutilated too, the stringy white hair hanging upside down, and a younger woman strapped to another bed, mouth blocked by an airway mask, the top of her skull removed and great veins or arteries or both pulsing in the blue-red loops and indentations of her exposed brain. I wanted to throw up, and couldn't afford to. Oh, fucking Hitler in hell, that was my aunt Miriam, and the brutalized man beyond, stretched out beside the table where Do Good flopped and yapped, was my brilliant violinist uncle Itzhak. Nightmare from some crazy mélange of bad movies. A Schwelle shredded the air and Toby stepped in, looked about him, agog, and strode at once lightly to Marchmain where the fellow cowered in his near-nakedness against an instrument panel.

"Where have you brought us, March?" His voice was rough, but he helped the man stand.

"He'll kill us all!" the butcher shrieked. "Get the fool of a boy away from here—do you want everything ruined?"

Toby's eyes darted. "Where? Oh. *Hanged Man,*" he said in a different tone. "Let me speak to the vessel's operating system."

An epicene male voice spoke from the air: *the spacecraft is on orbit in cissolar space. this unit is a limited-capacity observation bubble on polar orbit about the Xon star. please take care not to exceed regulation biosystems parameters.*

"Bullshit," Toby said. "This is a faux. Where *are* we, March?"

"Toby, for the love of Christ," I yelled, "look what the madman's been doing! We have to get these people to an emergency room!"

"Calm down, August. Tansy Seebeck, I presume, and the dog," Toby said thoughtfully. He stood between me and Marchmain, shielding the lunatic, as if accidentally. "I see. Rather obvious in hindsight, but it seems to have worked quite well, at least until recently. You've partitioned them."

"Am I to be permitted to finish my work?" Now Marchmain

was more indignant than frightened, looking poisonously at me. I was in turmoil, but kept my hand raised and pointed at them both. After a moment, Tansy groaned and struggled up like the return of the mummy. She made a shushing movement at me with one hand, and lapsed back to the bloodstained sheet. I went to her, leaned over her, tears in my eyes, wanting in a sort of childish impulse to pull her poor damaged scalp back into place. She whispered, "You're a good boy, August, a good son, but it's all right, everything's all right. This is our idea, our plan. Let Marchmain go ahead—you'll see."

What? What? I leaned away from her but clutched her hand the more fiercely.

"A brutally primitive methodology," Toby said with distaste, lips drawn back. "Couldn't Juni or Ruth provide some technique more subtle than this? Nanotechnology—"

"Don't be simpleminded. Go back to your huntin' and fishin' and leave the skull work to me." My brother Marchmain looked up with a grin from unconscious Itzhak, placing the bony crown of his skull in a steel container. I yearned to hurt him badly, I ached with the need, but instead I held Tansy's thin old hand and turned my face aside as he burned away enough cranial bone to remove her skullcap. Her grip never faltered; I guessed that his anesthetic techniques were more sophisticated than his horrible trepanning. I had done this to human remains in anatomy class not a year earlier, but then the corpse was long dead, shrunken, stinking of preservative. Tansy breathed, eyes closed, pulse steady in her wrist when I touch it lightly. Marchmain moved on to the next table, opened up the dog's head. Do Good growled, as if he dreamed of chasing a rabbit down a deep hole. Monitors sounded and blinked. I said, not knowing quite what I meant, "It's a semaphore."

"A metaphor," Marchmain corrected me, halfway between scorn and surprise.

"That's what I said. What's happening here is a coded message, a . . . a construct."

He wiped his bloody hands on his stained butcher's apron, favored me with a respectful nod.

"The boy's not the fool I took him for. How did you know?" He delved with glass-tipped electrode probes in the naked brains, pushing into the living tissue. Lines of blue laser light sprang into being, linking all four naked skulls in a web of electronic chatter.

I glanced at Toby, waved my hand at the displays. "This is some sort of . . . set, right?" I looked at the pulsing ring of violet light in deep blackness, and knew what it represented. My implants tingled in sympathy. "That's a recording of the Xon star?"

"Yes. He's playing spaceships. Always the theatrical one, our Marchmain."

"The Xon star was Tansy's discovery," I said, putting it all together. "Christ, what an extraordinary woman she was." I caught myself, horrified; I was acting as if my dear great-aunt were already dead. Yet surely she was, in the most important sense. "The star's a machine for turning our Vorpal implants off, most of the time, anyway. It's a . . . a timed lock on the inner door of the multiverse."

Marchmain toggled switches on displays; illumination drained from the cabin. Beyond the great window, imaginary stars brightened in black nowhere. Blue lines of radiance pulsed between the brain-engulfed electrodes, and something more: a haze enwrapped the four bodies, two female humans, one male human, one articulate brute. They furred, as if slipping away from our familiar dimensions, like some awful parody of human or canine flesh translated into one of the higher Tegmark levels where space and time traded places or multiplied into intolerable spacetimes with the wrong number of dimensions. It wasn't that their bodies flowed together, or drew away in some direction at right angles to everything else—but from moment to moment, it seemed as if something like that were happening, and worse.

Marchmain stood back, then, looking down at his work with satisfaction. "Identity is my forte, child. I am the master of alternatives. I make souls flow like water from one flesh to another. Nothing need remain frozen or concrete; all is in flux."

A high human voice screamed. My hand seemed locked inside the hazy globe of light which had been Tansy and the others. I jerked it free, stared about. The Vorpal implant tingled fiercely. A woman's voice had cried out in agony. A man's joined it in a threnody of rising pain. Toby, I saw, held a Schwelle open; he remained at its threshold, ready to flee or seek help, I couldn't tell. The globe of diffused light switched off. A naked man and woman, youths really, stumbled from the beds where Miriam and her husband had lain, and held each other, weeping, kissing, touching like two blind people given sight and desperate to reconcile the familiar feel of things with this new and baffling vision. Sick with confused grief, I looked from them to the two motionless, drained corpses on the other beds. I leaned over Tansy's sunken, waxy face, gazed at her closed eyelids. After a moment, I leaned down and kissed her thin dead lips. Gone. Yet, somehow, not gone.

"August?"

The young woman turned, eyes wet, and held out her arms to me. "August," she said. "My dearest child."

I stared wildly, yet at some deep level I knew perfectly well why Tansy was gone, and my strange old impossibly speaking dog, and the other two who had looked after me when my parents disappeared, whom I'd never known until Dramen and Angelina died. But my ageless Vorpal-resonant parents had not died, of course, not been killed in some Thailand aircraft crash nor by attack from the emotionally debauched K-machines scouring the universes, had not withdrawn from the Contest, either. Escaped into hiding, rather, purloined in plain sight, fractured into false identities safe even from self-disclosure.

"Mother," I said, and stepped forward with embarrassment into her naked, beautiful embrace. My father—younger than I, to look at him—stood tall and powerfully built at her back, nodding with approval.

She said, "Call me Angelina, sweetheart. And this is Dramen, of course. My, how you've shot up."

Marchmain said in a peeved voice, "Welcome back, you old bastards. If it's escaped your notice, I was the one doing all the heavy lifting here. Oh, do go away, Toby, and get the others ready for a moot. Don't let the Schwelle hit you in the ass on the way out."

Toby stayed put, eyes slightly averted from the reborn couple. "What do you mean, semaphore?"

"The universe is a computation," I said, "isn't that what you all believe? Isn't that what your Ontology Institution claims is the deep truth of reality?"

"Oh, now he's a philosopher," Marchmain said. "The boy's a veritable polymath in his own lunchtime. Speaking of which, you two must be hungry, why don't you let me—"

"Tansy could only do her psychic readings at a certain time of the day or night, and it kept shifting by four minutes every twenty-four hours."

"Local sidereal time," Toby said instantly, getting it. "Star time, not Sun time. So something relatively stationary against the fixed stars was causing her gift to switch on. Assuming she actually possessed a gift." He glanced clinically at the corpse of the old lady. "Which, given that she was an artifact of dear brother Marchmain's—"

"No," I said. "Christ, it's so obvious now, I had all the data right in my hand years ago. And Jan even told me, but she missed it herself. She called it an"—I searched my memory—"an ontology access well in the probability fields. Something was switching it *off,* not on."

"Tansy's access window opened as the constellation Sagittarius stood at the horizon," my mother said, nodding. She looked about sixteen years old.

Sagitt—My mind blipped. Surely not. The title of the K-machine Bible? I touched the slender volume on my breast pocket. Could that be radioastronomy jargon, *SgrA**? Jesus, of course it could. They must have known that. I was confused and excited and ready to chew on my own hand.

"I'm guessing Sagittarius is where the Xon star's located."

"Five parsecs from Earth," Angelina told me. "In that constellation, by line of sight from Earth. We thought for a long time that the radio source at Sagittarius A was responsible." She added, at my frown, "The galactic-center black hole. It's swallowed a million suns, but it's not responsible for the Vorpal occlusion."

"Oh." Marchmain looked deflated, annoyed at not being the one who worked it out. "Very well, that implies an increasing suppression of Vorpal access during the course of the sidereal day, after about . . . What hour?" He gave me a disdainful glance.

"About two o'clock in the afternoon, local star time, I think."

"The dawn of magic," he said with a smirk.

It came together fast in my mind, in strings and streamers of provisional logic. Start here: The human brain evolved in a fluctuating noisy environment. Most of the daily, monthly, seasonal rhythms, long ignored by medicine and psychology, are driven by solar cycles. But in the background of its functions, the human nervous system might be modulated as well by large-scale, feeble fluxes from beyond the solar system. As the Xon star sets, the world's turning mass blocks its photino radiation. Then a slow physiologic recovery peaks at optimum just around the next LST dawn of the Xon artifact.

Christ, this was sounding like Avril's astrological gibberish that they'd warned me against. Hey, but maybe she was right—what did I know? I shook my head, eyes unfocused. No, I *knew* the Xon star was out there in space, presumably even in this local cosmos. I retraced the argument, getting it straight in my mind. Suppose it affected me and the other Players by *suppressing* Vorpal activity during the hours when its photino emissions were biologically detectable, unscreened by the Earth's bulk. This inhibition would strengthen for several hours after sidereal dawn, peaking four or five hours later, as the nervous system clawed its way to equilibrium. Maybe suppression fell more slowly than it rose, reaching its lowest ebb again by the time the Xon star—and, coincidentally and misleadingly, Sagittarius A*—next lifted over the horizon. During this brief LST dawn-hour window, miracles worked best—and, I thought, deformer corpses might be deposited in Tansy's nexus collection-point bathroom, while she was safely distracted at her psychic work. Then biological inhibition started to rise once again, driven by Xon flux, and the cycle continued forever. Worse still, perhaps the initial burst of Vorpal recovery skewed probability space sufficiently that when the Xon star hung directly overhead, the probability deformation relaxed into a brief countervailing rebound, then once again settled to near-chance levels as the Sagittarius radiator dropped toward and then below the horizon. No wonder psychics had such a hard time replicating their paranormal feats.

And what of poor Jan on *The Hanged Man,* in a spacecraft deep in space, exposed to the filthy thing twenty-four hours a day? She'd had to fly her ship all the way home. In deep space, the Xon star's malign emanations must be unshielded,

"So who put the damned star up there?" I said in an angry growl, pointing to the image in the fake displays. "The Contest creator? If we're in some kind of computed Contest, I can't believe that's accidental."

"Shut up for a moment." Marchmain was clearing away the hospital apparatus, pushing to one side the two pitiful corpses in their wheeled beds. "I distrust this damned place, I don't like it one bit. The K-machines are hunting us, you know. It won't take them long to—"

"Marchmain, you *brought* us here."

"It had to be done *somewhere.* This world is far from the main stem, yes, but damn you, the longer we stay here the more visible and vulnerable we'll be." Irritably, he trailed off. With no evident sorrow, he wrapped the corpses of Tansy and Do Good in some sort of surgical cling-wrap. A terrifying concussion struck the habitat, the ground beneath our feet hammered upward.

"Oh, shit."

"They've found us again." The young woman—my impossibly recovered mother—reached for her husband, desperate, face distorted.

The other family members yelled and scrambled, seeking purchase. I saw Toby vanish across his threshold, and his Schwelle zip closed. A moment later it reopened and he crossed the crowded space, sparks spitting at his hair and fingers, Lune at his side with some heavy artillery in her arms. My heart convulsed at the sight of her. "Lune," I shouted, "get out of here!"

"You're under attack," she said savagely. "Where else should I be?" She was looking dartingly for the exit, looking for something to kill.

Explosions thumped terrifyingly, transmitted through the floor. I stared about me. A stench of burning metal and melted plastic filled my nostrils.

Again a crash. Lune said, "Deformer ship."

I felt myself spasm. The K-machines. "Yggdrasil Tree!" My blasphemy—and I knew, somehow, it was that—was heartfelt. I made a complicated gesture, something that rose up from the implanted grammar of the X-caliber device. Instantly, the faux bubble folded away.

And with that redescription, that recoding wrought by my guided act of intellect and will, we stood in the real local world, tall lush green grass under a brilliant multicolored aurora. I looked again. Saturn-like rings, spread across half the sky, sparkling, gorgeous. And no Moon. The rings, I guessed, marveling, were what remained of a fractured, gravity-smashed Moon.

"What place is this?" Dramen asked.

I said nothing, arms tight about Lune, waiting for understanding, poised trembling for danger.

"An Earth cognate well off the main stem," Marchmain said, staring about with white-rimmed eyes. "Smaller, lighter, unpopulated." On the far side of the grasslands, a large scaly saurian roared throatily, and another rose up on mighty hind legs to trumpet its challenging reply. Things chittered in the grass. "No people, I mean," Marchmain said, shivering, "but plenty of dinosaurs. How the hell did you do this, boy? I trust you have us well protected from the animals."

Fire stabbed in my foot and in my right palm. I thought for a moment that something in the grass had bitten me, but the Vorpal implants were howling. My nervous system accelerated further into shocked alert.

"Get out of here," I told them. "They must know where we are."

A shockingly bright light was scorching down the sky, trailing fire. It struck the ground in total silence. A searchlight beamed upward into its trajectory, luminous as the weapon burn from Phlogkaalik's Adamski saucer crystal. Lune's weapon spoke to the sky. Brilliant crimson light bloomed directly ahead of me, then, at the horizon. Before I could do much more, in the ominous silence, than seize Lune to me and throw us both to the grassy soil, covering her with my own body, a slamming gale of superheated air rushed over us faster than sound from the deformers' asteroid strike and all I could think as I died in agony, flesh macerated from bone and then ignited, through the desolation and anger at losing Lune and my recovered parents, was, "Oh fuck, they've totaled the dinosaurs again."

Yet even as I died, guttering Vorpal forces sustained some fragment of me, rebuilt my body and mind like the illusion it was. No, no, no, that was wrong, that was the temptation to simplify and demean the magnitude of what was here astonishingly revealed or confirmed. While the local world's algorithm ran on the deep ontological substrate of the T-multiverse ensemble, its output, its throughput, was as real as anything else in all the cosmos^{infinity}.

Into *code* space was where I stepped.

Twenty-one

After the mother was gone they came and took me for always. I have been their sting of the flesh, unwelcome burden, occasion for charity. They have never forgiven me. No father, of course. Whore, retribution. They cry out: It was her sin, yet we must bear the brunt of it.

Their words are noises in the air, mouth flappings, moth flappings. The fingers go to the ears when they speak of her. I listen for the birds, but at night the tree sleeps, only the rustle of sleepy feathers and wind in the leaves. I am not afraid while the tree stands tall, but when it guards itself in dream I can be lonely once again. They never understand the tears and the howling loss. The aunt, tall and sour. Her face shows the emotions of winter. Pressed between the harsh rolls of flesh, her eyes are dull and bitter curses. When she smiles the soul in her eyes is sick and mocking. While I lay still within the dark of the mother she took us with her out of obligation and for the satisfaction of pride. After the mother was gone she kept me. My burden she sighs, so I shit on her carpet. My body is her object, my flesh the world she is revenged upon. I drown in her pit and the furrows of her face. The soul crawling behind her eyes torments me in the wash of sleep, so I wake screaming.

The bottle she held was warm, with the heavy rubber nipple, but the breast was gone and the milk was sour and tasted of rubber. Clouds are white and soft in a billow of sweetness. Clouds float behind the branches. I hunger. It is easy to hate her. The uncle is a short square man with glass in front of his eyes and kind hands. He has lost his joy, though I have heard him whistle when she is away. His mouth is always opening and closing, talking to himself, for there is nobody to love him. I suppose he hates the aunt too. They sit in the house bickering all day, beyond the green and the tree. In his way he is kind so I am sorry it is his grass when I tear the green and throw back the food from the stomach. Often he held me, rocking me, before I grew old enough to refuse to speak. He lifts me now, grunting, from the bed to the wheelchair to the green beneath the tree. I am afraid. I am always afraid. The cousin's breasts are like the mother's, but not heavy. She giggles, and in the night with the boys under the window she moans, and is often cruel and sometimes kind. They do not love her but they care for her as they have never cared for me. She is their child. She is their flesh and her soul is their soul, glinting behind her pretty eyes.

The fucking system's locked up. Control-Alt-Delete doesn't do a thing. My fingers seem to have turned to stone. When I turn my head to speak to the doctor, it's as if my neck is grinding through rubble. Sounds slowing down. The wave function is spreading out like a, like a fucking wave, like a tidal wave, tsunami. The universes don't split. Oh my god, could that be it? They come together, they coalesce, they hunger for each other. We're separate, locked in our individual histories, decoherent, and the screaming goes on forever. But something there is that does not love a wall. Fuck, where did that come from? Did that leak out of doc's mind? Smears of locked light on the control panel. I open my mouth to shout at the doctor and Lissa's mouth opens, her voice slurred and drawn out like a, like a drag queen forgetting himself, no that's my voice she's speaking, fuck, fuck, the world is collapsing under his gaze, under his awful observing gaze, we're the cats in his—

TWENTY-TWO

I STEPPED INTO a place of scintillating light. Two men stood loosely wrapped in bedsheets, gazing out with blinded rapture through an immense blister window at the grandeur of the newborn Angels at sport.

"Decius," I called, voice breaking with emotion.

One man turned his head slowly, like a man in a dream. My brother.

"Aren't they lovely?" he said.

We looked for a timeless time on the Omega godthings, shaken by their music and their dance. Somehow I held to some thread of my grief and purpose.

"Decius, can you speak to them?"

"*May* I, that's the question." His tone was low-pitched and slow, clotted with a kind of worshipful dread. "I can call spirits from the vasty deep, but will they come when I do call for them?"

He was drunk, I saw. And from no grape.

"Decius, take command of yourself, sir. Our parents are dead."

"Ah, so you are the lost brother, eh? No matter. They died long ago, boy. Doomsday comes to us all, soon enough, consult with brother Jules if you doubt it. In this place, if the Angels wish it, they shall live again."

I took him angrily by the arm. His companion turned his head, looked at my passionate face with mild rebuke, swung back again to contemplation of the light-shot plenum.

"They were not dead. Dramen and Angelica withdrew into concealment. Now they are dead in truth, and our brothers Marchmain and Toby with them." My voice broke. "And one other."

"Ah, these are so beautiful! I have no parents. Hush, now."

"I am the child of their retreat. I love them, and I love Lune the more, you god-smitten imbecile," I raged, weeping, "and you *will* recover them for me!"

I drew back my arm and slapped his face, hard. Beyond the blister, eons were passing, worlds beyond worlds beyond worlds built in calculated simulation and recollection, histories rerun and devised from whole cloth. Somehow I knew all this, took instruction from the fringes of omniscient shadow that crossed Yggdrasil Station like currents in a great ocean tide at the shoreline of some insignificant atoll. Here, in this place, this closed space and time, the majesty and brutality of all the Tegmark levels was being rehearsed in infinite miniature, like half the sky captured perfectly in a single red droplet of wine at the bottom of a drained glass. I could have her here, in simulation, if I sought entry from the Angels. That was not what I desired. Let her live!

"Get her back for me," I told Decius and his companion, compelling them with my ardor, my steel-edged insistence. The Vorpal force in me blazed even in this radiant, numinous place. "It is not too much to ask."

"Very well," the man said, and closed his eyes.

An Omega Angel entered the blister.

TWENTY-THREE

A cloud has come to cover the face of the sun and has lost its own white blaze. The tree grows cool and climbs to the warmth. The tree does not need love, although I have offered it love and given it love. It climbs to the sky and sleeps in calm when the night has come. I know little yet of the tree. It is my life. If I have a hope it can grow only in the tree.

The yard is the same as ever. The lawn is wide and green, and the house is red beside it. My window is a burn of light now that the cloud has passed from the sun and light is bright on the glass. Pipes for water edge the wall, dull green with flakes of peeling paint. A gully-trap of concrete is shaded by an overhanging eaves. Here they throw the dead brown leaves from the teapot. I crawl there sometimes and find leaves stuck to the rough concrete and place my mouth against them. What has been warm and sweet and now is dead. Death brings a sour taste to tea. There are cracks in the concrete of the pathway, where the roots of the tree have heaved and fought their way. The grass is yellow and brown under fallen leaves. Along the edge of the red-tiled roof hangs guttering of steel and lead where the water runs in winter and the tissues of leaves gather. There is beauty in the house and yard. Only the inside of the house is drab and the colors have lost their meanings with too little wonder and three dead souls who have never reached across the gap.

I am the tree. I am in the tree. I am trapped in the sap rising from the deep roots of the history of all the earth. He is lying in the grass, not kicking his chubby legs. One eye is blue as the sky, green as the tree. He rubs at the other with the pointed end of a stick. Dear god in heaven, don't—But there is no heaven, no god. Dead souls. Reverberations without speech. We shall stand here forever, as clouds move across the sun and rains fall to drench our leaves until they tumble, long and brown, and the cycle run through again and again, as it must, and all the dead souls, all of us, suffer our damnation inside the red-tiled house, and Arthur waits and watches, watches, watches forever.

Twenty-four

SHE CAME UP out of muck, as if dragged by her hair. An Angel tore her back from corruption, knitted together the remnants left in the midst of mad voiceless terror, bombardment, the long, echoing drawn-out instant of death. Somehow, incredibly, her thoughts, drifting and tumbling as they were, fixed upon the mad book beloved of the K-machines, August's recent obsession. She tried desperately to recall some of the key threads of its simple, infinitely enfolded narrative. What was it—How did it—Pull it together. Her continued life, it seemed to her, depended on this understanding. All right. Linkollew's neuro doctor . . . what was his name? It didn't matter . . . and the quantum experimenter and the nurse are normal humans isolated within their own solitary mental/experiential/ interpretative worlds. So is the cousin, but she manages to attain some measure of empathy with the poor autistic man. With Aug . . . With Arthur. He, of course, is entirely solipsistic, in-turned, oblivious, except that eerily he's *not*—his awful condition lends him an astute—if—crude mythic perspective on the Real. Then the quantum experiment jams them all into a Schrödinger's Cat/Wigner's Friend superposition, and their minds bleed together. But autistic Arthur-Merlin-Odin is a sort of vortex that sucks them—and by extension *everyone*—into a deep Ur Reality that is terrible, icy, final, locked.

Knowledge burned and bubbled up in her from the Xon implant threading her Vorpal flesh, recalling to her references to myth and legend she had learned in her Ontology studies. Arthur under the hill waiting for release and the renewed call to duty, Merlin in dazed sleep trapped inside an oak, Odin in Fimbulwinter, under the shadow of the mighty Tree Yggdrasil, all of them one, the ultimate . . . observer. She felt, dying, that she, too, had watched, watched, watched forever, immobile, cold as ice, torn apart in the fireball of the K-machine attack that did not stint to murder an entire world in order to slay . . . who? Surely not her. She could not be the target. She was insignificant in the Contest. Certainly not Marchmain Seebeck, that slippery wizard of identity, nor Toby. The Seebeck parents? Dramen and Angelina, gone now a second time into the darkness, this time truly. Her mind skittered about like a mouse trapped in a bowl. Beloved August, then. His name was not Arthur. No, that was someone in a—

TWENTY-FIVE

A SMALL GOOD-humored man in early middle age entered through a mirror, jumping nimbly to the floor, carrying a large sack over one shoulder. He had the bleary eye of a drinker and a three-day growth of beard. On his tousled head he wore an old cloth cap. An appalling caterwauling came from the sack, which bounced of its own accord against his back.

"Morning, young August," the disposer said cheerfully. "Y've been in the wars, I hear. I was sorry to learn about that nice old house, and poor Mrs. Abbott, I could've been in with a chance there. Thought I'd fetch an old friend of yours."

Coop pulled open the drawstring to the burlap sack, and a furious moth-eaten tomcat hurtled from the opening, brindle hair sticking out all over him like the bristles on an old-fashioned toilet brush, spine arched, hissing and spitting and in no mood to be trifled with.

I felt sick and miserable nigh to death, which is where I'd been for an incalculable time, but I found myself smiling, for all that, recalling glory.

"Hello, Hooks," I said. "Hello, Mr. Fenimore. None of this makes any sense, you know. Robots and cats are barred from the afterlife."

"Ah, get over yourself," Cathooks growled in his abraded high-pitched way. "Nothing wrong with you that a good washing behind the ears wouldn't fix. Touch me again," he told the robot, "and I'll tear your fucking face off."

"I'd just put it straight back on again, old moggie," the disposer told him, and drew out his stinking meerschaum, tamped in some tobacco, lit up, puffed blue clouds. I sat in an ugly armchair in the Reverend Jules's manse living room, and the pipe smoke blew past me on a breeze from the nifty Schwelle air conditioner which apparently continued to function even in the absence of its opener. All the conveniences.

"Where's Lune?" I asked Coop in a choking voice.

The cat looked at the robot, put his ears back, one full ear and one stubby stump, settled down on the worn rose-patterned carpet. The robot looked at me, imperturbable. "Ask the Angel."

Ask the—

I was dead; I lived. The anguish of it terrified me anew.

I had found my own tattered flesh and put it back together, spun it like yarn about the armature of my Vorpal implants, my Xon metal ontology, my grammar coding. The world is computation; my numbers had been recrunched. Christ! Or rather, I saw (I swore): Ancient Intelligence! The once-and-future kinks in the substrate. Mad Avril was right after all. I need nobody to tell me anything. I said to the operating system of the multiverse, "Give me Lune."

The drab suburban room tore open and she turned to me. Tears like diamonds stood upon her cheeks. With a wondering cry, she ran forward, flung herself across the threshold to my ratty Alphaville, and stood weeping in my arms.

"You got me back," she said.

"The Angel," I told her, reluctant to accept any agency in the impossible deed. "The Omega Point godthing. Se . . . agreed to recover you." She was bussing my face and mouth again and again with little hot salty kisses. "Se said the Contest was not done. Se declared the K-machines had breached the Accord."

At that time I had no real understanding of what I was telling my beloved friend, but I trusted the Omega beings entirely. At my back, James C. Fenimore cleared his robot throat and gave a hoarse smoker's growling cough.

"All's well that ends well, then, eh?"

"Nothing is ended," I said with a deep angry growl of my own. "No, Coop, trust me, I've only just started with those fuckers. Lune, Lune." I spoke her name wonderingly, shivered with my release from fright, with my intoxicated love for her. "I would thank the Angel, if only I could find a way to—"

"Speaking," said a high-pitched grouchy growl from the floor.

"Hooks?"

He was licking his balls like a dog, like poor old Do Good who had hidden away and conserved from lethal attack some key part of my father's complex soul. I stifled my reflex laugh. Hooks was not the kind of person to welcome crass raillery. Instead, I said rather stupidly, reaching for the first safe topic that came to mind, "What's with this 'se' business, Cathooks? I've never met anyone in my entire life more palpably masculine than you."

"Yeah, well. I suppose you mean that as a compliment." Se jumped up on the armchair where I'd been having my postmortem nervous breakdown and butted ser head against my leg. "Whatever."

"Hooks, you're a god?"

"Damn near. When we juggled that cosmos through its shear convulsions and dropped the whole thing into the singularity hoop, we burned ourselves right into the substrate pattern. All the way down. Tegmark-zero. Talk about Ancient Intelligences. On a clear endless day, pal, you can see forever."

Lune's hand—the one that wasn't clutching me tight—went to ser head, and se graciously accepted her obeisance, rumbling, eyes squeezed nearly shut, until suddenly her stroking annoyed sem and se shook her off.

I asked ser: "Where are my parents? Are Dramen and Angelina dead? I mean, are they unrecoverable?"

Hooks gave me a long enigmatic look, purring like a pot on the boil on the stove, looked away. I opened my mouth again, closed it. My truest anguish, I realized, feeling it burn in the center of my chest, was not really for my mother and father. They had long been gone. For years I'd assumed that they were dead; I had made my peace with their loss. No, my grief was for poor dear lovable Great-aunt Tansy, who had been a snare and a delusion but by god she'd been a wonderful, kind, supportive, clever human being, and I'd loved her, I still loved her, and she was gone not once but twice. I pressed my face into Lune's shoulder, heard reality's fabric ripping.

When I straightened, wiping my eyes, I saw that we were standing in the main street of a busy fashionable enclave of some city I recognized but did not know. A man and woman dressed in batik strolled by, hand in hand, smiling in a friendly way. The woman gave me a concerned look as she noticed my red eyes and mournful countenance, but after only a momentary pause walked by politely, leaning across to whisper in her partner's ear. Gaily painted low vehicles floated past along the thoroughfare, half a meter above the prettily paved roadway, open to the fine weather, filled with children and old folks and one or two business types reading notepads or looking distractedly at the street life. We stood under a white wrought-iron awning. The store's window display, I found, was piled with glassware in a dozen, a hundred shapes, and daylight caught and splashed their hues of blood, cobalt, forest green, starry blues, yellows bright and delightful and crazy as van Gogh's, fluted and spherical, columnar and twining like viny candelabra. It was gay kitsch raised to the level of postmodern art. Worked into the stained-glass window of the doorway, below its old-fashioned sprung bell, was the store's name: THE HERO WITH 1000 VASES. I shook my head, smiled, turned to look for Cathooks. The Angel was gone, passing backward through time, perhaps, like Arthur's Merlin.

"I'm giving up studying medicine," I told Lune. An elderly man approached, munching on a souvlaki wrapped in brown paper; I smelled meat slashed from a gyro, lettuce and tomato and onion and green pepper, perhaps, and the tang of yogurt dusted with oregano, wrapped in a rolled sheet of Turkish pita bread. Juices spurted in my mouth. Christ, it had been ages since I'd had anything to eat or drink. "I'm starving," I added.

Instantly, to the passerby, Lune asked: "Excuse me, sir, where did you buy that wonderful meal?"

"Across the road," the distracted old gentleman told her, suspiciously until he took in her beauty, then falling into speechlessness. He pointed instead, gumming yogurt.

"Thank you." Lune searched for money, found square coins, gazed at them. "Never seen this sort before. Let's hope they do the job."

"They're bound to," I said. "Hooks wouldn't let us down."

We crossed at a break in the traffic and went into the Middle Eastern takeout parlor. I fished a couple of ice-cold cans of beer out of the cooler, snapped their pull tabs, handed Lune one.

"What will you do instead?" She wiped froth from her lips.

"What? Oh, philosophy, I suppose. I need to read your book on computational ontology."

"That should take you only five or six years." But she laughed in delight, and kissed me again full on the mouth, earning a pleased grin from the muscular young guy behind the counter. "Never mind," she added, "you'll have plenty of time. We'll both have plenty of time, August."

The souvlakis were delicious.

Afterword

NOSTALGIA IS A virtue oddly overlooked in most moral catalogs. For the traditional science-fiction fan, it's an unlikely key to the fullest enjoyment of this fertile mode of storytelling.

You might think that sf should push into totally unexpected territory, seeking novelty as its prime virtue. Yes, but what's also true is that sf should not cast off the best lessons, painfully learned, of the past. All too often, though, today's sf readers are cheated of our quite lengthy tradition, as many classic texts have been allowed to fall out of print. For those who do know and love the old wonders, I hope this novel rekindles fond memories. For those who don't, yet, may it lead you to search out tales by such writers as Roger Zelazny and Fritz Leiber. (I was surely influenced by Leiber's eerie 1945 short novel, *Destiny Times Three,* with its "Probability Engine" and Yggdrasil Tree.) At their best, which was attained often, both were witty poetic geniuses who placed their stamp indelibly on the development of the field. They stand above us, beckoning.

But it's also true that traditions need refreshing, as those good writers and their peers, forty or sixty years ago, renewed the imaginative narrative forms bequeathed by both science and fiction of sf's Golden Age. That fabled Age is often said to extend from the late 1930s to the mid-1940s, but I'd argue its true fruition was achieved in 1953, more than a full half-century ago as I write these grateful acknowledgments. That was also the year when DNA's structure was first cracked. In the decades since, we've seen immense, nearly inconceivable leaps ahead in the science and technology of computing, genomics, cosmology, quantum theory.

The Hubble telescope, the Chandra X-ray observatory, a dozen other superb instruments scan the depths of space and time, mapping the very birth of our cosmos. Meanwhile, mathematicians and physicists sketch out testable theories based on this new data, revealing, to our absolute astonishment, that the universe has not just grown from an explosion of the vacuum less than 14 billion years ago; now it expands ever faster, galaxies shoved away from each other by impalpable dark energies, the lambda factor. It starts to seem plausible that our local universe is no more than one infinitesimal bubble in an infinite expanse of universes, most of them utterly strange, marked by different fundamental constants and laws.

Perhaps the deepest and most challenging interpretation of these new data and theories is the computational cosmos. The infinite expanse of the multiverse, this theory claims, is not only subject to mathematical modeling, it *is* at bottom a discretized computation. This audacious idea was proposed in detail by Konrad Zuse (who built the first programmable computers in 1935–1941 and devised the first higher-level programming language in 1945), elaborated by Dr. Jürgen Schmidhuber, and explored by other brilliant thinkers such as Edward Fredkin, Dr. Max Tegmark and Stephan Wolfram. Luckily, much of their work is available for inspection on the World Wide Web. For example:

ftp://ftp.idsia.ch/pub/juergen/zuserechnenderraum.pdf
http://www.hep.upenn.edu/~max/
http://mathworld.wolfram.com/

Google to find the following intriguing papers, which I have rifled for this novel: "Investigations into the Doomsday Argument," by Dr. Nick Bostrom; Schmidhuber's "A Computer Scientist's View of Life, the Universe, and Everything"; Tegmark's "Is 'the theory of everything' merely the ultimate ensemble theory?"

I'm especially grateful to Professor Tegmark, whose four-level model of a computational cosmos I have adapted here, with his permission, in a shamelessly simplified fashion. His web site is an especially rich source, explaining how the universe can be regarded as a vast calculational ensemble that (perhaps) literally actualizes all possible variants of all possible worlds. See also Professor Frank Tipler's analysis of a hypertechnology-driven Omega Point at the end of time in a closed universe, in his formidable book *The Physics of Immortality.* Eliezer S. Yudkowsky allowed me to cite, as one of my epigraphs, a neat comment from a post to the Extropian email list. Oh, and fans of Isaac Asimov's fertile time-travel novel *The End of Eternity,* will have recognized Eric Linkollew's variora, which I filched.

Two other important sources of ideas and material are my friends Robert Bradbury and Dr. Anders Sandberg, two polymaths who have done a lot of serious and playful work on future directions life might take in an ever-complexifying cosmos. Bradbury's fertile, mind-boggling analysis of a Matrioshka Star—an M-Brain, or embedded system of Dyson spheres each made from a different kind of "computronium" sucking up all the heat and light of a central star—should be explored more widely by astronomers seeking evidence of stealthed alien life in the cosmos. Perhaps slightly nearer to future realization is Anders's more modest Jupiter Brain model ("The Physics of Information Processing Superobjects: Daily Life Among the Jupiter Brains," at http://www.transhumanist.com/volume5/Brains2.pdf), in which all the mass of a gas giant planet is converted into a single immense calculating engine encoding in excess of a billion billion bits per cubic centimeter.

My use of the hypothetical unified-force X-particles (or

Xons, as I've dubbed them here) is of course speculative in the extreme. What is not, surprisingly, is a claim that the measurable effect size of paranormal phenomena increases by a factor of four around 1350 hours local sidereal time, and goes significantly negative (psychics get the wrong answer more often than they should by chance) for a short time some four and a half hours later. This very odd finding, published in 1997 by physicist James Spottiswoode (*not* an astrologer), implies that something outside the solar system is modulating any demonstrable human psi capacity on a daily basis (assuming that the various databases James drew upon are reliable as evidence, which skeptics, naturally, will reject). Maybe it's the gigantic black hole at the galactic center, but James tells me the statistical fit is not especially good, which led me to imagine something even weirder and closer. See http://www.jsasoc.com/ docs/JSELST.pdf, "Apparent Association Between Effect Size in Free Response Anomalous Cognition Experiments and Local Sidereal Time."

As always, I thank the English Department in the University of Melbourne, where I am a senior fellow. I owe an immense debt to the Literature Board of Australia Council, whose generous grant helped support me as I worked on this complex novel. I'm grateful to a number of early readers of portions of the novel for useful hints, corrections and nice ideas, especially Lee Corbin and Anders Sandberg for some mathematics, Paul Voermans, Spike Jones, Liz Martin and Charles Stross for keen-eyed reading and suggestions, and especially my dear wife Barbara Lamar, whose love, enthusiasm and support kept me pushing forward through infinitely many universes . . . *and beyond!*

Melbourne, Australia,
San Antonio, USA
August 2004